Mary Fisher

A general survey of American literature

Mary Fisher

A general survey of American literature

ISBN/EAN: 9783337202750

Printed in Europe, USA, Canada, Australia, Japan

Cover: Foto ©Andreas Hilbeck / pixelio.de

More available books at **www.hansebooks.com**

A
General Survey
OF
American Literature

BY

MARY FISHER

AUTHOR OF "A GROUP OF FRENCH CRITICS"

"The most interesting books to me are the histories of individuals and individual minds; all autobiographies and the like. This is my favorite reading." — HENRY WADSWORTH LONGFELLOW.

CHICAGO

A. C. McCLURG AND COMPANY

1899

Preface

THE following book on American literature has grown largely out of the author's work in the class-room. There was no hurried daily flight from author to author, leaving upon the mind of the pupil a confused impression of dates, names, and lists of books; but a careful and prolonged attention was given to the author as a man and a thinker.

In preparing for recitation, the pupil was encouraged as much as possible to find the author in his works and to grow familiar with his thoughts and feelings. He was asked to discuss important questions suggested by his literary and biographical research, and every effort was made to make the study not a memory drill, but a stimulus to thought and a source of wider culture. For this purpose, the meagre and uninteresting information of the text-books, confined merely to external details, was found wofully deficient, and material from every available source was collected to eke it out.

To place this material within the reach of other students and to direct them to the intelligent study of American literature are ideas which have been continually before me in the preparation of this volume.

Each biographical sketch is accompanied with a critical estimate of the author's works founded upon an application of the recognized canons of sound criticism. To know why a given work is good requires a maturity of judgment which is not to be found in young students, although their healthy, untrammelled instincts may often lead them to select and enjoy what is really fine. This naturally correct taste is in no danger of being vitiated if the mind really perceives the reason for the existence of such a taste. Otherwise it is in danger of being seduced by plausible rhetoric or popular clamor into admiring what is far from admirable. Hence the necessity of teaching the young the principles of good taste in literature.

More attention has also been given to personal details in the biographical sketches than at a superficial glance may seem necessary; but it is these very details that individualize a man and help us to form a correct idea of him. There is too little of such individualizing in our text-books, and our authors do not stand out in them as men of striking character, but as mere names to which are appended a list of works. The value of biography lies in the stimulus given by acquaintance with what is fine, strong, and lovable in character, and no study of literature is complete in which this stimulus is wanting.

CONTENTS

Contents

A General Survey of American Literature

CHAPTER I

A GENERAL SURVEY OF AMERICAN LITERATURE

TO form a just conception of the comparative range and value of American literature, it is necessary to be acquainted with the masterpieces of other national literatures, and especially with those of England, in whose language it is written. There is necessary, too, on the part of the reader or thinker that broad, impartial spirit which rises above national prejudices and loses its limitations in presence of the larger thought of simple kinship in humanity. This spirit is the outcome of long and patient culture. It is not allied to the passionate enthusiasms of youth, but to the calm, broad, well-founded judgments of maturity and age.

The reader who brings to his study of American literature this spirit of impartiality and a mind trained by long familiarity with foreign classics is struck, at first, by the absence of supreme excellence. There is no name in American literature which he feels he can rank with that of Homer, Goethe, or Shakespeare. Neither can he find there the man of warm, large life, the very bone of our bone and flesh of our flesh, yet one to whom the whole world feels akin, — the Burns, the Heine, the Molière of his country. Our literature lacks the wide sweep, the uplift, the virility and solidity of the literatures of Europe. To refuse to acknowledge this is a tacit confession of inability to recognize excellence.

Our apologists say for us, "The people of the United States have had to act their Iliad and they have n't had time to sing it." We have made good use of this apology, and have written with pride of felled forests giving place to populous cities, of farms and fields now flourishing where buffaloes herded less than a quarter of a century ago, of mountains tunnelled and rivers bridged, of our vast commercial interests and our national growth; but though deeds are better than words, when words but stand for the deeds, they are not substitutes for literature, nor, if we inquire more deeply, are they in reality the reason for the absence of supremely excellent books. The burning word *will* be spoken, though gold lie in the mines for the digging and forests are to be felled and cities built. "The cheerless gloom of hermit with the unceasing toil of a galley slave" could not stifle the song on the lips of Burns. It never stifled music on the lips of any born musician. Had not the poor wool-comber's son a fortune to make, when he went up to London from Stratford, and held gentlemen's horses at the door of a theatre? Did that hinder him, o whom all the world was a stage, from seeing a better play outside the door than the gentleman whose horse he held could ever hope to see within?

The truth is that genius knows well its own royalty by right of birth, and all the kingdoms of the world cannot tempt it into silence or denial of its right divine. But it is also a truth that genius is not independent of race, environment, and political condition, and a democracy is probably that form of government most unfavorable to the production of a classical literature.

A democracy is based on the belief in the equal rights of all mankind and a faith in majorities. It offers a fair field and no favors to all forms of honorable ambition and energy. If abuses arise, they may be redressed at the ballot-box. A system of free public education opens the doors of learning to all who wish to enter. Responsibility for failure in life cannot easily be shifted from the individual to the social institution under which he was born. Hence, in an ideal democracy, there does not exist that restlessness, that brooding discontent, that deep, smothered consciousness of wrong and shame endured by toiling millions which finds eloquent expression in passionate taunt, pathetic cry, or vivid delineation in fiction. It is a noteworthy confirmation of this fact that in so far as our country has ever failed to reach, or has departed from, the principles of ideal democracy, or has been the scene of wrong and struggle, it has furnished material for eloquent literature. The Acadian outrage gave birth to the beautiful idyl of " Evangeline " with its tragic coloring. The struggles of the early settlers with the Indians is Cooper's territory. The echoes of the Revolution are heard in " The Spy " and in " Paul Revere." The dark stain of witchcraft and the unbending severity of Puritanism color the works of Hawthorne. Slavery gave us Whittier's stirring lyrics, " Uncle Tom's Cabin," and

Lowell's "Biglow Papers" and "Commemoration Ode." Freedom's voice is never so eloquent and far-reaching as when it is heard back of iron bars. The most revolutionary and radical literature is produced in those countries where the freedom of the press is most restrained and where social restrictions are the most galling.

Another disadvantage of a democracy lies in the fact that the temptations to a comfortable livelihood, and the ease with which power and honor are acquired with wealth, create a social atmosphere in which the artificial pleasures of civilized life are substituted for the simple and natural pleasures of the imagination. Few have the courage to remain poor in a country where poverty would seem to imply some lack of thrift and energy, and therefore few of our writers have devoted themselves exclusively to literary pursuits.

In no country in the world is the history of genius so comfortable a record of material prosperity and easily won recognition as it is in America. It is not the history of struggle, aspiration, despair, oftentimes life-long defeat, poverty, and woe, followed by statues and fame after death. It is, for the most part, the history of prosperous doctors, lawyers, college professors, editors, and public officials, to whom literature was not the first supreme aim, but an elegant accomplishment that waited on bread-winning. We have no cheery garret philosophers, no song birds whose music is the sweeter for their having been imprisoned in a darkened cage. But, on the other hand, we have escaped in a remarkable degree the sickly sentimentality of certain periods of literary decadence in other countries. We have no " Renés," " Werthers," or " Childe Harolds," no " Satanic school," nor, with the exception of Charles Brockden Browne, Edgar A. Poe, and possibly Hawthorne, is there any taint of morbidness in our literature.

From the life of intense activity in America, has sprung a literature breathing a confident, hopeful spirit, — the spirit of youth and health. It lacks, to be sure, what gives to youth its charm, — a strain of noble discontent and passionate aspiration. It is content with to-day and trustful of the future. It does not voice the heart hunger of the human race, nor the collected wisdom of its experiences. It does not lay bare the primitive passions of mankind, but it speaks to the prosperous, well-educated citizen of the world in the language of Christian philosophy. It is a clean and wholesome literature, — white wheaten bread, with here and there a toothsome brown crust.

The chief writers of America have been collegebred New England or Eastern men, and contemporaries of the period of the Civil War. Among this little band of contemporaries, Bryant, Emerson, Lowell, Longfellow, Hawthorne, Whittier, Holmes, there existed a warm friendship and mutual admiration, — a fact to which we owe the absence of anything like critical severity in their estimates of one another's writings. Friendship makes the best of focal distances from which to view character, but the critic's eye is far-sighted and needs a longer range. Even Coleridge, one of the acutest of critics, — a man who said that " praises of the unworthy are felt by ardent minds as robberies of the deserving," — over-praised his brother-in-law, Southey. But even when the critic's judgment is not warped by friendship, a delicate sense of loyalty to his friend must shut his lips to any expression of the weaknesses revealed to him by close companionship; and thus the very bond that makes him better able than another to pronounce a judgment is not an advantage to a critic, but rather an insuperable barrier, as it forbids him in honor to pronounce any verdict if unfavorable.

American criticism has suffered unavoidably from this circumstance of mutual friendship, for it has consisted chiefly of indiscriminate and extravagant laudation.   In the keen but kindly character sketches of Lowell's "Fable for Critics" we have a hint of what he was capable of doing in the criticism of American literature had not friendship tied his tongue and thrown shining dust in his eyes. Edgar A. Poe was deterred by no such scruples, but he lacked the first requisite of a great critic, — susceptibility to excellences as well as the quick perception of faults. To him a critic was simply a scourger of literary offenders.   Therefore we have no criticism of American literature by native writers which will stand the test of time and satisfy the verdict of posterity.

Before proceeding further, it is well to understand what we mean by " polite literature." We must not confound what DeQuincey calls " knowledge-literature " and " power-literature," the literature that simply teaches and the literature that moves. We restrict the term " literature " to that which brings the feelings into play, moving us not so much by appeals to our reason as to our sympathy and imagination. " The circle of human nature," says John

Tyndall, the eminent scientist, "is not complete without the arc of the emotions. The lilies of the field have a value for us beyond the botanical ones, — a certain lightening of the heart accompanies the declaration that Solomon in all his glory was not arrayed like one of these. The sound of the village bell has a value beyond its acoustical one. The setting sun has a value beyond its optical one. The starry heavens, as you know, had for Immanuel Kant a value beyond their astronomical one." It is this "value beyond" the purely practical and sense-apparent one in all things with which literature is concerned. This definition properly excludes the writings that belong to the departments of law, politics, theology, science, history, and metaphysics; yet there are cases in which a great imaginative genius treats a didactic subject with so much original power and enthusiasm, — so permeates it with his own striking individuality that he lifts it to the rank of pure literature. He moves while he instructs. To such works belong the sermons of Jeremy Taylor, the essays of Bacon, the criticisms of Sainte Beuve, the histories of Carlyle, and, though in lesser degree, the histories of our American writers, Prescott, Motley, and Parkman.

With this definition in mind, we can easily see why we must exclude, in our study of American literature, Jonathan Edwards, who is our most distinguished metaphysician, and Benjamin Franklin, probably the man of largest mind that America has as yet produced. The former devoted his genius to a field of thought largely speculative, and unprofitable for our purpose; while science, in its purely instructive form, was properly the domain of the latter. Neither can be rightly regarded as a representative of polite literature.

The gloomy theology of the Puritans reflected in their books belongs to a form of thought irrevocably past, and they, too, must be excluded from a title to consideration as contributors to American literature. Cotton Mather, their most distinguished representative, was a firm believer in witchcraft, and crowds his book " Magnalia Christi Americana " (The Mighty Works of Christ in America) with absurd and disgusting stories that have no value or interest beyond that of exciting pity and wonder at the credulity of the human mind. Here and there a fine sentence flashes out like the gleam of a jewel in a rubbish heap, as when he says of John Eliot, the apostle to the Indians : " He had a particular art of *spiritualizing* of earthly objects and raising of *high thoughts* from very *mean things ;* " but there are too few of such jewels to reward a long search through so much dust and rubbish.

Jonathan Edwards, whose book, " The Freedom of the Will," is oftener spoken of than read, was a close, acute reasoner from narrow premises. He argues that as the will is "that by which the mind chuses anything," and as the strongest motive always determines the choice, therefore the will cannot possibly be free. "The will," he says, " always is as the greatest apparent good is. . . . The will don't act in indifference; not so much as in the first step it takes, or the first rise and beginning of its acting. If it be possible for the understanding to act in indifference, yet be. sure the will never does; because the will's beginning to act is the very same thing as its beginning to chuse or prefer."

The Revolutionary period of our history produced orations and political essays of notable vigor. The most famous of these essays are Paine's " Crisis " and " Common Sense," and a series of eighty-five essays entitled collectively " The Federalist," written by Alexander Hamilton, James Madison, and John Jay. The " Federalist " essays first appeared in the newspapers of their day, and were first published in book form in 1788. The essays were written to interpret the new constitution of the United States to the people, and to create a feeling in favor of its adoption, which they ultimately did. The dangers of disunion from the arms of foreign nations and the effects of union upon commercial prosperity were ably dwelt on. "It has been said," says C. D. Warner, "and I think the statement can be maintained, that for any parallel to those treatises on the nature of government, in respect to originality and vigor, we must go back to classic times." But fine and vigorous as these essays are, the study of them properly belongs to political history and not to *belles-lettres*.

Our first novelist, Charles Brockden Browne, born in Philadelphia in 1771, published his first novel, " Wieland," in 1798. Of a sickly constitution, suffering all his life from acute attacks of nervous headache, dying before he had finished his fortieth year, his thought shared the morbid habit of his body. "When have I known," he writes to a friend in his thirty-ninth year, — "when have I known that lightness and vivacity of mind which the divine flow of health even in calamity produces in some men?

Never! scarcely ever! Not longer than half an hour since I have called myself man."

Browne's novels are revolting in their persistent accumulation of horror upon horror, unrelieved by any graces of style or skilful character drawing. His abrupt and stilted language abounds in awkward inversions; he has neither humor nor pathos; his world is a Bluebeard chamber of horrors, and his characters are its victims. He is no longer read, nor is it probable that he ever will be read so long as men seek in books what profits or delights them.

The profitable study of American literature may be said to begin with those of our writers who first acquired international renown by books that deserve to be remembered and read. These writers, in the order of their birth, are: William Ellery Channing (1780), Washington Irving (1783), James Fenimore Cooper (1789), William Cullen Bryant (1794), and William Hickling Prescott (1796). Born within the last decade of the eighteenth century, the works of these writers belong to the first half of the nineteenth century.

Our next group of chief writers clusters around the Civil War, and consists of Bancroft, Emerson, Hawthorne, Longfellow, Whittier, Poe, Holmes, Motley, Thoreau, Lowell, and Parkman. Bancroft, the eldest of this group, was born in 1800; Parkman, the youngest, in 1823. American literature, therefore, is a nineteenth-century product. If we except Jonathan Edwards's " Freedom of the Will," published in 1754, and Benjamin Franklin's " Autobiography," finished in 1788, but not published till 1817, the eighteenth century produced no noteworthy book in America.

Yet it was the century that gave to English literature Pope, Swift, Addison, Steele, Johnson, Goldsmith, Gray, Cowper, Thomson, Sterne, Gibbon, Robertson, Crabbe, Burns, and a host of inferior writers.

Benjamin Franklin's "Autobiography" and his "Poor Richard's Almanac" deserve more than a mere passing mention; indeed, their excellence in their own way is so undeniable that it furnishes reason to many for including Franklin among our great men of letters.   But if we recall our definition of literature, — if we believe that at its best it is not purely didactic, that it speaks, as DeQuincey says, "to the higher understanding of reason, but always *through* affections of pleasure and sympathy;" that it "does and must operate through the *humid* light which clothes itself in the mists and glittering iris of human passions, desires, and genial emotions;" that it "can teach only as nature teaches, as forests teach, as the sea teaches, namely, by deep impulse, by hieroglyphic suggestion;" that this teaching "is not direct, explicit, but lurking, implicit, masked in deep incarnations;"— if we believe this, there is no question that the character of Franklin's work excludes him from this classification.

Franklin's Muse has no wings; she never leaves the earth; she wears the form of the careful housewife, and always "brings her knitting in her pocket," to use Lowell's happy phrase. She knows the state of the market and the road to wealth by the way of thrift and prudence. She is sagacious, with all the shrewdness and experience of the successful business man, and her utterances are the collected wisdom of the world of trade.

Franklin is the ideal self-made man, and the incarnation of common sense. Born in Boston on the seventeenth of January, 1706; leaving school at the age of ten to help his father, a candle-maker and soap-boiler; apprenticed to his brother, a printer, at twelve, and running away at seventeen to escape further ill-treatment; turning up in Philadelphia, dirty from his journey, his pockets "stuffed out with shirts and stockings," fatigued and hungry, his whole stock of cash one Dutch dollar, but with indomitable pluck in his nature, and youth and strength to serve it; turning his hand to whatever he could find to do; making friends by his diligence, thrift, courtesy, and quick mind eager to know; going to London in his nineteenth year to better his fortune, and lodging in Little Britain with a companion at three and sixpence a week; returning to America after the varied experiences of eighteen months; marrying Deborah Read in 1730, and thereafter applying himself so diligently to business that at the age of forty-two he could retire with a competency and devote his leisure to scientific investigations; taking part in the political affairs of his country, bearing its honors with modesty and dignity abroad, and standing before kings; dying on the seventeenth of April, 1790, full of years and honors, with troops of friends and a record of services that will keep his name living while the world lasts; — this is, in brief, the story of Franklin's life. It is a story much of which he has told in detail and with charming simplicity in his famous " Autobiography." But the value of the book is not in its manner, it is in its matter. This record of a life so successful in every way and so cheerfully happy that Franklin could say of it he would have no objection to a repetition of it from the beginning, is quite unequalled as a picture of sturdy self-reliance, self-control, and hard work willingly done.   It wholly deserves the popularity it has, and should be in the library of every young man who aspires to make something of himself.

Franklin first began the publication of " Poor Richard's Almanac " in 1732, and continued it about twenty-five years.   It was a comic almanac, and its humorous prefaces and quaint bits of worldly wisdom soon made it immensely popular.   Franklin makes Poor Richard say of himself in the Almanac for 1734:

> " I'm not High Church nor Low Church, nor Tory nor Whig,
>   No flatt'ring young coxcomb nor formal old Prig,
>   Not eternally talking nor silently quaint,
>   No profligate sinner nor pragmatical saint.
>   I 'm not vain of my judgment, nor pinn'd on a sleeve,
>   Nor implicitly anything can I believe.
>   To sift truth from all rubbish, I do what I can,
>   And, God knows if I err — I'm a fallible man."

This sifting of truth from all rubbish was the chief concern of Franklin's life.

The verses scattered throughout his Almanac were not always original, any more than the proverbs in it. The latter, he said, " contained the wisdom of many ages and nations," and of the former he wrote: —

> " I know as well as thee that I am no poet born, and it is a trade I never learnt nor indeed could learn. . . . Why, then, should I give my readers *bad lines* when *good ones* of other people are so plenty?   'T is, methinks, a poor excuse for the bad entertainment of guests that the food we set before them, tho' coarse and ordinary, is ' *of one's own raising, off one's own plantation,*' etc., when there is plenty of what is ten times better to be had in the market."

But the verses, like the proverbs, were all well chosen to one end, — that of impressing upon his readers the importance of frugality, diligence, prudence, and virtue. They are what he said they were: "scraps from the table of wisdom that will, if well digested, yield strong nourishment to the mind." They flew far and wide; they lodged in the memory of thousands, and were repeated by young and old; and they inculcated those lessons of self-help which lie at the root of the greatness of nations as well as of individuals. Among the best and most familiar are the following: —

Early to bed and early to rise, makes a man healthy and wealthy and wise.

Eat to live, and not live to eat.

Great talkers, little doers.

God gives all things to industry.

Diligence is the mother of good luck.

God helps them that help themselves.

Forewarned, forearmed.

He that can have patience can have what he will.

If you have time, don't wait for time.

Have you somewhat to do to-morrow, do it to-day.

The noblest question in the world is, What good may I do in it?

He that pays for work before it 's done, has but a penny-worth for twopence.

If you 'd have a servant that you like, serve yourself.

Make haste slowly.

Beware of little expenses, a small leak will sink a great ship.

When the well 's dry we know the worth of water.

Be always ashamed to catch thyself idle.

Experience keeps a dear school, but fools will learn in no other.

Wars bring scars.

Grace thou thy house, let not that grace thee.

A man without ceremony has need of great merit in its place.

He that scatters thorns, let him not go barefoot.

God heals, and the doctor takes the fees.

Love, cough, and a smoke can't well be hid.

The use of money is all the advantage there is in having money.

He that can take rest is greater than he that can take cities.

> Grief often treads upon the heels of pleasure.
> Married in haste, we oft repent at leisure.

Fish and visitors smell in three days.

He that would catch fish must venture his bait.

If you would be loved, love, and be lovable.

The diligent spinner has a large shift.

There 's a time to wink as well as to see.

The tongue is ever turning to the aching tooth.

The muses love the morning.

If Jack 's in love, he 's no judge of Jill's beauty.

A good example is the best sermon.

Life with fools consists in drinking; with the wise man, living 's thinking.

Clean your fingers before you point at my spots.

Little strokes fell great oaks.

Love your neighbor, yet don't pull down your hedge.

In the affairs of this world, men are saved not by faith, but by the want of it.

If man could have half he wishes, he would double his trouble.

Generous minds are all of kin.

Constant dropping wears away stones.

Love and toothache have many cures, but none infallible except possession and dispossession.

Sloth, like rust, consumes faster than labor wears, while the used key is always bright.

There are no gains without pains.

Three removes are as bad as a fire.

If you would have your business done, go ! if not, send !

Dost thou love life?   Then do not squander time, for that 's the stuff life is made of.

Franklin's mind was remarkable for its assimilative power; the range of his love of knowledge knew no limits.   He had a great fondness for music, and invented an instrument, on the principle of musical glasses, which he called the " Armonica."   He discovered the fact of the identity of lightning and electricity, and invented the lightning-rod.   He invented a stove, and declined to take out a patent for it, on the principle that "as we enjoy great advantages from the inventions of others, we should be glad to serve others by any invention of ours; and this we should do freely and generously."   He delighted in natural history, and had the widest curiosity concerning plants and animals, and is said to have introduced the yellow willow into this country from a sprouting slip from a wicker basket of foreign make which he saw lying in a ditch.   For his valuable experiments and discoveries in electrical science he was made a member of the Royal Society of England, and received the degree of Doctor of Laws from the universities of St. Andrews and Oxford. During his residence in France as minister from the United States, he was appointed by the French king one of the commissioners to investigate the subject of animal magnetism, which was just then exciting a great deal of attention from the claims of Mesmer

and his credulous adherents.   Franklin's coolness
and common sense may be seen in the following
statement: —

" As to the animal magnetism so much talked of, I must
doubt its existence till I can see and feel some effect of it.
None of the cures said to be performed by it have fallen
under my observation, and there are so many disorders
which cure themselves, and such a disposition in mankind
to deceive themselves and one another on these occasions,
and living long has given me so frequent opportunities of
seeing certain remedies cried up as curing everything and
yet soon after totally laid aside as useless, I cannot but fear
that the expectation of great advantages from this new
method of treating diseases will prove a delusion.   That
delusion may, however, and in some cases, be of use while
it lasts.   There are in every great, rich city a number of
persons who are never in health, because they are fond of
medicines and always taking them, whereby they derange
their natural functions and hurt their constitutions.   If these
people can be persuaded to forbear their drugs in expectation of being cured by only the physician's finger or an iron
rod pointing at them, they may possibly find good effects
though they may mistake the cause."

Among many friends whom Franklin made in
France were the celebrities, Turgot, Buffon, D'Alem-
bert, Condorcet, La Rochefoucauld, and he had the
pleasure of meeting the great satirist Voltaire.

Franklin was not only interested in science, but in
whatever tends to the comfort and enlightenment of
humanity.   He was the first to suggest the forming
of fire-companies; the first to found a public subscription library in North America; the first to call
attention to the necessity of better systems of street

lighting and cleaning. He served on school committees. His own education had been acquired without direction, and the suggestions he had to offer on educational questions were practical and original. He had taught himself Latin, French, Italian, and Spanish. He had drilled himself in composition, and knew the value of terse, clear English. In his sketch of the work for an English School in Philadelphia, he insists that particular care be taken to make good spellers of the lowest class, declaring it a "shame for a man to be so ignorant of this little art in his own language as to be perpetually confounding words of like sound and different significations." This drill is to be followed in successive terms by drill in speaking properly and gracefully; drill in composition to be taught by putting the boys to writing letters to each other on various subjects, imaginary business, discussions of what they read or see, etc.; drill in paraphrasing, amplifying, and abridgment of fine passages; and, lastly, reading and discussion of the best English authors, whom he enumerates as "Tillotson, Milton, Locke, Addison, Pope, Swift," and adds for study "papers in the 'Spectator' or 'Guardian;' the best translations of Homer, Virgil, Horace, Telemachus, Travels of Cyrus, etc." By such a course he thinks the pupils "will come out of this school, though unacquainted with any ancient or foreign tongue, masters of their own." Such a mastery he valued very highly, and thought too much attention was given to the ancient languages at the expense of modern tongues. "He said," reports the historian, Jared Sparks, "that when the custom of wearing broad cuffs with buttons first began, there was reason for it, the cuffs might be brought down over the hands, and thus guard them from wet and cold. But gloves came into use, and broad cuffs were unnecessary; yet the custom was still retained. So likewise with cocked hats; the wide brim when let down afforded protection from the rain and sun. Umbrellas were introduced, yet fashion prevailed to keep cocked hats in vogue, although they were rather cumbersome than useful. Thus with the Latin language. When nearly all the books in Europe were written in that language, the study of it was essential in every system of education; but it is now scarcely needed except as an accomplishment, since it has everywhere given place, as a vehicle of thought and knowledge, to some one of the modern tongues."

Franklin's own mastery of his native tongue is admirable. He never uses a long word when a short one will do as well; nor does he add an extra word for the sake of emphasis when his meaning is clear without it. He never tries to say what he does not see clearly; he never ventures where he cannot walk securely. He is shrewdly humorous, and clenches his arguments with some apt and lively though homely illustration drawn directly from his own observation. For example, in an essay designed to show the nature of fault-finders and the discomfort arising from association with them, he says : —

" An old philosophical friend of mine was grown from experience very cautious in this particular, and carefully avoided any intimacy with such people. He had, like other philosophers, a thermometer to show him the heat of the weather, and a barometer to mark when it was good or bad; but there being no instrument to discover at first sight the un-pleasing disposition of a person, he for that purpose made use of his legs, one of which was remarkably handsome, the other by some accident crooked and deformed. If a stranger at the first interview regarded his ugly leg more than the handsome one, he doubted him. If he spoke of it and took no notice of the handsome leg, that was sufficient to determine my philosopher to have no further acquaintance with him. Everybody has not this two-legged instrument, but every one with a little attention may observe signs of that carping, fault-finding disposition, and take the same resolution of avoiding the acquaintance of those infected with it. I, therefore, advise those critical, querulous, dis-contented, unhappy people, that if they wish to be respected and beloved by others and happy in themselves, they should *leave off looking at the ugly leg.*"

Franklin's knowledge of men was very profound, his observation close. " The most trifling actions of a man, in my opinion, as well as the smallest lineaments of his face, give a nice observer some notions of his mind," he says. Yet he deals with men only on the practical side. He ignores wholly the world of senti-ment, imagination, and passion. Of ideality he had not a trace; he trusted his senses and lived in them soberly, cheerfully, happily. He rarely went to church, and Sunday was his day of study; but though he doubted the divinity of Christ, he believed in im-mortality and in God, and that " the most acceptable service we can render to Him is to do good to His other children."

He was about five feet nine or ten inches in height, and grew stout as he grew older. His complexion was fair, his eyes gray; his manner, dress, and speech plain and pleasing.   He suffered very much from gout in later life, but was uniformly cheerful, and retained his faculties unimpaired to the last.   He made himself famous in many ways: he was statesman, political economist, scientist, public speaker, and man of letters; and though the character of his mind and his studies make him first of all a man of science, he has lived close to the heart of every succeeding generation as the author of " Poor Richard's Almanac " and an incomparable Autobiography.

Franklin is often cited as a " typical American; " it would be better to say that he is the world's best type of good sense.   He belongs to us exclusively no more than Socrates belongs exclusively to the Greeks, or Montaigne to the French.   A man is great, not in proportion to what he reflects of national peculiarities, but in proportion to what he reflects of the whole human race; and Franklin reflects the homely instincts and common sense of civilized mankind.

The phrase " a typical American " is so great a favorite among our lesser critics that it is impossible to read their eulogy of our distinguished writers without encountering it in some form not once but many times.   It is a well-worn standard coin of literary criticism, and passes from hand to hand without question.   It is well to examine it in order to find out just what it is worth.   It undoubtedly originated in answer to the charge so frequently and senselessly brought against American literature, namely, that it lacks a distinctively national spirit, and that the influence of English models can be clearly traced in it.

Washington Irving reminds the English reader of Addison.   Bryant is the American Wordsworth; Cooper, the American Scott.   Motley savors of Carlyle to those who read only the headings of his chapters and the running titles of his pages; Emerson is the American Carlyle; Longfellow's " Hiawatha " has no flavor of the national soil, but might as well have been written within sound of the chimes of St. Paul. In short, grumbles the critic, these Americans act, think, talk, and write as their Christian brethren, the British Islanders.   To which we reply, Why not ? Literature is not a growth of the soil, like potatoes and Indian corn; it is a growth of feeling and understanding, and when men love and laugh, weep and work, think and hope, in a different manner on the banks of the Hudson from what they do on the banks of the Thames, we shall have a wholly different order of facts and feelings, and a distinctively national manner of recording them.   But when we do become thus differentiated from our kind, we shall produce a literature that nobody but ourselves will understand, enjoy, or care to read, because it is the oneness of humanity, the fundamental kinship of all nations recognized in literature, that makes its enduring value and its international fame.

When Ben Jonson sang of Shakespeare, " He was not of our age, but for all time," he uttered the epitome of all literary praise.   Had Shakespeare been nothing but an *English* poet of the sixteenth century, he would never be the poet of all mankind for all centuries.   It is, therefore, no discredit to our American writers, but rather the highest praise of them, that they do not exclusively voice America, but speak intelligently to England and other European nations; and our critics who in jealousy of our national honor proclaim of any given poet or novelist that he is "intensely and distinctively American," hoping thereby to give him the highest praise, in reality proclaim the limitations and not the universality of his genius. Burns is not "intensely and distinctively" Scottish, but intensely and distinctively natural and human; Goethe is not a typical German, but the world's most finished type of nineteenth-century culture. Byron is by no means a representative Englishman, but he stands for the restless activity of his age, its skepticism, its fierce revolt against conventionalities, and its insatiable hunger for happiness.

However, to speak with strict exactness, there is, to the acute and quickly perceptive mind, a very apparent national tone in our literature to which I have already alluded; namely, a thoroughgoing optimism, an absolute confidence in the future, and a healthy joy in life, that are singularly at variance with the pessimistic note of certain writers in other countries.

Contrast, for example, the attitude of Carlyle with that of Emerson. Friends and contemporaries, earnest seekers of truth and haters of cant, both of them; but the one, always "sunk in the bowels of chaos," utters his scorn of vice and folly, his impatience and despair, in words that burn and corrode like fire or acid; the other, with the mild serenity of a Hindoo sage, looks out on a world all light and slow, unceasing growth toward perfection, pronounces it good, and is content to bide its time.

If in this deep and steady faith in the ultimate victory of good over evil, — a faith that never fal-

tered in our best men even when the nation was con-
vulsed by civil war, our foreign critics do not discern
the national spirit, it is safe to say that they utterly
misconceive it.   An invincible good-nature characterizes us as a nation and pervades our literature.   Even
satire, which has been a scourge in the hands of Swift,
Voltaire, Heine, has never been more than a lithe,
tingling birchen rod in America.   Our humor is
broad and kindly, but lacks the mellow Elian flavor
and the exquisite keenness and delicacy of French
wit.   A sturdy good sense and practical shrewdness
are other elements of our literature.   One other indisputable quality it possesses, and that is purity.   With
the exception of Walt Whitman, there is no American
writer of note who would need to be edited for schools
in an expurgated edition.

Hawthorne is the writer to whom we can most confidently point when the question of original genius is at
stake.   Emerson is our broadest thinker, Longfellow
our most popular poet, Lowell our acutest critic, and
Motley and Parkman are our best historians.

CHAPTER II

WILLIAM ELLERY CHANNING, the leading Unitarian divine of America, says, in his remarks on the "Character and Writings of Fénelon" : —

"It is too true, and a sad truth, that religious books are pre-eminently dull. If we wished to impoverish a man's intellect, we could devise few means more effectual than to confine him to what is called a course of theological reading."

Had Channing's own works in any degree deserved this charge of theological dulness; had he stood aloof from his age, indifferent to its interests, yielding neither to its influence nor in turn reacting upon it, — it would be a great mistake to include him among the representatives of American literature. But he was not only a writer of great vigor and freshness, a thinker of unusual breadth and power, but a man of so marked an influence upon his age that "all America," says Emerson, "would have been impoverished in wanting him." More than any other man, he helped to free New England from the cramping influence of a narrow, dogmatic Puritanism. He not only helped to make literature possible, but he produced literature. His essay on Milton is a noble piece of work, dwelling with loving minuteness on Milton's lofty virtue, his love of freedom, his magnificent courage in poverty and blindness, and showing an acute, critical appreciation of his poetry and prose. His essay on Bonaparte is a remarkably fine piece of character analysis. His addresses on " Self-Culture " and on the " Elevation of the Laboring Classes " are so replete with good sense, high moral feeling, delicate sympathy and penetration, that they speak to the needs of the student and laborer as pointedly and helpfully to-day as they did in the hour in which they were written. His sermons have a glow, a fervor that rouses the feelings at the same time that it purifies them; for Channing had the temperament of a poet united with the aspirations of a saint. He had, too, the true literary instinct, and while he was no searcher after fine expressions, — indeed, had a horror of mere rhetoric, — so clear and compact was his thought and so nice his ear that his language is always terse yet harmonious.

Unitarianism, of which Channing is the chief exponent in America, had its martyr as early as 1553, when Michael Servetus was burned at the stake at the instigation of John Calvin; but the word " Unitarian " was first applied in 1568 to a religious organization in Transylvania, in the eastern part of the Austro-Hungarian Empire. Milton, Locke, and Newton were Unitarians in belief; but a Unitarian church was first established in England in 1774, when Theophilus Lindsey left the Episcopal church and transformed an old auction-room in Essex Street, London, into a place of worship. King's Chapel, an Episcopal church in Boston, was the first church in

New England to avow itself Unitarian, — in 1777, three years before the birth of Channing. Channing was not, therefore, the founder of a new sect, but he gave a new impulse and a new dignity to an old faith.

William Ellery Channing was born on the seventh of April, 1780, in Newport, Rhode Island. His father, a much respected lawyer, was of English descent; and his mother, Lucy Ellery, a careful, prudent woman, was the daughter of William Ellery, one of the signers of the Declaration of Independence. As a child, Channing was serious and reflective, and known among his schoolmates as " Peacemaker," the " Little Minister," or " Little King Pepin." But he was a fearless boy, with all his peaceful instincts, not inactive, a remarkable wrestler, and fond of long rambles alone. Large-hearted and generous in nature, money would not stay in his pockets, though he never spent it wholly upon himself; and so tender of life, so fearful of giving pain was he, that he would not crush the smallest insect at his feet, and never hurt a bird in his life. His nephew and biographer, William Henry Channing, relates as illustrative of his serious, earnest nature, the story of his being taken as a child to hear a famous preacher, whose glowing rhetoric and vivid representation of man's lost and evil state filled him with the profoundest grief and terror. On the way home he heard his father remark, "Sound doctrine, sir." " It is all true, then," was his gloomy reflection. His heart sank; the light of day seemed blotted out to him. He waited for his father to speak to him, and presently he heard him whistle; but when he got home and his father quietly removed his boots and began reading his newspaper, he said to himself: "Can what I've heard be true? No, father does n't believe it, people don't believe it; it was *not* true." He felt that he had not been seriously treated, and reflected long upon the inconsistency of living happily and at the same time expressing belief in a doctrine that, rightly apprehended, would make life a curse and torture.

As a pupil, young Channing was persevering and patient, but not quick; indeed, he was thought dull. Latin was especially difficult for him, and it is said that his father's office assistant, seeing the troubled boy poring over his task one day, called out to him: "Come, Bill! they say you're a fool, but I know better. Bring me your grammar, and I'll soon teach you Latin." The sensible, informal teaching soon bore good fruit, and Channing became a fine classical scholar, and, later, used to recall his early readings of Virgil as one of the keenest pleasures of his boyhood. For mathematics he had some aptness, but no particular relish; and in college, history and literature were his favorite studies.

In 1793 the boy's father died in his forty-third year, leaving a wife and family of nine children. At the time of his father's death William was living with his uncle Henry, a clergyman, preparing for Harvard, which he entered the following year. At that time no modern language was taught at Harvard, except French, and that only once a week. The library was scant, the course of instruction meagre. The president and professors were seen only in the most formal manner, and there was no social intercourse between the students and families of Cambridge. There was a certain class pride among the best scholars that offered an incentive to effort.

Channing was at this time small in stature, but muscular, in perfect health, and a hearty laugher. His fluent essays and orations gave him distinction in college, and were the result of careful study and preparation. In a letter to a youthful friend seeking advice, he gives us a glimpse of his aims as a student: —

" At your age I was poor, hardly able to buy clothes ; but the great idea of *improvement* had seized upon me. I wanted to make the most of myself. I was not satisfied with knowing things superficially or by halves, but tried to get some comprehensive views of what I studied. I had an *end*, and for a boy a high end, in view. I did not think of fitting myself for this or that particular pursuit, but for any to which events might call me. . . . I never had an anxious thought about my lot in life. When I was poor, ill, and compelled to work with little strength, I left the future to itself. I was not buoyed up by any hopes of promotion. I wanted retirement, obscurity. . . . What you want is to give tone, freedom, life to all your faculties, to get a disposable strength of intellect to use in whatever course you may pursue. A professional education, or one designed to fit you for a particular profession, would make but half a man of you. You are not to grow up merely for a particular occupation, but to perform all the duties of a man, to mix in society, to converse with intelligent men of all pursuits, to meet emergencies, to be prepared for new and unexpected situations. A general, liberal, generous education is what you need. Every study into which you throw your soul, in which you gain truth and exercise your faculties, is a preparation for your future course. I have found a good in everything I have learned."

On his graduation from Harvard in 1798, Channing went to Richmond, to become a tutor in the family of Mr. David M. Randolph, United States Marshal of Virginia. There he first saw the "iniquity and miseries of slavery," which always distressed him exceedingly. "Language," he says, " cannot express my detestation of it." Including Mr. Randolph's son, Channing had twelve boys under his care. His nephew relates that one day " an old colored woman came into the school to complain of some of the boys who had damaged her garden, broken her fence, and torn up her flowers, making loud complaints and wanting to see the master of the school. When he presented himself, she surveyed him for a moment and said, ' *You* de massa? You little ting, you can't lick 'em; dey put you out de window!'"

Channing's boyish stature and slender figure were always a matter of surprise to those who did not know him. It is related that a Kentuckian who ardently admired his works, exclaimed: " Dr. Channing small and weak! I thought he was six feet, at least, in height, with a fresh cheek, broad chest, voice like that of many waters and strong-limbed as a giant." On the contrary, he was small and slender to emaciation, with dark brown hair, hollow cheeks, and shining gray eyes deeply sunken in a pale spiritual face that told of lonely vigils and unremitting study. His health, robust enough in early boyhood, was ruined by his ascetic life in Virginia. Living in an outbuilding, giving his time to teaching during the day and seeing little of the family, the ardent, ambitious youth passed most of the night in study, remaining at his desk until two and three o'clock in the morning, and often seeing day dawn before he was content to relinquish his task. He had resolved to fit himself for the ministry; and, in accordance with his ascetic notions of purity and renunciation, he felt it his duty to subdue the animal nature and inure himself to all sorts of physical hardships. He slept on the bare floor, made experiments in diet, denying himself to the point of hunger. He spent his salary in buying books instead of clothes, and went all winter without an overcoat, though he was always extremely sensitive to cold. His shabby clothing forced him into a solitude whose advantages he praised in that it taught him to depend upon himself for enjoyment. But this ascetic life, by lowering his vitality and sowing the seeds of lurking disease that made a life-long invalid of him, seduced him into a state of melancholy revery and not active thought, to the harmfulness of which he alludes in a letter written to a young friend in later life: —

"Do anything innocent rather than give yourself up to *reverie*. I can speak on this point from experience. At one period of my life I was a dreamer, castle-builder. Visions of the distant and future took the place of present duty and activity. I spent hours in reverie. I suppose I was seduced in part by physical disability, but the body suffered as much as the mind. I found, too, that the imagination threatened to inflame the passions ; that if I meant to be virtuous, I must dismiss my musings. The conflict was a hard one ; I re-solved, prayed, resisted, sought refuge in occupation, and at length triumphed. . . . I have suffered, too, from a painful sense of defects, but on the whole have been too wise to waste in idle lamentations of deficiencies moments which should be used in removing them."

He tells us that in his youth he once handed a lady of active benevolence a poem of Southey's that had wrung tears from him. She read it coolly and said with a smile, "It is pretty." "Pretty!" was his indignant mental echo; but in reflecting on the circumstance at home, he saw that the mind is often just as passive under the stimulus of mere feeling as when it receives a sensory impression, and that there is no *moral merit* in possessing feeling. He says: —

"I went on to consider, whether there are not many persons who were still deficient in *active* benevolence. A thousand instances occurred to me, myself among the number. It is true, said I, that I sit in my study and shed tears over human misery. I weep over a novel. I weep over a tale of woe. But do I ever relieve the distressed? Have I ever lightened the load of affliction? My cheeks reddened at the question ; a cloud of error burst from my mind. I found that virtue did not consist in feeling, but in *acting from a sense of duty.*"

This discovery may have led to that systematic repression of emotion which later on passed for coldness among those who did not know him well. "My tears do not lie so near my eyes," he once replied to the question how he could be so unmoved during a pathetic appeal.

In these early years of struggle and search after truth and light, Channing fell into the dream of communism. He looked out into the world and saw that

"all is hurry, all is business. But why this tumult?" he asked himself. "To pamper the senses and load the body with idle trappings. Show me the man who ever toiled for wealth to relieve misery or unrivet the chains of oppression.

Show me the man who ever imported virtue from the Indies, or became a better Christian by increasing his hoard. Are not the mines of science forsaken for those of Potosi? . . . Ought man to provide most for his body or his mind? . . . I believe that selfishness and avarice have arisen from two ideas universally inculcated on the young and practised upon the old : (1) that *every individual has a distinct interest to pursue from the interest of the community* : (2) that *the body requires more care than the mind.*

"I believe these ideas to be false, and I believe that you can never banish them till you persuade mankind to cease to act upon them ; that is, till you can persuade them (1) to destroy all distinctions of property (which you are sensible must perpetuate the supposed distinction of interest) and to throw the produce of their labor into one common stock, instead of hoarding it up in their own garners ; and (2) to become really conscious of the powers and the dignity of their mind."

His grandfather Ellery, in a plain practical way, set forth his sensible arguments in opposition to this enthusiastic dream, and though he could not dampen his young grandson's ardor in benevolence, nor destroy his faith in the ultimate perfectibility of man, he did succeed in making plain to him some real objections to his schemes, and directed his enthusiasm into more practicable channels. Later, Channing often said that all that was worthy in his own life and influence grew out of the fidelity with which he had listened to objections offered to what he *wished* to believe or do.

Channing spent nearly two years in Virginia, and in 1800 went home to Newport broken in health. He stayed at home a year and a half, devoting himself to theological studies and at the same time taking charge of the education of his youngest brother and Mr. Randolph's son.   He began his study of divinity by a careful examination of the evidences of Christianity. He wished, he said, to know what Christ thought, and not what men have made him teach.   He thought ministers lost themselves in unimportant controversies, to the neglect of their most solemn charge, the saving of souls.

In 1801 he was elected regent in Harvard University; his duties were light, requiring only general superintendence of the students in the building where he roomed, and of the building itself.   The office supported him and gave him an opportunity to continue his studies.   He preached his first sermon at Medford in 1802, selecting for his text the words " Silver and gold have I none; but such as I have give I thee." He received two calls to settle in Boston, accepted that of the Religious Society in Federal Street, and was ordained in 1803.   He lived at first with some parishioners, but soon invited his mother and the family to Boston.   His brother Francis and he had agreed that for the support of their mother and the rest of the family one of them must remain unmarried for ten years, and William took upon himself the fulfilment of this obligation.   He chose the smallest room in the house for his study, and for a sleeping-apartment shared the attic with his younger brother; it was a cold, bare, cheerless room without a fire.   He dressed cheaply, though always with careful neatness; and though his salary was at first twelve hundred dollars a year, and later fifteen hundred dollars, — a very good salary for that time, — he did not save a cent of it. " Really," said his elder brother, " William should have a guardian; he spends every dollar as soon as he gets it." Yet the dollar was never idly spent, but always for the comfort of somebody else.

The other members of the Channing family were hilarious, outspoken, comfort-loving, — a strong contrast to our young saint; but he kept his own way among them, redeeming himself from any absurdity that might attach to his seriousness, by his real consideration for others and his rigid conscientiousness. But in later life Channing regretted this early repression of the fulness of his social and poetical nature, and used often to say to his nephew, " I am too serious." He was gentle and loving, in spite of an inherited tendency to irritability and sternness. Earnest and sincere, simple and natural in manner, he very much disliked to be called Reverend. His manner in the pulpit was as natural and unassuming as in private life. He had no grave pulpit intonations, made few gestures, and followed to the letter his advice to a young minister: —

" Put confidence in the power of pure, unsophisticated truth. Do not disguise it or overlay it with ornament or false colors to make it more effectual. Bring it out in its native shape and hues, and if possible in noonday brightness. Beware of ambiguous words, of cant, of vague abstractions, of new-fangled phrases, of ingenious subtilties. Especially exaggerate nothing for effect — that most common sin of the pulpit. Be willing to disappoint your hearers, to be unimpressive, to seem cold, rather than to ' o'erstep the modesty ' of truth. In the long run nothing is so strong as simplicity. . . . Prefer the true to the dazzling, the sunlight to the meteor."

Channing made it the business of his life to do good. "Let me remember, with Titus," he said, "that I have lost that day in which I have done no good to a fellow-man." Continual ill-health and a deep sense of his own unworthiness were the dragons he had to fight; but the battles were fought alone, and no one was ever pained or disturbed by them.

In the summer of 1814 Channing married his cousin Ruth Gibbs; four children were born to them, two of whom died in infancy. Channing was a wise and loving father. He says: —

"I wish my children to be simple, natural without affectation. Children are often injured for life by the notice taken of their movements, tones, sayings, which leads them to repeat what draws attention, and to act from love of observation instead of following the impulses of nature. A child should never be tempted to put on pretty airs or to think of itself and its looks. I have wished my children always to act in a free, natural, unstudied way, — without the desire of being observed, — and on this account I have been very willing to keep them out of society where they might have been taught, by injudicious notice, to turn their thoughts upon themselves, and to assume the behavior which they would have seen to attract attention. The charm of infancy is its perfect artlessness, and the immediate communication between its feelings and actions. I would prefer that my children should have any degree of awkwardness, rather than form an artificial style of conduct; for the first evil may be outgrown, but affectation is seldom or never cured."

In 1822 Channing's health had so far declined that he went abroad with his wife for rest. He visited France, Switzerland, Italy, and in England had the pleasure of meeting Wordsworth and Coleridge.

His health was little improved by his travels, and in 1824 the Rev. Ezra Stiles Gannett was ordained associate pastor with him. For eighteen years he and Channing toiled together, and gradually Channing's time and thought were given more and more to philanthropic and literary work, while Gannett assumed the duties of pastor. These later years, full of work and study, were the happiest years of Channing's life. He was accustomed to say that his childhood had been sad, and once, when asked at sixty what period of life he thought the happiest, he looked up with a smile and answered that he thought it was about sixty. The rigid asceticism of his youth had given way to more genial interpretations of life and its duties. He trusted his natural impulses more and more. " He changed his views from time to time," says Garrison, " but only to advance, never to retreat." Thus life with him was a growth, and he had not yet attained the limits of it when he died in 1842. He had been on a journey in Vermont, when he was taken ill of typhoid fever at Bennington in that State, where he died on the second of October. He was buried in Mt. Auburn Cemetery, near Boston.

Channing's name is associated with all the social reforms of his day. He sympathized with the temperance cause, and took an active part in the anti-slavery movement. He hated war, had a dread and abhorrence of the passion for power, and a reverence for liberty and human rights. He was intensely interested in the masses; he believed in manual-training schools, and one of his dearest ideas and hopes was the union of *labor* and *culture*. He did not think that the laboring classes were to be elevated by escaping labor or by pressing into a different rank. On the contrary, he had great faith in hard work. He says of the laboring classes: —

"I have no wish to dress them from a Parisian tailor's shop, or to teach them manners from a dancing-school. . . . Fashion is a poor vocation. Its creed, that idleness is a privilege and work a disgrace, is among the deadliest errors. Without depth of thought, or earnestness of feeling, or strength of purpose, living an unreal life, sacrificing substance to show, substituting the factitious for the natural, mistaking a crowd for society, finding its chief pleasure in ridicule, and exhausting its ingenuity in expedients for killing time, — fashion is among the last influences under which a human being who respects himself, or who comprehends the great end of life, would desire to be placed."

The elevation which Channing desired for the masses was elevation of soul; he wished every man to be a student and thinker. He saw the dangers arising from the love and spread of luxury among them: —

"Needless expenses keep many too poor for self-improvement. And here let me say that expensive habits among the more prosperous laborers often interfere with the mental culture of themselves and their families. How many among them sacrifice improvement to appetite! How many sacrifice it to the love of show, to the desire of out-stripping others, and to habits of expense, which grow out of this insatiable passion! In a country so thriving and luxurious as ours, the laborer is in danger of contracting artificial wants and diseased tastes; and to gratify these, he gives himself wholly to accumulation, and sells his mind for gain.

Our unparalleled prosperity has not been an unmixed good. It has inflamed cupidity, has diseased the imagination with dreams of boundless success, and plunged a vast multitude into excessive toils, feverish competitions, and exhausting cares. A laborer having procured a neat home and a wholesome table, should ask nothing more for the senses; but should consecrate his leisure and what may be spared of his earnings, to the culture of himself and his family, to the best books, to the best teachings, to pleasant and profitable intercourse, to sympathy, and to the offices of humanity, and to the enjoyment of the beautiful in nature and art. . . . The saddest aspect of the age to me is that which undoubtedly contributes to social order. It is the absorption of the multitude of men in outward material interests; it is the selfish prudence which is never tired of the labor of accumulation, and which keeps men steady, regular, respectable drudges from morning to night. The cases of a few murders, great crimes, lead multitudes to exclaim, How wicked this age! But the worst sign is the chaining down of almost all the minds of a community to low perishable interests. It is a sad thought that the infinite energies of the soul have no higher end than to cover the back and fill the belly and keep caste in society. A few nerves hardly visible on the surface of the tongue create most of the endless stir around us. Undoubtedly eating and drinking, house-building and caste-keeping, are not to be despised; most of them are essential. But surely life has a higher use than to adorn the body which is so soon to be wrapped in grave-clothes, than to keep warm and flowing the blood which is so soon to be cold and stagnant in the tomb."

Channing was an uncompromising defender of freedom in all its forms. When, in 1838, the editor of the " Boston Investigator " was sentenced to two months' imprisonment on a charge of blasphemy, Channing's was the first name on the petition for his release, because he thought it shocking for a man to be punished for his opinions. He befriended Garrison, the great champion of liberty, when he was the most hated man in Boston. But his best work for freedom of thought was done in the pulpit. To free the mind from servility to fear, to free religion of its terrors, to teach men to give due importance to their own free moral nature, was the task to which he gave himself heart and soul. He did not think that to rob man of his dignity was to exalt God, but that the glory of the Maker lies in his work. He did not believe that perfection consists in self-oblivion, but in an ever-growing activity. He thought that, "if Edwards's work on the Will really answered its end, if it could thoroughly persuade men that they were bound by an irresistible necessity, that their actions were fixed links in the chain of destiny, that there was but one agent, God, in the universe, — it would be one of the most pernicious books ever issued from the press." "False theories of religion," he said, "have done much to perpetuate those abject views of human nature which keep it where it is, which check men's aspirations, and reconcile them to their present poor modes of thought and action as the fixed and unalterable laws of their being." He had a strong faith in humanity, in progress, yet he was not blind to the difficulties in the way. James Freeman Clarke says: —

"I remember Dr. Channing's once telling me that of all the words of Jesus, nothing struck him more than his saying to the Jews around him, 'Be ye perfect, even as your Father in Heaven is perfect.' 'Why,' said he, 'when I consider what kind of people they were; when I consider the hardness of their hearts, the barrenness of their minds, — the faith in humanity which could inspire such a saying as that seems to me a marvel of the love of Jesus. You or I,' said he, 'would just as soon have thought of saying to these chairs and tables, "Be ye perfect, even as your Father in Heaven is perfect," as to those men.'"

In his discourse at the ordination of the Reverend Jared Sparks, delivered in 1819, Channing first gave full, free utterance to the doctrines of Unitarian Christianity. He defended the exercise of reason in matters of religion. He declared the Bible to be " a book written for men in the language of men, and that its meaning is to be sought in the same manner as that of other books." He objected to the doctrine of the Trinity, because, while acknowledging in words, it subverts in effect the unity of God, and he challenged his opponents to adduce one passage in the New Testament where the word " God " means three persons. He declared his belief that Jesus Christ is a being distinct from and inferior to God, and that he did not offer himself as a mediator between offending man and an offended, implacable God, but was sent to men as a great moral teacher by a merciful and loving God.

This address, which was published and widely read, excited much controversy; but though contention pained Channing, he never shrank from expressing what seemed to him true for fear of giving offence to the " majority, the fashionable or the refined." He had so great a dread of being creed bound, and thus losing the capacity for receiving new religious truths, that he even called himself little of a Unitarian, and stood aloof " from all but those who strive and pray for clear light, for a purer and more effectual manifestation of Christian truth." At the ordination of a fellow minister, he said: —

" Preach with moral courage ; fear no man, high or low. Honor all men, love all men, but fear none. Speak what you account truth frankly, strongly, boldly. . . . Wait not to be backed by numbers. Wait not till you are sure of an echo from the crowd. The fewer the voices on the side of truth, the more distinct and strong must be your own. . . . The noblest work on earth or in heaven is to act on the soul, to inspire it with wisdom and magnanimity, with reverence for God, and love towards men."

When we remember how few are able, or dare to think for themselves; how opinions, especially of a religious and political character, are propagated by contact and inheritance rather than by original thinking, we shall not be able to overestimate the influence of a fearless, original thinker like Channing. His works were widely circulated and read with avidity. James Freeman Clarke mentions a man in Wisconsin who, unable to buy a volume of Channing's, copied it with his pen, word for word, from beginning to end. "The timid, sensitive, diffident, and doubting needed this voice," said one. It awakened thought, inspired hope, cleared away mists, called men to their feet, directed them to their tasks, and taught them to find freedom, growth, and joy in doing it. It made straight the way for Emerson and that group of buoyant and strong writers that make the glory of New England. No man of his day had a finer feeling for what is excellent in literature, or a more delicate appreciation of art. Washington Allston, his brother-in-law and friend, said that there was no one whose judgment in pictures he valued more highly than Channing's. He recognized Wordsworth's greatness before the world had found him out, and after Shakespeare there was no poet whom he read so often. Had Channing devoted himself wholly to literature, his name would have been the first in criticism in the literature of his country; but he chose a nobler work, and he stands first as the champion of intellectual freedom.

CHAPTER III

IF sentiment were not perennial, if it did not properly belong to youth and genius, and that form of mind with a romantic coloring that defies time and disillusionment; if humor were not allied to a keen and loving insight into human nature, — Washington Irving would belong to a class of writers whose reign is over. Only three years younger in age than Channing, Irving is half a century younger than he in his attitude toward life and the problems of his time. In fact, these problems did not exist for him. He lived in a world remote from them. His mind brooded lovingly over the past, gathering to itself all that was picturesque and rich in coloring, all that was genial and human in character, and all that was generous, brave, and noble in sentiment. That which he gathered he put into his books with an ease, a grace, a gentle humor and pathos that make him one of the great masters of style. In selection and execution an artist, his fame rests secure in the domain of art.

Washington Irving was born in New York City on the third of April, 1783. His father was a Scotch Presbyterian, and his mother the granddaughter of an English curate. He was brought up with a strictness that led him to think that everything that was pleasant was wicked; but a naturally sound instinct protested against any particular horror of pleasant wickedness, and we have stories of stealthy visits to the theatre when his parents thought him asleep in bed. He was not remarkable as a child, and his brother relates that when he was about eight years old, he came home from school one day and said to his mother, "The Madame says I am a dunce; isn't it a pity!" But he made no particular effort to shine at school, shirking mathematics, which he disliked, and writing other boys' compositions while they did his sums for him. He was very fond of music and the theatre, a fondness that continued with him through life. He was fond, too, of reading books of travel, and used to take them to school for secret perusal under his desk. Out of school he wandered about the piers, looking out over the sea and wishing himself on the distant vessels whose sails he saw. He loved the Hudson and said of it: —

"I thank God I was born on the banks of the Hudson. I think it an invaluable advantage to be born and brought up in the neighborhood of some grand and noble object in nature, — a river, a lake, or a mountain. We make a friendship with it; we in a manner ally ourselves to it for life. . . . And I fancy I can trace much of what is good and pleasant in my heterogeneous compound to my early companionship with this glorious river."

At fifteen Irving left school, thus missing a collegiate training, — a fact that he always regretted. The next year he entered a law office, and the third advocate under whom he studied was Josiah Hoffman, whose house "became another home to him."

In this home he met the daughter Matilda Hoffman, with whom he fell deeply in love. The pathetic story of this attachment is best related in his own words, found after his death in a package of manuscript marked " Private Mems " : —

" We saw each other every day, and I became excessively attached to her. Her shyness wore off by degrees, the more I had reason to admire. Her mind seemed to unfold itself leaf by leaf, and every time to discover new sweetness. Nobody knew her so well as I, for she was generally timid and silent, but I in a manner studied her excellence. Never did I meet with more intuitive rectitude of mind, more native delicacy, more exquisite propriety in word, thought, and action, than in this young creature. . . .

" This passion was terribly against my studies. I felt my own deficiency, and despaired of ever succeeding at the bar. I could study anything else rather than law, and had a fatal propensity to *belles-lettres*. I had gone on blindly, like a boy in love ; but now I began to open my eyes and be miserable. . . . The gentleman with whom I studied saw the state of my mind. . . . He urged me to return to my studies, to apply myself, to become well acquainted with the law; and that in case I could make myself capable of undertaking legal concerns, he would take me into partnership with him and give me his daughter. Nothing could be more generous. I set to work with new zeal to study anew, and I considered myself bound in honor not to make further advances with the daughter until I should feel satisfied with my proficiency in the law. It was all in vain. I had an insuperable repugnance to the study ; my mind would not take hold of it, or, rather, by long despondency had become for the time incapable of any application. . . . In the mean time I saw Matilda every day, and that helped to distract me.

"In the midst of this struggle and anxiety she was taken ill with a cold. Nothing was thought of it at first, but she grew rapidly worse and fell into consumption. I cannot tell you what I suffered. The ills that I have undergone in this life have been dealt out to me drop by drop, and I have tasted all their bitterness. I saw her fade rapidly away; beautiful and more beautiful, more angelical to the very last. I was often by her bedside; and in her wandering state of mind she would talk to me with a sweet, natural, and affecting eloquence that was overpowering. I saw more of the beauty of her mind in that delirious state than I had ever known before. Her malady was rapid in its career, and hurried her off in two months. Her dying struggles were painful and protracted. For three days and nights I did not leave the house and scarcely slept. I was by her when she died; and all the family were assembled round her, some praying, others weeping, for she was adored by them all. I was the last one she looked upon. I have told you, as briefly as I could, what if I were to tell with all the incidents that accompanied it would fill volumes. She was but about seventeen years old when she died."

After her death Irving never spoke, even to his most intimate friends, of this beloved girl; but he was faithful to her memory throughout his life. Her Bible and Prayer-book he kept with him as long as he lived and wherever he went. "She died in the beauty of her youth, and in my memory she will ever be young and beautiful," he wrote of her in his note-book many years afterward; and his nephew records that one day, a few years before his death, speaking with his niece of the solitariness of unmarried life, he said, "You know I was never intended for a bachelor." Some hours afterward, he handed her in his own handwriting a copy of Campbell's "What's Hallowed Ground?" among the stanzas of which the following is most significant: —

> " For time makes all but true love cold,
>   The burning thoughts that then were told
>   Run molten still in memory's mould,
>   And will not cool
>   Until the heart itself be cold
>   In Lethe's pool."

Matilda Hoffman died in April, 1809. Irving was at that time in his twenty-seventh year, and had already given proof of unusual literary power. In 1802, over the signature of Jonathan Oldstyle, he had begun contributing clever sketches to a paper published by his brother. In 1804 he had gone to Europe for the sake of his health, as he had been troubled with a racking cough that seemed symptomatic of consumption. He sailed for Bordeaux, travelled in France, Italy, Sicily, and visited London, where he saw Mrs. Siddons and Kemble. In Rome he met Washington Allston, the artist, a young man three years his senior, and caught from him an enthusiasm for art that made him wish to become a painter. He returned to America in 1806, and passed his legal examinations, though sadly deficient in legal lore. The next year, assisted by his brother William and James K. Paulding, whose sister William had married, he commenced a series of social sketches published periodically, under the title of "Salmagundi." These sketches were written in evident imitation of Addison's "Spectator," and abound in good-natured satire of social follies. The law suffered by this attention to literature, but it was destined to suffer still further and finally to be abandoned. The Knickerbocker's " History of New York " was begun in the early part of 1809, and published in December of the same year. Written during the year in which he suffered the loss of Matilda Hoffman, it bears no mark of private grief, but is running over with humor and satire from beginning to end. After the publication of this history, which was favorably received in England as well as in America, Irving was for ten years variously occupied in politics, magazine writing, and in the hardware and cutlery business in partnership with his brothers. In 1815, in the interests of this business, he went to Liverpool, intending to stay but a few months, but he remained abroad seventeen years. The business in which he was engaged finally failed, and, thrown upon his own resources, he turned his attention again to literature.

The first fruits of his new leisure was the immortal " Sketch-Book " by Geoffrey Crayon, the publication of which began in 1819. It opens with the author's account of himself, whence we learn his taste for travelling, his preference for books of voyage and travel, and his subjection to the spell of Europe's " charms of storied and poetical association." The sketches that follow are interspersed with short legends and tales, the most beautiful as well as the most famous of which are the " Legend of Sleepy Hollow " and " Rip Van Winkle." Through them all runs that delightful style which Irving himself so finely praises in Goldsmith as " mellow, flowing, and softly tinted."

" Bracebridge Hall " and the " Tales of a Traveller "

followed the " Sketch-Book," and shared its character
and spirit.

Irving met many distinguished men while abroad,
among whom was Sir Walter Scott, whom he
described to his brother as " a sterling, golden-hearted
old worthy, full of the joyousness of youth, with an
imagination continually furnishing forth pictures, and
a charming simplicity of manner that puts you at ease
with him in a moment. . . . Everything that comes
within his influence seems to catch a beam of that
sunshine that plays round his heart." Irving visited
Paris, where he led what he called a " miscellaneous
kind of life," distracted by engagements in spite of his
efforts to keep out of society; and there he made the
acquaintance of Thomas Moore, the Irish poet, and
John Howard Payne, the young American actor and
playwright, author of " Home, Sweet Home."

In 1826 Irving went to Madrid to undertake the
translation of a new Spanish work on the voyages of
Columbus, but having access to much new material
on the subject, he gave up the idea of translating and
began to busy himself with a biography of Columbus.
He worked hard at his task, neglecting none of the
drudgery of research. Longfellow, who saw him at
Madrid, relates that —

" he seemed to be always at work. . . . One summer morning, passing his house at the early hour of six, I saw his study
window already open. On my mentioning it to him afterwards, he said, 'Yes, I am always at work as early as six.'
Since then I have often remembered that sunny morning and
open window, so suggestive of his sunny temperament and
his open heart, and equally so of his patient, persistent toil,
and have recalled those striking words of Dante, —

'Seated upon down
Or in his bed, man cometh not to fame,
Withouten which whoso his life consumes,
Such vestige of himself shall leave
As smoke in air, and in the water foam.'"

The result of this patient, persistent toil was the "Life and Voyages of Christopher Columbus," which immediately took rank as a complete and admirably executed historical work, and as such it has not yet been superseded. Irving, now thoroughly interested in Spanish investigations, found new themes for his pen as his studies continued. He wrote the "Conquest of Granada," and on the twelfth of May, 1829, he took up his residence in the Alhambra, an ancient royal Moorish palace and fortress of Granada. He writes to a friend: —

"Here then I am, nestled in one of the most remarkable, romantic, and delicious spots in the world. I have the complete range, and I may say control, of the palace, for the only residents besides myself are a worthy old woman, her niece and nephew who have charge of the building, and who make my bed, cook my meals, and are all kindness and attention to me. I breakfast in the salon of the ambassadors, or among the flowers and fountains in the Court of the Lions, and when I am not occupied with the pen, I lounge with my book about these oriental apartments, or stroll about the courts and arcades, by day or night, with no one to interrupt me. It absolutely appears to me like a dream, or as if I am spell-bound in some fairy palace."

In this quiet and romantic retreat he put the finishing touches to the "Legends of the Conquest of Spain," then left the Alhambra on the twenty-ninth of July, 1829. This same year he was appointed secretary of legation at London, and he spent the following three years in England.

Irving's remaining works on Spanish themes are: "Spanish Voyages of Discovery," "The Alhambra," "Moorish Chronicles," and "Mahomet and his Successors." Of these books "The Alhambra," styled by Prescott "the beautiful Spanish Sketch Book," is by far the most attractive.

Irving returned to America in 1832. During his seventeen years' absence his native country had made rapid strides forward, and he was eager to see the great prairies of the West toward which emigrants were hastening. He went down the Mississippi as far as St. Louis, travelled on horseback in Missouri and Arkansas, "leading," he says, "a wild life, depending upon game, such as deer, elk, bear, for food, encamping on the borders of brooks and sleeping in the open air, under trees to guard us against any surprise by the Indians." He writes from Independence, Missouri, that he has been out on a deer-hunt in the vicinity of that place, which led him "through some scenery which only wanted a gentleman's seat here and there interspersed to have equalled some of the most celebrated park scenery of England." "A Tour on the Prairies" was the result of this journey.

Irving was now anxious to make a home for himself in America, and bought a small farm at Tarrytown-on-the-Hudson, not far from Sleepy Hollow. He remodelled and enlarged the house, tastefully laid out the grounds, and gave to his new home the name of Sunnyside. His brother and family and a number of nieces were invited to share his home with him. Of these nieces, who later were his housekeepers and nurses, he used to say: "They take such good care of me, that really I am the most fortunate old bachelor in the world! Yes, the most fortunate old bachelor in all the world!" For ten years he enjoyed the tranquillity and domestic happiness of his home, but busy as ever with his pen, contributing to the "Knickerbocker Magazine" on a regular salary, writing the "Tour on the Prairies," "Astoria," "Abbotsford," "Newstead Abbey," "Captain Bonneville," and planning a history of the conquest of Mexico; but this plan was generously abandoned on learning that Prescott was collecting material for the same subject.

In 1842 Irving was appointed minister to Spain,— an appointment which he accepted not without reluctance, and which he gave up in 1846. He had now arrived at that age when a quiet home life is most fully appreciated. He had risen from obscurity and dependence to honor, fame, and opulence. He had indulged his love of travel; he had seen much of the world and shared little of its vanities. Nature had given him a big heart that no sorrow or disappointment could contract, and an imagination that turned the veriest prose of life into poetry. He writes to a friend from Madrid in 1845:—

"Though alone, I am not lonely. Indeed, I have been for so much of my life a mere looker-on in the game of society that it has become habitual to me, and it is only the company of those I truly like that I would prefer to the quiet indulgence of my own thoughts and reveries. . . . When I was young my imagination was always in the advance, picturing out the future and building castles in the air; now memory comes in the place of imagination, and I look back over the region I have travelled. Thank God the same plastic feeling which used to deck all the future with the hues of fairy land throws a soft coloring on the past, until the very roughest places through which I struggled with many a heartache lose all their asperity in the distance."

Settled once more in his beautiful home at Sunnyside, Irving resumed his literary work, and in 1849 published the " Life of Goldsmith," which for genial, sympathetic treatment is unsurpassed in biographical literature. It is easy enough with a little patience and diligence to collect written facts, make sure of dates, and arrange them in chronological order; but, to catch a glimpse of the real man through these facts, to select those that are vital and characteristic and to reject those that are not, and to recreate from this mass of inert material a man that lives and moves, whose hand we can touch and feel that it is warm, into whose heart we can look and read there secrets akin to our own, — to do this requires a sympathetic penetration, a subtle power of yielding one's individuality to the domination of another, a breadth of view that does not lose sight of the whole in its details, which are qualities that belong to creative genius of a high order. These qualities are admirably illustrated in the " Life of Goldsmith." It was a labor that he took delight in. He says of it in his preface : —

" It is a tribute of gratitude to the memory of an author whose writings were the delight of my childhood, and have been a source of enjoyment to me throughout life, and to whom, of all others, I may address the beautiful apostrophe of Virgil, —

'Tu se' lo mio maestro, e 'l mio autore ;
Tu se' solo colui, da che cu' io tolsi
Lo bello stile che m' ha fatto onore.' "[1]

The year following the publication of the " Life of Goldsmith," the " Life of Mahomet and his Successors " appeared. It is not a particularly strong book, but contains a good deal of valuable information. The last work that Irving wrote was a " Life of Washington," which is in reality a history of the American Revolution and only incidentally a biography of the hero. It was published in 1855, the year of the publication of another volume of miscellanies in the character of his earlier work and entitled " Wolfert's Roost."

Irving was now an old man, but life had not grown old to him nor were its joys exhausted. He writes on the fourth of April, 1853 : —

" Seventy years of age ! I can scarcely realize that I have indeed arrived at the allotted verge of existence, beyond which all is especial grace and indulgence. I used to think that a man at seventy must have survived everything worth living for ; that with him the silver cord must be loosed, the wheel broken at the cistern ; that all desire must fail, and the grasshopper become a burden. Yet here I find myself unconscious of the withering influences of age, still strong and active, my sensibilities alive, and my social affections in full vigor.

'Strange that a harp of thousand strings
Should keep in tune so long.'

[1] " Thou art my master, and my teacher thou ;
It was from thee, and thee alone, I took
That noble style for which men honor me."

While it does keep in tune, while I have still a little music in my soul to be called out by any touch of sympathy, while I can enjoy the society of those dear to me and contribute to their enjoyment, I am content and happy to live on."

But he was not destined to live on many years. An asthmatic affection had troubled him a long while; but the immediate cause of his death was heart-failure. On the twenty-eighth of November, 1859, as he was preparing to retire for the night, he fell backward to the floor dead. He had been ailing for some time, and in this last illness said, "I do not fear death, but I would like to go down with all sail set." His wish was granted; his work was done; he died

> " In the bright Indian summer of his fame.
>
> .   .   .   .
>
> How sweet a life was his, how sweet a death !
> Living to wing with mirth the weary hours,
> Or with romantic tales the heart to cheer;
> Dying to leave a memory like the breath
> Of summers full of sunshine and of showers,
> A grief and gladness in the atmosphere."

The memory of Washington Irving is very dear to Americans. So much of himself was written into his books, especially into his earlier sketches, that he needed no biographer to acquaint the world with his personality. Amiable, modest, affectionate, lenient to human frailties out of the cleanness of a heart that knew no evil, he seemed to carry the morning dew of youth into the noon of manhood and the twilight of old age. How much of this youthful freshness was due to his early disappointment and solitary life it would be hard to say, but writing of Byron's unfortunate love for Mary Chaworth, he says what seems singularly applicable to himself: —

"An early, innocent, and unfortunate passion, however fruitful of pain it may be to the man, is a lasting advantage to the poet. It is a well of sweet and bitter fancies; of refined and gentle sentiments, of elevated and ennobling thoughts; shut up in the deep recesses of the heart, keeping it green amid the withering blights of the world, and by its casual gushings and overflowings recalling at times all the freshness and innocence and enthusiasm of youthful days."

This freshness, innocence, and enthusiasm he had, at any rate, mingled with an unfailing humor that softened all the harsher realities of life; and, with all that, he was so plain and unassuming in his manner that no stranger ever suspected him to be a man of genius. There was nothing fastidious or eccentric about him. Writing in his youth of the miserable European inns and his lack of comforts in his travels, he said that if he could n't get a dinner to suit his taste, he tried to get a taste to suit his dinner, adding characteristically, "There is nothing I dread more than to be taken for one of the Smell-fungi of this world." Neither was there anything extraordinary in his appearance; he was about five feet seven inches in height, somewhat inclined to stoutness; had black hair and fine dark-gray eyes that lighted up when he talked, but talking was not his forte; he had a slight catch or huskiness in his voice, and it was a tradition among wits that he was always sleepy at dinner-parties and often fell sound asleep there. Moore says of him that he was "not strong as a lion, but delightful as a domestic animal." His nephew accounts for this drowsiness at dinner by saying that his sleep at night was always fitful, and that he read and sometimes wrote in bed. "He often had a peculiar shambling gait," says one, "that would attract the attention even of those who did not know him." His dress was neat, but he avoided peculiarities and extremes of fashion. The following anecdote related by one who knew him will illustrate his modesty: —

A contractor for building the Croton aqueduct which passed through Tarrytown, was accustomed to meet, at the temporary building erected for the reception of his tools, a plainly dressed, simple-mannered old gentleman, with whom he fell into conversation. These chance meetings continued for upwards of six months, when, one day travelling on the Hudson and in earnest conversation with the same old gentleman, the contractor was surprised by hearing the bell of the steamer suddenly ring out. He left his companion, went to the captain, and asked what all the noise was about. The captain replied that they were opposite Sunnyside, and Washington Irving being on board, they wished to give notice to his servant to be ready with a carriage at the landing. The contractor with great enthusiasm exclaimed, "Washington Irving! he on board! why, point him out to me; there is no living man whom I would more like to see." The captain looked surprised, and replied to the great astonishment of the contractor, "Why, sir, you have just left Washington Irving's company, and from the number of times I have seen you in familiar conversation with him on this boat, I supposed you were one of his most intimate friends."

Irving was a member of the Episcopal church, loved its services, and was to be seen in his pew at the village church every Sunday. His pastor relates that one Sunday morning Irving approached him and asked why the "Gloria in Excelsis" could not be sung every Sunday. The pastor replied that he had no objection, and that there was nothing whatever to prevent it, and asked in his turn, "Do you like it?" "Like it! like it!" replied Irving, "above all things. Why, it contains the sum and substance of our faith, and I never hear it without feeling better and without my heart being lifted up."

Though Irving was social by nature and went a good deal into society, he was not indifferent to the folly of wasting much time this way; and when we remember that he left school at fifteen, and yet that he subsequently contrived to make himself a good Spanish, German, and French scholar in addition to his literary work, it is evident that he did not neglect weighty matters for social pleasures. "When you have leisure," he cautions his nephew, " do not waste it in idle society; by idle I mean what is termed fashionable society." And writing to a lady in Paris on the education of her girls, he advises her not to "attempt to make remarkable women of them. Let them acquire those accomplishments which enliven and sweeten home, but do not seek to fit them to shine in fashionable society. Keep them as natural, simple, and unpretentious as possible. Cultivate in them noble and exalted sentiments, and above all the feeling of veneration, so apt to be deadened, if not lost, in the gay, sensuous world by which they are surrounded."

Of Irving's literary habits N. P. Willis gives us some account in his report of a visit to Sunnyside made in the summer of 1857 : —

"Our conversation for the half hour that we sat in that little library turned first upon the habits of literary labor. Mr. Irving, in reply to my inquiry whether, like Rip Van Winkle, he had arrived at that happy age when a man can be idle with impunity, said, ' No,' that he had sometimes worked even fourteen hours a day, but that he usually sits in his study occupied from breakfast to dinner, both of us agreeing that in literary vegetation the 'do' is on in the morning; and that he should be sorry to have more leisure. He thought indeed that he should die in harness. . . . He was never more astonished, he said, than at the success of the Sketch-Book.   His writing of those stories was so unlike an inspiration — so entirely without any feeling of confidence which could be prophetic of their popularity. Walking with his brother one dull, foggy Sunday, over Westminster Bridge, he got to telling the old Dutch stories which he had heard at Tarrytown in his youth, when the thought suddenly struck him : ' I have it!   I 'll go home and make memoranda of these for a book ; ' and leaving his brother to go to church, he went back to his lodgings, and jotted down all the data, and the next day, the dullest and darkest of London fogs, he sat in his little room and wrote out 'Sleepy Hollow' by the light of a candle."

Irving never read any criticism of his works, good or bad, saying that if his writings were worth anything they would outlive temporary criticism; if not, they were n't worth caring about. That they *have* outlived temporary criticism, we know; that the best of them — the "Sketch-Book," "Brace-bridge Hall," "Tales of a Traveller," "The Alhambra," "The Life of Goldsmith" — belong to what is imperishable in our literature, we are equally safe in saying that we know. The romantic coloring of much of Irving's historical work lessens its value to a scientific age, and it will be read rather from an interest in the writer than for its own sake. The Knickerbocker "History of New York" made our ancestors laugh while the memory of the Dutch settlers whom it ridicules was with them; but it does not amuse the present generation as it did the one for whom it was written, and very likely our descendants will not be otherwise affected by it. But we pity the age that will not have smiles and tears for the "Sketch-Book," that will not see the broad humanity of it, that will not feel the influence of its perfect style, as rich and mellow in its subdued glow as the Indian summer the author loved so well. It belongs to a class of books that time cannot touch. These books blossom from the heart of man, and strike roots again into every heart that has preserved its sweet humanity.

CHAPTER IV

JAMES FENIMORE COOPER (1789–1851)

JAMES FENIMORE COOPER, the first American novelist to win distinction outside of his own country, was born in Burlington, New Jersey, September 15, 1789. His father, William Cooper, moved into New York State, then a wilderness, in 1790, and began the settlement of Cooperstown on the southwestern shore of Lake Otsego. He built a mansion there, and called it Otsego Hall. He was of Quaker descent, a benevolent, energetic, vivacious man who loved a joke at any expense. A little village rapidly grew up where he had settled, and he was elected the first county judge of Otsego County. His wife, Elizabeth Fenimore, was of Swedish descent, a woman of energy and cultivation, fond of romance reading, and the mother of twelve children, of whom James Fenimore was the eleventh.

The boy, known as "Jim Cooper" among his school-fellows, inherited the robust frame and healthy activity of his parents, and spent more time riding, fishing, shooting, skating, and roaming the forests than in studying his lessons; yet he was noted in the village school for his spirited recitations of poetry. After a few years' schooling in Cooperstown, he was placed under the instruction of a clergyman in Albany and prepared for Yale, which he entered at thirteen. He was still more conspicuous for love of play than of books, and after spending nearly three years at college was sent home for his participation in some boyish mischief. Fond of adventure and wishing to see something of the world, he induced his father to let him go to sea, and at sixteen he made his first voyage to England and Spain in a merchant-vessel.

In 1808 he was made United States midshipman, and he served in the navy for three years. At the end of that time he left the sea, married Miss De Lancey, and settled for some time on a farm in Westchester County, New York. Later he lived three years at Cooperstown, and was the first secretary of the first Agricultural Society of Otsego County. He delighted in farming and took pride in it; he loved animals, and they soon learned to know him and follow him about; he had a particular interest in his vegetable garden, and liked to boast having on his table the earliest green peas and new potatoes in that part of the country.

At this time there was nothing about him to indicate that he was soon to be ranked among the foremost novelists of his age. He even disliked writing, and looked, as an English journalist subsequently described him, "like a bluff English farmer," and not like a man of imagination and sentiment. He had a huge, strong frame above the ordinary height, and inclining in later years to corpulency; "a very castle of a man," says Irving, — with a large strong face, forehead broad and high and prominent over the eyes, — deep-set "vigilant eyes," says one, — and a firm, inflexible mouth.

His first novel, as has been often related, was written in consequence of his disgust at a feeble English novel which he had been reading. " I believe I could write a better story myself," was his impatient exclamation as he threw down the book; and at the urgency of his wife to do it, he wrote and published " Precaution " in 1820. The novel, a story of English life, is conventional in subject and treatment, but it met with success enough to encourage the author to try again. This time he chose a theme from American history in the time of the Revolution, and the next year published " The Spy," whose hero, Harvey Birch, was hailed as a new and noble creation in fiction.

In 1822 Cooper moved with his family to New York, where he took part in the social life of the city and belonged to a club of which the poets Halleck and Bryant, and S. B. Morse, the inventor of the telegraph, were members.

The first of the Leatherstocking series was begun in 1822 by the publication of the " Pioneers," a story of frontier life whose freshness and originality made it a worthy successor to " The Spy." In December of the next year he published " The Pilot," regarded by many as the best of his sea stories. In later years Cooper, who had modelled the pilot after his conception of John Paul Jones, regretted that he had overdrawn the character, as he thought, and given to it a strength and a nobility that did not in every respect belong to the original. He also regretted that he had not more fully worked out the character of Long Tom Coffin, who was a great favorite with him. But the public found no fault with the book, and waited eagerly for its successor. It came in the form of another Leatherstocking tale, "The Last of the Mohicans," published in 1826, and pronounced by some critics the best of the series. This same year Cooper sailed for Europe, and he remained abroad with his family for seven years. Most of this time was spent in France, where he was consul at Lyons for nearly three years. Among the numerous works that he wrote during his residence abroad, were: "The Prairie," "The Wept of Wish-ton-Wish," "The Red Rover," and "The Water Witch."

In 1833 he returned to America, and after a short stay in New York City, settled for the rest of his life in Cooperstown. He lived in the old homestead, Otsego Hall, and indulged his rural tastes in beautifying his estate with shrubbery, plants, and flowers in abundance. His habits were methodical; he rose early, and after a morning walk usually wrote till late in the afternoon and then took a walk again. He walked with a cane, and his erect, portly figure was a familiar sight in the streets of Cooperstown, though he seldom spoke to any one on the street. Indeed, at this time, he was on very ill terms with his countrymen, being engaged in a long controversy with them that embittered his later years, and obscured to a great degree the natural goodness and sincerity of his heart. He had left America a passionate lover of his country and defender of her institutions and manners. He had published in London a book in two volumes entitled "Notions of the Americans Picked up by a Travelling Bachelor," in which he tried to set forth to English eyes the superiority of the United States to any other country on the globe. He predicted the time when she was to be the first marine nation in the world.   He lauded the common sense, coolness, frankness, energy, and courage of her citizens.   He praised the modesty, delicate beauty, and sweet domestic virtues of her women.   He dwelt with particular pride on the absence of caste feeling, and the general respect entertained for honest worth independent of wealth or station.   But the book was not particularly well received, either in this country or in England. Moreover, Cooper did not in his own manners convey a pleasing idea of American independence.   He was brusque to rudeness; he was absolutely destitute of tact; and so far from concealing his democratic views where they were most offensive, he took care to announce his contempt for kings as superfluities, and of lords as expensive luxuries.   Yet, with all his democratic principles, he had that fastidious aloofness of feeling which we call aristocratic.   " A man of unquestioned talent, almost genius," says Horace Greeley, " he was aristocratic in feeling and arrogant in bearing, although combining in his manners what a Yankee once characterized as ' winning ways to make people hate him. ' "

In England he was welcomed everywhere for the sake of his great fame as a novelist; he dined with lords and ladies, and met the most distinguished writers of his time, among whom were Scott and Coleridge.   But he did not make a favorable impression upon strangers.   His brusque, self-important manners, his violence when contradicted, his lack of tact which made him always say the wrong thing, and his supersensitiveness that kept him ever on the alert for slights and causes of offence, made him a disagreeable guest where his talents as a novelist had recommended him to particular favor. He records once quoting to Scott a Frenchman's disparaging criticism on Scott's "Life of Napoleon," and then naïvely comments on Scott's evidently not liking it. He published in several volumes a detailed account of his experiences abroad, under the general title of "Gleanings from Europe." There is little of dignity or acuteness of observation in these gossipy gleanings, but they are still readable, and hardly deserved the fierce attack upon them in the "Quarterly Review" which pronounced them an "autobiography of excoriated vanity."

Having made for himself rather a disagreeable personal reputation in Europe by his obtrusive patriotism, Cooper returned to America only to find that his long residence abroad had unconsciously produced a change in his feelings and his point of view. He now found himself out of touch with the country he had so passionately loved and defended. He found America altered for the worse, not the better; he saw a great increase in wealth, but not in knowledge. Instead of the simplicity of dress and manner that he had so often praised as peculiarly American, he saw everywhere foolish extravagance, vulgar display, and pretentious ignorance. The boastful and exclusive love of country which in his own case he had so prominently displayed under the name of patriotism, and of which he saw irritating evidence in silly, blatant Fourth of July orations, he called the "governing social evil of America, — provincialism." The rule of the masses, in which he had once felt such profound faith, he now saw not to be necessarily right.   And what he saw, Cooper felt that he must say in a manner as unmistakable as possible. Had he possessed the humor of Dickens or the genially satiric power of Thackeray, he might have tickled or gently stung his readers into reform.   But the genius of the humorist or the satirist was not his. He could write stories of adventure on sea or land; he could depict the wild, free life of forest or prairie; but he had no power to delineate character or to catch the vital facts of social life beneath passing forms, no skill to touch follies and incongruities with that humorous exaggeration that amuses without offending.   But what he could not do, he tried to do in pamphlets and novels, of which " Homeward Bound " and " Home as Found " are notable examples. These books and pamphlets, now quite forgotten, exasperated his countrymen, and led to attacks from the press which he angrily resented by bringing suit after suit for libel, and he nearly always won his case.   The most notable of these suits were brought against Thurlow Weed of the " Albany Evening Journal," and Horace Greeley of the " New York Tribune."   Though Cooper rarely kept a copy of any of his books (his daughter Susan says the " family never owned a complete series of his works until after his death "), and though he never re-read them, he diligently read all the criticisms about them, and was galled to the quick by anything that he thought false or unfair in notices concerning himself, and resented them accordingly.

In addition to his quarrels with the newspapers, he had had the misfortune to embroil himself with his fellow-citizens in Cooperstown on the subject of a point of land belonging to his estate. This point of land, known as Three Mile Point or Myrtle Grove, was a prettily wooded piece of land, less than an acre in extent, jutting out into Otsego Lake. During Cooper's absence in Europe it had been used as a public picnic-ground and pleasure-resort, but on his return he claimed it as private property and forbade the public the use of it. Indignation meetings of the citizens were called; resolutions were drawn up denouncing him, and it was recommended that his books should be removed from the public library. But Cooper was not the man to be intimidated into renouncing a claim that he felt to be just, and he persisted in it until it was recognized even at the expense of his popularity. But it would be wrong to infer from this that Cooper was naturally a quarrelsome and illiberal man. He was really a good-hearted, sincere, impulsive, passionate man, generous to liberality; but he had a quick sense of *meum et tuum*. It annoyed him excessively to have any one cross his grounds without permission; but he would have marched an army through them of his own accord, if a good end were to be served by it. He would have given his apples away by the bushel, or picked his flowers by the handful; but woe to the boy who dared take an apple by stealth, or to the woman who would pull a rose without asking leave to do it. "It is just as bad to take my flowers as to steal my money," he shouted one day to a woman whom he saw picking a rose, and he accented the angry words with a threatening flourish of his cane that put the poor woman to flight. But his faults were not much deeper than the surface. "His character," says

Bryant, " was like the bark of the cinnamon, a rough and astringent rind without, and an intense sweetness within. Those who penetrated beneath the surface found a genial temper, warm affections, and a heart with ample place for his friends, their pursuits, their good name, their welfare."

In his own household he was full of vivacity and cheer. Like his father, he loved a joke, and when he came upon a good thing in his reading, he was never satisfied till all his family had shared the fun of it. He never willingly talked of himself and his writings, and entered easily into the interests of others. His favorite game was chess, which he frequently played in the evenings with his wife. He was a man of deep religious convictions, and was strongly attached to the Episcopal church.

In 1840, after the controversial novels and letters had had their day, Cooper returned to the field in which he had won his fame, and published " The Pathfinder." The next year " The Deerslayer" appeared, and with this novel the Leatherstocking series was completed. Two more sea tales, " Wing-and-Wing" and " The Two Admirals," followed in 1842, and were succeeded at varying intervals by eleven other books now little read or heard of. Cooper lived to see himself again respected and admired after years of unpopularity and detraction; he died of dropsy on the fourteenth of September, 1851. His wife died four months later, and was buried by his side, in the graveyard of Christ Church, Cooperstown.

Cooper had a great dislike of publicity, and on his deathbed asked his family to allow no authorized life of him to be published. Owing to their scrupulous fidelity to his wish, we are without those interesting biographical details which are so indispensable to a complete and correct idea of the personality of a writer whose books do not reflect it; but the ample and sometimes tedious prefaces with which he introduced his books throw light enough upon his aims as a novelist. The hero of the five Leatherstocking tales in which Cooper's best and most popular work is done, is variously known as Natty Bumppo, Leatherstocking, Deerslayer, and Hawkeye. In his preface to " Deerslayer," Cooper gives us his idea of Natty Bumppo, and defends his romantic conception of the Indian : —

" Taking the life of the Leatherstocking as a guide, ' The Deerslayer ' should have been the opening book, for in that work he is seen just emerging into manhood ; to be succeeded by ' The Last of the Mohicans,' ' The Pathfinder,' ' The Pioneers,' and ' The Prairie.' . . .

" The author has been often asked if he had any original in his mind for the character of Leatherstocking. In a physical sense different individuals, known to the writer in early life, certainly presented themselves as models, through his recollections ; but in a moral sense the man of the forest is purely a creation. The idea of delineating a character that possessed little of civilization but its highest principles, as they are exhibited in the half-educated, and all of savage life that is not incompatible with these great rules of conduct, is perhaps natural to the situation in which Natty is placed. He is too proud of his origin to sink into the condition of the wild Indian, and too much a man of the woods not to imbibe so much as was at all desirable from his friends and companions. In a moral point of view it was his intention to illustrate the effect of seed scattered by the wayside. To use his own language, his 'gifts' were 'white gifts,' and he was not disposed to bring on them discredit. On the other hand, removed from nearly all the temptations of civilized life, placed in the best associations of that which is deemed savage, and favorably disposed by nature to improve such advantages, it appeared to the writer that the hero was a fit subject to represent the better qualities of both conditions, without pushing either to extremes. . . .

" It is the privilege of all writers of fiction, more particularly when their works aspire to the elevation of romance, to present the *beau idéal* of their characters to the reader. This it is which constitutes poetry, and to suppose that the red man is to be represented only in the squalid misery or in the degraded moral state that certainly more or less belongs to his condition is, we apprehend, taking a very narrow view of an author's privileges. Such criticisms would have deprived the world even of Homer."

Whatever may be said of the waning popularity of Cooper and of the failure of his novels as higher creations of art, it is an incontestable fact that his sea tales and Leatherstocking stories still find a ready sale, and that his name was once coupled with Scott's as a master of fiction. His novels were translated into French, German, Spanish, and even into the Persian tongue, and wherever they were read it was with admiration and keen delight. That much of his popularity was due to the novelty of his themes cannot be doubted. An English writer in " Colburn's New Monthly Magazine," 1831, says : —

" We are not hazarding much in saying that no writer ever possessed the advantages enjoyed by the author of 'The Spy' on his first outset in literary life. The very peculiarity of his situation rendered it next to impossible for him to fail in charming that large portion of the English people denominated the novel-readers. Scott had set his seal upon us. The author of ' Waverley ' — the great Napoleon of novelists — had conquered the country from one end of it to the other. Nothing then could be more fortunate as regards time, and as to place, what region could be so pregnant with interest, or what subject so calculated to gratify the cravings of an excited curiosity as America? — a country which had hitherto been considered alike destitute of writers and readers, whose soil had even been pronounced by the learned in these matters to be essentially unfavorable to the growth of genius, and in which one could no more think of looking for the golden graces of literature than for dancers among the Dutch. An Esquimau poet brought over by Captain Parry could hardly have excited more wonder than the great American novelist when he made his first appearance in Europe. The world fell into a fit of admiration at the first sign of a genius on the barren waste of America, and stared at it as the bewildered Crusoe did at Friday's foot-mark on the sand."

The writer continues his article with lavish praises of Cooper's knowledge of human nature, his invention, his talent for description, and " the refined power and delicacy which he displayed in his delineation of the female character." It is a curious fact that these very gifts for which the English critic praised Cooper over half a century ago, are those which our own later critics deny him, and for the absence of which he is no longer read with pleasure by cultivated readers out of their teens. His women, says Lowell, —

"from one model don't vary,
All sappy as maples, and flat as a prairie."

His characters show no development; they are ready made from the start; we know that his heroes will always behave with intrepidity and coolness in every situation, and that his women will always live up to the author's standard of feminine meekness and decorum. As for his invention, we shall let Mark Twain speak of that, only premising that there is a good deal of truth under his humorous exaggeration: —

" Cooper's gift in the way of invention was not a rich endowment; but such as it was he liked to work it; he was pleased with the effects, and, indeed, he did some quite sweet things with it. In his little box of stage properties he had six or eight cunning devices, tricks, artifices, for his savages and woodsmen to deceive and circumvent each other with, and he was never so happy as when he was working these innocent things and seeing them go. A favorite one was to make a moccasined person tread in the tracks of the moccasined enemy, and thus hide his own trail. Cooper wore out barrels and barrels of moccasins in working that trick. Another stage property that he pulled out of the box pretty frequently was his broken twig. He prized his broken twig above all the rest of his effects, and worked it the hardest. It is a restful chapter in any of his books when somebody does n't step on a dry twig and alarm all the reds and whites for two hundred yards around. Every time a Cooper person is in peril and absolute silence is worth four dollars a minute, he is sure to step on a dry twig. Cooper requires him to turn out and find a dry twig; and if he can't do it, to go and borrow one. In fact, the Leatherstocking series ought to have been called the Broken Twig series."

Fortunately for Cooper's reputation, our ancestors were not so critical as we; they were under no subjection to facts; they could enjoy Natty Bumppo without questioning his phenomenal skill with the rifle, and accept the " noble red man " with his civilized virtues and refinements of feeling as a correct delineation of the North American savage. It was not human nature in itself that the great mass of novel-readers understood or were so much interested in. The faultless hero and virtueless villain were two favorite types of human nature. Even Charlotte Bronté, with all her knowledge of the human heart that kept her from falling into insipidity in her own work, was enraged with Thackeray for " making Lady Castlewood peep through a keyhole, listen at a door, and be jealous of a boy and a milkmaid; " and yet there is not a more striking instance of Thackeray's genius than this very perception that an essentially noble nature may be betrayed into weakness by the dominance of a master passion. But our ancestors preferred their heroes and heroines unalloyed with weakness. They cared less for the spectacle of the drama of a soul in conflict with passions or in a struggle with circumstances, than for thrilling accounts of adventures that endanger the body. In this field Cooper had a new world all to himself, and he made excellent use of his advantages. He wrote rapidly and very often with slovenly inaccuracy in grammatical construction and the selection of words, but there was the breath of the prairies and the odor of forests in his books. They depicted a beautiful, wild, free, unconventional life of adventure on sea and land that came like a revelation to those who knew nothing of woods and waters beyond the suggestions of a city park. There were no taints of sewers and gutters in

his books. They were clean and sweet as a wild rose;
and for this reason, though the Leatherstocking tales
have lost their hold upon maturer readers, they may
still be recommended to the young as the most
wholesome and entertaining of novels.

CHAPTER V

WILLIAM CULLEN BRYANT, the first distinguished poet of America, was born in the little town of Cummington, in western Massachusetts, November 3, 1794. On his mother's side, he was descended from the Puritan John Alden and his wife, Priscilla Mullens. His father, a country physician, was a man of decided literary tastes, and in the good library which he had collected the boy had access to the writings of the best English authors of his time. He was a precocious lad, and at ten years of age wrote verses for the local papers; at thirteen he published a satire on Jefferson's administration, entitled "The Embargo;" and before the completion of his eighteenth year he had composed the poem, "Thanatopsis," with which his name is most generally associated, and which is usually considered his masterpiece.

The gravity of these early poems — a gravity which characterizes all Bryant's works — is singularly in harmony with the tone of thought prevalent in New England during the early years of the nineteenth century. In an autobiographical fragment Bryant gives us a pleasant glimpse of his youthful environment. He tells us of the profound respect entertained for the clergy, so that the mere presence of a minister of the gospel was as effectual in quelling a disturbance as that of a police force.   Church-going was universal.   Men called tithing-men were appointed to keep order in church.   There was an especially keen surveillance of the boys, and if two were caught whispering, one was led away by the button to sit beside the stern keeper of the peace. These tithing-men were also empowered by law to see that no one unnecessarily absented himself from church.   If he did so, he was fined.   Parental discipline was severe.   Says Bryant: —

"The boys of the generation to which I belonged, — that is to say, who were born in the last years of the last century or the earliest of this, — were brought up under a system of discipline which put a far greater distance between parents and their children than now exists. The parents seemed to think this necessary in order to secure obedience.   They were believers in the old maxim that familiarity breeds contempt.   My own parents lived in the house with my grandfather and grandmother on the mother's side.   My grandfather was a disciplinarian of the stricter sort, and I can hardly find words to express the awe in which I stood of him, — an awe so great as almost to prevent anything like affection on my part, although he was in the main kind, and certainly never thought of being severe beyond what was necessary to maintain a proper degree of order in the family. . . . With my father and mother I was on much easier terms than with my grandfather.   If a favor was to be asked of my grandfather, it was asked with fear and trembling ; the request was postponed to the last moment and then made with hesitation and blushes and a confused utterance."

Huskings, apple-parings, house-raisings, social intercourse at the singing-schools, furnished the simple and wholesome amusements of the villagers. The hurry and fret and feverish anxieties of modern life were as remote from them as from the villagers of Goldsmith's "Sweet Auburn." The effect of this simple and regular life, and the influence of religious teaching in familiarizing the mind with images and thoughts of death, are very apparent in Bryant's poetry.

In his sixteenth year Bryant entered Williams College, where he remained seven months preparing himself for Yale. But his father's means would not allow him to bear the expense of a course at Yale, and he returned home, where he busied himself a year or more with farm-work, meanwhile reading assiduously from his father's library and growing acquainted with the wild flowers of forest and field. "I was always from my earliest years," he writes, "a delighted observer of external nature, — the splendors of a winter daybreak over the wide waste of snow seen from the windows, the glories of the autumnal woods, the gloomy approaches of the thunder-storm, and its departure amid sunshine and rainbow, the return of spring with its flowers, and the first snow-fall of winter."

In 1812 he entered a law-office, dividing his time between the study of law and the writing of poetry. Three years later he passed his examination, and settled for practice at Plainfield, a village seven miles from his home. To a circumstance connected with his settling there, we owe one of the most beautiful short poems in our literature, the lines "To a Water-fowl."

It was a chill December afternoon on which he

started to walk from home to Plainfield.   He was in the flush of youth, just twenty-two, — conscious of powers not untried that could give him hope to attain eminence some day.   He was about to enter a profession to which he had not given his heart, but must give his time, if he wished to make even a livelihood by it.   He was alone, depressed by the uncertainty of the future, impatient of the exactions of the present; suddenly, at sunset, across the flush of the western sky, he saw a solitary waterfowl winging its way southward.   He was in that susceptible mood in which the poet finds his lessons and sets them to the music of eloquent speech, and as he paused to watch the bird's unerring flight across the crimson sky, his desolation and despair softened into the tenderest and deepest trust that the Power whose care taught this waterfowl its

> " way along that pathless coast
> The desert and illimitable air,
> Lone wandering, but not lost,"

would of a surety lead his steps aright in the long way that he must tread alone.   That night the poem " To a Waterfowl " was written.   It is a picture and a mood wrought into exquisite verse.   The dreary winter landscape, the sunset glow, the solitary bird, the thought of Infinity guiding its flight, the calm, deep trust growing out of this thought, are faultlessly rendered.

Bryant's law practice proved fairly successful, and he did not abandon it until his assumption of the control of the " Literary Review " and his removal to New York in 1825.   Four years prior to this event he had married a farmer's daughter, Miss Fanny Fairchild, and published a small volume of poems that had secured a widespread recognition of his merits.

The "Literary Review" did not prove a successful venture, and during his second year's residence in New York Bryant was appointed assistant editor of the "New York Evening Post."   Three years later he became the editor-in-chief, which connection he retained for the rest of his life.   Poetry was not entirely abandoned for journalism, but it certainly suffered from the exactions of its rival.   The best and the greater part of his poetry was written before his fortieth year.   His connection with the "Post" brought him a handsome income, and enabled him to indulge a taste for travel.

He made six visits to Europe, saw Egypt and the Holy Land, and travelled in Cuba and Mexico.   His descriptive letters to the "Post" during his travels rarely rise above mediocrity.   The best of them have been collected in two volumes, entitled, respectively, "Letters of a Traveller" and "Letters from the East."   Besides these two volumes, Bryant's prose consists chiefly of orations, addresses, and editorial criticisms and comments.   But his prose is of little enduring value.   It lacks elasticity, nervous energy, the terseness, directness, and glow of thoughts that have forced their utterance and made a style for themselves.   It is even and dignified, but it bears the impress of hack work, — themes selected for him by societies that clamored for addresses, and newspaper columns that clamored to be filled.

His criticisms lack vitality, for he was not a profound thinker.   He did not assimilate the far-reaching scientific generalizations of his age, but sneered at evolution without taking the pains to comprehend its teachings.

But, viewed as a journalist, Bryant was a most painstaking and conscientious writer.   Until the close of the Civil War, he was almost a daily contributor to the " Evening Post," but he was never unmindful of the responsibilities of his position.   Says a writer in the " Post," at the time of Bryant's death : —

"According to one theory of journalism, to-day is the whole of life, and to let to-morrow take care of itself is a part of newspaper religion.   It cannot be denied that the practice of this theory is effective.   To treat what is uppermost to-day, simply because it is uppermost, without caring what may be uppermost to-morrow ; to fix the reader's attention to-day, no matter where his attention may be to-morrow, — to do this, certainly is to make an entertaining newspaper, if not a useful one.   This was not Mr. Bryant's theory.   To him to-day was by no means the whole of life, and he was not disposed to let to-morrow take care of itself.   On the contrary, to-day was chiefly valuable to him so far as it provided for to-morrow.   That is to say, he used the newspaper conscientiously to advocate views of political and social subjects which he believed to be correct.   He set before himself principles whose prevalence he regarded as beneficial to the country or to the world, and his constant purpose was to promote their prevalence.   He looked upon the journal which he conducted as a conscientious statesman looks upon the official trust which has been committed to him, or the work which he has undertaken, — not with a view to do what is to be done to-day in the easiest or most brilliant way, but so to do it that it may tell upon what is to be done to-morrow, and all other days, until the worthiest object of ambition is achieved. This is the most useful journalism, and, first and last, it is the most effective and influential."

In politics Bryant never servilely followed any party, but criticised men and measures opposed to his judgment, irrespective of party. He was an advocate of free trade, a supporter of President Jackson's course in regard to the United States banks, a zealous opponent of the Texas annexation, and, at first, a Free Soil Democrat. He joined the Republican party in 1856 to oppose the extension of slavery. Reciprocity treaties with other countries were the subject of his last journalistic work.

In 1866 Bryant's wife died. He had already made translations from the " Odyssey " some three years before the death of his wife, and now, feeling the need of that distraction from grief which is most successfully found in occupation, he set himself the task of making a complete translation of Homer, and finished his task in 1872. He was now an old man, but still hearty and hale and in frequent requisition for orations and addresses. On the twenty-ninth of May, 1878, he delivered an oration in Central Park, New York, at the unveiling of a statue to the Italian patriot, Mazzini. He spoke with uncovered head in the glaring sunlight, and shortly afterward, in ascending the steps of the house of a friend with whom he had been invited to dine, he suddenly fell backward, striking his head against the platform step. Concussion of the brain resulted. He was driven home, but never recovered. His death took place two weeks later, on the twelfth of June. He was buried at Roslyn, Long

Island, in which place he had made his home for many years. Some time before his death, and in anticipation of it, his fine library was divided between his native village, Cummington, and his later home, Roslyn.

In person, Bryant was spare and short of stature. In his youth he had a profusion of light brown hair, which became snowy white in age. Hawthorne, who saw him in Rome in 1858, describes him as having "a forehead impending yet not massive; dark, bushy eyebrows, and keen eyes without much softness in them; a dark and sallow complexion, and a slender figure bent a little with age." Hawthorne also gives it as his opinion that Bryant was "rather cold," and says that "he shook hands kindly but not with any warmth of grip." A few years before this, while travelling in Germany, Bryant had written Dana that a Leipsic paper had described him as "a little, dry, lean, old man."

In disposition, Bryant is said to have been retiring even to the point of bashfulness. This reserve, often associated with deep and tender feeling, is apt to be mistaken for coldness and pride. But Bryant was neither cold nor proud. He never thought highly of his achievements in verse, and when on his return from Europe in 1836, a complimentary dinner was tendered him by the New York authors and public men, he declined it on the plea that he had done nothing to merit such a distinction.

An associate editor, speaking of Bryant's tenderness for the feelings of others, says that he cautioned him once in this way: "I wish you would deal very gently with poets, especially with the weaker ones."

"Later," continues the editor, "I had a very bad case of poetic idiocy to deal with, and as Mr. Bryant happened to come into my room while I was debating the matter in my mind, I said to him that I was embarrassed by his injunction to deal gently with poets, and pointed out to him the utter impossibility of finding anything to praise or even lightly to condemn in the book before me. After I had read some of the stanzas to him, he answered: 'No, you can't praise it, of course; it won't do to lie about it, but,' turning the volume over in his hands and inspecting it, 'you might say that the binding is securely put on, and that — well, the binder has planed the edges pretty smooth.'"

Bryant had no affectations either in personal manner or in literary style. There is extant a letter of his filled with valuable advice to a young man who had asked for a criticism upon an article he had written. In the course of his reply, Bryant says: —

"Be simple, unaffected; be honest in your speaking and writing. Never use a long word when a short one will do as well. Call a spade by its name, not a well-known oblong instrument of manual labor; let a home be a home, and not a residence; a place, not a locality; and so on of the rest. When a short word will do, you will always lose by a long one. You lose in clearness, you lose in honest expression of meaning, and in the estimation of all men who are capable of judging, you lose in reputation for ability.

"The only true way to shine in this false world is to be modest and unassuming. Falsehood may be a thick crust, but in the course of time truth will find a place to break through. Elegance of language may not be in the power of us all, but simplicity and straightforwardness are."

Simplicity and straightforwardness were eminently in Bryant's power. There is neither an artificial nor an obscure line in all the poetry he has written. To be sure, this is not the highest praise that can be given to a poet, but it is one of the elements of the highest praise that can be given to expression. Bryant is not a poet of the widest range. Neither the ardors and generous enthusiasms of youth, nor the calmer affections of social and domestic life, find a place in his verse. A few of his poems will die only with the English tongue, but the bulk of his poetry is not of a character to take a deep hold on the heart.

Bryant has been called the American Wordsworth, but in vigor of thought, in range, and in feeling, he ranks far below his English rival. Both are poets of nature in the sense that nature is the chief source of inspiration and the theme of both, but the difference between Bryant and Wordsworth is the difference between I like and I love, — between the whitish blue of the noonday sky and the morning and evening red. With Bryant, the love of nature produces a grave and calm elevation of sentiment tinged with gentle melancholy. Thoughts of death, pious resignation, and unfaltering faith in immortality are almost invariably aroused in him by the contemplation of natural beauty. An ever-recurrent thought with him is the impassiveness of nature, her unchanging beauty and incessant variety in the presence of the life, birth, and death of the individual. This thought is the keynote to " Thanatopsis," his first masterpiece. It reappears in his lines " To the Apennines" : —

"Below you lie men's sepulchres, the old
   Etrurian Tombs, the graves of yesterday;
   The herd's white bones lie mixed with human mould,
   Yet up the radiant steeps that I survey
   Death never climbed, nor life's soft breath with pain
   Was yielded to the elements again."

"The Rivulet" voices the same sentiment: —

   "Thou changest not
      Since first thy pleasant banks I ranged;
      And the grave stranger come to see
      The play-place of his infancy,
      Has scarce a single trace of him
      Who sported once upon thy brim.
      The visions of my youth,
      Too bright, too beautiful to last, are past.
      I 've tried the world, — it wears no more
      The coloring of romance it wore.
      Yet well has nature kept the truth
      She promised to my earliest youth;
      The radiant beauty shed abroad
      On all the glorious works of God,
      Shows freshly to my sobered eye
      Each charm it wore in days gone by.

      .   .   .   .   .

      And I shall sleep — and on thy side,
      As ages after ages glide,
      Children their early sports shall try
      And pass to hoary age and die;
      But thou, unchanged from year to year,
      Gayly shalt play and glitter here;
      Amid young flowers and tender grass
      Thy endless infancy shall pass,
      And singing down thy narrow glen
      Shall mock the fading race of men."

Wordsworth, on the contrary, feels in the presence
of nature a deep joy, — a rapturous stirring of the

pulses that arouses in him a sense of fulness of life. In his exquisite ode " Lines on Revisiting the Banks of the Wye," perhaps the finest expression of love of nature ever penned, Wordsworth shows the extraordinary character of the emotions awakened in him by natural beauty : —

> " For nature   .   .   .   .   .
> To me was all in all, — I cannot paint
> What then I was.   The sounding cataract
> Haunted me like a passion ; the tall rock,
> The mountain, and the deep and gloomy wood,
> Their colors and their forms, were then to me
> An appetite, a feeling, and a love
> That had no need of a remoter charm
> By thought supplied, or any interest
> Unborrowed from the eye ; that time is past,
> And all its aching joys are now no more,
> And all its dizzy raptures."

There are no " aching joys," no " dizzy raptures " in Bryant's love.   Contrast these lines of Wordsworth with the following lines from Bryant's " Winter-Piece," in which he expresses the same thought, and the charge of coldness so often brought against the American poet will be understood : —

> " The time has been that these wild solitudes
> Yet beautiful as wild, were trod by me
> Oftener than now ; and when the ills of life
> Had chafed my spirit, — when the unsteady pulse
> Beat with strange flutterings, I would wander forth
> And seek the woods.   The sunshine on my path
> Was to me a friend.   The swelling hills,
> The quiet dells retiring far between,
> With gentle invitation to explore
> Their windings, were a calm society

That talked with me.   Then the chant
Of birds and chime of brooks and soft caress
Of the fresh sylvan air, made me forget
The thoughts that broke my peace, and I began
To gather simples by the fountain's brink,
And lose myself in day-dreams; while I stood
In nature's loneliness I was with one
With whom I early grew familiar, one
Who never had a frown for me, whose voice
Never rebuked me for the hours I stole
From cares I loved not, but of which the world
Deems highest, to converse with her."

Bryant seeks nature to allay the excitement of worldly cares, to calm and soothe him, and afford him matter and opportunity for quiet thought or pleasant reverie.   Wordsworth seeks nature to find an excitement the world cannot give, a joyous abandonment, a spiritual exaltation.   With the one, nature was a source of recreation; with the other, a passion.   It is the emotional element that gives to verse its heart-stirring power, and it is this element that is feeble in Bryant.   He had, however, a true conception of poetry.   He believed that it should touch the heart, excite the imagination, and appeal to the understanding.   "To write fine poetry," he says, "requires intellectual faculties of the highest order, and among these not the least important is the faculty of reason."

The most general favorites among his poems, and those by which he will most likely be remembered, are "Thanatopsis," "To a Waterfowl," "Forest Hymn," "June," "The Death of the Flowers," "The Gladness of Nature," "To a Yellow Violet," "The Planting of the Apple-Tree," and "The Fringed Gentian."

In his poem entitled " The Battlefield " are to be found these often quoted lines: —

> " Truth crushed to earth shall rise again ;
> The eternal years of God are hers :
> But error, wounded, writhes with pain,
> And dies among her worshippers."

CHAPTER VI

CARLYLE'S definition of history as a biography of nations is as good as it is brief. This definition implies in the historian not only that which we look for in a successful biographer, — sympathy with his subject, familiarity with facts concerning it, the power of selection, knowledge of man, the ability to tell clearly and vividly what he knows and feels, — but it implies a still rarer faculty, that of perceiving the subtle influences that work out events, embodying themselves now in a creed, now in a political institution, and again in the indomitable passions of men in power. We ask, too, of an historian that he shall be more impartial than the biographer, that he shall have no pet theory by which to interpret what he relates, — that, rather than this, he shall give us the bare facts and let us draw our own conclusions. But if he be a man of feeling and judgment like Motley, we shall not quarrel with him if in narrating infamous wrongs, he lets us feel the beatings of his own heart and see the flush of indignation in his cheeks. Or if he have the vivid descriptive power of Prescott, who sometimes abuses it, we shall be glad of the play of life and color in his pages.

Our best historians, Prescott, Motley, and Francis Parkman, had these gifts in a more or less marked degree.   Bancroft's voluminous history of the Colonial and Revolutionary periods preceding the adoption of the Constitution of the United States is a storehouse of valuable facts, and has many admirable pages, but these facts are not presented in an attractive way, and the book, as a whole, lacks compactness, as it lacks perspective.   Bancroft views everything too close at hand, and thus events do not assume with him their relative proportions.   Prescott chose for his themes the reign of Ferdinand and Isabella, the conquest of Mexico and Peru, and the history of Philip the Second of Spain; Motley chose the struggle of the Netherlands against Spanish tyranny, and Parkman the conflict between France and England for the possession of North America.

Few lives are more encouraging than Prescott's and Parkman's as a story of successful achievement in the face of almost insurmountable obstacles.   Both men struggled with failing sight in the midst of a mass of material for study that might have wearied the strongest pair of eyes, and both wrote with a vividness and minuteness of descriptive power that recall Milton's keen and far-searching inward sight.

William Hickling Prescott was born in Salem, Massachusetts, May 4, 1796.   His grandfather, Colonel Prescott, commanded the Americans at the battle of Bunker Hill.   His father, an eminent and wealthy lawyer, removed with his family to Boston in 1808, where young William was prepared for Harvard. He entered the Sophomore class in his sixteenth year, and was a good Greek and Latin scholar, so far as an acquaintance with the principles of these languages goes, but he hated mathematics.   Having proved to his instructor in geometry that he could commit to memory the required demonstrations without understanding a word of what he was reciting so glibly, he was excused from further displays of memory, and allowed to follow his own tastes in study. He was a handsome, fun-loving, social boy, not naturally studious, but ambitious, and with a proper estimate of the advantages of a good education. Therefore he spurred himself to his tasks by making resolutions and binding himself to pay a forfeit if they were not rigidly kept, — a practice that he continued throughout life.

The accident whose terrible consequences deprived him of the use of one eye and permanently weakened the other, occurred in his Junior year. One day just after dinner, as he was leaving the dining-hall at college, he looked back to see the cause of some disturbance that was going on in the room. A hard piece of bread thrown at random by one of the students, struck his left eye and felled him to the ground. The retina was paralyzed, and though the eye showed no evidence of blindness, no mark of the blow, he never again saw with it. The right eye, weakened through sympathy, so seriously troubled him at intervals all his life, that for months at a time he was obliged to be shut in a darkened room. He was also subject to acute attacks of rheumatism, and the necessity of preserving his health for the sake of his eyes induced him to form regular habits of retiring and taking exercise. He went to bed at half-past ten, rose early, but not without effort, charging his servant to call him, and paying him a forfeit whenever he failed to respond to the call. He took daily exercise on horseback in his early years; and, later, walked from four to six miles daily. Ticknor, his biographer, says: —

" If a violent storm prevented him from going out, or if the bright snow on sunny days in winter rendered it dangerous for him to expose his eye to its brilliant reflection, he would dress himself as for the street, and walk vigorously about the colder parts of the house, or he would saw and chop firewood, under cover, being, in the latter case, read to all the while."

He had intended to follow the law as a profession, but the state of his eyes interfered with unremitting application; and in 1815, in the hope of improving his health, he set sail for the Azores. His mother's father, Thomas Hickling, was then United States Consul at St. Michael's Island, one of the Azores, and had a charming country-house near the capital of the island.   Here William stayed with his grandfather about seven months, and then set sail for London to consult the best oculists there.   But nothing could be done for his eyes, and he visited Paris, passed the winter in Italy, revisited England, and returned to America in 1817.

His sight had not improved, and he was forced to abandon his project of studying law, and began to think of literature as a profession.   His father's circumstances assured him a competency, and he could afford to give himself ample time for preparation.   In 1820 he was happily married to Susan Amory.

Ticknor says that at the time of his marriage Prescott was one of the finest-looking men he had ever seen, — " tall, well-formed, manly in his bearing but gentle, with light brown hair that was hardly changed or diminished by years, with a clear complexion, and a ruddy flush on his cheek that kept for him to the last an appearance ot comparative youth, but above all with a smile that was the most absolutely contagious I ever looked upon."

This smile was the index of the cheeriest nature with which a man was ever gifted. No difficulty ever frightened him; no pain, no trial ever eclipsed the sunshine within him. A friend once said of him, " He could be happy in more ways, and more happy in every one of them, than any other person I have ever known." Even when shut up in his darkened room on account of his eyes, or confined to his bed with rheumatic pains, his irrepressible gayety made his room the cheeriest in the house.

Before entering upon any definite literary work, Prescott planned for himself, in 1821, a course of study beginning with that of English, as follows: —

" 1. Principles of grammar, correct writing, etc.

" 2. Compendious history of North America.

" 3. Fine prose writers of English from Roger Ascham to the present day, principally with reference to their modes of writing, — not including historians, except as far as requisite for an acquaintance with style.

" 4. Latin classics one hour a day."

He went to work with Blair's Rhetoric and Lindley Murray's Grammar; then read all the great English classics for nearly a year. He next took up French, reading from Froissart to Chateaubriand; then he mastered Italian and wished to take up German, but the weakness of his sight led him to give up for the time the pursuit of so difficult a language, and he began the study of Spanish instead.   This was a fortunate choice, for it soon led him into those researches which culminated in a resolve to write the history of Ferdinand and Isabella.

In 1826 he earnestly set about collecting material, undismayed by all the difficulties he had to encounter. The shades and shutters in his study had to be regulated to admit just the amount of light, and no more, that his weak eye could bear.   Sometimes he could use it only half an hour a day.   He employed a secretary to read for him, and trained his memory so that he could carry in it sixty printed pages for dictation.   He had received his material from Madrid, and " in my disabled condition," he writes in one of his prefaces, "with my transatlantic treasures lying around me, I was like one pining from hunger in the midst of abundance.   In this state, I resolved to make the ear if possible do the work of the eye.   I procured the services of a secretary who read to me the various authorities, and in time I became so familiar with the sounds of the different foreign languages (to some of which I had been previously accustomed by a residence abroad) that I could comprehend the reading without much difficulty."   He wrote with an ivory style, and to guide his hand in writing, employed a framework similar to that used by the blind, enclosing sixteen parallel brass wires.   These wires rested on blackened paper, underneath which was a sheet of white paper.

In June, 1836, he had finished the last chapter in the " Reign of Ferdinand and Isabella," and offered the book to the London publisher Murray, who declined it. Longman also declined it; but it was finally accepted by Richard Bentley, and published in December, 1837. It was a decided success from the first. In 1839 the " Conquest of Mexico " was begun, and it was published in 1843. A period of what Prescott called " literary loafing " followed, and then he set to work on the " Conquest of Peru," which appeared in 1847. The next year he began preparations for the " History of the Reign of Philip the Second," only three volumes of which he lived to complete.

In 1850 he sailed for England, where he was a great favorite wherever he went. He was presented to the Queen, and met Macaulay, Dean Milman, Hallam, Lockhart the son-in-law and biographer of Scott, the Duke of Wellington, and Sir Charles Lyell the eminent geologist.

On the fourth of February, 1858, he was stricken with apoplexy in his home in Boston, but recovered from the attack. He suffered a second and fatal stroke on the twenty-eighth of January, 1859. Longfellow records speaking with him in Boston just a few days before his death: —

" I met him in Washington Street just at the foot of Winter Street. He was merry and laughing as usual. At the close of the conversation he said: 'I am going to shave off my whiskers, they are growing gray.' 'Gray hair is becoming,' I said. 'Becoming!' said he, 'what do we care about becoming who must so soon *be going?*' 'Then why take the trouble to shave them off?' 'That's true!' he replied with a pleasant laugh, and crossed over to Summer Street. So my last remembrance of him is a sunny smile at the corner of a street."

It was a pleasant remembrance of one whose scholarly labors could not suppress his sunny social nature, nor prevent him from finding time to endear himself to a multitude of friends.

As an historian, Prescott still retains his popularity with the great majority of readers, in spite of his later critics who find him wanting in philosophical insight, and complain that his books read like tales from the "Arabian Nights." It is true that he loaded his palette with too many colors, that he has an eye for all romantic episodes and dramatic situations, and that all those external details which a staid historian suppresses to get at his fact sometimes seem that for which Prescott relates his fact. But he wished to produce the life, color, and movement of a panorama; and he succeeded. This is why he continues readable in spite of the critics. Yet he censured Carlyle severely to Bancroft for running altogether into dramatic or rather picturesque effect, and thought the "French Revolution" a work in very bad taste, and could not read it through with patience. Prescott, however, has nothing of Carlyle's strained, spasmodic style, nor is he a violent partisan. Indeed, we often miss in him the burst of honest indignation, the stinging sarcastic lash at infamy which make us feel in Motley and Carlyle that they wrote with the heart as well as with the head.

The "History of the Reign of Ferdinand and Isabella" comprises a view of the Castilian monarchy before the fifteenth century; the establishment of the Inquisition, and the expulsion of the Jews; the conquest of the Moorish kingdom of Granada; the Italian wars, and the discoveries of Columbus.

The "Conquest of Mexico" opens with a view of Aztec civilization. The country of the ancient Mexicans or Aztecs, part of which the Spaniards denuded of trees so that its bareness might remind them of their own Castile, is graphically described. The story of the Aztecs in so far as it can be gleaned from tradition is admirably told. Their mythology, sacerdotal rites, and progress in the arts are minutely described. The subsequent history of the discovery of Mexico during the reign of Charles V.; the expedition of Cortés under the auspices of the governor of Cuba; the deliberate burning of the ships, that, hope of return being taken from the faint-hearted, they might throw themselves into the new venture with the courage of desperation; the almost incredible sufferings of the Spaniards; the barbaric splendors of the city of Mexico; the superstitions of the people; their horrible religious rites; their pusillanimous Emperor Montezuma; the long parley; the dreadful retreat; the final siege of three months; the horrible sufferings of the starving inhabitants; the fall and plunder of the city, and the subsequent career of Cortés,—all this is told with a fulness of description, an energy of movement, that never cease for a moment. The reader is hurried on breathlessly from spectacle to spectacle, and in his lively interest forgets to be critical, forgets everything but the narrative before him. Such an absorption on the part of an intelligent reader is an evidence of uncommon skill in the author. Prescott undoubtedly makes his readers see and feel, and it is useless to argue against a sensation.

Prescott is inclined to believe in an Asiatic origin

of Aztec civilization. He bases his belief upon comparative analysis, and upon traditions of a Western or Northwestern origin preserved among the Mexicans orally and in their hieroglyphical maps. The physical traits of the Aztecs approached the Mongolian type; the pyramidal structure, the terrace-formed bases of their architectural remains so like those of the East, suggest an Asiatic origin, as does also " the peculiar chronological system of the Aztecs," he says, "their method of distributing the year into cycles and reckoning by means of periodical series instead of numbers. A similar process was used by the various Asiatic nations of the Mongol family, from India to Japan. A correspondence quite as extraordinary is found between the hieroglyphics used by the Aztecs for the signs of the days and those zodiacal signs which the Eastern Asiatics employed as one of the terms of their series."

Later investigations do not sustain Prescott's theory. " At whatever point we touch the subject of ancient America," says John Fiske, " we find scientific opinion tending more and more steadily toward the conclusion that its people and their culture were indigenous."

Though not insensible to the cruelties necessarily attendant upon the conquest of Mexico nor to the mixture of refined fanaticism and barbarity in these Spanish soldiers who celebrated the mass and then marched to their work of slaughter, Prescott finds the conquest justifiable in consideration of the overthrow of the barbarous and cruel religion of the Aztecs,. which required the annual sacrifice of many human beings. He admires the courage, resolve, skill, and address of Cortés, who died at sixty-three, in debt, embarrassed, and out of favor with the court. Speaking of his heroic qualities, his constancy of purpose even in the presence of defeat and ruin, Prescott says: "When his own men deserted him, he did not desert himself."

It is this element of heroism in Cortés that redeems the conquest of Mexico. There is nothing like it in the " History of the Conquest of Peru," which follows the same plan as that of Mexico. It opens with a detailed account of the institutions of the Incas or nobility of ancient Peru, and follows this description with the story of the conquest under Pizarro. The whole story of this conquest, filled as it is with cold-blooded butcheries and even worse atrocities, and descriptions of the greed, cruelty, and perfidy of these low, ignorant Spanish adventurers (Pizarro himself could not even read or write), is so revolting that the reader sickens over it, and feels none the richer for knowing that there could be wretches so inhuman as these in the world. Pizarro's success was that of good fortune backed by a rapacious cruelty that knew no compunctions of conscience or dictates of honor. The only pleasing and valuable part of the history is that in which the civilization of the Peruvians is described.

The ancient empire of Peru stretched along the Pacific coast from the second to the thirty-seventh degree, and spread toward the east considerably beyond the mountains. But it was for the most part a strip of sand on the sea-coast which the ingenuity of the Peruvians had rendered fertile by irrigating canals and underground watercourses. The ruins on the shores of Lake Titicaca belong to an older race than the Peruvians, who knew nothing of their founders. The capital of the Peruvian empire was Cuzco. The government of the empire was a singular union of communism and despotism; its religion, a worship of the sun, whose sister wife, the moon, also received religious honors. The hereditary nobility of Peru, the royal race of Incas, boasted themselves descendants of the sun, and their emperor, representing the sun, was the chief of the priesthood. All the inhabitants of Peru except the Incas and the priesthood worked together at agriculture. The land was parcelled out among the Incas, the people, and the sun, — the land of the latter being designed for the maintenance of the priesthood. Divisions of the soil were made every year, and increased or diminished for the people according to the size of the family. It was a crime in Peru to be idle. At break of day all the inhabitants upon whom the lot of labor fell, were summoned by proclamation to their work in the fields. They worked first on the land of the sun, then on that of the old, sick, or infirm, then on that of the Incas, and at last for themselves. The Peruvian was an altruist by compulsion; he labored not for himself, but for others. Says Prescott: —

"However industrious, he could not add a rood to his possessions, nor advance himself one hair's breadth in the social scale. The great and universal motive to honest industry, that of bettering one's lot, was lost upon him. The great law of human progress was not for him. As he was born, so he was to die. Even his time he could not properly call his own. Without money, with little property of any kind, he paid his taxes in labor. . . . The Peruvian laboring all his life for others might be compared to the convict in a treadmill going the same dull round of incessant toil, with the consciousness that however profitable the results to the state they were nothing to him. . . . No man could be rich, no man could be poor in Peru, but all might enjoy and did enjoy a competence. . . . No Peruvian was too low for the fostering vigilance of government. None was so high that he was not made to feel his dependence upon it in every act of his life. His very existence as an individual was absorbed in that of the community. His hopes and his fears, his joys and his sorrows, the tenderest sympathies of his nature which would most naturally shrink from observation, were all to be regulated by law. He was not allowed even to be happy in his own way. The government of the Incas was the mildest but the most searching of despotisms. . . . It is not easy to comprehend the genius and the full import of institutions so opposite to those of our own free republic, where every man, however humble his condition, may aspire to the highest honors of the state, — may select his own career, and carve out his fortune in his own way; where the light of knowledge instead of being concentrated on a chosen few is shed abroad like the light of day, and suffered to fall equally on the poor and the rich; where the collision of man with man wakens a generous emulation that calls out latent talent, and tasks the energies to the utmost; where consciousness of independence gives a feeling of self-reliance unknown to the timid subjects of a despotism; where, in short, the government is made for man, — not as in Peru, where man seemed to be made only for the government. The New World is the theatre on which these two political systems, so opposite in their character, have been carried into operation. The empire of the Incas has passed away and left no trace. The other great experiment is still going on, — the experiment which is to solve the problem so long contested in the Old World, of the capacity of man for self-government. Alas for humanity if it should fail!"

The " History of Philip the Second," the last and unfinished work of Prescott, is well written; but the author's propensity to forgive the enormities of his hero on the score that they are to be referred to the influences of his age, forgetting that that age could also produce William of Orange, mars the spirit of the book.   Writing of Philip the Second to Lady Lyell, Prescott says: "With all my good nature, I can't wash him even into the darkest French gray. He is black and all black."   The reader feels, too, that this is his color; but he perceives constant efforts at washing in Prescott's history, and is glad to know that Philip's character has been painted in its real hues by the firmer, more masterly hand of Motley.

CHAPTER VII

TRANSCENDENTALISTS AND THE TRANSCENDENTAL
MOVEMENT IN NEW ENGLAND

BEFORE proceeding to a study of Emerson it is necessary to give some attention to his associates and to the time in which he lived, for Emerson is emphatically a man of his time. His writings reflect its eager, restless, intellectual curiosity; its separation from old forms of thought; its irreverence for the past; its rash and arrogant confidence in the future; its ideal aspirations and vagaries; its attempt to assimilate the new and startling discoveries of science, and its newly aroused enthusiasm for Oriental philosophy. It was a time of intellectual ferment; a new leaven had been poured into the old materials of thought, and the minds of thinking men stirred anew under its influence. They began to inquire into their spiritual and social relations as they had not done before. In New England this spiritual movement took the form of what is known as Transcendentalism. The best explanation of this term is to be found in the words of one of its earliest teachers, George Ripley.

GEORGE RIPLEY was born on the third of October, 1802, in Greenfield, Massachusetts. He was educated at Harvard, taught school for a time, prepared for the ministry, and in 1826 was ordained pastor of the

Unitarian Society of Boston.   The following year he married Sophia Willard Dana.

Ripley was a serious, reserved man, giving little outward token of an idealistic turn of mind that led him later into extravagant experiments in social reform.   He was a fine scholar, and had collected an unusual library, particularly rich in German philosophy.   He was one of the founders of a club known as the Transcendental Club, which assembled for the purpose of discussing philosophical questions and such as bear upon the conduct of life.   This club held its first meeting at his house on the nineteenth of September, 1836.   Emerson, F. H. Hedge, C. Francis, James Freeman Clarke, and A. B. Alcott were all that were present, besides Ripley.   The next year Caleb Stetson, Theodore Parker, Margaret Fuller, and Elizabeth Peabody joined the club.   The subjects discussed were Law, Truth, Individuality, and the Personality of God.   The utmost freedom was permitted in these discussions, and Ripley found in them an outlet for the thoughts growing up in him, but so often concealed from his congregation lest he should shock them by uttering what might be construed as heresy.   But the love of freedom grows with its exercise, and in a few years the longing for a freer mode of worship impelled him to resign his pastorate.   His resignation was accepted in 1841.   In a letter to his congregation in 1840, he defines Transcendentalism as follows : —

"There is a class of persons who desire a reform in the prevailing philosophy of the day.   These are called Transcendentalists because they believe in an order of truths which transcends the sphere of the external senses.   Their leading idea is the supremacy of mind over matter. Hence they maintain that the truth of religion does not depend on tradition nor historical facts, but has an unerring witness in the soul. There is a light, they believe, which enlighteneth every man that cometh into the world; there is a faculty in all — the most degraded, the most ignorant, the most obscure — to perceive spiritual truth when distinctly presented; and the ultimate appeal on all moral questions is not a jury of scholars, a hierarchy of divines, or the prescriptions of a creed, but to the common sense of the human race. These views I have always adopted; they have been at the foundation of my preaching from the first time that I entered the pulpit until now. The experience and reflection of nearly twenty years have done much to confirm, nothing to shake them; and if my discourses in this house or my lectures in yonder vestry have in any instance displayed the vitality of truth, impressed on a single heart a genuine sense of religion, disclosed to you a new prospect of the resources of your own nature, made you feel more deeply your responsibility to God, cheered you in the sublime hope of immortality, and convinced your reason of the reality and worth of the Christian revelation, it was because my mind has been trained in the principles of Transcendental philosophy, — a philosophy which is now taught in every university on the continent of Europe, which is the common creed of the most enlightened nations, and the singular misunderstanding of which, among ourselves, illustrates more forcibly, I am ashamed to say, the heedless enterprise than the literary culture of our clergymen."

Thus Transcendentalism found one of its most eager American expounders in George Ripley, under whose influence it was not long before it had its literary organ. In the same year, 1840, in which he had addressed his congregation in the language quoted above, he founded " The Dial," in conjunction with Emerson and Margaret Fuller. " The Dial," a monthly magazine devoted to religion, literature, and art, was designed to do in public what the Transcendental Club had done in private. Emerson sent the first number of " The Dial " to Carlyle; and the sturdy Scotchman, who loved a fact and was not to be moved from his allegiance to it by the prettiest "rose-pink dreams," replied, in acknowledging the receipt of it:

" I read it with interest : it is an utterance of what is purest, youngest in your land, — pure, ethereal as the voices of the Morning ! And yet — you know me — for me it is too ethereal, speculative, theoretic : all theory becomes more and more confessedly inadequate, untrue, unsatisfactory, almost a mockery to me. I will have all things condense themselves, take shape and body if they are to have my sympathy."

The general public was like Carlyle. It wanted more body in its spiritual nutriment, and " The Dial," after languishing for four years, quietly died.

Ripley's next venture was the beautiful but unsuccessful socialistic experiment of Brook Farm. Before giving an account of this experiment, it is well to state that the inquiry into man's social relations at this time had led earnest enthusiasts into as many vagaries as the investigation of his spiritual relations. The outcome of this inquiry was a deep and widespread discontent with social institutions, and a firm belief that they were responsible for existent poverty, degradation, and misery. Nowhere was this belief so generally and so fiercely maintained as in France, where the horrors of the Revolution might have taught men that governmental restraints are still wholesome and necessary.

The founder of French socialism was a count named ST. SIMON, who at the age of nineteen assisted the American colonies in their revolt against England. He took no part, however, in the French Revolution, — wanted, perhaps, a revolution of his own conducted peacefully by which the law of inheritance should be abolished, and society at large assume the sole management of all commercial enterprises and public improvements. He stringently insisted upon the recognition of merit, — each man's retaining his position on the score of his merit, — and advocated the complete emancipation of woman. He appealed to Louis XVIII. to inaugurate the new order of things. He gave his valet orders to awaken him every morning with the words, "Monsieur le Comte, remember that you have great things to do." But no great things came of all his restless energy. He completely impoverished himself, found few followers, and was at last obliged to work hard at an absurdly low salary and to live on the generosity of a former valet.

FOURIER (1772–1837), another famous socialist of France, was the son of a rich merchant. He believed in the free development of human nature, the free indulgence of all desires and passions, and advocated co-operative industry. According to him, society should be divided into communities or phalanges numbering about sixteen hundred persons, all of whom should live in one common building or phalanstery and have a certain portion of ground allotted to them for cultivation. Out of the common gain five-twelfths should be given to labor, four-twelfths to capital, and three-twelfths to talent. The institution of marriage was to be abolished. Fourier's theories on the relations of the sexes gave great offence to society; but his theories of co-operation soon attracted widespread attention, not only in France but in other countries, and were in a great degree the inspiration of Ripley's attempt in America.

PROUDHON, a third notable French figure in this movement of dissatisfaction with society, denounced the systems of St. Simon and Fourier. He was the son of a brewer's cooper, and herded cattle in his youth, afterwards becoming a printer and journalist. In opinion, he was an anarchist, and asserted that government of man by man in any form is oppression. He thought that all kinds of labor should be equally paid; that the most menial service should receive the same reward as that of the greatest sculptor, poet, artist, claiming that a day's labor balances a day's labor whatever its nature.

LASSALLE (1825–1864) was the originator of the social-democratic movement in Germany, and founder of the association known as the United Workmen of Germany. Lassalle was of Jewish extraction, the son of a prosperous merchant. He was a violent agitator, and ambitious of overturning the German Empire and forming a Republic, of which he was to be president. He had great difficulty, at first, in arousing the working-men of Germany to a rebellious attitude. He wished to abolish the present relations of capital and labor and raise the working-men into a great political power. In private life he was a great dandy and spendthrift, living sumptuously and giving costly banquets. He was killed at the age of thirty-nine in a foolish duel over a woman.

In England the founder of socialism was ROBERT OWEN (1771–1858). He was born at Newton, Montgomeryshire, North Wales. Owen's father was a saddler and ironmonger. So thrifty and energetic was young Robert that at nineteen he was managing a cotton-mill at Manchester, England. During a Glasgow visit he fell in love with Miss Dale, daughter of the proprietor of New Lanark Mills. He married the daughter, bought an interest in the Lanark mills, and finally assumed control of them. The business proved a great commercial success. His improvements in the condition of his workmen resulted in a community where drunkenness was unknown, and health, plenty, and contentment reigned.

In a report to the House of Commons in 1817, he recommended the establishment of communities of about one hundred and twenty persons, who should be settled on land comprising from one thousand to fifteen hundred acres, and that they should all live in one large building in the form of a square, with a public kitchen and dining-halls. Work and the enjoyment of its results were to be common. In 1825 an experiment of this kind was attempted by Abram Combe at Orbiston, near Glasgow; and Owen himself commenced another in America at New Harmony, Indiana, where most of his wealth was sunk. Both experiments proved complete failures, but they brought the word "socialism" into currency, and a vast quantity of ephemeral communistic literature which was not without its influence.

From the preceding account of the growth of socialistic ideas, Ripley's experiment at Brook Farm may be more easily understood. It is of especial interest to us in connection with the literature of our country, for the Brook Farm community numbered among its first members our foremost writer of fiction and greatest imaginative genius, Nathaniel Hawthorne, whose experiences there suggested to him " The Blithedale Romance."

The Brook Farm Association for Education and Agriculture, as it was called, was founded by George Ripley in the spring of 1841. The association bought a tract of two hundred acres of farm land in West Roxbury, Massachusetts, about nine miles from Boston. The object of the association was to secure to all its members, with perfect social equality, the greatest amount of culture with the least amount of manual labor, or, as a writer in " The Dial " expressed it, " This community aims to be rich, not in the metallic representation of wealth, but in the wealth itself which money should represent, namely, *leisure to live in all the faculties of the soul.*"

The plan of the community was to allow shareholders an interest of five per cent on funds invested in the common property of the farm. The members could either keep house or board in common, as they chose. Their living expenses were to be paid from the interest accruing to them or from the wages they received for their labor for the community. The price of board, including fire, light, room, and washing, was four dollars a week. The members could work at what they liked and as many hours as they chose; but whatever the nature of the labor, intellectual or manual, they were to be paid the same rate of wages, on the ground that it is a greater sacrifice to work at manual than at intellectual labor, which in a great measure is its own reward.

Community warehouses were to supply material comforts at the cost of production, and in course of time it was hoped that all the arts and all the trades would flourish in harmonious brotherhood without the stimulus of gain or competition, — that life would be rendered easy to all, and poverty and crime become unknown.

It was a beautiful dream, and the dreamers of that first community were noble men and women. Charles A. Dana was recording secretary, and Minot Pratt, treasurer. Ripley placed his fine library at the service of the community; and the advantages of a superior training were offered to pupils not only in its use, but in the association with so many men and women of culture. The community soon became known as a desirable place for the education of young people, and a limited number of pupils was received on very liberal terms. They could either pay their board and tuition fees by money, or by sharing the labors of the community. It is possible that they may have missed something of the accuracy and method of college training; but they got what was better, — an inspiration to a simpler, purer life, an uplifting into a higher atmosphere of intellect and morals, that reacted upon them in the most beneficial way.

The community soon numbered eighty members; but it was not long before it was discovered that there are certain weaknesses inherent in human nature which cannot be eradicated by phalansteries or life in common, even in surroundings so idyllic as those of

Brook Farm. Theory and practice refused to be reconciled. The indolent were indolent still, and the energetic bore the heavy end of the burden of labor. Financial difficulties arose, and at the end of three years the community was increased in numbers and transformed into a Fourier phalanx. But in 1846 the phalanstery, or building in which the members were housed, burned down, and the association dissolved.

The failure left Ripley poor, and burdened by a debt which hung over him for fifteen years. He went on the " New York Tribune " at a salary of five dollars a week, which was increased from time to time until it reached the sum of seventy-five dollars a week. He wrote for the popular magazines of the day, and in association with C. A. Dana edited the " American Encyclopædia." Ripley died in 1880. A Lutheran Orphans' Home now occupies the site of his famous experiment, but the memory of it is one of the pleasant and wholesome lessons of the nineteenth century. W. H. Channing, nephew of W. E. Channing, the great Unitarian leader, said of it in 1871 :

" We tried to bloom our buds while the snow was still on the ground — amidst the first golden streaks of sunrise. So dear Brook Farm, blossom of Eden as it was, paled, grew brown, fell from the stalk, and left as if in mockery a pauper union ! The breath of its fragrance has scented the atmosphere of our whole nation, however. But the process of forcing such blossoms is too wasteful. The fruit cannot set or ripen ; and that fruit, remember, is the fruit of the Tree of Life. We do injustice to our faith by potting a small specimen twig of this tree, even if we can force it to flower. It was an heroic effort that the Brook Farmer made, but quite too tragic a one to be repeated."

Transcendentalism had its practical expounder in George Ripley, but its typical philosopher was Amos Bronson Alcott (1799–1888), its typical poet, Jones Very of Salem, Massachusetts, and its finest feminine type, Margaret Fuller.

In certain particulars Alcott might have been the prototype of Wordsworth's hero of " The Excursion." Like him, Alcott was a pedler in his youth, and, like him, he was given to philosophical speculations. But there the likeness ends. Alcott gave up peddling and tried teaching in Boston. He was master of a private school in one of the rooms of the Masonic Temple.

He furnished his room with busts of Shakespeare, Milton, Scott, Socrates, and Plato, — an unusual proceeding then, but common enough now. He adopted the Socratic method of teaching by questions and conversations on various subjects, and read aloud a great deal to his pupils, requiring the most earnest attention from them. On the whole, he was an uncommonly fine teacher so far as he went. But he wholly ignored external nature. He directed the eye inward, not outward ; he made the child think about thoughts, instead of helping him to accumulate the material of thought; and carried his methods of self-analysis so far as to insist upon autobiographical journal-writing from his pupils, and in this way over-stimulated their imagination and self-consciousness. His school at first numbered about twenty pupils, boys and girls, ranging from the age of three to twelve. But the publication of a little book entitled " Conversations on the Bible," the result of his class-work, created an unfavorable prejudice against him.

His pupils were withdrawn, and his school-keeping ended.

In 1842 Emerson, who had an extravagant estimation of Alcott's ability, contributed to a fund to send him to England to commune with growing, liberal minds for the purpose of coming at some definite plans for introducing social reforms into America. He returned in October of the same year, with two English socialists, Charles Lane and Henry C. Wright, and undertook at once the disastrous experiment at Fruitlands in the town of Harvard. His daughter Louisa, whose fame as a writer of stories for children has eclipsed that of her father, has given us in her autobiography a half-humorous, half-pathetic account of this experiment, in a chapter entitled " Transcendental Wild Oats."

Emerson had given Alcott a letter of introduction to Carlyle, and the keen-eyed Scotchman had pierced at a glance what was nebulous, magnifying, and mystifying, and got at once to the small nucleus of him. " He is a genial, innocent, simple-hearted man," writes Carlyle, " of much natural intelligence and goodness, with an air of rusticity, veracity, and dignity withal, which in many ways appeals to one. The good Alcott with his long, lean face and figure, with his gray, worn temples and mild radiant eyes; all bent on saving the world by a return to acorns and the golden age; he comes before me like a venerable Don Quixote, whom nobody can even laugh at without loving." But later, he speaks with more frankness, and warns Emerson to keep " rather a strict outlook on Alcott and his English tail. I mean as far as we have any business with it. Bottomless imbeciles ought not to be seen in company with Ralph Waldo Emerson, who has already *men* listening to him on this side of the water."

Alcott had proposed to some English men of letters a new international journal to be called "The Janus: An Ephemeris of the Permanent in Religion, Philosophy, Science, Art, and Letters." Neither the proposal nor the title receiving the approval he expected, Alcott remarks: "My idea was obviously too broad and daring for them, and so we separated." The tone of this consolatory reflection is characteristic of the Transcendentalists. They never explained their failures to interest and arouse the public by their own vagueness and want of common sense. They explained it as the result of the public's obtuseness, cowardly conventionalism, and lack of spirituality.

Alcott continued for some time to sow "Transcendental wild oats" in lectures that did not pay expenses, and which he persisted in calling conversations, and finally, in the spring of 1879, he founded the Concord School of Philosophy. This school afforded him an opportunity to exercise his particular gift of conversation, in which gift he took so much delight as to declare that his definition of heaven was "a place where you can have a little conversation."

Among the notable men who assisted in the first session, which lasted six weeks, Emerson was the most distinguished. Lectures were delivered on art, psychology, the Platonic philosophy; and such subjects as the personality of God, the immortality of the soul, pre-existence, fate, and freedom of the will, were freely discussed.

In the second year's program Alcott discussed mysticism, St. John the Evangelist, Behmen, Swedenborg. Other lecturers expounded speculative philosophy, Oriental and mystical philosophy. The philosophies of Hegel, Fichte, and Kant were the chief topics of the third, fourth, and fifth years. The sixth year, the genius and character of Emerson was the principal subject of discussion; and Goethe and modern science furnished the theme for the seventh year.

It will be seen by this list of subjects that it was chiefly with the unknowable, not the knowable, that the Transcendentalists were concerned, and that in this respect they showed a spirit directly contrary to that of patient scientific research, with its humble consciousness of the limitations of human knowledge. They closed their eyes to the phenomena without them, and gave themselves up to idle speculations. The Transcendentalists were ambitious of " stringing worlds like beads upon their thought," but nothing more than a glittering necklace came of this pretty pastime. Infected with the teachings of Oriental philosophy, they regarded the soul of man as a pre-existent, external part of the divine soul of the universe. In this arrogant belief they fell into a mild kind of intellectual anarchy, in which every mind by virtue of its own right divine was privileged to claim an incontestable authority for its wildest opinions. This belief, to be sure, gave to the holder a certain dignity and self-reliance that was not without its positive value, and it must be acknowledged that the Transcendentalists cannot be charged with any mean or trivial interpretation of life. On the contrary, they gave to it a nobly spiritual significance. They stripped it of its vulgar material wrappings, its greed of gain, its hurry and fever of ignoble strife. They broke the old Puritan fetters of thought, and gave the mind liberty to go whither it would, and they gave to the world two men of incontestable power, Ralph Waldo Emerson and Henry David Thoreau.

JONES VERY, the typical poet of Transcendentalism, was born at Salem, Massachusetts, August twenty-eighth, 1813. His father, a sea-captain, married his own cousin Lydia Very, and died when his son was eleven years old. At fourteen young Very became an errand-boy for an auction-room at Salem, reading greedily all books that passed through his employer's hands. He fitted himself for a tutorship in a private Latin school in Salem, and in 1834 entered the Sophomore class at Harvard. He was graduated two years later, and received an appointment as tutor in Greek at the Divinity School, where he was studying theology. An overweening vanity and persuasion of his own purity made him lose all sense of relation and proportion. He said that he felt it an honor to wash his own face, because it was the temple of the spirit. But he saw only vileness in the world and in those about him. He told Emerson one day that it was a day of hate with him, — a day when the bad element in every person repelled him and he shrank from giving his hand to those whom he met; that the world looked to him like a huge ink-blot, and he only went to see men to do them good.

This morbid frame of mind soon became so alarming that he was put for a time in an insane asylum

at Somerville, a suburb of Boston.   After a few
months' detention he was released, and in 1843, when
his health was sufficiently restored, he received a
license to preach.   He was never a popular preacher
and received no regular pastorate, but occasionally
supplied a Unitarian pulpit.   He never married, but
after the death of his mother lived quietly in the
family home with his sisters.   His mornings were
spent in study, and his afternoons in rambling alone
over the fields and hills.   His love of nature, he says,

> "is deeper far
> Than strength of words, though spirit-born, can tell;"

and he certainly gives no expression to that keen
delight in natural beauty that speaks so unmistakably
in Cowper, Wordsworth, and certain of Burns's poems.
His love for nature never rises above a comfortable
sensation of being undisturbed in his self-commun-
ings.   This drowsy comfort is expressed in the following poem, "The Columbine," which, as well as
any that might be selected, gives the range of the
poet's mind in this direction: —

> "Still, still my eyes will gaze long fixed on thee,
>   Till I forget that I am called a man,
> And at thy side fast-rooted seem to be,
>   And the breeze comes my cheek with thine to fan.
> Upon this craggy hill my life shall pass,
>   A life of summer days and summer joys,
> Nodding our honey bells mid pliant grass,
>   In which the bee half hid his time employs;
> And here we 'll drink with thirsty pores the rain,
>   And turn dew-sprinkled to the rising sun,
> And look when in the flaming west again
>   His orb across the heavens its path has run:
> Here left in darkness on the rocky steep,
> My weary eyes shall close, like folding flowers, in sleep."

With the exception of the religious sonnets and hymns, the subjects of Very's poems are mostly natural objects met in his rambles, notably flowers and trees; as "The Yellow Violet," "The Houstonia," "The Oak and the Poplar," "The May Flower," "The Wind Flower," "The Sabbatia," etc.

Jones Very thought himself a reed through which the Master Musician spoke. The monotonous burden of his rhymes is, "I am the Lord's: He speaks through me; I am but a passive instrument of His will." But never was there more foolish overrating of a humble power of rhyming. He has not written a quotable line, unless it be the opening lines of the sonnet entitled "The True Light," which are a pretty rhetorical rendering of the familiar thought that the kingdom of God is within you : —

> "The morning's brightness cannot make thee glad,
>   If thou art not more bright than it within,
> And naught of evening's peace hast thou e'er had,
>   If evening first did not with thee begin."

Once only did he break through the monotonous circle of ideas to which he gave expression, and write true poetry, and that was when he wrote "The Arab Steed." Perhaps for this one poem he deserves grateful remembrance. There is in it a fire, a swift energy, an imaginative vigor of which he gives no proof elsewhere. His weakness is the weakness of the monotone, — the weakness of the man in whom is lacking that fine common-sense born of experience, and who has nothing, therefore, to hold him back from yielding to the extreme conclusions of his theories. His love of God crowded from his heart the love of man. He was pure; but his purity was that of white, dry sand in which not even a nettle will grow; and so " our brave saint," as Emerson calls him, has done less for the world than many a sinner with the gift of song.   He died on the eighth of May, 1880.   In manner, he was reserved yet courteous; in person, tall, straight, and haggard in his leanness.   His portrait represents a long, thin face, the cheeks drawn in and covered on the lower part with a scant fringe of hair, the mouth pursed up, the eyes sunken and dreamy, the forehead bald, the top-head high and pointed arched.   It is the face of one to whom the world is but a place of unwilling sojourn, the face of one who would be solitary in crowded places, and in whose heart there is an unstilled hunger for the unknown.

Jones Very represents wholly the dreamy poetic side of Transcendentalism with its coloring of religious mysticism.   Alcott is its theorizing philosopher, with his head in the clouds and his feet in the mire. George Ripley is its benevolent man of action, attempting to put into practice its theories, and learning through disastrous experience that man has matter as well as spirit to contend with in this world. But in no one has Transcendentalism so complete a representative as in that brilliant, restless, romantic, daring, arrogant spirit known as Margaret Fuller. Quick to feel and quick to think, she brought to her intercourse with men of genius that subtle sympathy which is the sunshine and dew of the spirit, brightening and vivifying all who come under its influence, and she will live to posterity in their generous and grateful eulogies rather than in the value of anything she has written.   She will live as the representative of Transcendentalism in all its varied aspects, — in its poetry of boundless aspiration and theoretic activity, in its prose of humble achievement, and in its stimulating influence. She was the richest fruit it produced in New England.

SARAH MARGARET FULLER OSSOLI was born at Cambridge, Massachusetts, on the twenty-third of May, 1810. Her father, Timothy Fuller, a lawyer and politician of some prominence, was noted among his associates for a certain irritating arrogance, which trait he bequeathed in no less degree to his gifted daughter. T. W. Higginson says that had the father "lived next door to an imperial palace, he would have thought that it was he who did the favor by mingling with his neighbors." This inherited pride and unwarrantable self-assertion were curiously present in Margaret in a belief cherished in her childhood that she was not the real daughter of her parents, but a changeling European princess. Father and daughter were too much alike to be congenial; neither would bend to the mood of the other, and as the father undertook the charge of his daughter's early education, there often resulted an unhappy conflict of wills that made them both wretched.

She began studying Latin at six, Greek somewhat later, and her father listened to her recitations when his office hours were over. The natural result of this undue stimulation of an intellect originally precocious and associated with an ardent, excitable temperament, was a deplorable state of the nerves, in which horrible nightly visions drove sleep from her pillow or made a somnambulist of her. As she grew older, her ill-health was further aggravated by the unwise mode of dressing then prevalent, and by the fact that she was allowed to go into society at thirteen. Naturally, at seventeen, we find her writing verses lamenting the vanishing of " life's primal freshness all too soon," and invoking the " breath of dawn to rouse to the draught of life the wearied sense." The story of her childhood and girlhood is not a pleasing one. The grave defects of her passionate and imperious nature were not softened or concealed by any womanly graces. W. H. Channing, who became in her later womanhood her ardent friend, and praised her heroism, her devotion to truth, and the quickening power of her keen intellect, speaks of her repellent qualities in her twentieth year, — her exaggerated intensity, arrogance, satire, and her romantic friendships in which " she seemed to walk enveloped in a shining fog of sentimentalism." "In brief," he adds, " it must be candidly confessed that I then suspected her of affecting the part of a Yankee Corinne."

As her reading at this time was chiefly in French and Italian, and as her exorbitant vanity craved nothing so much as admiration, Channing's suspicions are probably well founded. Extremely plain in person, she craved the gift of beauty for the power that lies in it. But she very early learned that a higher and rarer power might be hers, — the power of intellectual vigor. It would be difficult to prove that her love of learning at this time was not rooted in a longing to be admired. With all her passionate admiration of genius and her belief that she had its power, it never seems to have occurred to her that the very soul of genius is a boundless tenderness that overruns humanity and spends itself, as it spent itself in Burns, even on the daisy at one's feet or on the cowering mouse of the field. She seems never to have known that its other characteristic is a sweet humility, not weak or fawning, but strong and simple, the result of that clear insight into the relation of one man to the vast unknown about him. But this was not then, nor was it ever, Margaret Fuller's ideal of genius.

It is necessary to emphasize this fact, for it lies at the bottom of her failure as a critic and writer. She had formed herself after the model of the French sentimentalists, and like them she never associated strength with serenity. Her idea of intellectual activity was never disassociated from that of a delirious intoxication of the senses. She loved to be excited. She did not think she lived when her pulse beat normally, but only when it ran at fever rate. The heat of blood which belongs to youth and passes with it was the inspiration of Margaret Fuller's talent, and nothing can be more certain than that with increasing years her gifts would not have ripened but would have shrivelled.

The removal of the Fuller family from Cambridge to Groton in 1833, and the death of her father two years later, were turning-points in Margaret's life. The beautiful, fearless courage in her awoke to the responsibilities of her situation, and she became the heart and stay of the home. In 1837 she taught for a few months in A. B. Alcott's school in Boston, and then received an appointment in the Green Street Academy of Providence, Rhode Island, at a salary of one thousand dollars a year. She disliked teaching, and in December, 1838, she left Providence for Boston, hoping to find a fuller field of activity for her remarkable gifts. For a time she took private pupils in Boston at two dollars an hour, and then started her famous conversation classes. The first class, consisting of twenty-five ladies, met on the sixteenth of November, 1839, at Miss Peabody's rooms on West Street. The class met once a week at noon, and remained together for two hours. The first series of conversations lasted for thirteen weeks, and the subject was Grecian mythology. The ladies took part in the discussion by questions and answers, but the burden of the labor naturally fell to the shoulders that could carry them best, and those were Margaret's. The topic of the next year's series of thirteen weeks was the Fine Arts. These classes were so successful that they were continued each winter until Margaret's removal to New York in 1844. "What is life?" "Culture," "Ignorance," "Vanity," Prudence," were other subjects of discussion.

In 1839 Margaret published a translation of "Eckermann's Conversations with Goethe," and in 1840 she undertook for two years the editorship of the new Transcendental organ, "The Dial." Among other things, she wrote for its pages the series of articles called "The Great Lawsuit," afterward published in book form under the title of "Woman in the Nineteenth Century." "Summer on the Lakes," her first original publication in book form, appeared in 1844; it brought her no pecuniary recompense, but it added to her growing reputation, and in December of the same year Horace Greeley offered her the position of literary critic on the "New York Tribune."

She at once went to New York, and became an inmate of the Greeley household.

She was not a ready writer, but dependent upon moods and inspirations, and the punctual demands of newspaper work taxed her severely. She was glad to escape them and realize a long-cherished wish when, in the summer of 1846, she set sail for England. She visited Carlyle and Wordsworth, and met DeQuincey. She made a tour of Scotland, and then went to Paris, where she visited George Sand. From France she journeyed to Italy, and settled in Rome, where the romance and the tragedy of her life began.

Italy at this time was still engaged in her long struggle to become a united kingdom, and at the time of Margaret Fuller's arrival three parties were organized whose object was national unity. One party, known as Young Italy and led by Joseph Mazzini, desired a republic; another party desired a confederation of states with the Pope at its head; the third party wished a constitutional monarchy with the King of Sardinia on the throne. The last party, through the efforts of Count Cavour, was destined to see its wishes fulfilled, and to give to Italy the peace of unity.

Margaret Fuller threw herself ardently into the cause of young Italy; she became the friend and counsellor of Mazzini, and in December, 1847, she secretly married a young Italian patriot, Marquis Ossoli. This young man, who was some eight or nine years her junior, was of very handsome person, tall, dark-haired, dark-eyed, and gentle-mannered, but intellectually far beneath her. But the hungry-hearted woman, once so scornful of an intelligence beneath her own, had learned the worth of heart as well as head. The secret of her marriage was carefully kept even from her American relatives and friends until some time after the birth of her child, which took place in September, 1848, at Rieti, a classical old town of Italy. The reason given for the concealment was that the announcement of the marriage of the young Marquis to a Protestant and a Republican would endanger such hopes of favor as his family and social relations might offer him in case of the failure of the Republican party.

During the siege of Rome by the French in 1848, Margaret left her infant at Rieti with an Italian nurse, and hurried on to Rome to offer her services in the care of the wounded and dying at the soldiers' hospitals. A brief respite of peace and happiness with her husband and child in Florence followed the terrors and anxieties of her life in Rome. But her money was nearly spent, the necessity for further exertion pressed upon her, and she determined to return to America. She sailed with her husband and child Angelo, from Leghorn on the ship "Elizabeth" in May, 1850. The pathetic story of that voyage homeward bound; the death of the captain by small-pox; the anxious watch over the little Angelo stricken with the same dread disease; the child's recovery; the violent tempest in sight of land, and the wrecking of the vessel on Fire Island beach, — all this has been graphically told by the few survivors of that wreck. But Margaret Fuller and her loved ones were not among them. The child's body was washed ashore and was buried in Mt. Auburn Cemetery, Cambridge, at the foot of a stone erected to the memory of Margaret Fuller, her husband, and her child.

Never was woman more fortunate in her friendships than Margaret Fuller. She knew intimately most of the best men and women of New England. Theodore Parker, W. H. Channing, George Ripley and his wife, James Freeman Clarke, Dr. Hedge, Alcott, Thoreau, Hawthorne, and Emerson were her friends, and all in a greater or less degree admired her. To have had the power to form and keep such friendships argues no slender fibre of actual worth in the woman; but when we turn from the story of her life of struggle and aspiration, and the friendly eulogies of her genius by those who knew her, it is impossible to escape a feeling of intense disappointment. The best of her critical articles collected from the columns of the " New York Tribune " are to be found in a volume entitled " Art, Literature, and the Drama." " Life Within and Life Without " is the title of another volume prepared from the unpublished manuscripts which she left at her death, while the record of her travels is to be found in a book called " At Home and Abroad." These volumes, together with " Summer on the Lakes " and " Woman in the Nineteenth Century," are sufficient, if the quality were equal to the quantity, to have established her fame on a solid basis. But there is infinitely more whey than curd in her books. Her talent has been called critical, not creative, and as such has been highly praised; but the true test of a critic's power is time. It is easy enough to pronounce judgment according to one's individual tastes; but to pronounce it according to a fixed standard, established upon a knowledge of human nature and a close familiarity with the masterpieces of human art in all ages and countries, is so difficult that the literature which can boast its two or three fine critics to its scores of creative geniuses, may be considered rich in criticism.

Margaret Fuller's standard was false. It was not the natural but the unnatural that appealed to her. She had a decided bias toward the romantic, the exaggerated, and the eccentric. By nature superstitious, a believer in charms, fated days, talismans, presentiments, she ignored real science, but gave a ready acquiescence to the preposterous claims of "mesmerism and its goblin brood." "Subject," she says of herself, "to the sudden revelations, the breaks in habitual existence, caused by the aspect of death, the touch of love, the flood of music, I never lived, that I remember, what you call a common natural day. All my days are touched by the supernatural, for I feel the pressure of hidden causes and the presence, sometimes the communion, of unseen powers." Now, it is by the pure light of a common day that the true critic views his subject. The light by which Margaret Fuller viewed objects was broken by prismatic coloring; she saw by red, blue, yellow, or violet rays, therefore her criticisms simply voice an idiosyncrasy. They have no value in themselves aside from that which belongs to a unique and interesting personality. Time has in almost every case refuted them, and all her predictions fail. She thought, for example, that the novels of Charles Brockden Browne should be the pride of his countrymen. She hailed Henry Taylor, by virtue of his now almost forgotten "Philip Van Artevelde," as a bright poetic star of the first magnitude. Of Bailey, the author of "Festus," she speaks in terms of extravagant praise, finding no poet of his day worthy to stand beside him. But while she was thus hailing meteors for stars, there was shining in England a clear steady light destined to shine on through the ages. The new star was Wordsworth, but she did not recognize him. Longfellow she thought artificial and inartistic, and Lowell "absolutely wanting in the true spirit and tone of poesy," and predicted that posterity would not remember him. On the other hand, of Ellery Channing, her brother-in-law, whom posterity has not remembered, she said that "some of the purest tones of the lyre are his, the finest inspirations as to the feelings and passions of men." Of Goethe, whom she was said to understand better than any one in America, she has left no memorable word. She had no adequate conception of either Carlyle or Emerson, while of Disraeli, the most factitious of writers, she said that he "shows not only the heart but the soul of men; he wishes to care wisely for all." Her best critique, that on Sir James Mackintosh, owes what merit it has to the truthfulness of an undercurrent of self-analysis, made possible and proper by a partial likeness between herself and her subject. Like Mackintosh, she eagerly desired literary distinction, and found in conversation an outlet for her intellectual activity. She speaks, therefore, with rare penetration of the charms of conversation, and of the tact and ability that it requires.

The romantic cast of her imagination, which is her weakness as a critic, gives to her descriptive writing a feeble Chateaubriandish coloring that robs it of fidelity and originality. Had she been capable of reproducing simplicity and truth, and shunned the "bombast spates o' nonsense swell, and snap conceits," she would have needed no memorial cairn to preserve some record of a life so full of ambition. Her books would have been what they are not now, her cairn, and posterity would have remembered her with gratitude. She had a daring, impetuous, passionate, arrogant nature, with a substratum of coarseness; like George Sand's Helène, whom she admired, "she could hear so well the terrene voice, yet keep her eyes fixed on the stars." To love what is beyond one's reach and to aspire after it, to try to silence the discords of one's nature and attune it to a sweet and noble harmony, are not aspirations and endeavors so common that they can pass without comment. However glaring her defects, there was no littleness in Margaret Fuller. She was never a rich woman, but her purse was always open like her heart and mind, and she gave generously of it, often to her own actual discomfort, and without hope of return. Fearless and stanch in friendship she knew how to be. "Do not, I implore you," she writes, "wish to exile me from the dark hour. The manly mind might love best in the triumphant hour; but the woman could no more stay from the foot of the cross than from the transfiguration."

All who have written of her have spoken of the extraordinary power that she exercised over the persons whom she met, drawing confidences from those who were not confidential, melting the glassy reserve of the cautious, and possessing herself of secrets hidden even from the revealer's dearest friends. This power belonged to a rare social instinct, a wide sympathy, a sure tact. Margaret Fuller liked to know people. She loved to listen to the beating of a human heart. Her intellectual curiosity gave her a large tolerance in which one felt secure from a narrow interpretation. Her eager desire to know life in all its varied activity found a deep satisfaction in learning its experiences from others. The opportunity to praise or reproach gratified her innate love of power, and the ability to attract others in such a way that they gave her, not the superficial life which the world had of them, but the very depths and centres of their being, gratified her vanity in no common degree. That she never abused these confidences, that she never used her power for vulgar ends, but held every one whom she met ever level, ever true to his highest duty, is worthy of all praise. "We never met," said James F. Clarke of Margaret, "without my feeling that she was ready to be interested in all my thoughts, to love those whom I loved, to watch my progress, to rebuke my faults and follies, to encourage within me every generous and pure aspiration; to demand of me always the best I could be or do, and to be satisfied with no mediocrity, no conformity to any low standard."

"Persons were her game," says Emerson of Margaret; and so they were, but they were dangerous game to her inflammable temperament, her "sultry Southern nature," and good and evil came of it. Good came of it, in that it broadened and ripened her, softened the asperities of her nature, and made her fitter for the work that she aspired to do. But evil came of it, in that she ended with being scorched by her own fire. A feverish emotionalism poisoned her enjoyment of a calm, rational friendship with Emerson, whose cool reserve she could not melt with all her arts and tricks of sympathy. Moonlight could not have been sweeter and milder than his attractive and irritating serenity. She would have given the world to break it; to see a new light in the eyes, a faint flush of color on the cheeks, a nervous trembling in the calm, cool hand outstretched to hers. But she never saw that change in him, and all her efforts rather chilled him into a more helpless silence, though they did not break a friendship which she learned at last to value and be grateful for as it was given her.

She was a woman of remarkable talent, who mistook a passionate love of beauty and a passionate desire to reproduce it for the power to fulfil that desire, and lost herself in futile excitements. She was not content to see things as they are but as she thought they ought to be, and lost the real world for a romantic dream world of her own creation. She was impatient of slow, intellectual growth, incapable of loving knowledge for itself alone and of bearing the privations and lonely obscurity of the earnest scholar's life, and sacrificed enduring glory for the fleeting glory of an hour. But if she missed the literary fame she coveted, her life was by no means a failure, but had its beauty and meaning, of which no uncertain reflections have come down to us. To those who knew her she was an intellectual stimulus, a source of inspiration, and many lives were enriched by her influence.

CHAPTER VIII

R ALPH WALDO EMERSON was born in Boston, May 25, 1803. In many respects he is one of the most interesting men of America; the descendant of a long line of New England ministers, himself a Unitarian clergyman in his early youth, he illustrates in a remarkable degree both the influence of heredity and that of environment. His ancestors on his father's side were men of stern enthusiasm and rectitude. His mother, an energetic woman of sweet and serious piety, was left a widow with six children, her husband having died at the early age of forty. To support herself and children, Mrs. Emerson took boarders, worked hard, lived frugally, but managed to give her children the best education within reach.

There were times when poverty sorely pinched the little household, making it necessary to choose between material comforts and educational advantages, but the choice was always rightly made. Ralph and his brother Edward, says Emerson's biographer, Cabot, "had but one great coat between them, and had to take turns in going without and in bearing the taunts of vulgar-minded school-fellows inquiring 'Whose turn is it to wear the coat to-day?'" The edge of hunger was sometimes dulled by stories of heroic endurance. The teller of these stories, Mary

Moody Emerson, an aunt of the children, was a woman of remarkable vigor of intellect, though eccentric to a degree approaching unsoundness. It was she who stimulated her nephews to intellectual exertion by keeping before them the loftiest ideals, and awakening in them a sense of the incalculable superiority of mental riches to any form of material wealth.

It was to this aunt more than to any other person that Emerson was indebted for certain tastes, notably his love of nature, and certain lofty strains of thought, — a hatred of what is mean and trivial in life, a scorn of anything that disturbs the soul's serenity and blocks its view of what is true and eternal with what is false, merely eye-dazzling, and temporary. Years afterward, in recognition of the value of the discipline of these early years of poverty and struggle, Emerson wrote : —

"The wise workman will not regret the poverty or the solitude which brought out his working talents. . . . A Fifth-avenue landlord, a West-end householder is not the highest style of man ; and though good hearts and sound minds are of no condition, yet he who is to be wise for many must not be protected. He must know the huts where poor men lie, and the chores which poor men do. The first-class minds, Æsop, Socrates, Franklin, had the poor man's feeling and mortification. A rich man was never insulted in his life, but this man must be stung. A rich man was never in danger from cold or hunger or war or ruffians, but you can see he was not, from the moderation of his ideas. 'T is a fatal disadvantage to be cockered and to eat too much cake. What tests of manhood could he stand ? Take him out of his protections. He is a good bookkeeper or he is a shrewd adviser in the insurance office, perhaps he could pass a college examination and take his degree; perhaps he can give wise counsel in a court of law. Now plant him down among farmers, firemen, Indians, and emigrants. Set a dog on him; try him with a course of mobs. Send him to Kansas, to Pike's Peak, to Oregon; and if he have true faculty, this may be the element he wants and he will come out of it with braver wisdom and manly powers. Æsop, Saadi, Cervantes, Reynard, have been taken by corsairs, left for dead, sold for slaves, and know the realities of life."

Emerson was but three years old when he was first sent to school. He was not precocious, and distinguished himself neither at school nor at Harvard, which he entered in his fifteenth year. As a youth, he was much what he was as a man, mild, equable in temper, kind and affable, observing and self-contained. He was not fond of athletic sports, and was hardly spirited enough to be popular with the average student. He wrote verses, and, like most youthful writers of verses, hated mathematics, diligently read the poets, and studied languages.

Edward Everett was at that time professor of Greek at Harvard, and George Ticknor filled the chair of modern languages. Emerson was a faithful attendant at the lectures of these two scholars; but, according to his classmate Josiah Quincy, he gave " no sign of the power that was fashioning itself for leadership in a new time. He was quiet, unobtrusive, and only a fair scholar according to the standard of the college authorities."

After his graduation from Harvard, in 1821, Emerson taught school for three years, but he so heartily disliked his occupation that his biographer refers to

this period as the " one gloomy passage in his life."
Writing to a friend in 1822, Emerson says : —

" To judge from my own happy feelings, I am fain to
think that since commencement a hundred angry pens have
been daily dashed into the sable flood to deplore and curse
the destiny of those who teach. Poor, wretched, hungry,
starving souls ! How my heart bleeds for you ! Better tug
at the oar, dig the mine, or saw wood : better sow hemp or
hang with it than sow the seeds of instruction."

In this same letter Emerson, who had up to this
time been called Ralph, warns his correspondent that
he has altered his name from Ralph to Waldo, and
wishes him to " be sure and drop the first." From
this time his letters are always signed Waldo.

A year later we find him deliberately attempting to
cultivate a delight in nature, and perhaps there is not
a better instance anywhere of the success attending
the cultivation of a taste than this experience of one
of our foremost nature-lovers. In his early youth he
had been quite indifferent to the charms of which his
aunt Mary had so repeatedly written and spoken to
him, hoping to disunite him, so she said, " from
travelling with the souls of other men; of living and
breathing, reading and writing, with one vital, time-
fated idea, their opinion." Now he is resolved upon
enjoying these delights of which the poets and his
aunt speak so promisingly, and in a letter to a friend
written in 1823 we have a relation of his experience : —

" I am seeking to put myself on a footing of old acquaintance
with nature as a poet should ; but the fair divinity is rather
shy of my advances, and I confess I cannot find myself quite

as perfectly at home on the rock and in the wood as my ancient and I might say my infant aspiration led me to expect. My aunt (of whom I think you have heard before, and who is alone among women) has spent a great part of her life in the country, is an idolater of nature, and counts but a small number who merit the privilege of dwelling among the mountains, — the coarse thrifty cit profanes the grove by his presence, — and she was anxious that her nephew might hold high and reverential notions, regarding it as the temple where God and the mind are to be studied and adored, and where the fiery soul can begin a premature communion with the other world.

"When I took my book therefore to the woods, I found nature not half poetical, not half visionary enough. There was nothing which the most froward imagination would construe for a moment into a satyr or dryad. No Greek or Roman or even English fantasy could deceive me one instant into the belief of more than met the eye. In short, I found that I had transplanted into the new place my entire personal identity, and was grievously disappointed."

A good many years were to pass before Emerson learned that the lovers of nature do not woo her with a book in the hand, nor seek for satyrs and dryads, nor suggestions of them, instead of common flowers and trees. It is plain by the tone of this letter that Emerson regarded himself as a poet, but he had as yet no definite literary plans, but was preparing himself for the ministry as the calling most in harmony with his character and with his aspiration to be of some service to the world.

He was ordained in 1826, and preached his first public sermon at Waltham. About this time his eyesight and general health were affected from excessive study and deficient exercise, and the year following his ordination a pain in his lungs drove him South, where he spent the winter at St. Augustine, Florida. In view of the fact that during the antislavery agitation prior to the Civil War, Emerson's was one of the most eloquent and emphatic voices to be heard against the evils of slavery, it is singular that though he witnessed the buying and selling of slaves during his stay in the South, there is no evidence of his indignation at the sight, no scathing and burning word spoken then for justice and humanity.

The truth is, Emerson's was a sluggish temperament, slow to feel, slow to think; but he had a susceptible though not strong imagination, a passionate admiration for eloquence, an unerring instinct that taught him the sources of power, and a supreme wish to lay hold of them. None knew his limitations so well as he. " Can you not awaken," he writes to his aunt, " a sympathetic activity in torpid faculties? Whatever Heaven has given me or withheld, my feelings, or the expression of them, is very cold, my understanding and my tongue slow and unaffecting."

On his return from the South, Emerson was chosen to fill the pulpit of the First Church in Boston during the absence of its pastor, Frothingham. In the spring of 1829 he was appointed colleague of Mr. Ware, minister of the Second Church in Boston. In September of the same year he married Ellen Louisa Tucker, a frail, consumptive young girl, who died two years later. Mr. Ware resigned a few weeks subsequent to the appointment of Emerson, who was thus left in sole charge of the pastoral work. This work soon grew to be as much of a stricture to him as teaching had been. He had an extraordinary catholicity, and truth of any character did not seem to him to be the special property of any particular sect. He did not always feel himself in the mood which he believed suitable for the fulfilment of his duties, and the performance of them in an alien frame of mind seemed nothing else than sacrilege. Nor was he by temperament a man of warm sympathies yielding easily to the personality of others, and he was therefore unfitted for the happy performance of pastoral duties. There is a story told of a Revolutionary veteran's calling Emerson to his death-bed for spiritual consolation, and in his wrath at the latter's hesitancy, saying, "Young man, if you don't know your business, you had better go home." However, whether he knew his business or not, Emerson retained his connection with the church for three years, and then resigned his charge on the plea that he could not regard the Lord's Supper as a sacrament, and could not conscientiously administer it as such.

This resignation was not made without a severe struggle. In spite of the fact that he had never felt himself entirely in harmony with his work, he valued it highly as an opportunity for the utterance of the noblest spiritual truths and the exercise of the finest spiritual influence. The temptation to compromise, or to yield this point in question, was strong in him. He reasoned with himself that it is " not worth while for them who charge others with exalting forms above the moon to fear forms themselves with extravagant dislike ; " that he ought not to bury his " talent in the earth with his indignation at this windmill." He writes in his journal : —

"'Though the thing may be useless and even pernicious, do not destroy what is good and useful in a high degree rather than comply with what is hurtful in a small degree. . . . I will not, because we may not all think alike of the means, fight so strenuously against the means as to miss of the end which we all value alike. I think Jesus did not mean to institute a perpetual celebration, but that a commemoration of him would be useful. Others think that Jesus did establish this one. . . . I know very well that it is a bad sign for a man to be too conscientious and stick at gnats. The most desperate scoundrels have been the over-refiners. Without accommodation, society is impracticable. But this ordinance is esteemed the most sacred of religious institutions, and I cannot go habitually to an institution which they esteem holiest with indifference or dislike."

This ended the matter. Whatever virtue there might be in tolerance or accommodation, there was certainly none in hypocrisy for the high-souled Emerson, and the resignation was reluctantly given and unwillingly accepted. The young pastor was somewhat chagrined at the result, hoping that his congregation would agree to his terms; but he was suffering in health again, and decided to leave for a time the scene of his disappointments and chagrins. In December, 1832, he sailed for the Mediterranean, visited Sicily, Italy, neither excited by nor thoroughly interested in all the wonders of the old world, seeking ever intellectual excitement, — seeking the man who was to inspire him. In Rome he received from a friend of Carlyle's a letter of introduction to the great Scotchman, who was then a comparatively obscure writer, although his articles in the English reviews had impressed Emerson with a conviction of his unusual powers.

In Florence, Emerson met Walter Savage Landor. From Florence he went to Switzerland and France; Paris he thought "a loud modern New York of a place." In London he saw Coleridge, and hoped to see Carlyle in Edinburgh, but learning of his lonely residence at Craigenputtock, he drove across the moors from Dumfries and spent the afternoon and night there. From this interview there sprang up an affection and life-long friendship between these two men, so wholly unlike except in their deep love and reverent seeking for the truth; and in the correspondence which resulted from this new tie we have a most beautiful record of fine, manly friendship. At Rydal Mount Emerson visited Wordsworth. He had now seen what was more to him than mountain or ocean, city or woodland, — the faces of the greatest living English writers, — and in his journal at sea, his tentative thoughts, his yearnings for a great teacher, are crystallized into those solid convictions that make the burden of his subsequent essays, namely : —

"A man contains all that is needful to his government within himself. He is made a law unto himself. All real good or evil that can befall him must be from himself. He only can do himself any good or any harm. Nothing can be given to him, or taken from him, but always there's a compensation. . . . The purpose of life seems to be to acquaint man with himself. He is not to live to the future as described to him, but to live to the real future by living to the real present. The highest revelation is that God is in every man. Milton describes himself in his letter to Diodati as enamored of moral perfection. He did not love it more than I. That which I cannot yet declare has been my angel from childhood until now. It has separated me from men. It has watered my pillow. It has driven sleep from my bed. It has tortured me from guilt. It has inspired me with hope. It cannot be defeated by my defeats. It cannot be questioned, though all the martyrs apostatize. It is always the glory that shall be revealed ; it is the open secret of the universe."

A man has made great strides toward culture and toward moral dignity and rectitude of conduct when he learns to be self-reliant, — learns to recognize and obey the law of his own being. Emerson had sought in great men some extraordinary and contagious virtue, some happy inspiration by which the dark places in his own life were to be made light. He had gone to meet them in the romantic spirit in which he had gone to nature to find satyrs and dryads, or gone as he said to the wonders of Italian painting, fancying " the great pictures would be great strangers ; some surprising combination of color and form ; a foreign wonder, barbaric pearl and gold ; " but finding instead that " genius left to novices the gay and fantastic and ostentatious, and pierced directly to the simple and true ; that it was familiar and sincere ; that it was the old eternal fact . . . the plain you and me I knew so well." In the same manner he found that great men were not the fortunate possessors of all forms of truth, but humble seekers like himself, — differing only from ordinary men in their passionate devotion to the search of it, and in their capacity to receive it whether painful or pleasant.

On his return from Europe, Emerson continued for four years to preach from various pulpits, without accepting any regular charge, or making any claim to ministerial authority. The settlement of the Tucker estate in 1834 brought him a comfortable income from his dead wife's portion, and relieved him from any pressing pecuniary care. The same year brought other notable changes in his life. The death of his brother Edward occurred under painful circumstances. A young man of remarkable gifts and commonly considered much more brilliant than his brother Waldo, he had ruined his health by excessive study and brought on an attack of acute mania. After a short confinement in an asylum in Charlestown, he recovered, but exiled himself to the West Indies, where he died. Not long after Edward's death, Waldo and his mother were invited by Dr. Ripley, of Concord, to make their home with him in the Old Manse. Another brother, Charles, was engaged to Miss Elizabeth Hoar, of Concord, and intended to begin practising law there. The beautiful little village was within easy reach of Boston, and offered temptations of privacy to the scholar which Emerson could not resist. In the course of a year he married Miss Lydia Jackson, of Plymouth, — a stately, dignified woman, a few years his senior, — bought a house in Concord, and settled there for life.

To Miss Jackson, who wished that they should live in her old colonial mansion at Plymouth, he writes of Concord and himself: —

"I must win you to love it. I am born a poet, — of a low class without doubt, yet a poet. That is my nature and vocation. My singing, to be sure, is very husky, and is for the most part in prose; still I am a poet in the sense of a perceiver and dear lover of the harmonies that are in the soul and in matter, and especially of the correspondence between these and those.   A sunset, a forest, a snow-storm, a certain river-view are more to me than many friends, and do ordinarily divide my day with my books.   Wherever I go, therefore, I guard and study my rambling propensities."

At Concord these "rambling propensities" were indulged in the afternoon, while the morning was spent in study and the evening in the company of his family.

The year 1836 was another eventful one to Emerson. It saw the death of his brother Charles, the birth of his first child, — a beautiful boy whom he called Waldo, who died at the age of five, — and the publication of his first work, "Nature," — a slender volume that attracted little attention, and sold so slowly that twelve years elapsed before the first edition of five hundred copies was exhausted.   But this want of success did not disconcert the author.   If the public would not read his book, it listened willingly to his lectures;   and this intercourse with the public not only satisfied his desire to be heard, but it proved a wholesome discipline whose value he was not slow to recognize.

"It is because I am so ill a member of society," he writes, "because men turn me by their mere presence to wood and stone, because I do not get the lesson of the world where it is set before me, that I need more than others to run out to new places and multiply my chances for observation and communion."   Forty years he remained in the lecture field.   There he tested his ideas; there he learned more of his fellow-men, whom no man was ever more eager or more unfitted to understand.   His lectures subsequently formed the material of his Essays, the first volume of which appeared in 1841. Five years later his poems were published: if they often lack the music and emotion of verse, they are not the less a hearty and condensed expression of his delight in beauty and nobility of character among men, and the lessons of cheer and encouragement nature had taught him.

In 1847 he made a second visit to England, where he was received with marked favor. He revisited France, and this time pronounced Paris " a place of the largest liberty in the civilized world," and declared that in case of ever needing a place of diversion and independence Paris should be his " best bower anchor." In 1850 he published " Representative Men," following it six years later with " English Traits," — a work which has always been more admired in America than in England, where it elicited many unfavorable comments and provoked a caustic letter directed to the author by Walter Savage Landor.

As Emerson's reputation increased, his lecture tours, which had been mostly confined to the Eastern States, were extended to the West. His comment on this new experience is interesting: —

"This climate and people are a new test for the wares of a man of letters. All his thin, watery matter freezes; 't is only the smallest portion of alcohol that remains good. At the Lyceum the stout Illinoisian, after a short trial, walks out of the hall. The committee tell you that the people want a hearty laugh; and Saxe and Park Benjamin, who give this, are heard with joy."

To a man like Emerson, who disliked to laugh and was never heard to laugh aloud, a severer test of his powers could not have been made.   But we find traces of his efforts to meet this test in his preservation of witty and pointed anecdotes, and in his Essay entitled "The Comic."   The wit of shrewdness and good sense he had in abundance, but of sportiveness, or of the flashing wit that comes from a keen and quick perception of incongruities, he had not a particle.   He confessed that he could never turn a page in Don Quixote or in Dickens without a yawn.   This deficiency in perception was a result of his lack of sympathetic understanding of the coarser elements of human nature, — the substratum of animalism in man.   He had too lofty, sweet, and noble a nature to take any account of human infirmities.   One feels like addressing to him Aurelia's speech to Meister: —

"In hearing you expound the mysteries of Shakespeare, one would think you had just descended from a synod of the gods, and had listened there while they were taking counsel how to form men ; in seeing you transact with your fellows, I could imagine you to be the first, large-born child of the creation, standing agape and gazing with strange wonderment and edifying good nature at lions and apes and sheep and elephants, and true-heartedly addressing them as your equals, simply because they were there and in motion like yourself."

With more weakness, more susceptibility on the emotional side of his nature, Emerson's power would have been immensely increased.   But his susceptibility was wholly intellectual.   He divined men intellectually, not emotionally; that is, he saw them through the mind's eye ; he did not draw near them through the sympathetic pulsations of his own heart.

His own contact with men was a continual violation of his temperament which kept him inexorably apart from them. He knew this defect in himself, he realized what it cost to his power, and he strove all his life to overcome it; but it was a struggle against heredity, a struggle against the accumulated reserve and systematic repression of five generations of clergymen, and Emerson never won more than half the victory. He won that half-victory in a tolerance so broad that it hardly escapes the license of intellectual anarchy; and he won it in a manner so tactful, so attractive, that it seemed a continual promise of the largest and most intimate friendship. Yet the victory went no farther; the sweet, low-pitched voice, the placid smile, the deferential attention were only a beautiful mask for the concealment of the most impenetrable reserve.

Henry James, the elder, writing of Emerson's personality, says: —

"On the whole, I may say that at first I was greatly disappointed in him, because his intellect never kept the promise which his lovely face and manners held out to me. He was to my senses a literal divine presence in the house with me; and we cannot recognize literal divine presences in our households without feeling sure that they will be able to say something of critical importance to our intellect. It turned out that any average old dame in a horse-car would have satisfied my intellectual capacity as well as Emerson . . . and though his immense personal fascination kept up, he at once lost all intellectual prestige to my regard. I even thought that I had never seen a man more profoundly devoid of spiritual understanding. . . . In his books or public capacity he was constantly electrifying you by sayings full of divine inspiration.   In his talk or private capacity he was one of the least remunerative men I ever encountered.   No man could look at him speaking (or when he was silent either, for that matter) without having a vision of the divinest beauty.   But when you went to him to hold discourse about the wondrous phenomena, you found him absolutely devoid of reflective powers."

Again, when asked for letters that had passed between him and his eminent correspondent, James replied : —

"I cannot flatter myself that any letter I ever wrote to Emerson is worth your reading. . . . Emerson always kept me at such arm's length, tasting him, sipping him, and trying him, to make sure he was worthy of his somewhat prim and bloodless friendship, that it was fatiguing to write him letters. I remember well what maidenly letters I used to receive from him, with so many tentative charms of expression in them that if he had been a woman, one would have delighted in complimenting him ; but, as it was, you could say nothing about them, but only pocket the disappointment they brought. It is painful to recollect now the silly hope that I had along the early days of our acquaintance, that if I went on listening, something would be sure to drop from him that would show me an infallible way out of this perplexed world, for nothing ever came but epigrams, sometimes clever, sometimes not."

In explanation of this singular frigidity it is interesting to read Emerson's own account of it.   He says in his journal : —

"Some people are born public souls, and live with all their doors open to the street.   Close beside them we find the lonely man, with all his doors shut, reticent, thoughtful, shrinking from crowds, afraid to take hold of hands ; thankful for the existence of the other, but incapable of such performance, wondering at its possibility, full of thoughts, but paralyzed and silenced instantly by these boisterous masters; and though loving his race, discovering at last that he has no proper sympathy with persons but only with their genius and aims. He is solitary because he has society in his own thought, and when people come in, they drive away his society and isolate him. We would all be public men if we could afford it. I am wholly private, such is the poverty of my constitution. Heaven 'betrayed me to a book and wrapped me in a gown.' I have no social talent, no will, and a steady appetite for insights in any or all directions to balance my manifold imbecilities. M. Fuller writes me that she waits for my lectures, seeing well, after much intercourse, that the best of me is there. She says very truly; and I thought it a good remark which somebody repeated here, from S. S., that I 'always seemed to be on stilts.' It is even so. Most of the persons I see in my own house I see across a gulf. I cannot go to them, nor can they come to me. Nothing can exceed the frigidity and labor of my speech with such. You might turn a yoke of oxen between every pair of my words, and the behavior is as awkward and proud. I see the ludicrousness of the plight as well as they. But never having found a remedy, I am very patient of this folly or shame, — patient of my churlishness in the belief that this privation has certain rich compensations."

Though he was a public lecturer all his life, Emerson never attained easy, spontaneous utterance, and rarely attempted even the shortest speech without careful preparation. "I remember," says his biographer, "his getting up at a dinner of the Saturday Club on the Shakespeare anniversary in 1864 to which some guests had been invited, looking about him tranquilly for a minute or two, and then sitting down, serene and unabashed, but unable to say a word on a subject so familiar to his thoughts from boyhood." Yet this hesitancy, this coolness were associated with a sweetness and nobility of character and a rectitude of conduct rarely equalled. Life was no mere play-day to him: it was an arena for heroic struggle and endurance, and he was intent on training every faculty for the contest, not grimly and despairingly, but cheerfully and confident of victory. But his lot had fallen on evil times. "The dark slavery question" was to him, as he said, "like Hamlet's task imposed on so unfit an agent as Hamlet." The Fugitive Slave Law of 1850, "making every man in Massachusetts liable to official summons in aid of the return of escaped slaves," roused his indignation to white heat. He felt, he said, "an infamy in the air," that "justice and mercy had been ordained subject to fine and imprisonment," and "a crime had been written into the statute books." Then the slow tongue quickened, and uttered swift burning words in denunciation of Webster, the abettor of the law; and when at Cambridge he was interrupted by hisses, shouts, and cat-calls, he stood unmoved until the tumult had subsided, and then continued "as if nothing had happened," narrates a spectator. "There was no repetition, no allusion to what had been going on, no sign that he was moved, and I cannot describe with what added weight the next words fell."

In the beginning of the slavery agitation Emerson advocated peaceful measures, the buying and freeing of the slaves, and was not at all in sympathy with the ultra-abolitionists who preferred disunion, war, general ruin,—anything to the outrage of slave-holding. But the dastardly assault upon Sumner in the Senate Chamber and John Brown's insurrection kindled him into pure flame, burned away all his hesitancy, and when the war broke out he could say: " We have been homeless, some of us, for some years past, say since 1850, but now we have a country again." And when he viewed the warlike preparations in Charlestown navy-yard, he said, " Ah! sometimes gunpowder smells good."

Emerson wrote little after 1866, and in 1870 his memory began to fail him. He could not recall the right word in conversation, as when he said to some one standing in the sunlight, while he himself was sheltered by a large tree, " Is n't there too much *heaven* on you there?" In the summer of 1872 his house burned down. A check for five thousand dollars and a contribution of nearly twelve thousand dollars were immediately sent to him by friends; and he was persuaded to take another trip to Europe, including Greece and the Nile, in company with his eldest daughter, Ellen. He saw Carlyle again at Chelsea, visited Paris, Rome, made a tour in Egypt, returned to England and thence home. All Concord was at the station to meet him, and he was escorted with music and a band of school-children to his own house rebuilt as it had been before the fire.

In the spring of 1882 a cold culminating in pneumonia resulted in his death shortly before his seventy-seventh birthday. He was buried in Sleepy Hollow Cemetery at Concord,— a beautiful bit of natural woodland, where the squirrels still hold possession of the trees, and all sorts of wild-flowers, shrubs, and berries grow in undisturbed profusion.

French's bust of Emerson, made in 1879, is a most satisfactory and beautiful representation of his nobly intellectual face, with its sharply cut outlines, its large, hawklike nose, firm, wide, sweetly smiling mouth. According to French's statement, there was a great difference in the formation of the two sides of Emerson's face, and there was more movement on the left side than on the right; but it is very probable that this difference was not so marked as to be generally noticeable. His eyes were of a bright blue color, and though weak in youth, subsequently became so strong that he did not use glasses in reading his lectures till he was sixty-four. His brown hair was abundant, and retained its youthful color until late in life. In figure he was tall and spare, six feet in height, and ordinarily weighed one hundred and forty and one-half pounds.

In his social and domestic relations, Emerson left no duty or attention unperformed. He was public-spirited, ready with the helpful word and deed on all important occasions. He served on the school-board and was a member of a town club, the Social Circle. Though he had freed himself from all conventional claims of creed or sect, he recognized their social value and gave his support to them. He disliked going to church himself; but he liked to have other people attend religious services, and when a motion to dispense with compulsory attendance on morning prayers was made before the Harvard board, of which he was a member from '67 to '79, he voted against it. He likewise once advised a friend not to resign a pastoral charge on the ground of difference of opinion, although he himself had pursued a contrary course. Though no one was ever more fearless or more free in his utterance of offensive truths, there was a noble sweetness, a high moral tone in his utterance of them that took away their sting. He was the very gentlest of image-breakers, " an iconoclast," says Holmes, " who took down our idols from their pedestals so tenderly that it seemed like an act of worship."

In his family he was kind, affectionate, generous, and particularly solicitous for the comfort of his domestics. Perhaps no man ever "respected the burden" more than he. His son Edward says that he built his own fire, and always insisted upon carrying his own valise to and from the train. His life was undoubtedly one of noble endeavor, lofty aspiration, and in perfect harmony with the teachings of his pen.

His literary methods were peculiar. His biographer assures us that he was by no means so great a reader as the variety and number of his quotations suggest, and that there is reason to think that " even where the coincidence (as with Fichte, Schleiermacher, Hegel) seemed too close to be accidental, he had no first-hand acquaintance with the books." He was in the habit of keeping a journal; and he recorded in it the thoughts awakened in him by reading, observation, or any remarkable saying that he had heard. Dr. Hedge relates that he came to him late one evening to get the particulars of some anecdote they had both heard that day. He could not sleep, he said, until he had made a note of the whole. This vigilant, tireless attention resulted in the accumulation of a vast number of brilliant observations and aphorisms, from which his essays and lectures were built up by selection and combination. Fiction, in the shape of novels, he could not read. " Pope and his school," he said, "wrote poetry fit to be put around frosted cake." Walter Scott "wrote a rhymed traveller's guide to Scotland." Than Tennyson's, he thinks, " there is no finer ear nor more command of the keys of language. . . . But he wants a subject, and climbs no mount of vision to bring its secrets to the people." Wordsworth's " Ode on Immortality " he calls the " high-water mark which the intellect has reached in this age," and he thought Coleridge's " Biographia Literaria " the best work of criticism in the English language. Two expedients for literary culture he deems indispensable: " First, sit alone. In your arrangements for residence, see that you have a chamber to yourself, though you sell overcoat and wear a blanket. Second, keep a journal. Pay so much honor to the visits of truth to your mind as to record them."

Of the character of Emerson's intellect, it is difficult to speak with certainty. It presents the most puzzling contradictions. It produces, at first, the impression of phenomenal breadth and assimilative power. But a closer scrutiny reveals the fact that what was mistaken for assimilation is only collection. The fundamental characteristic of this mind is an insatiable curiosity. It pushes into the remotest corners of the intellectual world. It gathers up all the ideas that attract it, and the result is a heterogenous collection that interests and stimulates, but is utterly lacking in anything like plan or consistency. Never was a mind more fatally lacking in logical power than Emerson's. He utters half-truths with the force of whole truths. He makes sweeping generalizations on insufficient data. He never sees the whole truth at once; he sees only a fragment of it, but he views it at so close a range that the fragment assumes the proportions of the whole to him, and he falls into extravagance when he describes it. Another point of view brings another fragment of truth into prominence, and he at once forgets what he has seen, and falls into equally extravagant valuation of that which now absorbs his attention. Hence those almost incomprehensible oscillations from idealism to materialism, from the wildest of fanciful speculations to the sternest of scientific truths, and a practical shrewdness as serviceable as that of any day-laborer who earns his bread and butter by it, — from the most extravagant laudations of Swedenborg to the warmest appreciative sympathy with Montaigne. Hence, too, the comparative worthlessness of a great deal of his criticism. Anything that stimulated his intellect and gave him a new outlook into the world, were it ever so strange a one, blinded him to its real value to the world at large. This is the reason of his singular overrating of such eccentric men as Alcott, Jones Very, and Walt Whitman.

Certainly no man ever feared inconsistency less. He follows to the letter his own advice : " Speak what you think to-day in words as hard as cannon-balls, and to-morrow speak what to-morrow thinks in hard words again, though it contradict everything you said to-day." At one time he tells us that the poet can articulate the world, that he is in possession of all the secrets; at another, he laments the world's inarticulateness, talks of the unfathomed secret, says that there is no such thing as touching reality, and that an "innavigable sea washes with silent waves between us and the things we aim at and converse with." At one time he is pure idealist and affirms the exterior world to be but the "externization of the soul, an appearance that bursts into life in its presence and vanishes with it." At another time he is the most uncompromising and scornful of materialists, comes to his own, as he says, and "makes friends with matter which the ambitious chatter of the schools would persuade us to despise, and is ashamed out of his nonsense." There are times when he prefers twilight to daylight, ghosts to living men, and is avid of an intellectual sensation at any price, and longs to pass from dream to dream in a kind of mental intoxication. It is at such times that he thinks "nothing of any value in books excepting the transcendental and extraordinary." Then, again, he thinks he will read only the commonest books, the Bible, Homer, Dante, Shakespeare; sings the commonplace, and relishes every hour and what it brings him, "the pot luck of the day as heartily as the oldest gossip in the bar-room." At one time we find in him a childish credulity in the perfectibility of man: he believes that "we are all the children of genius, the children of virtue;" he does not believe that the difference of opinion and character in men is organic; there come to every soul visitations of a diviner presence. "I see not," he cries in indignation, "if we be once caught in this trap of so-called sciences, any escape from the links of the chain of physical necessity. Given such an embryo, such a history must follow. On this platform one lives in a sty of sensualism and would soon come to suicide." Yet, in his essay on Fate, he drops cheerfully into this hated "sty," and pertinently inquires : —

" How shall a man escape from his ancestors ; or draw off from his veins the black drop which he drew from his father's or mother's life ? . . . Men are what their mothers made them. You may as well ask a loom which weaves huckaback why it does not make cashmere, as expect poetry from this engineer or a mathematical discovery from that jobber. Ask the digger in the ditch to explain Newton's laws ; the fine organs of his brain have been pinched by over-work and squalid poverty from father to son for a hundred years. When each comes forth from his mother's womb, the gate of gifts closes behind him. Let him value his hands, and feel he has but one pair. So he has but one future, and that is already predetermined in his lobes and described in that little fatty face, pig eye, and squat form. All the privilege and all the legislation of the world cannot meddle or help to make a poet or prince of him."

At one time he speaks of that "extraordinary and incomputable agent," personal influence, the " occult power that men exert on each other," and again he says that " human life and its persons are poor empirical pretensions. A personal influence is an *ignis-fatuus*."

In his essay entitled " Nominalist and Realist," he classes Swedenborgianism with Mesmerism, Fourierism, and the Millennial Church, and calls them all " poor pretensions enough ; " but in " Representative Men " he writes of Swedenborg in terms of extravagant laudation, calls him the last Father in the Church, predicts that it is not likely to have another, styles him a colossal soul lying vast abroad on his times, uncomprehended by them, and lauds his scientific discoveries, when, to quote Maudsley, a genuine scientist, "scientifically he [Swedenborg] is as sounding brass or a tinkling cymbal." The truth is, Emerson was incapable of scientific criticism, but he had in a large measure the gift of panegyric, and he used it unsparingly, evidently clinging fast to his dictum, "It is fatal to spiritual health to lose your admiration." When he writes of Plato, he says that his are the only books that deserve Omar's fanatical compliment to the Koran, "Burn the libraries, for their value is in this book." When he writes of Swedenborg, he declares that "his writings would be a sufficient library to a lonely and athletic student," that "Plato is a gownsman" to him, and that he "is awful to Cæsar, and Lycurgus himself would bow to him." Wilkinson, his English translator, is a pupil "with a coequal vigor of understanding and imagination comparable only to Lord Bacon's." But later we find him telling us that "Shakespeare is as much out of the category of eminent authors as he is out of the crowd. He is inconceivably wise; the others conceivably. A good reader can in a sort nestle into Plato's brain and think from there, but not into Shakespeare's;" but when we come to Goethe, we are told that "the old eternal genius who built the world has confided himself more to this man than any other."

But besides wanting the faculty of combination so necessary to a critic, Emerson was equally wanting in a no less essential faculty, — the dramatic power, —

the power of losing one's self in the personality of another. In his " Representative Men " we find nothing like the vivid portraiture of its prototype, Carlyle's "Heroes and Hero Worship." It is rich in isolated sentences of acute penetration, but its final judgments are unsound, and its attempts at portraiture fail to give an impression of harmonious unity. Character-painting is not analysis, it is synthesis. It is the inextricable blending of light and shade into a lifelike whole. Emerson's method is directly the opposite of this. In his characterization of Napoleon, for example, he really sketches two men. He draws up all Napoleon's excellences on one side, and all his defects on another, and so gives us two catalogues instead of one man.

This remarkable peculiarity of Emerson's intellect by which he could perceive only in fragments is as remarkably illustrated in his style. He excels in short, graphic sentences of wonderful freshness and vigor, but he is incapable of continuity. He thinks, not in continuous sequences, but by flashes that are sometimes sparks and sometimes pale gleams. He writes : —

" If Minerva offered me a gift and an option, I would say, give me continuity, I am tired of scraps, I do not wish to be a literary or intellectual chiffonier. Away with this Jew's rag-bag of ends and tufts of brocade, velvet and cloth of gold, and let me spin some yards or miles of helpful twine ; a clew to lead to one kingly truth, — a cord to bind wholesome and belonging facts."

But Minerva never conferred this gift. To the end of his life, he continued to get over the ground like a kangaroo, by what he calls "successive saltations." To read him is like crossing a brook on stepping-stones instead of plunging into the stream and either wading or swimming across. You are not immersed in thought; you lave in no genial, bracing current. You walk dry-shod from point to point of thought, but in a bracing wind, to be sure. Whatever his subject, he has but one manner of expression, which comes at last to bear the same relation to the varied and flexible utterance of imaginative genius that the sharp terse click of the telegraph does to the marvellously expressive human voice. But there are times, and they are not infrequent, when the message is of so noble and sweet a character that the expression of it sings to the ear like music; then, nothing can be richer, nothing finer than his periods.

Every man whose influence on the world has been a wholesome one has a right to be judged by what is best in him, and few men have a better claim to such a right than Emerson. If we must deny to him the title of a deep thinker, because he is not logical, because he sometimes follows intellectual sensations rather than truths, because he dreads scientific conclusions that disturb his ideals, and so seems, at times, not to love truth herself so well as what he thinks *ought* to be true; if we must deny to him the right to be called a great poet because he speaks not to the universal but to the particular consciousness, and because his verses are only his essays cut up into regular lines and tagged with rhyme which is not always faultless, by reason of his inability, as he once confessed to Lowell, "to apprehend the value of accent in verse;" if we must deny critical acumen at times to a man who could speak of Alcott as "the most extraordinary man and the highest genius of his time," — there is one office of a great man which cannot be denied him: he is a great teacher, an incomparable character-former. "My special parish," he was wont to say, "is young men inquiring their way of life." That was true.

However numerous his contradictions and vagaries, they are not vital; he was sound at core, and it is with this sound and constant element in him that we have most to do. He allowed his intellect the freedom of all sorts of eccentricities, but in practice he is firmly rooted in common sense. He is everywhere the scholar's friend, the friend of thought, *par excellence,* — the defender of the intellectual life. This is the one indisputable territory in which he reigns supreme. It is the burden of all he has to say. Over and over again he asserts the beauty of fearlessness and independence, self-centrality and calmness, the supremacy of the moral law, and the union of the highest intelligence with the willing obedience to that law. He teaches a fine scorn of worldliness:

"What is rich? Are you rich enough to help anybody? to succor the unfashionable and the eccentric? rich enough to make the Canadian in his wagon, the itinerant with his consul's paper which commends him 'to the charitable,' the swarthy Italian with his few broken words of English, the lame pauper hunted by overseers from town to town, even the poor insane or besotted wreck of man or woman, feel the noble exception of your presence and your house from the general bleakness and stoniness; to make such feel that they were greeted with a voice which made them both remember and hope? What is vulgar but to refuse the claim of an acute and conclusive reason? What is gentle, but to allow it and give their heart and yours one holiday from the national caution? Without the rich heart, wealth is an ugly beggar. The king of Schiraz could not afford to be so bountiful as the poor Osman who dwelt at his gate. Osman had a humanity so broad and deep that although his speech was so bold and free with the Koran as to disgust all the dervishes, yet was there never a poor outcast, eccentric or insane man, some fool who had cut off his beard, or who had been mutilated under a vow, or had a pet madness in his brain, but fled at once to him. That great heart lay there so sunny and hospitable in the centre of the country that it seemed as if the instinct of all sufferers drew them to his side. And the madness which he harbored he did not share. Is not this to be rich? this only to be rightly rich?"

Something of this generous, intellectual hospitality Emerson himself had, and during his long lifetime Concord was the Mecca of all the intellectually lame, halt, and blind who could find their way to him for assistance in foisting their new universal panacea upon the notice of the world. But it was not only the intellectually lame and halt that looked to him for guidance. Young men with earnest purposes, and mental and moral vigor to carry them out, listened to him with reverent delight. Speaking in America of the eloquent voices to which he had listened when an undergraduate at Oxford, — Newman's, Carlyle's, Goethe's, — Matthew Arnold says: —

" And, besides those voices, there came to us, in that old Oxford time, a voice from this side of the Atlantic, a clear and pure voice, which for my ear, at any rate, brought a strain as new and moving and unforgettable as the strain of Goethe and Carlyle. . . . To us at Oxford, Emerson was but a voice speaking from three thousand miles away. But so well he spoke, that from that time Boston Bay and Concord were names invested to my ear with a sentiment akin to that which invests for me the names of Oxford and of Weimar. Snatches of Emerson's strain fixed themselves in my mind as imperishably as any of the eloquent words which I have been just now quoting."

Lowell, too, pays an eloquent tribute to Emerson's electrifying power over the young men of his time. He spoke to all that is best and noble and inspiring in human nature. He was uniformly hopeful, optimistic. " A low, hopeless spirit," he says, " puts out the eyes." He had brave words for the lonely thinker to whose lot discouragement and failure fall more frequently than to that of any other worker. He told him that the scholar has drawn the white lot in life, even though he must bear poverty, insult, weariness, and repute of failure: that the scholar is here " to fill others with love and courage by confirming their trust in the love and wisdom which are at the heart of all things; to affirm noble sentiments, to hear them wherever spoken, out of the deeps of ages, out of the obscurities of barbarous life, and to republish them; to untune nobody, but to draw all men after the truth, and to keep men spiritual and sweet."

Those essays in which Emerson himself fulfils this office — " The Man of Letters," " The Scholar," " Self-Reliance," " Heroism," " Spiritual Laws," " Friendship," and others of that strain — are the fullest of that fine, helpful tonic thought which made his power, and which assure him an immortal place among the great teachers of mankind.

In the light of the preceding chapter on the Transcendentalists in New England, it is easy to recognize that element which makes the vague unsatisfactory note in much that Emerson has written, — that note which produces in his readers the painful doubt entertained by the author of " Sartor Resartus " in regard to Herr Teufelsdröckh, — whether they are to find firm ground to stand on, or only a cloud-covered abyss. Emerson was of his time; he spoke its convictions, and in so far as these convictions fall short of permanent truth, he is perishable. But there is in him an imperishable element, a vein of pure gold that time cannot tarnish. The German critic Hermann Grimm, writing of Emerson, says that the great literary artists reconcile him to life: —

" What oppressed me delights me now. I no longer flee from it, and it is transformed into beauty in my hands. All that the artists touch becomes gold, is beautiful as if God's finger were pointing to it, and a mysterious voice whispered, ' Look at it and know it,' and I have the strength to recognize it as long as they show it to me. This feeling Emerson, too, produces in me in the purest degree."

John Tyndall, in an address to students, said: —

"The reading of two men, neither of them imbued with the spirit of modern science, — neither of them, indeed, friendly to that spirit, — has placed me here to-day. These men are the English Carlyle and the American Emerson. I must ever gratefully remember that through three long, cold German winters Carlyle placed me in my tub, even when ice was on its surface, at five o'clock every morning, — not slavishly, but cheerfully, meeting each day's studies with a resolute will, determined, whether victor or vanquished, not to shrink from difficulty. I never should have gone through

Analytical Geometry and Calculus had it not been for these men.   I never should have become a physical investigator, and hence without them I should not have been here to-day. They told me what I ought to do in a way that caused me to do it, and all my consequent intellectual action is to be traced to this purely moral force.   To Carlyle and Emerson I ought to add Fichte, the greatest representative of pure idealism. These three unscientific men made me a practical scientific worker.   They called out, ' Act ! '   I hearkened to the summons, taking the liberty, however, of determining for myself the direction which· effort was to take."

We can pardon many shortcomings to the writer who can exert so wonderful and noble an influence as this.   Emerson exerts it on all intellectual readers. He stimulates, he guides, he consoles, he encourages; his faults are the faults of his age; his virtues are all his own.

CHAPTER IX

IN our practical American life, lying all firmly out-lined in the clear light of modern times, with no shadowy background stretching far into the un-chronicled past to temper our riotous, youthful vigor with memorials of the brevity of nations and of individuals, — Nathaniel Hawthorne stands as ideal and unexpected a figure as his own beautiful little snow image before the Heidenberg stove in Mr. Lindsey's parlor. Only he is in no danger of melting away so suddenly. Of no other American writer can we be so certain that the incommunicable gift of genius, which made him delight his contemporaries, will delight those who are to come after them to the remotest time. And of so rare a character, so dependent on prenatal influences, surroundings, and constitutional idiosyncrasies, was his genius, that it is probable the world will sooner see another Shakespeare than another Hawthorne. It is as if the dark, blood-stained soil of Puritanism had yielded a delicate, shrinking, sensitive-leafed plant with a stainless blossom and exquisite odor, and its growth were possible in no other soil. And so long as the delight in beauty and fragrance gives an added value to life, so long will this sweet, fair blossom delight mankind.

In the old burying-ground of Salem, Massachusetts, there stands a slate gravestone erected to the memory of "Colonel John Hathorne, Esquire," who died in 1717. The man whose dust lies here was a harsh and relentless persecutor of innocent men and women during that terrible period of the witchcraft delusion in the early history of Salem. His father before him had persecuted the Quakers with the same relentless cruelty. The immediate descendants of these old Puritans were seafaring men who continued to make Salem their home, and the last of these sailors, Captain Hawthorne, was the father of the great novelist Nathaniel Hawthorne, who was born in Salem on the Fourth of July, 1804. Captain Hawthorne died of yellow fever in South America. Mrs. Hawthorne, who was passionately devoted to her husband, lived, after his death, in the strictest seclusion with her boy and two little girls, Elizabeth and Louisa. Some idea of the closeness of this seclusion may be found in the fact that though Hawthorne and his future wife, Sophia Peabody, passed their childhood on the same street within a stone's-throw of each other, they never met until they were both of mature years.

But to the boy, Nathaniel, this retirement was in harmony with an inherited reserve and constitutional shyness that distinguished him all his life. Fortunately, he had sound lungs and a good digestion, and was in no danger of suffering from those morbid moods of profound dissatisfaction with life which so often accompany a romantic imagination. When he was nine or ten years of age, his mother spent a year on the shore of Sebago Lake in Maine, and there the boy hunted, fished, and roamed the woods after the manner of boys in general. On his return to Salem, he was placed under the tutorship of Joseph Worcester, the lexicographer, and prepared for Bowdoin College, which he entered in his eighteenth year. Among his classmates at Bowdoin were the poet Longfellow, and the distinguished naval officer, Horatio Bridge, with the latter of whom Hawthorne formed an intimate and lifelong friendship. In the class ahead of him was Franklin Pierce, subsequently president of the United States and another of Hawthorne's warm friends. We are told that though Hawthorne was a fine scholar, he was not a brilliant one, — a statement which is frequently made of youths who subsequently distinguish themselves in literature. A mind with a strong, native bent toward any particular calling, instinctively turns toward that which will nourish it. It may conform to a certain extent to a prescribed course of instruction, but its best energies are spent on that to which its strong inclinations guide it. Hawthorne was obeying such an inclination in a wide reading, thus giving himself the best possible education for his future work.

After his graduation from Bowdoin in 1825, Hawthorne returned to his mother's home in Union Street, Salem, and devoted himself exclusively to literature. There, for twelve years, he lived the life of a recluse, studying and writing incessantly. His meals were often left at his locked door. If he went out at all, it was for the most part at night, when nobody saw him; not half a dozen people in Salem outside of his own family knew of his existence. For a man who was to make life and its realities the subject of his pen, it was hardly the best possible training, but for the preservation of that exquisite veil of romantic ideality through which youthful eyes see all the coarse and vulgar realities of life softened and beautified, nothing could have been better. Just before his marriage in 1842, Hawthorne writes in his journal of this period of his life : —

" Here I sit in my old accustomed chamber, where I used to sit in days gone by. Here I have written many tales, — many that have been burned to ashes, many that doubtless deserved the same fate. . . . If ever I have a biographer, he ought to make great mention of this chamber in my memoirs, because so much of my lonely youth was wasted here, and here my mind and character were formed, and here I have been glad and hopeful, and here I have been despondent, and here I sat a long, long time, patiently waiting for the world to know me, and sometimes wondering why it did not know me sooner or whether it would ever know me at all, — at least till I were in my grave. And sometimes it seemed as if I were already in the grave, with only life enough to be chilled and benumbed. But oftener I was happy, — at least as happy as I then knew how to be or was aware of the possibility of being. By and by the world found me out in my lonely chamber, and called me forth, not indeed with a loud roar of acclamation, but rather with a still small voice, and forth I went, but found nothing in the world preferable to my old solitude till now. And now I begin to understand why I was imprisoned so many years in my lonely chamber, and why I could never break through the viewless bolts and bars ; for if I had sooner made my escape into the world, I should have grown hard and rough and been covered with earthly dust, and my heart might

have become callous by rude encounter with the multitude.
. . . But living in solitude till the fulness of time was come,
I still kept the dews of my youth and the freshness of my
heart. . . . I used to think I could imagine all passions, all
feelings and states of the heart and mind, but how little did
I know ! "

The first production of these years of solitude was
a romance, entitled " Fanshawe," published anony-
mously in 1828. It is a somewhat maudlin story,
named after its hero, a solitary student, who " scorned
to mingle with the living world and to be actuated
by its motives," and who died of over-study. As
might be expected, the book shows neither knowledge of the world nor of the human heart, and is
interesting only because of its unconscious autobio-
graphic touches that reveal something of the mental
peculiarities of the youthful dreamer, its author.
" Fanshawe " attracted little or no attention, and
when Hawthorne reached the maturity of his powers,
he was ashamed of it and tried to suppress it.

The book which first made the reading world at
all curious about him was the " Twice Told Tales,"
a collection of sketches and tales that were first
given to the public in various periodicals and newspapers. The book appeared in 1837. The subtle
analytical power it revealed, and the pure limpid
style in which it was written, proclaimed it the work
of a man of genius. But though it was recognized
as such by those who were capable of judging, it was
not of a character to meet with widespread popularity. There were still many years of struggle and
effort to be endured by this solitary and sensitive
genius, who had already known the sickening dis-

couragement of failure and the bitterness of hope deferred. The " Twice Told Tales " was followed by "Grandfather's Chair," an admirably written little volume of New England history, consisting of clear and picturesque sketches of the chief events and characters in the history of Massachusetts, from the landing of the Puritans to the death of Samuel Adams in 1803. Nowhere else can so vivid a panorama of our early history be found.

In 1839 Bancroft procured Hawthorne an appointment as weigher and gauger in the Boston customhouse. He retained this situation during the remaining two years of the Democratic administration, and lost it by the victory of the Whigs on the election of Harrison. In the mean time he had become interested in Ripley's social reform at Brook Farm, and willingly entered his name among the first shareholders, contributing one thousand dollars toward the general fund. It is not difficult to understand why Hawthorne joined this little band of enthusiasts, any more than it is difficult to see why, of all lives, that which they had planned was the least suited to his character and genius. He was irresistibly attracted by whatever promised to give a romantic tinge to life. Mingled with this attraction, yet perhaps less strong, was the hope of securing an economical and congenial home for himself and future wife, — and the larger hope that a more generous, less ignoble life were possible for all in new social forms, governed, as he said, by other than the false and cruel principles on which human society has all along been based. He writes in " The Blithedale Romance ": —

"We had divorced ourselves from pride, and were striving to supply its place with familiar love.   We meant to lessen the laboring man's great burden of toil, by performing our due share of it at the cost of our own thews and sinews.   We sought our profit by mutual aid, instead of wresting it by the strong hand from an enemy or filching it craftily from those less shrewd than ourselves (if indeed there were any such in New England). . . . Therefore, if we built splendid castles (phalansteries, they might be more fitly called), and pictured beautiful scenes among the fervid coals of the hearth around which we were clustering, and if all went to rack with the crumbling embers and have never since arisen out of the ashes, let us take to ourselves no shame.   In my own behalf I rejoice that I should once think better of the world's improvability than it deserved.   It is a mistake into which men seldom fall twice in a lifetime, or, if so, the rarer and higher is the nature that can thus magnanimously persist in error."

On the thirteenth of April, 1841, Hawthorne made the first entry in his journal from Brook Farm, where he had arrived in just such a snow-storm as he afterward described in "The Blithedale Romance."   "I intend," he says, "to convert myself into a milkmaid this evening; but I pray heaven that Mr. Ripley may be moved to assign me the kindliest cow in the herd, otherwise I shall perform my duty with fear and trembling."   Being a milkmaid, or, as he later expressed it, "a chambermaid to cows and pigs," soon lost all its poetical glamour, and became the veriest prose to poor Hawthorne; and he writes, under date of the twelfth of August: —

"Joyful thought! in a little more than a fortnight, I shall be free from bondage, free to enjoy nature, free to think and feel.   Even my custom-house experience was not such

a thraldom and weariness. Oh! labor is the curse of the
world, and nobody can meddle with it without becoming
brutified. Is it a praiseworthy matter that I have spent five
golden months in providing food for cows and horses? It
is not so."

He had learned, too, that no system of artificial
levelling can eradicate the natural inequalities among
men, and that men's hands may touch whose minds
are separated by impassable gulfs. He pronounced
his life at Brook Farm

"an illusion, a masquerade, a pastoral, a counterfeit Arcadia,
in which we men and women were making a play-day of the
years that were given us to live in. . . . If ever I have
deserved (which has not often been the case, and I think
never), but if ever I did deserve to be soundly cuffed by a
fellow-mortal for secretly putting weight upon some imaginary social advantage, it must have been while I was striving
to prove myself ostentatiously his equal and no more. It
was while I sat beside him on his cobbler's bench, or clinked
my hoe against his own in the cornfield, or broke the same
crust of bread, my earth-grimed hand to his at our noon-
tide lunch. The poor, proud man should look at both sides
of sympathy like this."

Hawthorne soon put an end to this unnatural life
by abandoning Brook Farm and setting up a household for himself. He had been engaged for some
time to Sophia Peabody, a woman whose nature in
its exquisite delicacy and susceptibility was akin to
his own. They were married in the summer of 1842,
and went to housekeeping in the "Old Manse" at
Concord. In this beautiful and quiet retreat nearly
four years of unbroken happiness were passed. An-

other little book of sketches, the " Mosses from an Old Manse," was the fruit of this seclusion. It was published in 1846, and in the same year Hawthorne received an appointment as surveyor of the revenue at the custom-house of Salem, and removed thither with his family.

With regard to Hawthorne's intellectual development, this removal was one of the most important events in his life. It brought him into touch with that homely, practical, every-day life of the world, so distasteful to him, but at the same time so essential to the perfect development of his genius. He knew it, and said of this experience: —

" It contributes greatly to a man's moral and intellectual health to be brought into habits of companionship with individuals unlike himself, who care little for his pursuits, and whose sphere and abilities he must go out of himself to appreciate. . . . After my fellowship of toil and impracticable schemes with the dreamy brethren of Brook Farm; after living for three years within the subtle influence of an intellect like Emerson's; after those wild free days on the Assabeth, indulging fantastic speculations beside our fire of fallen boughs with Ellery Channing; after talking with Thoreau about pine-trees and Indian relics in his hermitage at Walden; after growing fastidious by sympathy with the classic refinement of Hillard's culture; after becoming imbued with poetic sentiment at Longfellow's hearthstone, it was time, at length, that I should exercise other faculties of my nature, and nourish myself with food for which I had hitherto had little appetite. Even the old Inspector was desirable as a change of diet to a man who had known Alcott. I look upon it as an evidence, in some measure, of a system naturally well-balanced, and lacking no essential part of a thorough organization, that with such associates to remember, I could mingle at once with men of altogether different qualities and never murmur at the change.

"Literature, its exertions and objects were now of little moment in my regard. I cared not at that period for books; they were apart from me. Nature — except human nature — the nature that is developed in earth and sky, was in one sense hidden from me, and all the imaginative delight where-with it had been spiritualized passed away out of my mind. A gift, a faculty, if it had not departed, was suspended and inanimate within me."

But the literary gift awoke again, stirred into vigor by an appeal to an imagination always susceptible to the mysteries of sin and its terrible consequences. One rainy day, in a dusky, cobwebbed corner of an old deserted room of the custom-house, Hawthorne's attention was attracted by some old barrels stored with rubbish. Burrowing in this waste of ancient official documents, he came upon a package once the property of one Jonathan Pue, a local antiquarian who had been surveyor of customs under Governor Shirley. On opening the package, he discovered a small roll of manuscript wrapped in a moth-eaten rag of scarlet cloth richly embroidered with the letter A. The manuscript contained a brief relation of the story of Hester Prynne, who had lived in Massachusetts about the middle of the seventeenth century. The dormant fancy was all alert again. The revenue officers, hearing the unwearied tramp of the musing author as he paced the custom-house day after day, used to remark to one another, "The surveyor is walking the quarter-deck." But the surveyor, obliv-ious of weighers and gaugers, was standing with Hester Prynne on the platform of the pillory, or walking with Arthur Dimmesdale among the early Puritans of Boston.

The inauguration of Taylor in 1849 produced a change in the civil-service employees, and Hawthorne lost his position. It was a fortunate circumstance for the literary world, because in the leisure which he now enjoyed Hawthorne wrote "The Scarlet Letter," and published it in 1850. By many critics this work is considered his masterpiece. The author, who had called himself the "obscurest man of letters in America," suddenly found himself on the heights of fame and popularity. Success stimulated him to further effort. He removed to Lenox, and there among the Berkshire Hills he wrote "The House of Seven Gables," which he himself thought superior to "The Scarlet Letter." It appeared in 1851, and was followed the same year by the "Wonder Book," and in 1852 by "The Blithedale Romance," suggested by his Brook Farm experience. This same year Hawthorne went back to Concord, and bought a home for himself on the old Lexington Road, near Alcott and not far from Emerson. He called his new home The Wayside, and there he wrote the "Tanglewood Tales," and a brief biography of Franklin Pierce, who was a candidate for the presidency. On his election, he offered Hawthorne the consulate at Liverpool, which he accepted. The next four years were spent in England. They were not years of unmixed happiness, for the publicity attendant upon the discharge of his official duties was exceedingly painful to Hawthorne.

"What would a man do if he were compelled to live always in the sultry heat of society and could

not bathe himself in cool solitude?" he once asked.
If he were a man of Hawthorne's temperament, he
would do as Hawthorne did, — protect himself from
the sultry heat by the assumption of another character, faultlessly automatic and regular in its discharge of social functions, but giving no hint of the
real, living man beneath it.   In the chapter on civic
banquets in "Our Old Home," Hawthorne gives a
frank confession of his feelings at the delivery of an
after-dinner speech, saying that he could speak of it
quite as indifferently as if it were the experience of
another person, because it was not he, in his own
proper and natural self, that sat there at table, or
subsequently rose to speak, and that if the choice
had been offered him whether the mayor should let
off a speech at his head or a pistol, he would unhesi-
tatingly have taken the latter alternative.

There is probably little exaggeration in this statement.   Never was an organization more sensitive, or
more correct in its intuitions than Hawthorne's.   It
was as if a sixth sense had been given him by which
he divined at once the spiritual nature of all with
whom he came into contact, and if that nature had
nothing in common with his own, it thrilled no fibre,
awoke no music in him.   He became mute and cold as
the strings of an untouched harp.   This muteness was
often mistaken for an effect of ordinary diffidence,
but it was not; it was the muteness of an untouched
chord.   Speaking of an interview with Miss Bremer,
with whom he could not get on in conversation, he
says: "There must first be close and unembarrassed
contiguity with my companion, or I cannot say one
real word.   I doubt whether I have really talked with

half-a-dozen persons in my life, either man or woman."
This peculiarity made at once the strength and the
limitations of Hawthorne's genius.   It gave him un-
rivaled analytical power.   The mysteries of the
human heart, its agonizing struggles in the grasp of
sin, the desolate bitterness of loneliness, the withering
of the soul in the fierce heat of a master-passion, he
depicts with incomparable power and naked truthfulness.   But the sunshine of life does not lighten his
pages; only its pale moonlight gleams and its shadows are there.   "I wish God had given me the faculty
of writing a sunshiny book," he says in his journal,
just before writing his last romance.   But the faculty
was denied him.   What he somewhere calls the
"white sunshine of actual life" dazzled and bewildered him.   Over all he wrote hangs the shadow of
a vague yet profound melancholy.   His books give
as much pain as pleasure, and only the stern wholesome moral underlying them all relieves them from
the charge of being morbid.   Hawthorne's genius was
unquestionably of the highest order, but it was limited in its range.   Real life lay all about him, offering
him subjects for study, but he had not the hearty
assimilative power of those great creative geniuses
who seize upon the present and transform it.   Deeply
rooted in Puritan soil, drawing his sustenance from it,
he returns again and again to the past for material
for his work.   But he has revivified that past; he has
made of it an immortal picture gallery, with New
England for a background.

Hawthorne resigned the Liverpool consulate in
1857, and the following year went on the Continent,
where he spent most of his time in Italy.   His resi-

dence in Italy furnished him with suggestions for a new romance, which he published in 1860 under the title of "The Marble Faun." In the same year he returned to America, and settled for the remainder of his life in Concord, at his old home the Wayside. The Wayside is an unpretentious frame cottage, painted dark yellow. On the top of the roof Hawthorne built for his study a rather ungainly-looking square room, called by courtesy "the tower." The tower was entered by a trap-door, upon which Hawthorne placed his chair, when writing, to secure himself from interruption. The cottage is beautifully located at the foot of a steep, long hill thickly grown with hemlocks and pines. On the crest of this hill, among the sweet-fern and brambles, under the gloomy shade of the pines, Hawthorne was accustomed to take his solitary walks while he brooded over his last romance. Mrs. Hawthorne called this hill his Mount of Vision.

Thoreau had told Hawthorne of a tradition concerning a former occupant of the Wayside, a man who thought he could never die. Hawthorne seized upon this idea as the theme of his last-planned romance, "Septimius Felton," later worked out in the unfinished "Dolliver Romance." It is the story of an old doctor who had a bottle of the elixir of life; but there is little in the fragment left us to indicate that it would have equalled Hawthorne's earlier romances. Before its conclusion, the great author was dead. He had been in failing health for some time, and in May, 1864, he was induced to take a carriage journey through southern New Hampshire with his old friend, ex-President Franklin Pierce. It was hoped that the rest and change would bring back something of his old vigor; but he died on the nine-teenth of May at a hotel in Plymouth, New Hampshire, and four days later was buried in Sleepy Hollow Cemetery, Concord. A low, plain marble headstone, with the one word HAWTHORNE carved upon it, marks his grave. The wife whom he loved so tenderly, and who returned his love with equal devotion and tenderness, died in London some years later, and was buried in Kensal Green Cemetery.

Hawthorne had requested that no biography of him should be written; but the successive publication of his note-books, and later the publication of a biography by his son Julian, entitled " Nathaniel Hawthorne and his Wife," have furnished us with more satisfactory biographical material than we possess of any other American author. The tall, robust frame; the large, finely shaped head with its thick, dark-brown hair; the handsome face with its keen gray eyes and sensitive mouth shaded by a heavy mustache, are more familiar to the mind's eye of his present readers than they were to the bodily eyes of his neighbors. The cloudy veil which, he said, stretched across the abyss of his nature, though he had no love of secrecy and darkness, is thinner to our eyes than it was to theirs, and we look into a heart in which there was no guile, only an unutterable longing for the beautiful, and an inextinguishable desire to express it.

Alcott says, in his reminiscences entitled " Concord Days," that during all the years Hawthorne lived beside him, he rarely caught sight of him. Emerson has a like report to give; Cabot, Emerson's biographer, says that Emerson and Hawthorne liked each other personally, but that they were very unlike in nature, and of an unlikeness that had no mutual attraction. They "interdespised" each other's moonshine, as very amiable and pretty but childish. When Hawthorne died, Emerson wrote : —

"I thought there was a tragic element in the event that might be more fully rendered in the painful solitude of the man ; which, I suppose, could not longer be endured, and he died of it. I found in his death a surprise and a disappointment. I thought him a greater man than any of his words betray : there was still a great deal of work in him, and he might one day show a purer power. . . . It was easy to talk with him, there were no barriers, only he said so little that I talked too much, and stopped only because, as he gave no indications, I feared to exceed. He showed no egotism, no self-assertion, rather a humility, and at one time a fear that he had written himself out. . . . I do not think any of his books worthy of his genius. I admired the man, who was simple, amiable, truth-loving, and frank in conversation, but I never read his books with pleasure : they are too young."

There is no doubt that Hawthorne's unerring intuition divined this secret disapproval in Emerson, and moreover divined the reason of it in a constitutional difference of thought and feeling that made a full, free, and affectionate friendship between them impossible. Emerson demanded of men an intellectual stimulus. The fire in him could best flash out in a flint-like collision of mind with mind. For any other contact with men, he cared little or nothing at all. It was the teacher among them he sought, not the comrade. Hawthorne, on the contrary, belonged to that order of sensitive geniuses in whom the feminine need of loving and being loved is a marked characteristic.   Quick, warm sympathy, loving appreciation and responsiveness, were as necessary to the full and happy development of his powers, as warm sunshine and refreshing rains are essential to the blooming of plants.   "He was feminine," said his friend Hillard, "in his quick perception, his fine insight, his sensibility to beauty."   Nothing can be more certain than that his marriage with a woman of artistic temperament and warm human sympathy mellowed and ripened his genius, and saved him to the world as a great artist.   She strengthened his trust in himself: she never questioned the majesty and beauty of that ideal world in which he lived; she brought him a large, childlike faith, and a passionate womanly devotion that answered the needs of his heart.   With women of such a temperament Hawthorne was always at his best, and conversed with nothing of that reserve and caution that characterized his intercourse with men.   In his Italian note-book he records the pleasure he felt in the society of Mrs. Browning, because of her quick sympathy and responsiveness.

This peculiarity of Hawthorne's temperament, associated with the circumstances of his early life, explains the morbid, introspective character of much of his early work.   The man of adamant, turned to stone from his refusal to open his heart to the beneficent influences of love to his fellow-men; Ethan Brand, who went in search of the unpardonable sin, and found it to be "the sin of an intellect that triumphed over the sense of brotherhood with man and reverence for God, and sacrificed everything to its own mighty chains;" the artist of the beautiful, to whom had often come " a sensation of moral cold that makes the spirit shiver as if it had reached the frozen solitudes of the pole; " the man at the Christmas banquet with his heavy brow bent downward, naturally earnest and impassioned, feeling himself the bearer of a message to the world, essaying to deliver it, but finding no ear to listen; Osborn, surrounding himself with shadows that bewilder him by aping realities and drawing him into a strange solitude in the midst of men where nobody wishes for what he does, nor thinks and feels as he does; — all these characters are transparent veils through which Hawthorne's own despair and yearning are revealed. They are the cries of a chilled and sensitive heart for the warmth of human love and sympathy, — the cries of a heart that makes its own loneliness through an almost terrible fastidiousness. He had all that exquisite poetic sensibility which, while it opens regions of inexpressible delight to its possessor, also renders him abnormally susceptible to painful impressions. Of this fastidiousness Mrs. Hawthorne gives us some inkling in her comments on Hawthorne's complaints of grimy pictures, tarnished frames, and faded frescos in his French and Italian note-books. She says : —

" They were distressing beyond measure to eyes that never failed to see anything with the keenest apprehension, . . . and he suffered in a way not to be readily conceived from any failure in beauty, physical, moral, or intellectual. . . . The ' New Jerusalem, even like a jasper stone, clear as crystal,' ' wherein shall in no wise enter anything that defileth, neither that maketh abomination nor maketh a lie,' would alone satisfy him, or rather not give him actual pain."

Another peculiarity of Hawthorne's intellect is embodied in the constant reappearance in his works of one character under various forms; namely, the analytic observer, cool, self-poised, profoundly interested in the mysteries of the human heart, but interested for the most part through his intellect and not through his emotions. This character goes by the name of Miles Coverdale in "The Blithedale Romance," Mr. Holgrave, the daguerreotypist, in "The House of the Seven Gables," and Roger Chillingworth in "The Scarlet Letter." But under whatever name he reappears, he is, undoubtedly, representative of that curious twist in Hawthorne's mind that made him say: —

"The most desirable mode of existence might be that of a spiritualized Paul Pry hovering invisible round man and woman, witnessing their deeds, searching their hearts, borrowing brightness from their felicity and shade from their sorrow, and retaining no emotion peculiar to himself."

One of the most admirable examples of this dramatic power to enter into the feelings of another is to be found in the " Mosses from an Old Manse " in the wonderfully lifelike sketch entitled "The Old Apple-Dealer." The subject seems at first sight as unpromising as an attempt to represent the soul of a lamp-post. But with an exquisite, almost super-human sympathy, the author depicts the " frost-bitten, patient despondency " of the little withered old man, until the reader puts aside the sketch with a lump in his throat, an ache in his heart, and a new and vivid consciousness of the tie that unites us all to the very humblest and meanest of our kind. The power to awaken this consciousness belongs to the highest order of art. The French moralist, Joubert, speaking of the fiction of his day, says: "Viewed from the standpoint of art, the problem of the romance is to paint a flame; and it is the fireplace that is painted instead." All fiction that depends upon external accessories, mere show and movement, to interest the reader, instead of relying upon the growth of thought and feeling and the development of character, falls short of the highest art. Hawthorne is eminently a psychologist. It is not the deed but the motive or impulse behind it, and the condition of mind that follows it, that sets his fancy astir.

Therefore his work answers the highest demand that can be made of it: it paints the flame, not the fireplace. Bare of incident, it is crowded with the life of the soul. Dealing with the mysteries of sin and guilt, it preserves an austere purity. Concerning itself with those problems in human life that breed despair and pessimism, it is tainted with no morbid wailing, but breathes a manly spirit of trust and resignation. "The Scarlet Letter" is the most dramatic and most richly colored of Hawthorne's longer works, and these qualities have made it the most popular of his romances. But in acuteness and delicacy of analytic power, in variety and naturalness of character drawing, in the skilful blending of the lights and shades of humor and pathos, it is surpassed by "The House of the Seven Gables." "To see clearly," says Herbert Spencer, "how a right or wrong act generates consequences, internal and external, that go on branching out more widely as years progress, requires a rare power of analysis."

" The House of the Seven Gables " rests upon such a theme, that had long haunted Hawthorne's imagination in the story of that Puritan ancestor who had persecuted and wronged the Quakers. There are few characters in the story, and no extraordinary incidents. Its whole power, and it is a rare and wonderful power, centres in the analysis of character and emotion. And never was analysis more searching or more faithful. Never were the quivering, sensitive nerves of a shy, proud, fond woman's nature laid bare to human view with sharper distinctness than those of poor old Hepzibah Pyncheon. " The Blithedale Romance," which Emerson calls a disagreeable story, failing to do justice to the Brook Farm experiment, embodies Hawthorne's views on the perfectibility of human society. The cold-hearted, selfish Hollingsworth, with his philanthropic dream of reforming criminals by appealing to their better instincts; the restless, nervous, brilliant Zenobia, eager to lose herself in some absorbing passion, or larger life that would tax all her faculties; the poor waif, Priscilla; the analytic observer, Miles Coverdale, —were certainly, as Hawthorne emphatically protests, *not* drawn after the life, but they are lifelike types of human character. Many a profound problem of human life is worked out in this brilliant romance for those who have understanding to follow its analysis. It was a great favorite with the poet Browning. In " The Marble Faun " Hawthorne approaches once more the old mystery of human sin, and works out his solution of it, in the awakening of the intellectual life in Donatello.

Besides being a great psychologist, a great writer

of fiction, Hawthorne was a master of style. His language, while reflecting the rich glow of his imagination, is at all times pure and simple. It lends itself to his subtlest or boldest thought with exquisite delicacy and chasteness. He once wrote his publisher that he was never good for anything till after the first autumnal frost, which had somewhat the same effect on his imagination that it had upon the foliage about him, multiplying and brightening its hues. Something of this rich, warm, autumnal hue tinges his style, and gives to the reader a pleasure of its own, independent of his subject matter. America has not as yet produced his equal in genius nor in finished artistic skill.

CHAPTER X

IN his essay on the poet, Emerson says: —

"I took part in conversation the other day, concerning a recent writer of lyrics, a man of subtle mind, whose head appeared to be a music-box of delicate tunes and rhythms, and whose skill and command of language we could not sufficiently praise. But when the question arose whether he was not only a lyrist but a poet, we were obliged to confess that he is plainly a contemporary, not an eternal man. He does not stand out of our low limitations, like a Chimborazo under the line, running up from a torrid base through all the climates of the globe with belts of the herbage of every latitude on its high mottled sides ; but this genius is the landscape garden of a modern house, adorned with fountains and statues, with well-bred men and women sitting and standing in the walks and terraces. We hear through all the varied music the ground tone of conventional life. Our poets are men of talent who sing, and not the children of music. The argument is secondary. The finish of the verse is primary."

It is impossible to state with absolute certainty who was the particular poet of whom Emerson spoke in this recorded conversation ; but it is very probable that it was Longfellow, because of no other American poet can this admirable criticism be more aptly made. Longfellow, though the most popular of American poets, does not rank with the great singers of the human race. The poetic flame that glowed in him was not native and original like that which burst from the volcanic breast of the mighty world poets. It was a decent, well-controlled fireside flame that owed its existence to other than spontaneous sources. But the fireside flame has its meaning as well as the inextinguishable fires of nature. Sweet and tender associations cluster round it. The gentler affections, the joys and griefs of home, crowd into the memory when we name it, and these are the themes of Longfellow's verse. This is why he is so aptly called the " Household Poet." So little of the turbulent appears in his poetry, so smoothly does it reflect his own gentle character, that he might have sung to his genius in his youth what he sang to his heart: —

> " Stay, stay at home, my heart, and rest.
>   Home-keeping hearts are happiest;
>   For those that wander they know not where
>   Are full of trouble and full of care.
>   To stay at home is best."

Henry Wadsworth Longfellow was born in Portland, Maine, on the twenty-seventh of February, 1807. His mother, Zilpah Wadsworth, was a descendant of John Alden and Priscilla Mullens. His father, Stephen Longfellow, was an able lawyer and successful politician who at one time represented his district in Congress. Longfellow entered Bowdoin College in his fifteenth year. He was a sunny-natured, practical, and sensible youth, who loved his books, but loved good health better, and finding exercise necessary to it, took long walks when walking was practicable, cut wood when it was n't, or boxed with an imaginary pugilist chalked out on his closet door. "I have very resolutely concluded," he writes to his father, in his seventeenth year, "to enjoy myself heartily wherever I am. I find it most profitable to form such plans as are least liable to failure." One of these plans was a determination to fit himself for literature. "Somehow," he confides to a friend in 1824, "and yet I hardly know why, I am unwilling to study any profession. I cannot make a lawyer of any eminence, because I have not a talent for argument. I am not good enough for a minister, and as to physic, I utterly and absolutely detest it." About the same time he wrote his father that he wished to spend a year at Cambridge in order to read history and learn Italian, as after leaving Cambridge he designed to attach himself to some periodical and live by writing. In urging this project upon his father, he writes confidently, "I *will be eminent* in something." However, the autumn and winter after his graduation were spent in his father's law-office reading Blackstone. But this same year a professorship of modern languages was established at Bowdoin; and Longfellow, whose translations from Horace and original literary work had attracted the attention of one of the trustees, was offered the position with a proposal that he should visit Europe to prepare for his work.

The proposal was eagerly accepted, and on the fifteenth of May, 1826, Longfellow sailed for Europe to be gone three years. He settled first at Paris, where he spent eight months, enlivening his French studies by little pedestrian journeys to the neighboring country and towns. We have a pleasant record of

these journeys in his published " Life and Letters,"
but the record is chiefly interesting as a revelation of
Longfellow's dependence at this time upon precon-
ceived ideas for his inspiration. Nature does not
appeal to him at first hand, but through what he
has read about her. In a pedestrian journey to
Tours, for example, he overtakes a band of village-
girls on their way home, and he joins the party. He
says : —

" I wanted to get into one of the cottages, if possible, to
study character. I had a flute in my knapsack, and I
thought it would be very pretty to touch up at a cottage-
door, Goldsmith-like, though I would not have done it for
the world without an invitation. Well, before long, I determined to get an invitation if possible, so I addressed the girl
who was walking beside me, told her I had a flute in my
sack, and asked her if she would like to dance. Now, laugh
long and loud ! What do you suppose she answered ? She
said she liked to dance, but did not know what a flute was.
What havoc that made among my romantic ideas ! My
quietus was made. I said no more about a flute the whole
journey through, and I thought nothing but starvation would
drive me to strike up at the entrance of a village door as
Goldsmith did. The company I was with conducted me to
the village of Tivher, the most beautiful and romantic village
I was ever in. I found the village inn, and fell asleep at
night with the thought that perhaps a great part of ' The
Traveller ' was written in that very village."

It is safe to say that it could never have been
written there, nor anywhere else, had Goldsmith, like
Longfellow, looked upon a band of young girls as if
they were puppets in a romantic theatre, instead of
feeling himself a real flesh-and-blood peasant among

them, in that generous overflow of youthful spirits and hearty comradeship that annihilates caste. It is this thinking and seeing at second hand that robs Longfellow's youthful letters and journal of buoyancy and sparkle, and gives to them, in spite of their romantic tinge, a certain insipid, almost leaden, staidness.

From Paris, for which he cared little, Longfellow went to Spain and took up his residence in Madrid. He had seen no city in Europe, he said, that pleased him so much as Madrid. He had also the good fortune to meet Washington Irving in Spain. After a stay of eight months he left Spain for Italy, where he remained a year; but Italy excited no enthusiasm in him. He was, he said, "homesick for Spain. The recollection of it completely ruins Italy for me."

In the midwinter of 1828 he received a letter from home saying that the Bowdoin professorship offered him had been withdrawn on the score of his being too young, and that a tutorship was tendered him instead. He wrote back proudly to his father: —

"They say I am too young. Were they not aware of that three years ago? If I am not capable of performing the duties of the office, they may be very sure of my not accepting it. I know not in what light they may look upon it, but for my own part, I do not in the least regard it as a favor conferred upon me. It is no sinecure, and if my services are an equivalent for my salary, there is no favor done me : if they be not, I do not deserve the situation."

From Italy, Longfellow went to Dresden, and began the study of German, which he continued at Göttingen. From there, he took a run over to England and back to Germany by way of Holland. In the fall of 1829, as he had declined the tutorship, the Bowdoin trustees voted him the professorship at a salary of eight hundred dollars, with an addition of one hundred dollars as librarian.

He was twenty-two when he commenced his professional duties. He was an earnest, sympathetic, cordial teacher, and in these early years he was delighted with his work. He published some text-books for the use of his pupils, translated Spanish poetry, and led what he called " a very sober jog-trot kind of life." He began contributing to the " North American Review" in 1831. In September of the same year he married Mary Potter, a beautiful girl, of Portland, Maine.

His first book, a translation from the Spanish, a small volume of fewer than one hundred pages, was published in 1833. It was followed in the same year by a volume of prose entitled " Outre Mer." The book is filled with the impressions of a joyous young traveller to whom the land beyond the sea is a kind of holy land, — a land of immortal memories. The reminiscences of famous places are interspersed with graceful tales, and, on the whole, " Outre Mer" is decidedly the pleasantest of Longfellow's prose works.

In 1834, on the resignation of George Ticknor, Josiah Quincy tendered Longfellow the professorship of modern languages at Harvard, with a salary of fifteen hundred dollars a year, and a residence in Cambridge required. He was permitted to spend a year or eighteen months in Germany at his own expense, if he liked. He sailed for Europe in the spring of 1835, spent three weeks in London, where he met Carlyle, sailed for Hamburg and thence to Copenhagen and Stockholm. Settling in Stockholm, he began the study of Swedish and Danish, and later took up Dutch in Amsterdam. In this city his wife fell ill. She recovered sufficiently to remove to Rotterdam, but suffered a relapse and died there.

Longfellow then went to Heidelberg, where he met for the first time the poet Bryant. He travelled in Tyrol and Switzerland, and on the wall of a little chapel at St. Gilgen he read the inscription which he afterward made the motto of " Hyperion " : —

" Blicke nicht trauernd in die Vergangenheit, sie kommt nicht wieder. Nütze weise die Gegenwart, sie ist dein : der düstern Zukunft geh ohne Furcht mit männlichen Sinne entgegen."

The brave, manly spirit of these lines breathed new hope and courage into him. He no longer allowed his grief to absorb him, but turned resolutely to the accomplishment of his task. He went back to America in 1836, and took up his residence in the old Craigie House at Cambridge. He writes to a friend two years later : —

" I live in a great house which looks like an Italian villa ; have two large rooms opening into each other. They were once General Washington's chambers. I breakfast at seven on tea and toast, and dine at five or six, generally in Boston. In the evening I walk on the Common with Hillard or alone, then go back to Cambridge on foot. If not very late, I sit an hour with Felton or Sparks. For nearly two years I have not studied at night, save now and then. Most of the time I am alone. I smoke a good deal, wear a broad-brimmed black hat, black frock coat. . . . Molest no one. Dine out frequently.   In winter go much in Boston society. . . . I do not like this sedentary life.   I want action; I want to travel. Am too excited, too tumultuous inwardly, and my health suffers from all this."

There were no street-cars running from Cambridge into Boston at that time, and Longfellow's frequent journeys there were made on foot.   In returning from Boston, he would stop on the bridge that crosses the Charles River, and watch the waters rolling beneath it.   The restless waves symbolized the restlessness of his own heart.   Life was bringing its lessons to him; his thought was deepening and broadening; he was learning to speak the universal experiences, and that which had satisfied him once no longer answered his needs.   He was beginning to tire of having his " mind constantly a playmate for boys, constantly adapting itself to them instead of stretching and grappling with men's minds."   The fruit of this unrest appeared in the publication in 1839 of another prose volume, " Hyperion," and his first volume of original verse, " Voices of the Night."

Of the success of "Hyperion" he was very confident, and wrote his father that it would take a great deal of persuasion to convince him that the book was not good.   To a friend he wrote : —

" The feelings of the book are true ; the events of the story mostly fictitious.   The heroine bears a resemblance to the lady without being an exact portrait.   There is no betrayal of confidence, no real scene described.   Hyperion is the name of the book, not the hero.   It merely indicates that here is the life of one who in feeling and purposes is a ' son of Heaven and Earth,' and who, though obscured by clouds, yet 'moves on high.' Further than this, the name has nothing to do with the book and, in fact, is mentioned only once in the course of it."

Of the success of "Voices of the Night" the author was equally confident, and it did succeed; at the end of a fortnight only forty copies were left out of an edition of nine hundred. "Hyperion" is not so fresh and healthy a book as "Outre Mer." The joyous young traveller of the latter work has become a melancholy dreamer in "Hyperion," and the sentiment has, in great part, become a kind of wan, sickly sentimentalism. But the collection of poems "Voices of the Night" contained many of those poems that have since become household favorites, — "The Psalm of Life," "Footsteps of Angels," "The Beleaguered City," "The Reaper and the Flowers." Another volume of verse, "Ballads and Other Poems," appeared in 1841, and still further increased the poet's reputation.

With his success with the public, the literary man gained the ascendency, and the professor began to decline; university life grew intolerable to him. "I will not consent to have my life crushed out of me so. I had rather live awhile on bread and water," he writes to his father. His eyes began to trouble him, his health failed. He secured a leave of absence for six months in 1842, went abroad again and took the water-cure at Marienberg. On his return to America he was married, in the summer of 1843, to Frances E. Appleton, whom he had first met in Switzerland six years before. At the time of their meeting she was a lovely girl of nineteen, the Mary Ashburton of "Hyperion." Mr. Appleton, the father of the bride, purchased Craigie House and presented it to his daughter and her husband. Another notable event of 1843 was the publication of the drama of " The Spanish Student" and a little volume of poems on slavery.

Longfellow's masterpiece, " Evangeline," was published in 1847. It had been begun two years before under the title of " Gabrielle." It is a pathetic rendering in hexameter verse of an incident connected with the exile of the Acadians in 1755. The Acadians were of French descent, and before their exile occupied what is now called Nova Scotia. By the terms of the treaty of Utrecht closing the war of the Spanish Succession in 1713, France lost to England Newfoundland and what is now Canada. The Acadians were not inclined to acknowledge the English rule, and at the outbreak of the fourth French and Indian war in 1754, they were accused of secretly aiding their countrymen against the English. In retaliation, the English seized their forts, laid waste their villages, and at the point of the bayonet drove more than six thousand unhappy Acadians into English ships and scattered them far from their homes along the Atlantic coast. In this cruel exile husbands were separated from their wives, parents from their children, and dear friends parted never to meet again. Among those who were separated, tradition speaks of a beautiful young girl and her lover who, after years of fruitless wanderings in search of each other, met when both were old and one was on his death-bed. " Evangeline " is the story of the separation and wanderings of these lovers. The story is told with exquisite feeling and in melodious language which has the rhythm of verse and the perfect freedom of prose. Its success was instant and unmistakable.

" Evangeline " was followed, in two years, by a prose tale called " Kavanagh." It is a feeble story, not unpleasant to read, but giving an impression of the author's inability to create characters or incidents that win the sympathy or excite the interest of the reader. The tale is evidently based on the author's own experiences of the difficulty of realizing literary ambitions in the face of professional duties and claims upon his sympathy and time. While writing " Evangeline," he makes this entry in his journal : —

" I am in despair at the swift flight of time and the utter impossibility I feel to lay hold upon anything permanent. All my hours and days go to perishable things. College takes half the time, and other people with their interminable letters and poems and requests and demands take the rest. I have hardly a moment to think of my own writings and am cheated of some of life's fairest hours. This is the extreme of folly, and if I knew a man far off in some foreign land doing as I do here, I should say he was mad."

In this entry we have the germ of " Kavanagh ; " and Mr. Churchill, the schoolmaster, the " dreamy poetic man," and not Kavanagh, the clergyman, for whom the book is named, is the real hero. Mr. Churchill, who ardently longs to write a romance, continually defers beginning his task, because of the importunate claims of the moment. It is always the coming hour that is to find him resolutely at work, but the hour brings its duty or its exaction, and the task is once more set aside. A slight thread of a love story — the love of two young girls for the minister — is interwoven.   The minister's wooing and winning of one of them and the death of the other serves to show that Churchill had under his eyes, at his very feet, the material for an immortal romance, had he but possessed seeing eyes and the skill to use poetically what he saw.   The story closes with the following quotation, which Churchill thought "worthy to be written in letters of gold and placed above every door and every house as a warning, a suggestion an incitement!" —

> "Stay, stay the present instant !
> Imprint the marks of wisdom on its wings !
> Oh, let it not elude the grasp, but like
> The good old patriarch upon record,
> Hold the fleet angel fast until he bless thee."

"Kavanagh" has the defect of all Longfellow's dramatic and prose work, — conventional character drawing and feeble sentimentality.   It bears the mark of immaturity and ideality, and depends for what attention it receives on the reputation his poetry has won for him.

The college work, which he said was like a great hand laid on all the strings of his lyre stopping their vibrations, ceased at last in 1854.   The chair which he resigned was immediately filled by James Russell Lowell, whose recently delivered lectures on the English poets had attracted a great deal of attention. About the time of his resignation the first idea of an Indian epic occurred to Longfellow.   He designed at first to call it Manabozho, but later changed the name to Hiawatha.   His idea was to weave the myths and traditions of the Indians into a metrical narrative.

The metre chosen was eight-syllable trochaic, after a Finnish epic. The poem, which he calls an Indian Edda, is feigned to be sung by an Indian bard, Nawadaha. The scene is the southern shore of Lake Superior, between the Pictured Rocks and the great sand-dunes. The traditions are, in general, those of the tribe called Ojibways. Hiawatha is the teacher of the nations. He taught them how to make the canoe and to cultivate the maize; he taught them picture-writing and the care of the dead. He fought with the mighty magician, the creator of pestilential diseases, fogs, and deadly marsh exhalations. The woodpecker told him what vulnerable spot to aim at, and in return for this service, Hiawatha stained his top-knot with blood, for which reason the wood-pecker wears to this day a tuft of scarlet feathers on his head. Many of the myths are very pretty; as, for example, that the rainbow is the flower-garden of heaven, where the wild flowers of the forest and the lilies of the prairie bloom again when they wither on earth.

The story of the maize is another pretty myth. For three days Hiawatha wrestled with a celestial visitor, and conquering him at last, received the command to bury him under light, loose earth, and to let no ravens nor worms come at him. After nine days the green-leafed tasselled maize sprang from the stranger's ashes. Another pretty legend is that of the South Wind's love for the dandelion of the prairies, mistaking it for a beautiful maiden with yellow hair. The entire poem of Hiawatha is graceful, but not epic. All the stern, masculine Indian traits have been re-jected for what is beautiful and poetic. Though the imagery is carefully chosen from the simple, familiar objects of nature, the poem is pervaded by a sweetness and gentleness, the outgrowth of years of culture, that mark it the performance of a scholarly poet, and not, as feigned, that of a native bard. It has no rude Ossianic vigor. Hiawatha and Minnehaha are not Indians. Minnehaha is a Priscilla in Indian costume, and Hiawatha, for all his magic gloves that rend the rocks asunder, and his magic boots by which he measures a mile with every stride, is a hero of our own race and century. The poem is a forest idyl; a poet's dream of the youth-time of a savage nation. As a sweet and refreshing picture of life in nature such as Rousseau might have dreamed, it gratifies the imagination. In its reproduction of some of the most poetical of Indian legends, it interests the understanding. As an " Indian Edda " taken from the lips of a native bard, it is the prettiest and most transparent of fictions, breathing everywhere the gentle spirit of its author, the fireside poet of America.

"Hiawatha" was published in 1855, and made a sensation at once. It was ridiculed and parodied, and it was extravagantly admired. Noted public readers recited selections from it on the stage. Steamboats were named Hiawatha and Minnehaha. It sold at the rate of three hundred copies a day. But its author, unmoved by criticism or undue admiration, quietly set to work on another theme, "The Courtship of Miles Standish," and in the summer of 1858 he wrote, " I have just·finished a poem of some length, — an idyl of the Old Colony Times, a bunch of Mayflowers from the Plymouth woods." It would be difficult to characterize the freshness and sweetness of the poem in fewer or better words. And now the happy and busy life of the poet was soon to be interrupted by a terrible and fatal accident. On the ninth of July Mrs. Longfellow, sitting in the library sealing with wax some little packages containing locks of her children's hair, let fall a lighted match upon the floor. Her thin summer dress caught fire, and she was so badly burned that she died the next day. A long silence fell upon the poet. He had not the art of turning his grief into words. But when once more he could master quiet hours, he busied himself with the translation of Dante, and published the first series of the " Tales of a Wayside Inn."

In 1868 he went again to Europe, making a tour of the Scottish Lakes and revisiting Italy. After eighteen months' travel, he returned to America and continued the publication of the "Tales of a Wayside Inn" in two successive series. Other poems and ballads followed, some of them not inferior to what he had written in his youth, though none of the more ambitious works of this period equalled " Evangeline," " Miles Standish," or " Hiawatha."

Longfellow died of peritonitis on the twenty-fourth of March, 1882, and was buried in Mt. Auburn Cemetery. His " Life and Letters," published by his brother, the Rev. Samuel Longfellow, confirms the impression which his poems give, of a singularly sweet and noble character. And to these graces of disposition were added the charm of a fine, tall figure, a handsome head and face, brown wavy hair, and frank, kind blue eyes. George H. Hillard once wrote to Longfellow, " Your fine organization and poetical genius make you a sort of Italy among human beings." And indeed there was a sunny geniality, a sweet, sympathetic, companionable simplicity in the man that endeared him to all who knew him. From childhood he had a hearty dislike of everything violent. When a little boy, he used to beg the maid to fill his ears with cotton on the Fourth of July, that he might not hear the roar of the cannon. And in the same spirit, in manhood he shut out of his life the bluster and tumult of political life, the angry, envious noise of critical censure, and the fierce blaze of consuming passion. His poems on slavery are not indignant lashes, but mournful pictures of the pathetic side of slavery. Even his pleasures were not tumultuous. "With me," he once said, "all deep impressions are silent ones. I like to live on and enjoy them without telling those around me that I do enjoy them;" and again he writes in his journal: "Decidedly the calm, dull husbanding of one's nervous energies, though less conducive to swift intellectual effort, is more so to happiness. Let us be calm and happy, rather than excitable and nervous-minded." And, as might be expected, his journal is a very quiet chronicling of ordinary events, meetings with strangers and friends, records of sunshine and storm, blossoming trees and falling leaves, notes of books read and work planned; but nowhere is there a quick flashing insight into life, nowhere a profound, brain-stirring thought, nor an acute, far-reaching criticism of contemporary literature. The calm cheerfulness of the record is broken only here and there by a vague, half-melancholy restlessness and longing for travel.

So serene and uniformly healthy a temperament

will guard its fortunate possessor from all excesses, and help him to

> "Make the house where Gods may dwell
> Beautiful, entire, and clean."

If the susceptibility of genius accompany such a temperament, it will manifest itself in works of quiet beauty and purity. Delicacy of sentiment, melody, and finish in execution rather than fervor, originality, and strength will mark these works; and such are the characteristics of Longfellow's verse. He had warmth of fancy rather than ardor of feeling, artistic appreciation and delicacy, but nothing of that quick, original, and contagious rapture which our French neighbors call *verve*. The romantic and picturesque strongly attracted him, and led him in youth and early manhood to think and feel too closely after the manner of the books he admired. Yet this romantic leaning led him into no extravagances in practical life. He had a fine common sense that preserved him from the intellectual delusions of Transcendentalism. He detected the unsound vein in Emerson's thinking, and said of him: "He is one of the finest lecturers I ever heard, with magnificent passages of true prose-poetry. But it is all *dreamery*, after all." Longfellow's romanticism was the natural result of a youth of ease, culture, and foreign travel on a susceptible, poetical temperament; but when life's harsh experiences had matured him, he learned the austere beauty of reality, and expressed its common lessons in simple melodious verse, and in so doing he fulfilled his ardent wish that he might not pass away and leave no mark of his existence. He has admirably characterized his

own poetry in "The Day is Done."   He himself is
not one of " the grand old Masters," or

> " bards sublime
> Whose distant footsteps echo
> Through the corridors of Time."

But he is the humbler poet whose

> " songs have power to quiet
> The restless pulse of care,
> And come like the benediction
> That follows after prayer."

CHAPTER XI

JOHN GREENLEAF WHITTIER belongs to a class of poets who " grow upon us," to use an expression of approval for that which is essentially good but which does not recommend itself by anything superficially striking or dazzling. He is rarely a favorite with the young, unless they are old-fashioned enough to believe that simplicity is a virtue and calmness an indication of strength, or have

> " The eye to see, the hand to cull
> Of common things the beautiful."

But he steals into the affections, — he sits a restful, cheering presence at the hearth of those who have known the storms of life and are now thankful for its calms and harbors. He, too, knew life's storms and perils, but weathered them bravely and came to port in calm. He gave the vigor of his youth and manhood to the antislavery cause; and though the poetry by which he is to be remembered is not that which he wrote in defence of freedom, it is impossible to read his early antislavery poems without feeling a tingle of the blood, and realizing that he spoke the solemn truth when he said to his fellow-worker Garrison : —

"I am not insensible to literary reputation. I love, perhaps too well, the praise and good-will of my fellow-men; but I set a higher value on my name as appended to the anti-slavery declaration of 1833 than on the titlepage of any book.

. . . .

'My voice, though not the loudest, has been heard
  Wherever Freedom raised her cry of pain.'"

The echoes of this voice full of passion and pain have almost died away with the wrong it strove to right; the voice that we listen to now is restful without dulness, full of peace and sweetness. It brings to us beautiful memories of family affections, of country life, glimpses of green fields and woods, the scents of wild-flowers, and the babble of brooks, — and interwoven through them all a rich, low undertone, freighted with a message of trustful hope and calm that makes us fling with him "the windows of the soul" "wide open to the sun," and say: —

"No longer forward nor behind
  I look in hope or fear;
But grateful, take the good I find,
  The best of now and here.

. . . . .

"Enough that blessings undeserved,
  Have marked my erring track;
That wheresoe'er my feet have swerved,
  His chastening turned me back.

. . . . .

"That care and trial seem at last
  Through memory's sunset air,
Like mountain-ranges overpast,
  In purple distance fair.

"That all the jarring notes of life
  Seem blending in a psalm;
And all the angles of its strife
  Slow rounding into calm.

> " And so the shadows fall apart,
> And so the west winds play;
> And all the windows of my heart
> I open to the day."

John G. Whittier was born on a farm near the town of Haverhill, Massachusetts, on the seventeenth of December, 1807. His parents were Quakers in moderate circumstances: the boy helped with the farm work, milked seven cows, and until he was nineteen had no other educational advantages than those afforded by the district school with its change of teachers every winter. Among these teachers of Whittier's boyhood only two were fit to be instructors, and to one of them Whittier owed his introduction to the poems of Robert Burns. There were not above twenty volumes in his father's home, and they were chiefly of a religious character, the journals of pioneer ministers in the Society of Friends, and the boy would now and then walk a mile to borrow a book of biography or travel when he heard of it. He was fourteen when his schoolmaster lent him Burns's poems; it was about the first poetry he had ever read, and it had a lasting influence upon him which he recalls in his poem to Burns on receiving a sprig of heather in blossom: —

> .   .   .   .   .
>
> "Wild heather bells, and Robert Burns,
> The moorland flower and peasant,
> How at their mention, memory turns
> Her pages old and pleasant!
> .   .   .   .   .
> " Sweet day, sweet songs ! the golden hours
> Grew brighter for that singing,
> From brook and bird and meadow flowers
> A dearer welcome bringing.

"New light on home-seen nature beamed,
New glory over woman,
And daily life and duty seemed
No longer poor and common.

"I woke to find the simple truth
Of fact and feeling better
Than all the dreams that held my youth
A still repining debtor.
        .   .   .   .   .

"I saw through all familiar things
The romance underlying,
The joys and griefs that plume the wings
Of fancy skyward flying.
        .   .   .   .   .

"Let those who never erred forget
His worth in vain bewailings,
Sweet soul of song ! I own my debt
Uncancelled by his failings."

It was the songs of Burns that first awoke the gift
of song in Whittier. Some of his youthful verses
were printed in the Newburyport " Free Press," then
edited by William Lloyd Garrison, who was only
three years his senior. Young Garrison was the first
to recognize the genius of his unknown contributor,
and one summer day in 1826 he called on the young
poet. John was hoeing in the cornfield, barefooted
and in his shirt-sleeves. He was called to the house,
and dressed himself properly to meet his new friend.
Garrison urged the family to give the boy an education befitting his genius. But the father had not the
means to do so, though he consented to spare him
from the farm, if he could pay his own expenses at
the Haverhill Academy. A laborer in the neighborhood taught him to make slippers retailing at twenty-
five cents a pair, and in the winter of 1826 he earned

enough to buy a suit of clothes and to pay his expenses for six months at the academy. He took up the study of French in addition to the ordinary English branches, and read with avidity all the books that came in his way. He boarded with the editor of the "Haverhill Gazette," and was a great favorite with the young people of the village on account of his courtesy, liveliness, and kindly wit. He was a tall, slender, handsome youth, having attained his full height, five feet ten and a half inches, at the age of fifteen. His complexion was a clear olive, his hair and eyes black.

After a term in the academy, he taught a district school in the winter of 1827 to pay his expenses for another term's tuition. He did not enjoy his experience as a teacher. It was the day of the reign of arithmetic, and the big boys used to bring him mathematical puzzles to work out; to save himself from disgrace in the eyes of his pupils, he spent many a weary night over the solution of these useless problems. Writing to a friend of his future work in November, 1828, he says : —

"School-keeping, out upon it ! The memory of my last year's experience comes up before me like a horrible dream. No, I had rather be a tin-pedler, and drive around the country with a bunch of sheepskins hanging to my wagon. I had rather hawk essences from dwelling to dwelling, or practise physic between Colly Hill and Country Bridge.

" Seriously — the situation of editor of the ' Philanthropist ' is not only respectable, but it is peculiarly pleasant to one who takes so deep an interest as I do in the great cause it is laboring to promote. I would enter upon my task with a heart free from misanthropy, and glowing with that feeling that wishes well to all. I would rather have the memory of a Howard, a Wilberforce, and a Clarkson, than the undying fame of Byron."

Another six months in the Haverhill Academy and his school-days were over. Then he edited a paper in Boston for a short time, but he was needed on the farm and went back home again. He still continued to write, however, and for a time edited the " Haverhill Gazette." In 1830 he went to Hartford to succeed George D. Prentice as editor of the " New England Weekly Review." But after a year and a half he resigned his editorship on account of ill-health, and returned to the farm. His father's death in 1831 left him the main support of his widowed mother and the family. He worked hard and faithfully, now at the plough, now with the pen. Through his strict economy he was always able to save money, and even when earning but nine dollars a week in Boston he was able to save half of it to help to pay off the mortgage on the farm. His ambitions at this time were political and philanthropic. He longed to be in a position to speak and act with power against the curse of slavery. Garrison had begun in 1831 his publication of the " Liberator " with its famous declaration : —

" I will be as harsh as truth, and as uncompromising as justice. I am in earnest, I will not equivocate, I will not excuse, I will not retreat a single inch, and I WILL BE HEARD !"

Whittier, too, *would* be heard. He published at his own expense, in 1833, an antislavery pamphlet, and followed it by frequent newspaper articles on the

subject. Three years later he was made corresponding secretary of the Haverhill antislavery society.
The word "abolitionist" was then a hated one, and in making his opinions public, Whittier several times incurred the dangers which arise from infuriated mobs. He was once pelted with rotten eggs, mud, and stones. In 1838, while editing the "Pennsylvania Freeman" in Philadelphia, his printing-office was burned by a mob. "For twenty years," he writes to a friend in 1866, "I was shut out from the favor of book-sellers and magazine editors, but I was enabled by rigid economy to live in spite of them, — and to see the end of the infernal institution which proscribed me. Thank God for it." In memory of this long struggle and its triumphant close, Whittier once said to a boy: "My lad, if thou wouldst win success, join thyself to some unpopular but noble cause."

In 1839 we find the Whittier family removed to Amesbury, where a cottage had been bought from the proceeds of the sale of the farm three years before. This cottage continued to be Whittier's home for the rest of his life. He never married, and after the death of his mother his housekeeper for a number of years was his younger sister, Elizabeth, a brilliant and noble-hearted woman, between whom and her brother there existed the tenderest affection. Her death in 1864 was a blow from which he never fully recovered.

The first complete edition of Whittier's poems was published in 1857. His antislavery poems had appeared in 1849, under the title of "Voices of Freedom," but it was not until 1866 that his masterpiece,

"Snowbound," was given to the world. There is not in our language a more exquisite poem descriptive of domestic joys and sorrows than "Snowbound." It is a bit of New England country life transfigured by immortal verse. It is no picture of the imagination; it is as real as the soil under our feet. It is a man's recollections of the home of his boyhood, — a man upon whom the snows of age are beginning to fall, but so lightly that they have no power to chill the warmth of his heart or the glow of his fancy. It is a description of the home from whence come the sinews and brain of our nation; a home in which character can ripen; in which duty and labor have a large part to play; in which the inmates, dependent upon one another for solace and happiness, are bound together by ties of deathless affection; in which the pleasures are of that innocent, wholesome character that leaves no bitter after-sting of regret or weariness; in which nature seems large because it is close at hand, and the world's tumult small, because its echoes, softened by distance, hardly reach the inattentive ear.

"Snowbound" is rich in beautiful character sketches. The duty-loving father and mother, with their stories of early days; the dear aunt in whom

> "The morning dew that dries so soon
> With others, glistened at her noon;"

the elder sister with "full rich nature," and the youngest and dearest, in whose death the poet felt "a loss in all familiar things;" the genial uncle "innocent of books," but "rich in lore of fields and brooks;" the young schoolmaster, "large-brained, clear-eyed;" the stranger guest, — all these are drawn with exquisite precision and delicacy. "Snowbound" found its way at once to the heart of the public and has never left it. It was followed in 1867 by the "Tent on the Beach," a collection of poetic tales feigned to be related by the poet and his two friends, Bayard Taylor and James T. Fields, while encamped on Salisbury Beach.

Among Whittier's minor poems the following have always been popular favorites, and show the poet at his best: "The Barefoot Boy," "Maud Muller," "Barbara Frietchie," whose story was communicated to the poet by Mrs. Southworth, the novelist, "Mary Garvin," "The Witch's Daughter," "Telling the Bees," "The Robin," "Hampton Beach," "In School Days," "My Psalm," "My Triumph," "The Eternal Goodness," "Last Walk in Autumn," "Ichabod," and "Skipper Ireson's Ride."

No American poet has so thoroughly infused his own personality into his work as Whittier. In all that he has written, and he has written much prose as well as poetry, there is a distinctively individual note, quickly recognizable to the lover of Whittier, and endearing him more and more to the poet, as he learns the rarity and fineness of it. There was in him a remarkable blending of Quaker severity and chasteness with the poet's susceptibility and passionate love of beauty; a tolerance wide as the world for all human frailties and human doubts, and a faith in God as simple and unquestioning as a little child's; a nervous sensitiveness almost fastidious, and yet so sane and tender a love for all simple, homely joys, — so restful a calm sought and kept amidst all the poetic oscillations of a fiery spirit.

He has given us in his poem "My Namesake" an analysis of himself which is remarkably true : —

> "In him the grave and playful mixed,
>   And wisdom held with folly truce,
>   And nature compromised betwixt
>   Good fellow and recluse.
>   .   .   .   .
> "He loved the good and wise, but found
>   His human heart to all akin
>   Who met him on the common ground
>   Of suffering and of sin.
>   .   .   .   .   .
> "His eye was beauty's powerless slave,
>   And his the ear which discord pains,
>   Few guessed beneath his aspect grave
>   What passions strove in chains.
>
> "He had his share of care and pain,
>   No holiday was life to him ;
>   Still in the heirloom cup we drain,
>   The bitter drop will swim.
>
> "Yet heaven was kind, and here a bird
>   And there a flower beguiled his way ;
>   And, cool, in summer noons, he heard
>   The fountains plash and play.
>
> "On all his sad or restless moods
>   The patient peace of nature stole ;
>   The quiet of the fields and woods
>   Sank deep into his soul.
>
> "He worshipped as his fathers did,
>   And kept the faith of childish days,
>   And, howsoe'er he strayed or slid.
>   He loved the good old ways,
>
> "The simple tastes, the kindly traits,
>   The tranquil air and gentle speech,
>   The silence of the soul that waits
>   For more than man to teach."

Whittier's health was never robust, yet in spite of his semi-invalidism he lived to be eighty-five, suffering a light stroke of paralysis shortly before his death, which occurred on the seventh of September, 1892.

"I inherited from my parents," he says, "a nervous headache, and on account of it have never been able to do all I wished to do." In middle and later life he could not read or write for half an hour without severe pain. He suffered, too, from a frequent pain in the region of the heart; any little excitement, an animated conversation, the presence of strangers, brought on these severe headaches and pains and drove him into solitude to avoid them. This shrinking from society was often wrongly attributed to shyness. He was a poor sleeper but an early riser, and we are told that in forty years he rarely missed seeing the sun rise. He was color-blind, being wholly unable to distinguish green from red. S. T. Pickard, his biographer, relates that his mother discovered this defect when he was a little boy picking wild strawberries. He could see no difference between the color of the berry and that of the leaf. Only white or yellow roses were pretty to him, and the golden-rod was his favorite flower. The autumn foliage had no beauty of color to him unless yellows predominated in it, and the radiantly colored rainbow looked to him like a bright yellow arch. He was partially deaf after middle life, and took refuge in this deafness at times to excuse himself from taking part in conversations that bored him; for like all men who have made their mark in the world, he had to pay the penalty of publicity by obtrusive visits from curious and impertinent sight-seers. Says Pickard: —

"It would be a mistake to suppose that gentleness was a necessity of his nature; it was in reality the result of resolute self-control and the habitual government of a tempestuous spirit. He was quick and nervous in movement, but never otherwise than dignified and graceful. In conversation he spoke slowly and with precision, hesitating occasionally without the slighest nervousness for the word he wanted. . . . He religiously curbed his tongue, and said of himself that he was born without an atom of patience in his composition, but that he had tried to manufacture it as needed."

In early youth he habitually wore the Quaker gray, but later wore no outward sign of his faith but a black broadcloth coat cut in Quaker style. But he clung all his life to the Quaker form of speech, the familiar thee and thou which he had learned at his mother's knee; and he clung with the same tenacity to the simple and early forms of Quaker worship. In a letter addressed to the editor of the " Friends' Review " in Philadelphia, he says in regard to some changes in the Society: —

"There is a growing desire for experimenting upon the dogmas and expedients and practices of the sects. . . . But for myself I prefer the old ways. With the broadest possible tolerance for all honest seekers after truth, I love the Society of Friends. My life has been nearly spent in laboring with those of other sects in behalf of the suffering and enslaved; and I have never felt like quarrelling with Orthodox or Unitarian who were willing to pull with me side by side at the rope of Reform. A very large proportion of my dearest personal friends are outside of our communion; and I have learned with John Woolman to find ' no narrowness respecting sects and opinions.' But with a kindly and candid survey of them all, I turn to my own Society, thankful to the

Divine Providence which placed me where I am; and with an unshaken faith in the one distinctive doctrine of Quakerism — the light within — the immanence of the Divine Spirit in Christianity."

Whittier never went to a theatre or a circus in his life. On his first visit to Boston as a boy, he promised his mother that he would not go to the theatre, and he kept the promise as long as he lived. He was no traveller in foreign countries, and did not think that he had lost much of the world's beauty by seeing no country but his own, since

> " he who wanders widest lifts
> No more of beauty's jealous veils
> Than he who from his doorway sees
> The miracle of flowers and trees,
> Feels the warm Orient in the noonday air,
> And from cloud-minarets hears the sunset call to prayer."

He had a quaint frankness of speech that often amused his friends. Mrs. Fields relates that once when pressed to stay as a guest after he had risen to go, he replied to his host's question, " *Why* can't you stay? " "Because, I tell you, I don't want to." He heartily disliked being a chief object of interest anywhere, and much preferred the society of children and young people to that of effusive literary admirers. He liked the old English classics, and especially enjoyed reading Milton's prose. He liked strength in repose, not in tumult. "Elizabeth has been reading Browning's poem (Men and Women), and she tells me it is great," he writes to a friend. "I have only dipped into it here and there, but it is not exactly comfortable reading. It seemed to me like a galvanic battery in full play — its spasmodic utterances and intense passion make me feel as if I had been taking a bath among electric eels. But I have not read enough to criticise."

His own literary method is as far as possible removed from this. It grew out of his life: —

> " No dreamer [he] but real all, —
> Strong manhood crowning vigorous youth,
> Life made by duty epical
> And rhythmic with the truth."

And elsewhere he sings : —

> "Better to stem with heart and hand
> The roaring tide of life, than lie
> Unmindful, on its flowery strand,
> Of God's occasions drifting by !
> Better with naked nerve to bear
> The needles of this goading air,
> Than, in the lap of sensual ease, forego
> · The godlike power to do, the godlike power to know."

Whittier used his poetic gift, as we have seen, in the service of liberty, and when that service was over, he used it to give expression to what he saw of pure and good in life and nature, — to sing his own deep faith and trust and calm, and his gratitude for all the sweet, free, common gifts of life. To read him is like taking a solitary walk at sunset in summer, along a high ridge with a glorious sweep of radiant sky bending over fields of ripening grain and deep green, distant woodland. The bustle and heat and glare of day are over, and as we yield to the sweet influence of the beautiful hour, we taste again the exquisite serenity of perfect possession of ourselves. It is as if we were penetrated by some subtle, holy influence,

— a sacred hush in which all restlessness is stilled, all desires dead, yet the ecstasy of life thrills every nerve; we drink deep, full draughts of it, and feel *clean* through and through.　We have come under the influence of the poet's

> " prayer of Plato old,
> God make thee beautiful within;
> And let thine eyes the good behold
> In everything save sin."

The poet who can influence us in this way has an assured place in the literature of the world.

CHAPTER XII

IT often happens that certain traits of character or peculiarities of disposition, ugly and repulsive in themselves, are associated with some graces of person or wonderful mental gifts that blind us to their true nature. Instead of any longer repelling us, they are sources of a mysterious fascination. We do not love the possessor less but more for them. The egotism we laugh at and depise in Boswell, we admire and stand in awe of in sturdy Sam Johnson, and dearly love in such amiable egotists as Charles Lamb and La Fontaine. The more they speak of themselves, the more they delight us. Their egotism has the innocence and freshness of childhood, and appeals to our common human nature in the same artless and lovable way. Even the imperfections of such men as Burns soften reproach into pity, and teach us the charity that suffereth long and is kind.

Probably no man ever stood in greater need of that charity, or ever received more of it, than Edgar A. Poe. Of brilliant but erratic genius; inheriting an unfortunate temperament, the legacy of the unnatural and irregular life of his parents; spoiled by indulgence in his childhood; left to his own resources in manhood; isolated from his kind by want of sympathy with their aims and pursuits, — his life was a tragedy, in memory of which censure grows mute, and sympathy is apt to become an unwise admiration.   What the man really did is lost sight of in what he might have done.   The fascination of a personality so extraordinary and difficult to understand is blended with the estimate of his genius, and unduly enhances it.   In bright sunlight objects are seen with a distinctness that brings out every spot, every protuberance, and leaves nothing to illusion.   It is the dim light of a misty morning that gives confused and enlarged images, and leads us to suspect unknown forms in a vague background that leaves all to the imagination. Viewed in an analogous way, Edgar A. Poe is regarded by many critics, especially in France, as the most original and powerful genius America has produced.   But in the light of the most intelligent modern criticism, this estimate shrinks to true proportions.   Genius is not denied him; but far from being of the highest order, it is seen to be very narrow in its range, and within that range morbid and analytic rather than sound and creative.   An unprejudiced study of his life and works cannot fail to make the truth of this assertion apparent.

Edgar Allan Poe was born in Boston on the nineteenth of January, 1809.   On his father's side he was a descendant of General David Poe, a hero of the Revolution, the sod of whose grave Lafayette once kissed as he said, "A noble heart rests here."   On his mother's side he was descended from a family of English actresses.   His mother, Elizabeth Arnold, married Mr. Hopkins, a member of the troupe to which she belonged; later, as Widow Hopkins, she captivated David Poe, and was married to him within a month of her first husband's death. David Poe was never more than a third-rate actor, having abandoned the study of law to go upon the stage, much against the wishes of his family. But Mrs. Poe, a piquant, arch little woman, was an actress of some ability in light comedy and melodrama. Three children were born to them: William, Edgar, and Rosalie. From Boston, where they remained three years, the Poes went to New York and subsequently South, where their poverty and misfortunes attracted the charitable notice of the public of Richmond, Virginia. Mrs. Poe was taken ill and died in Richmond. Her husband had died of consumption shortly before, and the three orphan children were left to the care of charity. The eldest boy, William, fell to the charge of a friend of the father's in Baltimore; a lady in Richmond took charge of Rosalie, and Edgar was adopted by Mr. John Allan and his wife, who had no children of their own. Mr. John Allan was a Scotchman and a wealthy tobacco-merchant. The pretty and precocious boy was petted and made much of by the Allan family and their friends.

In 1815 Mr. Allan took his wife and Edgar to England, and placed the latter in the Manor House School, Stoke Newington, a London suburb. Traces of his pleasant remembrance of this school are to be found in the tale "William Wilson," where he writes lovingly of the "old, large, rambling Elizabethan house," and speaks of the dreamlike and spirit-soothing influences of the venerable old town.

"The ardor, the enthusiasm, the imperiousness of my disposition rendered me a marked character among my schoolmates," he writes. His teachers thought him a clever lad, but spoiled by too liberal an allowance of pocket-money. He remained five years in this school. On his return to Richmond, in 1820, he was sent to school in that city. Though he was a leader among his fellow-students, both in scholarship and athletic sports, his self-will, caprice, and fitful temper made him unpopular. When, through misconduct, he had justly incurred punishment at school, his foster-parents indignantly resented his being punished, and thus further increased his naturally wayward and wilful disposition. He had, too, that reserve which precludes close intimacy, and is sometimes the result of shrinking delicacy and sometimes the result of pride. In Edgar A. Poe it was, undoubtedly, pride, — a mingling of boundless pride in his gifts as if they set him apart from his associates, and a haughty indifference to the claims of others. "My whole nature utterly revolts," he once said in later life, "at the idea that there is any being in the universe superior to *myself.*" His foster-parents were kind, liberal, even unwisely indulgent to him, but he seems to have felt himself an alien, and no real heart-tie of gratitude or affection bound him to them.

He entered the University of Virginia in 1826, and pursued his study of the ancient and modern languages. He joined the fun-loving set of students, and became addicted to the vice of gambling. He was a reckless player, and incurred a debt of twenty-five hundred dollars, which his foster-father refused to pay. Moreover, when he went home in December, Mr. Allan put him to office work instead of permitting him to return to the University. The work was displeasing to him, and in a fit of petulance he left Richmond for Boston, with a collection of youthful poems, which he succeeded in getting published under the name of "Tamerlane and Other Poems." The volume brought him neither reputation nor money, and poor, friendless, and solitary, he enlisted at eighteen in the army of the United States, giving his age as twenty-two and his name as Edgar A. Perry. He must have faithfully discharged his duties, for in 1829 he was made sergeant-major.

Learning of his enlistment and service, Mr. Allan procured his discharge by substitute and sent him to West Point. Before going there, Poe published a long poem of no merit called "Al Aaraaf."

At West Point he showed a particular aptitude for French and mathematics, but was neglectful of military duties, absenting himself at pleasure from roll-calls and drills. Any form of restraint was particularly distasteful to him, and six months of service satisfied him that life at West Point was wholly unsuited to his disposition, and he systematically set himself to incurring charges for dismissal.

He was tried for offenses against discipline, found guilty and dismissed penniless. About the time of Poe's admission to the academy, Mr. Allan, whose wife had died some time before, married again, and Poe, who had conducted himself so ungratefully toward his foster-father, soon discovered that he had nothing to hope from him in the way of inheritance or of immediate assistance. He published a second and subscription edition of his poems, to which new ones were added, and with the small sum received he went to Baltimore. There he made several unsuccessful attempts to find employment. At last an offer of one hundred dollars for a prize story in the "Saturday Visitor," edited by Lambert A. Wilmer, attracted his notice. He sent a number of tales, of which the "Manuscript Found in a Bottle" received the first prize. This bit of good fortune relieved him for a time from the wretched poverty in which he had been living. His aunt, Mrs. Clemm, his father's sister, took him into her house to board, and there he made the acquaintance of his child-cousin, Virginia Clemm, whom he afterward married.

In 1835 he removed from Baltimore to Richmond, having secured employment on the "Southern Literary Messenger" at a salary of ten dollars a week. His marriage to his cousin, who was not quite fourteen at the time, took place the next year, and Mrs. Clemm accompanied her daughter to Richmond, hoping to add to the income of the little household by keeping boarders.

Poe's literary ability soon made itself felt. He undertook the editorship of the "Literary Messenger," and wrote for its pages a number of his weird tales and much of his trenchant criticism. Unfortunately, those intemperate habits which ultimately led to his ruin were already fixed upon him, and his connection with the "Messenger" was of short continuance. It is said that no one could work more faithfully and regularly than Poe under the stress of necessity; but he belonged to that unfortunate class whom prosperity renders madly capricious and self-indulgent.　No one could do more than temporarily aid him, for the element of self-destruction lay within himself.　His connection with the "Messenger" was severed in 1837, and he went to New York. There, in the following year, he published his longest story, "The Narrative of Arthur Gordon Pym."　It was not a successful financial venture, and Poe left New York for Philadelphia to work on the "Gentleman's Magazine."　His irregular habits in a short time caused his dismissal.　He found work again on "Graham's Magazine," and about this time wrote some of his best short stories: "The Gold Bug," "The Fall of the House of Usher," "The Murders in the Rue Morgue," and "The Mystery of Marie Roget."

After six years' stay in Philadelphia, Poe returned to New York in 1844, and for a short time worked for N. P. Willis on the "Evening Mirror."　His poem, "The Raven," was published in this paper in 1845.　It attracted wide-spread notice, and in the same year another edition of his poems appeared, containing all his later and now better known work.　His literary reputation was now of such a character that he might have easily earned a comfortable income, but it was just at this period that the severest distress of his life began.　He moved into a little frame cottage at Fordham, just out of the city.　His wife, who had broken a blood-vessel while singing, was frail and ailing and threatened with death from consumption.　Writing of the agony he endured at this time, Poe says: "I am constitutionally sensitive — nervous in a very unusual degree.　I became insane, with long intervals of horrible sanity." This is, perhaps, the most charitable as well as the truest explanation of those incessant fits of intemperance that drove him from paper to paper, and involved him in quarrels with all who tried to befriend him.   His extreme poverty and the sufferings of his invalid wife were dragged into the glare of publicity by that pseudo-charity which is always so extremely solicitous that the left hand shall know all that the right hand doeth.   The proud-spirited poet bore this humiliation with a manly attempt to conceal his real condition, but it was only too apparent.

In January, 1847, his wife died, and after this event a marked intellectual decline was noticeable in him; and he was, undoubtedly, not responsible for his irrational behavior toward two women whom he wished to marry and to whom he wrote frantic and despairing love-letters.   During all this time he was the object of the devoted love and care of one woman, to whom, more than to any other, he owed all the happiness that life had ever brought him.   That woman was Mrs. Clemm, his aunt and the mother of his wife.   She sat by him in the long watches of the night while he worked at a new book of which he entertained the most extravagant hopes.   He told Putnam, the publisher, that the book contained discoveries of more interest and importance than the discovery of gravitation.   He called the new book "Eureka: A Prose Poem," and said of it: "What I have propounded will in good time revolutionize the world of physical and metaphysical science."   But the book attracted no attention.

In the fall of 1849 Poe visited Richmond in order to make arrangements for his marriage to a lady of that city. On his return home, he stopped at Baltimore. Of what befell him there, little is positively known beyond the sad fact of his death at a hospital on Sunday, the seventh of October, 1849. Many years after his death, the physician who attended him at the hospital made public a statement with reference to his condition at that time. According to that statement, Poe was found in a stupor lying on a bench in front of a mercantile house. He was not recognized until ten o'clock A. M., although he had been lying there since early morning, the subject of the idle curiosity of gathering crowds. No smell of liquor was perceived on his breath or clothing. He was taken to a hospital, and when aroused from his stupor, he showed consciousness of his strange surroundings, but lapsed into a delirium and spoke incoherently. Just before his death, he revived and said: "Doctor, it is all over; write Eddy is no more." He was buried in Baltimore the next day, and his grave was left unmarked by a stone until 1875. Mrs. Clemm survived the poet twenty years, and dying at the same hospital in Baltimore, was buried, as she had requested, by his side.

According to Mrs. Clemm, the poet at home "was simple and affectionate as a child, and during all the years that he lived with me," she adds, "I do not remember a single night that he failed to come and kiss his ' mother,' as he called me, before going to bed." The testimony of other women who enjoyed his friendship shows that he must have been singularly winning and gracious in manner when he chose to be. Then, too, his handsome person created a favorable impression for him independent of his gifts. He was of slender build, and five feet eight inches tall. His soft, black, curly hair framed a pallid, melancholy face lighted by luminous, dark eyes. He very likely portrayed his own physical features with some slight idealization in his description of Roderick Usher. It is worthy of remark that the description of Ligeia's personal beauty closely follows that of Roderick Usher. There is the same pallor, the same lofty brow, jetty hair, Hebraic outline of nose, and luminous black eyes. These were also characteristic features of his wife's beauty, and he was evidently partial to them.

But though Poe seems to have been capable of warm, domestic affections and sentimental friendships for women, he made few friends among men, and was by temperament one of those unfortunates who are shut out from their kind by almost complete self-absorption. The largest natures are those of widest sympathy. They typify the race, not an idiosyncrasy. They understand its healthy desires, its aspirations, its sorrows, its joys, its weakness, and its strength. Nothing that is human is alien to them. They absorb by sympathy the experiences of all with whom they come in contact. Heart and intellect are enriched by this quick susceptibility and ready assimilation. That is the reason that if we wish to praise a man's acuteness and sanity of intellect, even in common social life, we say, "He understands human nature." It is said of Count Cavour, Prime Minister of Italy, that he seemed to take pleasure in everything, and had the gift which cannot be acquired, of being within reach of every one. The commonest, most ignorant day-laborer felt at home with him by an instinctive consciousness of his large humanity. He was not one man but many men. If to this gift of large humanity there be added the gifts of imaginative vigor and musical speech, we shall have genius of the highest order, — the genius of Homer, Shakespeare, Goethe. There is no question here of the sanity of genius. These men typify intellect in its clearest and highest form.

But there is another order of mind and temperament exactly the opposite of this. The eye in this case is turned inward, not outward. The mind is imprisoned within a narrow circle of ideas. Instead of that warm love of humanity that leads to a broad, sympathetic understanding of our common nature, distrust and suspicion lead to indifference and hatred. Human nature is comprehended not in its strength and nobility, but in its weakness and degradation. In such a temperament the heat and ferment of the imagination is mistaken for warmth of heart and feeling. The victim of this morbid temperament lives in a fantastic dream world, and because he cannot reconcile the world of his imagination with that of reality, and has not the will-power or the inclination to abandon the unreal for the real, he suffers daily from shattered illusions, and ends in misanthropy and pessimism, if not in downright madness. All his sympathies are with revolt and emotionalism. He lives in sensations and reverie, not in action and thought. The genius of such men is of that type that is allied to madness.

Their works may have the charm of exquisite diction and wonderful analytic skill; but the analysis is confined to that of self-torturing emotions, or depraved and criminal impulses. Another remarkable limitation of this morbid intellectual power is an absence of anything like humor. The laughter of these men is sardonic, a convulsion and not the natural relief of a tickled midriff. Rousseau, Chateaubriand, Senancour and St. Pierre are the most striking examples in foreign literature of this type of genius, and Edgar A. Poe is the most striking example in the literature of America. But though essentially of the same type, Poe's genius manifested itself in a manner peculiar to himself, and in a marked degree influenced by his era and the spirit of his country. The peculiar form of the sentimentalism of Rousseau and his followers — its exaggerated estimate of the passion of love, its melancholy, its restlessness and discontent — belongs to the eighteenth century and to France. The nineteenth century, with its scientific discoveries, exciting curiosity, and directing the attention from the individual himself to that which is without him, has furnished new and widely different subjects of study. Then, too, the absence of any insurmountable barrier of caste in America, and the consequent possibility of gratifying worthy aspirations by honest effort, removes any legitimate cause, with regard to existing institutions, for envious dissatisfaction and sullen resentment. Poe's works, therefore, are neither in subject-matter nor in style at all like those of the great French sentimentalists; but he belongs to their order of genius by reason of a certain moral obliquity or perverseness, an impatience of law and order, a self-will, caprice, and passion that mark a highly excitable and diseased nervous organization.

Poe's literary work covers three distinct fields, — poetry, fiction, and criticism. It was as a critic that he first attracted attention, as a writer of tales that he first established a reputation for original genius, and as a poet that he was most ambitious to be remembered and is at present most widely known. A brief consideration of his work in these three departments of literature will give a sufficiently clear idea of the peculiarities of his genius.

Poe's strongest and most characteristic work is to be found in his prose tales. These tales, with few exceptions, are stories of impossible adventures told with grave minuteness of detail, or studies of crime and incipient madness. Poe had no humor, and the few sketches he has written with the intention of being funny are as feeble and arrant nonsense as ever was penned. But he is anything but feeble on his own ground. His analysis of monomania reads like the pages of a pathological journal and affects the reader like a visit to a mad-house. The circumstantial fidelity of his adventurous narratives sometimes surprised unthinking readers into a belief that they were true. The balloon hoax, for example, an account of a journey performed by balloon from an estate in North Wales to Charleston, was published in the "New York Sun" under sensational head-lines and was for a time actually believed. Poe delighted in mystifications of this sort, and diligently read scientific works in order

to give an air of probability to what he wrote.
"The Adventures of Hans Pfaal" is an account of
a journey to the moon in a balloon.   "Von Kempe-
len and his Discovery" is a feigned account of the
discovery of the philosopher's stone, by which lead
may be turned into gold.   "The Manuscript Found
in a Bottle" is the story of a sailor who was storm-
tossed from his own ship to a phantom ship and
went down in a whirlpool near the south pole.
The theme of another tale, entitled "The Descent
into the Maelstrom," is sufficiently indicated by the
title.   "The Narrative of Arthur Gordon Pym" is
the story of the horrible adventures that befell a
shipwrecked crew after mutiny among the sailors.
Cannibalism and its horrors, a ship with putrescent
corpses floating upon the waste of waters, are
some of the loathsome incidents with which the
story is crowded.   All the wonderful scientific discoveries and inventions of the age give him hints for
the "Thousand and Second Tale of Scheherazade."
"The Gold Bug" is the account of the discovery of
Captain Kidd's treasure under a tulip-tree, by means
of the chance finding of a piece of parchment on
which the hiding-place of the treasure was indicated
by cipher.   Poe had a remarkable talent for decipher-
ing cryptographs, and a great many specimens of
cipher writing were sent him to be read.   Mystery
in any direction fascinated him, because it brought
into action his wonderful analytic skill.   The story
of the "Murders in the Rue Morgue" reveals the
analytic power of a young Frenchman, who dis-
covers that the perpetrator of a horrible murder in
Paris is an orang-outang escaped from a Maltese

sailor. This young Frenchman's morbid love of darkness is illustrated in a remarkable manner. He closes all his shutters in daylight, draws the curtains, and lights candles; but when real night comes, he opens his shutters, puts out his candles, and sallies forth for a walk.

This trait is admirably symbolic of Poe's own genius. Turning away from the bright, wholesome sunshine of life, scornful of all that gives warmth, color and joy to it, he gropes in the chill gloom of night. He burrows into the cryptlike recesses of the human heart and draws forth its mould and decay. To do him justice, he leaves untouched its grosser foulness and corruption. A fine sense of decency, the instincts of a gentleman, kept him clean of the stain of obscenity. "Let what is to be said, be said plainly. True; but let nothing vulgar be ever said or conceived!" he once wrote of a poet who had offended decency; and he followed his own dictum.

"The Mystery of Marie Roget" is the unravelling of another murder case, the particulars of which were actually reported in the daily papers at the time in which it was written. "The Purloined Letter" is another clever detective story. In this story Poe denies that mathematical studies develop the reasoning faculties. "Mathematical truths," he says, "are only truths within the limits of relation," "finite truths," as it were.

"The Black Cat" is the story of the crimes of a man driven insane by the intemperate use of alcohol. The criminal relates his own story, and it is remarkable for its faithful portrayal of the growth of criminal impulse in association with the ruin of the mind.   The dominance of a fixed idea; the helplessness of a broken will in the storm of wayward and morbid impulses; the frightful change of all the sweet affections of the heart into cruel hatred; the apathy following the commission of the crime; the hideous vanity that exults in its perpetration are well known to pathologists.   Another story of a deliberately planned murder under the dominion of a wicked impulse, and then a confession of the crime induced by an equally irresistible impulse, is related in "The Imp of the Perverse."   In this story Poe says:—

"I am not more certain that I breathe than that the assurance of the wrong or error of any action is often the one unconquerable *force* which impels us, and alone impels us, to its prosecution.   Nor will this overwhelming tendency to do wrong for the wrong's sake admit of analysis or resolution to ulterior elements.   It is a radical, a primitive impulse, elementary."

This statement is made in ignorance of the fact that though such impulses to perversity undeniably exist, they do *not* accompany a sound and mature organization.   They indicate disease or weakness, and accompany the morbid conditions of hysteria and insanity, or the weakness of immaturity and ignorance.   It cannot be too often repeated that morality is simply obedience to law recognized or unrecognized.   Organic beings are no more exempt than the universe from the dominion of law.   All right living, all individual and social progress depend upon conformity to law, not caprice.   Says Maudsley:—

"Good moral feeling is to be looked upon as an essential part of a sound and rightly developed character in the present state of human evolution in civilized lands: its acquisition is the condition of development in the progress of humanization. Whoever is destitute of it is to that extent a defective being; he marks the beginning of race degeneracy."

In "Berenice," a story of catalepsy and monomania, Poe makes his hero say: "In the strange anomaly of my existence, feelings with me *had never been* of the heart, and my passions *always were* of the mind." This anomalous trait is curiously characteristic of Rousseau and his school, of whom it was said that they had no real or lasting attachment to any but the persons of their own invention, nor sincere affection for anything but nature, in whose name they adored their own moods and feelings.

Loathsome stories of metempsychosis, mesmerism, and pestilence are to be found among other tales that Poe has written; but enough has been said of his fictitious work to show its pathological character, and to suggest that the intellect which could delight in and produce it was perilously near the morbid state it could so faithfully depict. He, too, knew that nameless terror that haunted Roderick Usher. We know from Mrs. Clemm that he had a childish fear of the dark, and would not stay alone at night. With him, too, feelings were of the mind, not the heart. Outside of his narrow household no tie of love or gratitude could bind him long. And for this reason, Lowell, whom he attacked after valuable services rendered him, said that he "was wholly lacking in that element of manhood which for want of a better name we call character." He was untruthful and the slave of his impulses. But while this admission is made, the pity of it must silence censure on the lips of every generous reader. When we know why the rose has its canker and the lily its worm, we shall know why genius, the fairest gift to man, may be poisoned in its sources, and then we may pronounce judgment.

As a critic, Poe has left no work valuable in itself, — partly because he chose especially to review the works of those of his contemporaries who deserved to be forgotten, and partly because he misconceived the true spirit of criticism. He believed that criticism should busy itself with defects, not excellences, because excellence is not excellence if it requires pointing out. On the contrary, the chief business of criticism is not to point out defects, but to point out excellences, on the principle that a beautiful object is more worthy of attention than an ugly one, and that perfect taste is cultivated by the study of what is beautiful and not of what is ugly. It is not true that excellence is not excellence if it needs pointing out. The perfect taste that can discern beauty in simplicity and strength in quiet harmony, is the fruit of long and patient training, and they are few who acquire it. The uneducated taste delights in gaudy coloring and profuse ornamentation, and mistakes convulsive activity for strength. This is the taste of the vast majority of readers, to correct which by dwelling upon the beauty of classic models is the chief task of the critic. If it is none the less his duty to point out defects, it is still a secondary duty, because the mind that has once apprehended a type of ideal beauty has within itself a standard by which to measure what is presented to its consideration.

But Poe's criticism was not based upon a sincere wish to correct public taste by furnishing it with such a type. There was more of perversity than honesty in it, and it consists almost wholly of censure and ridicule, rarely of praise. The charge of plagiarism on grounds the most absurd and far-fetched, is so frequently made that it would be laughable if it were not an indication of lamentable weakness. But Poe was by no means devoid of a natural feeling for what is strong and fine in literature, and no clamor of popular applause deafened him to the false ring of what would fain pass for sterling coin. This critical instinct and his absolute fearlessness might have made him a power in American literature at a time when real criticism did not exist in it. But unfortunately his distrust, or his envy, of popularity degenerated into a belief that a popular writer was necessarily a worthless writer, and he criticised indiscriminately in accordance with this opinion. He attacked Longfellow and Lowell, and wrote always with rude scorn of the Transcendentalists, — or "muddle-pates," as he called them, — spoke contemptuously of Carlyle, but praised Hawthorne, whom the public ignored, though he denied him originality and likened him to Tieck. Of Wordsworth he could make nothing; but he revered Coleridge, and thought Tennyson "the noblest poet that ever lived."

Poe was guided in his criticisms by a few principles afterward summed up in his essays, "The Philosophy of Composition" and "The Poetic Principle." These critical principles deserve examination in so much as they help us to an estimate of his own work, from which he evidently deduced them.

The object of poetry he conceives to be beauty, not truth, and to give pleasure, not instruction. An epic or a long poem is "a flat contradiction in terms," because "all high excitements are necessarily transient. Thus a long poem is a paradox." For the same reason he contends that the short prose tale is superior to the long work of fiction. Music he called "the perfection of the soul or idea of poetry," and affirms it of "so vast a moment to poesy as never to be neglected by him who is truly poetical." As for truth, that is altogether of minor importance. "That the chief merit of a picture is its truth is an assertion deplorably erroneous. . . . If truth is the highest aim of either painting or poesy, then Jan Steen was a greater artist than Angelo, and Crabbe is a more noble poet than Milton." Of beauty he says that, "whatever its kind, in its supreme development it invariably excites the sensitive soul to tears. Melancholy is therefore the most legitimate of all poetical tones." He declares humor to be "directly antagonistic to that which is the soul of the muse proper."

Let us examine these principles, and learn in what degree they underlie the recognized masterpieces of art. To say that a long poem cannot exist because the elevating excitement which a true poem creates cannot be sustained for any length of time, is to confound a work of art with a condition of mental susceptibility. It is equivalent to saying that the pictures in an art-gallery are no longer works of art because the eye wearies of pictures before it has seen them all, or that the myriad-starred sky is not a sublime spectacle because it arches above us night after night, and the wonder of it is lost in familiarity, — just as the marvellous beauty of Alpine sunsets is lost on the eye of the peasant that looks on them daily. The Iliad and the Odyssey, " Paradise Lost," and the " Divine Comedy" are none the less poems because they cannot be read at a sitting.

Moreover, the idea that a poem is of necessity the production of "a high excitement necessarily transient" is a very false one. Poe himself, in his account of the composition of the " Raven," the most successful of his poems, shows that it was not dashed off at a heat, but was the slow and labored result of deliberate and logical thought. He carefully selected the theme and refrain, aiming from the first at a certain effect. The stanza beginning " Prophet, said I, thing of evil!" was written first, to establish a climax. His own verses were not, therefore, the spontaneous outpourings of his heart, the musical products of high and transient excitements; they were fantastic compositions deliberately planned and composed after set theories.

Sidney Lanier, the young Georgia poet and critic, who died in 1881 with half the music in him yet unuttered, took pains to teach his hearers, in his Johns Hopkins lectures, that poetry is not the product of a frenzy, but of the sanest, coolest wisdom;

that it is not at all antagonistic to science, but draws its deepest inspirations from the profoundest knowledge. "Genius, the great artist," he says, "never works in the frantic vein, vulgarly supposed; a large part of the work of the poet, for example, is selecting; a dozen ideas in a dozen forms throng to his brain at once; he must choose the best; even in the extremest heat and sublimity of his *raptus*, he must preserve a godlike calm. . . . 'He who will not answer to the rudder must answer to the rocks.'" Poe himself, when it answered his purpose in critical articles, declared that poetry has nothing to do with profound emotion. "We agree," he says, "with Coleridge, that poetry and passion are discordant;" and elsewhere he repeats: "It is precisely this unpassionate emotion which is the limit of the true poetical art. Passion proper and poesy are discordant. Poetry in elevating tranquillizes *the soul*. With *the heart* it has nothing to do."

But if we accept his other theory, which certainly contradicts this one, how are we to classify the beautiful "Elegy in a Country Churchyard" which Gray was so many years in writing, or that exquisite series of pictures, reflections, and sentiments which makes up Goldsmith's "Deserted Village" and "The Traveller," Goethe's "Hermann and Dorothea," or Whittier's "Snowbound"? Were these the products of high and transient excitements, and do they require a similar state of mind for their enjoyment? To apply such a test as this to poetry would exclude from that title nearly all the verse that ever was written.

Poe's argument for the superiority of the short

prose tale over the longer work of fiction is equally indefensible. Admirable as the short prose tale may be, it reveals neither the imaginative vigor, power of reasoning, versatility, nor knowledge of the world implied in a long work of fiction of the highest type. Says the great French critic, Edmond Scherer: —

" A well-written novel is a biography. We witness the development of a principal character whom the incidents of the story but serve to bring out into relief. The chief character alternately rules and submits to the events around which are grouped other characters who influence his destiny. Art in this species of writing consists in giving to the invention of facts and the portrayal of character all the variety that is compatible with biographical unity. The more varied and interesting the details in themselves thus revealing the author's inventive resources and the correctness of his observation, the more the characters will be distinguished, — but always on the condition that these details are subordinated to the aim, which is, I repeat, the exhibition of one sovereign personality."

Now, this development of character, this reaction of thought and feeling upon the destiny of a human being, requires for its exhibition more than the narrow limits of a brief tale; hence the necessary superiority of the longer work of fiction. Compare, for example, Dickens's " Christmas Stories " and " Sketches " with " David Copperfield " or " Martin Chuzzlewit; " George Eliot's " Clerical Tales " with " Middlemarch " or " Adam Bede; " Hawthorne's " Mosses from an Old Manse " with " The Scarlet Letter " and " The House of the Seven Gables."

The assertion that truth is not the aim of art, that its sole object is beauty, not truth, and the effect it produces pleasure, not instruction, is equivalent to saying that beauty is not truth nor instruction capable of giving pleasure. On the contrary, truth is the vital principle of beauty, and the highest pleasures are those in which the intellect is active, not passive. Not that truth is always beautiful; there are ugly truths as well as beautiful ones. A rubbish heap is as real as a fine cathedral, but it is not beautiful; a rose is as real as an unsightly weed, but the weed cannot give the eye the same pleasure. Sin is as real as virtue, but the sage mind can find no delight in it. The truths that Jan Steen and Crabbe chose to portray are the truths of the rubbish heap and the weed. The truths that Milton and Angelo chose to depict are the higher truths of harmony, design, and beauty. The highest art instinctively makes this selection. But there is still another beauty, — the beauty of mere color and form, the beauty that appeals to the senses wholly, — and this is the beauty of which Poe speaks, and of which Gustave Flaubert said in his youth : —

"For my part, I admire tinsel as much as gold. The poetry of tinsel is much superior in that it is sad. For me there is nothing in the world except beautiful verses, well-tuned harmonies, resonant phrases, glorious sunsets, moonlight, colored paintings, antique marbles, and shapely heads. I would sooner have been Talma than Mirabeau, because he lived in a sphere of purer beauty. Caged birds stir my compassion as much as enslaved peoples. In all politics there is only one thing I understand, and that is revolt."

The concluding sentiments of this confession are the natural result of its first admissions. The worship of beauty entirely for itself, dissociated from any sense of design or regard for essentials and ethical value, inevitably degrades the worshipper. He loses all sense of values; surfaces content him; he becomes the vulgar victim of show and glare, and, like the savage, he would exchange an unpolished jewel for a glittering glass bead. He shuns the sweet, austere lessons of life, and steeps himself in sensual indulgence. He talks much of "art for art's sake," by which he means simply delight for the senses and an opiate for the intellect. The art that lasts, the art that gave renown to Greece and Italy, the art that makes the literature of England her consummate gift to the world, is not the art of surfaces, but the art of the centres of life and thought.

> " Not from a vain or shallow thought,
> His awful Jove young Phidias wrought.
> Never from lips of cunning fell
> The thrilling Delphic oracle ;
> Out from the heart of nature rolled
> The burdens of the Bible old;
> The litanies of nations came,
> Like the volcano's tongue of flame,
> Up from the burning core below, —
> The canticles of love and woe ;
> The hand that rounded Peter's dome
> And groined the aisles of Christian Rome
> Wrought in a sad sincerity :
> Himself from God he could not free ;
> He builded better than he knew,
> The conscious stone to beauty grew."

The idea that beauty in its supreme development awakens melancholy in the sensitive soul may be true if the sensitiveness is morbid, but if it is healthy in character, the emotion excited is exactly the contrary; it is that of pure exhilaration or deep joy that may sometimes lie close to tears, but they are tears of gratitude and reverence, not tears of depression. There is no surer sign of a healthy organization than its capacity for joy, and art in its highest manifestation appeals to this capacity.

We have now arrived at some definite conclusions which help us to judge Poe's work as an artist. No poet, not even Gray, ever went to the tomb with a slenderer bunch of immortelles in his hand. When six or seven short poems are named, we have given in his title to remembrance. These poems are "The Raven," "The Bells," "The Haunted Palace," "The Conqueror Worm," "The City in the Sea," "To One in Paradise," and "Annabel Lee." Perfect in their kind, they belong, however, to the "poetry of tinsel," which depends for its charm on melody and a vague suggestion of perishable beauty that excites a pleasing melancholy. But the tinsel is hopelessly tarnished in such absurd jingles as "Ulalume," where the grief is so evidently an affectation, the choice of expression so evidently intended to be effective, that the simplest reader cannot be deceived by it. He knows that the pallor of the hero is the pallor of powder, and his horror a theatrical pose.

Poe's poetical world was a fantastic dream world. He sympathized neither with love as men ordinarily feel it, with friendship, domestic joys, nor delight in natural beauty. He shunned these grand commonplaces in which the great poets find their inspiration. His love of the odd and fantastic as well as the musical is shown in his choice of names, — Ligeia, Ulalume, Lalage, Ianthe, Morella, Lenore. He cared more that his verses should have the charm of melancholy and novelty than of thought. But that he knew the value of thought is shown in his criticism of an unfortunate poet, whose sounding verses he reduced to plain prose in order to exhibit their nonsense. How many of his own poems would bear the same proof of their value?

Poe's first work as a poet was written in evident imitation of Moore's Oriental poems. As Poe had not yet concluded a long poem to be a paradox, he wrote long poems, with a result that certainly favored his theory and probably gave birth to it.

Poe's tales do not rank among works of the highest art, because they do not embody the most beautiful forms of truth. They exhibit no character drawing, no elevating or enlivening incident. Their truths are the ugly realities of madness and crime. Their lessons are in manner and subject those of the Spartan helot to his master's sons.

As for Poe's criticism, it does not reach the highest order of criticism, because it does not recognize the ethical value of art.

Poe's last work, "Eureka, an Essay on the Material and Spiritual Universe," can hardly be said to be necessary to a complete study of the poet. It was written in the decline of his powers and bears evidence of the fact. But it is a curious instance of the mind's persistence in a given direction while at the same time yielding to the influence of its era. Poe, who loved mystery and sought its solution in various fields, audaciously attempts in this essay to solve the great mystery of the origin of the universe. Contrary to all his theories of music in poetry, he called this work a poem, and it was written in prose. Moreover, it is long, not short; and so far from aiming simply at a reproduction of beauty according to his theory of art, instruction is its real aim, although he declares the contrary, and is didactic in the dryest of all possible ways, — the metaphysical way. For what is still more singular in this utter repudiation in practice of his cherished theories, he adopted in his reasoning the method of the Transcendentalists whom he had so bitterly ridiculed.   The dedication of " Eureka " will sufficiently testify to this : —

"To the few who love me and whom I love, to those who feel rather than to those who think, — to the dreamers and those who put faith in dreams as the only realities, — I offer this book of truths, not in its character of truth-teller, but for the beauty abounding in its truths constituting it true. To these I present the composition as an art product alone, let us say as a Romance, or if I be not urging too lofty a claim, as a Poem.   *What I here propound is true :* therefore it cannot die ; it will rise again to the life everlasting.   Nevertheless, it is as a poem only that I wish this work to be judged after I am dead."

The book opens with a silly punning on the names of Aristotle and of Bacon, whose system of arriving at knowledge Poe attempts to demolish, while he asserts the superiority of his own, — namely, the Transcendental method of trusting to the untrammelled intuitions or imaginations of the soul.   His theory of the existence of the universe in its present form is indebted to La Place's theory for its central conception, while his theory of man's relation to the universe is equally indebted to the teachings of Hindoo philosophy; and why he should have proclaimed himself the discoverer of a new truth in his promulgation of well-known theories it would be hard to tell.

But with all his defects and limitations, with all his unhappy mistakes so tragically expiated, it must not be forgotten that this man *did* have the gift of genius, if not in its highest and purest manifestations, at least in such manner as to give him a place among the immortals.

CHAPTER XIII

OLIVER WENDELL HOLMES, poet, essayist, novelist, was born at Cambridge, Massachusetts, on the twenty-ninth of August, 1809. He was fond of saying that the year of his birth was that which also gave to the world Gladstone, Tennyson, Lord Houghton, Darwin, and Abraham Lincoln, — making it seem " like an honor to have come into the world in such company." He also liked to observe that just a hundred years before him, Samuel Johnson was born; and every year he followed, with a curiosity quickened by sympathy, the events of Johnson's life as narrated by Boswell, to see, as his biographer, John T. Morse, remarks, " what Johnson was about in that year of his age to which he himself had then come."

Holmes's mother, Sarah Wendell, was a little woman of great vivacity and intelligence, and lived until her ninety-third year. Her ancestors were Dutch, while those of his father, the Reverend Abiel Holmes, were English.

Young Oliver was a very human, lively boy, taking more pleasure in a jack-knife and a gun than in books, of which his father's library contained between one and two thousand. He says he read few books through, but read *in* many of them, — a practice he kept up through life. His father was a Congregational clergyman, and from the frequent presence of ministers as guests in the household, the bright boy had a lively sense of the depressing influence of ministerial gravity, and in later days, contrasting the genial clergymen of his acquaintance with their opposites of his boyish recollections, he says in the "Poet at the Breakfast-Table": —

"What a debt we owe to our friends of the left centre, the Brooklyn and the Park Street and the Summer Street ministers: good, wholesome, sound-bodied, sane-minded, cheerful-spirited men, who have taken the place of those wailing *poitrinaires* with their bandanna handkerchiefs round their meagre throats, and a funeral service in their forlorn physiognomies: I might have been a minister myself, for aught I know, if this clergyman had not looked and talked so like an undertaker."

As it was, the boy early revolted from dogma, shrewdly suspecting human ingenuity rather than divine benevolence underlying its formulas; yet terrified in the dark by a vague, nameless horror born of the superstitions of the time, and from that terror developing a hatred of all books that owe their origin to harsh creeds, such as Jonathan Edwards's "Sermons," Bunyan's "Pilgrim's Progress," and Dante's "Inferno," of whose spirit he speaks as "the hideousness, the savageness of that mediæval nightmare." Of Jonathan Edwards he says with harsh truth: —

"The practical effect of Edwards's teaching about the relations of God and man has bequeathed a lesson not to be forgotten. A revival in which the majority of his converts fell away; nervous disorders of all sorts, insanity, suicide among the rewards of his eloquence ; Religion dressed up in fine phrase and made much of, while Morality, her Poor Relation, was getting hard treatment at the hands of the young persons who had grown up under the reign of terror of the Northampton pulpit ; alienation of the hearts of the people to such an extent as is now rarely seen in the bitterest quarrels between pastor and flock, — if this was a successful ministry, what disaster would constitute a failure ? "

This feeling of strong antagonism to creeds, of horror at any cramping of the soul to make it fit a set theological mould, appears in all Holmes's prose works, but it began in his boyhood as he sat, a silent but rebellious and uncomfortable listener, to the " wailing *poitrinaires* " around his father's dinner-table.

At fifteen he was sent to Phillips Academy, Andover.   In 1825 he went to Harvard, and was graduated from there four years later.   He then studied law for a year, but dropped the law to take up medicine.   He had already written verses of a humorous character for a college periodical, but his first poem of any particular merit was the stirring " Old Ironsides," written when he was twenty-one. An order had been given for the destruction of the old frigate " Constitution," then lying disabled in the Charlestown navy-yard.   The ringing lines " Ay, tear her tattered ensign down ! " saved the old ship, and first carried the name of Oliver Wendell Holmes beyond the college circle of his native town.

In 1833 Holmes sailed for Europe to continue his medical studies in Paris.   He took lodgings in the Latin Quarter, attended hospitals and lecture-rooms, studied diligently, and wrote home that he had fully learned at least three principles : " not to take authority when I can have facts; not to guess when I can know; not to think a man must take physic because he is sick." But while pursuing his medical studies, he was not indifferent to the means of general culture; and in urging his father to allow him to prolong his stay abroad, he said, " Economy in one sense is too expensive for a student," and used his vacations in seeing something of Europe. He took a run into England, and in London heard Carlyle's brilliant friend, Edward Irving, preach, and described him as a " black, savage, saturnine, long-haired Scotchman, with a most Tyburn-looking squint." At the royal opera he saw Victoria, then a princess of fifteen, " a nice, fresh-looking girl, blonde, and rather pretty." In 1835 he made a short journey into Italy, and wrote with enthusiasm of the wonders of Rome.

The next year he was back in Boston, and had commenced the practice of medicine. But he never became a brilliantly successful practitioner. The wit and the poet were uppermost in him ; his social gifts, his gayety, the versatility of his genius were prejudicial to him as a physician. They made of him a most charming companion, but to the general public they hardly seemed compatible with the grave discharge of duties that required exhaustive study and patient bedside observation. A volume of lively verses that appeared in 1836 did not increase the faith of the doubting public in the poet physician; but that he could also write a valuable medical paper was proved by his winning the Boylston prize in the same year, for an essay on "Intermittent Fever in New England." The next year he was appointed professor of anatomy at Dartmouth College.

In 1840 Holmes married Amelia Lee Jackson, an intelligent, attractive young woman, who made a happy home for him. Seven years later he was elected to the chair of anatomy and physiology in Harvard University. His connection with this university continued for thirty-five years. His position was a difficult and, in many respects, a trying one: he was assigned the fifth-hour lecture, beginning at one o'clock, because he alone could hold the attention of the wearied students at that late hour. But he was eager, ardent, and had a perennial flow of youthful spirits. He clothed his instruction in the language of wit and sentiment, and charmed while he informed. He was patient with dulness, and uniformly addressed his lectures to the ordinary intelligence rather than to the higher; feeling sure that the latter can make its way, but that the former needs all the help it can get, and is vastly in the majority.

In 1857 a new literary magazine was founded in Boston, and named, at the suggestion of Holmes, "The Atlantic Monthly." For this magazine Holmes wrote the first book that made him widely known, "The Autocrat of the Breakfast-Table." This was the first of that admirable series of good talk known as the Breakfast-Table series, of which "The Professor at the Breakfast-Table" followed the "Autocrat" in two years, appearing in 1860; and twelve years later, "The Poet at the Breakfast-Table" was published. In the mean time the poet and essayist had become a novelist by the publication of "Elsie Venner," in 1861, and "The Guardian Angel," six years later. A life of Motley, in 1878, and one of Emerson, in 1884, were followed, in 1885, by another novel, entitled " A Mortal Antipathy." The following year Holmes made another trip to Europe, commemorating the event in a chatty record entitled " A Hundred Days in Europe."

Holmes was now an old man, unless we apply to him his own lines to the old player: —

> " Call him not old whose visionary brain
> Holds o'er the past its undivided reign.
> For him in vain the envious seasons roll
> Who bears eternal sunshine in his soul."

Lowell, who saw him in Europe, delighting and delighted with everybody, wrote that he envied him the freshness of genius that made him take " as keen an interest in everything as he would have done at twenty." The rich vein of talk was not yet exhausted, but revealed itself again in his last volume, " Over the Teacups," published in 1890.

Holmes was troubled with asthma a great part of his life; but with the exception of a natural dimming of sight and dulling of hearing, his old age was clouded with no painful or humiliating infirmity; to the last day of his life he was up and about, and he died, peacefully sitting in his chair, on the seventh of October, 1894.

In person, Holmes was a plain, wiry little man, about five feet five inches tall. His eyes were blue, his hair brown, his bright, homely face full of shrewdness and fun. " I do not think my face a flattering likeness of myself," he writes humorously to a friend on sending a photograph; and again to Lowell, " I have always considered my face a convenience rather than an ornament." Holmes was very ingenious with his fingers, and invented the hand-stereoscope, but took out no patent for it. He liked racing, rowing, and was n't above taking an interest in pugilism so far as admiration of physical strength and skill go. He had a pronounced taste for music, and once tried to learn to play on the violin, but without any marked success. He loved the blue hyacinth, the smell of crushed lilac leaves, had a veritable passion for great trees, and used to visit a few fine old big-trunked New England elms with as great an enjoyment and regularity as if they had been living men or women.

Holmes was naturally somewhat of an aristocrat in feeling, preferring, on his own confession, " other things being equal, a man of family traditions and accumulative humanities of at least four or five generations." "I go for the man with the gallery of family portraits," he continues, "against the one with the twenty-five cent daguerreotype, unless I find out that the last is the better of the two." That " blood will tell " is an insistent point with him ; it crops out all through his novels, and in his frequently asserted horror in one form or another of those mésalliances that last " fifty years to begin with, and then pass along down the line of descent, breaking out in all manner of boorish manifestations of feature and manner." But he believes in " no aristocracy without pluck in its backbone." He had a wide and eager intellectual curiosity, but he was not a student in the strictest sense of that word. "My nature," he writes, " is to snatch at all the fruits of knowledge, and take a good bite out of the sunny side, — after that let in the pigs." He was deeply interested in his profession, but it was rather because of its psychological bearings than its practical results as an art of healing. He had little faith in taking medicine, though that did not bring him any nearer the Homeopathists, for whom he had great contempt as logicians and practitioners. He says in one of his medical essays: —

"Throw out opium, which the Creator himself seems to prescribe, for we often see the scarlet poppy growing in the cornfields as if it were foreseen that wherever there is hunger to be fed, there must also be pain to be soothed; throw out a few specifics which our art did not discover and is hardly needed to apply; throw out wine, which is a food, and the vapors which produce the miracle of Anæsthesia, and I firmly believe that if the whole materia medica, *as now used*, could be sunk to the bottom of the sea, it would be all the better for mankind, — and all the worse for the fishes. ... But if the materia medica were lost overboard, how much more pains would be taken in ordering all the circumstances surrounding the patient (as can be done everywhere out of the crowded pauper districts) than are taken now by too many who think that they do their duty and earn their money when they write a recipe for a patient left in an atmosphere of domestic malaria, or to the most negligent kind of nursing! I confess that I should think my chance of recovery from illness less with Hippocrates for my physician and Mrs. Gamp for my nurse, than if I were in the hands of Hahnemann himself, with Florence Nightingale or good Rebecca Taylor to care for me."

The volume of "Medical Essays" from which the above extract is taken amply repays reading, but it is not as a medical writer that we are particularly concerned with Holmes, nor is it as such that he wished to be remembered. He once wrote: —

"If I should confess the truth, there is no mere earthly immortality that I envy so much as the poet's. If your name is to live at all, it is so much more to have it live in people's hearts than only in their brains! I don't know that one's eyes fill with tears when he thinks of the famous inventor of logarithms, but a song of Burns's or a hymn of Charles Wesley's goes straight to your heart, and you can't help loving both of them, sinner as well as saint."

But it is not as a poet that Holmes will be endeared to the readers of coming generations: he has written some beautiful lines, it is true, and a great quantity of lively after-dinner verse; but he has sung no song that goes straight to the heart, unless it be that half-smiling, half-tearful poem "The Last Leaf," one stanza of which Lincoln said contains the most pathetic lines in the English language: —

> "The mossy marbles rest
>   On the lips that he has prest
>   In their bloom,
>   And the names he loved to hear
>   Have been carved for many a year
>   On the tomb."

"The Chambered Nautilus," which was Holmes's own favorite, is sometimes regarded as his best poem, and its last lines ring on the ear with an awakening call: —

> "Build thee more stately mansions, O my soul,
>   As the swift seasons roll!
>   Leave thy low-vaulted past,
>   Let each new temple, nobler than the last,
>   Shut thee from heaven with a dome more vast,
>   Till thou at length art free,
>   Leaving thine outgrown shell by life's unresting sea!"

"Under the Violets," "The Old Man Dreams," " Bill and Joe," "My Aunt," "The Wonderful One-Hoss Shay," are other popular favorites. But if Holmes had left nothing but his verses as a memorial of himself, he would have left no deeper mark upon his times than Drake, Halleck, or Willis. He was not possessed by poetry, but he possessed in no mean degree the poet's gift of musical speech and felicitous imagery. In his dedicatory poem " To My Readers " he says : —

> " Our whitest pearls we never find ;
> Our ripest fruit we never reach;
> The flowering moments of the mind
> Drop half their petals in our speech."

This was eminently true of himself. He was a born talker. Witty, genial, shrewd, sympathetic, quickly responsive to touches of pathos or sentiment, strongly individual but without eccentricity of any kind, his talk continually revealed himself, and pleased in proportion as it revealed the more of him. When he wrote the Breakfast-Table series, he simply talked on paper to the public, making shrewd, genial, running comments on men and things in general, not without a piquant flavor of kindly satire at times, and here and there a genuine poetic flight both in prose and verse. Now, whenever a man of cleverness, tact, observation, and wit chooses to take the public into his confidence, and to pour out unreservedly his tastes, his feelings, his ideas, and his witty sallies, the public will lend the ear of a delighted listener. " I shall say many things," says the Poet of the Breakfast-Table, " which an uncharitable reader might find fault with as personal. I should not dare to call myself a poet if I did not;

for if there is anything that gives one a title to that name, it is that the inner nature is naked and is not ashamed."

Holmes has found few uncharitable readers of that sort. No man since "Elia" has put himself so directly into his work, though Holmes has not the mellowness, the *naïveté*, the indescribable quaintness that make Charles Lamb so delightful. All that was rich and unctuous and *human* in the antiquated literature of England had filtered through Lamb's intellect, and we get the essence of it in those incomparable soliloquies in public which he calls his essays. Holmes, on the contrary, is very new, brisk, and modern : we even catch now and then an unpleasant whiff of varnish and hear the creak of his boots; but on the whole he, too, is a genuine bit of human nature, with the dear, familiar foibles that the tailor's art can never hide. Nor would he have hidden them if he could. " We must have a weak spot or two in a character, before we can love it much. People that do not laugh or cry, or take more of anything than is good for them, or use anything but dictionary words, are admirable subjects for biographers. But we don't always care most for those flat-pattern flowers that press best in the herbarium," remarks the professor; and it is true. With all his intellectual sparkle and wisdom, and his deep admiration of genius, he never for a moment swerves from his allegiance to the better qualities of the heart. "The brain is the palest of all the internal organs, and the heart the reddest. Whatever comes from the brain carries the hues of the place it came from, and whatever comes from the heart carries the heat and color of its birthplace."

And again, " When a strong brain is weighed with a true heart, it seems to me like balancing a bubble against a wedge of pure gold."

This is why the " new woman " with her intellectual aspirations and ambitions that may endanger her affections does not mean much to him. He says : —

" A woman who does not carry a halo of good feeling and desire to make everybody contented about her wherever she goes, — an atmosphere of grace, mercy, and peace of at least six feet radius which wraps every human being upon whom she voluntarily bestows her presence, and so flatters him with the comfortable thought that she is rather glad that he is alive than otherwise, — is n't worth the trouble of talking to, *as a woman;* she may do well enough to hold discussions with. . . . The brain women never interest us like the heart women : white roses please less than red. But our Northern seasons have a narrow green streak of spring as well as a broad white zone of winter, — they have a glowing band of summer and a golden stripe of autumn in their many-colored wardrobe ; and women are born to us that wear all these hues of earth and heaven in their souls."

He has no patience with deception in a woman : —

" I would have a woman as true as death. At the first real lie which works from the heart outward, she should be tenderly chloroformed into a better world, where she can have an angel for a governess, and feed on strange fruits, which shall make her all over again, even to her bones and marrow."

A slender story runs through each volume of the Breakfast-Table series, giving it coherence and a more general interest, but the real value of the series lies in the fact that it gives us a finished and artistic portraiture of the author himself as thinker, poet, and professor.   It is Holmes's best work, and his title to future remembrance.

Holmes's novels hardly repay a second perusal, and even the witty sentences in them cannot save them from oblivion.   They are inartistic in the sense that they depict abnormal, not normal types as their central characters, and that they seem not so much to be written to give a faithful picture of life as to illustrate a theory.   The man of medicine, not the artist, is too apparent in them.   The question of the influence of heredity and of physical organization interested Holmes profoundly, too much so to make him a good novelist; for the novelist's power of reproducing life and character faithfully is no more dependent upon a knowledge of the laws of heredity than portrait-painting upon a knowledge of the ramifications of nerves and blood-vessels under the skin.   " Elsie Venner," the best of Holmes's three novels, discusses the question of prenatal influence and moral responsibility. The mother of Elsie Venner had been bitten by a rattlesnake shortly before the birth of the child.   The foreign element thus supposed to be introduced into the child's blood shows itself in certain peculiarities of temperament that are alien to human nature.   While writing this novel, Holmes was not satisfied with reading all that he could find about venomous reptiles, but procured a live rattlesnake and kept it for several weeks, studying all its ways.   Says Holmes, in a letter to Mrs. Stowe : —

" To make the subject of this influence interest the reader ; to carry the animalizing of her nature just as far as can be done without rendering her repulsive ; to redeem the character in some measure by humanizing traits which struggle through the lower organic tendencies; to carry her on to her inevitable fate by the natural machinery of circumstance, grouping many human interests around her, which find their natural solution in the train of events involving her doom, — such is the idea of this story."

In his preface to "The Guardian Angel," a novel which continues the discussion of hereditary influence and moral accountability, he says of the probability of the story of Elsie Venner: —

"Whether anything like this ever happened or was possible mattered little : it enabled me at any rate to suggest the limitations of human responsibility in a simple and effective way."

This idea is a dominant note in all Holmes's prose work. The conclusions that he comes to are as follows : —

"I believe much, and I dare not say how much, of what we call 'sin' has no moral character whatever in the sight of the great Judge. I believe much of what we call 'vice' is not only an object of the profoundest compassion to good men and women, but that the tenderest of God's mercies are in store for many whom the so-called justice of the world condemns. . . .

"We are all tattooed in our cradles with the beliefs of our tribe ; the record may seem superficial, but it is indelible. You cannot educate a man wholly out of the superstitious fears which were early implanted in his imagination ; no matter how utterly his reason may reject them, he will still feel, as the famous woman did about ghosts, '*Je n'y crois pas, mais je les crains.*' . . .

"Our natural instincts and tastes have a basis which can no more be reached by the will than the sense of light and darkness, or that of heat and cold. . . .

" It is very singular that we recognize all the bodily defects that unfit a man for military service and all the intellectual ones that limit his range of thought, but always talk at him as if all his moral powers were perfect. I suppose we must punish evil-doers as we extirpate vermin ; but I don't know that we have any more right to judge them than we have to judge rats and mice, which are just as good as cats and weasels, though we think it necessary to treat them as criminals. . . .

" *Treat bad men exactly as if they were insane.* They are *in-sane*, out of health morally. Reason which is food to sound minds is not tolerated, still less assimilated, unless administered with the greatest caution, perhaps not at all. Avoid collision with them, so far as you honorably can, — for one angry man is as good as another : restrain them from violence promptly, completely, and with the least possible injury, as in the case of maniacs, — and when you have got rid of them, or got them tied hand and foot, so that they can do no mischief, sit down and contemplate them charitably, remembering that nine tenths of their perversity comes from outside influences, drunken ancestors, abuse in childhood, bad company from which you have probably been preserved, and for some of which you, as a member of society, may be fractionally responsible."

" A Mortal Antipathy," like Holmes's other novels, smells of the medicine case. It is the story of a young man who had an unconquerable antipathy to beautiful young women, owing to a fright he had received in his infancy from a young and pretty cousin. The antipathy was finally overcome by his rescue during a state of convalescence from a burning house. His rescuer, a beautiful, athletic young woman, became his wife. The progress of the story is interrupted by accounts of antipathies and quasi-medical information. On the whole, it is a disagreeable and feeble book.

Holmes's biographies of Motley and Emerson, though readable, do not belong to his best work, any more than his novels do. That best work is, as we have said before, the Breakfast-Table series, and it is as the Autocrat and the Professor that Oliver Wendell Holmes is to see his wish fulfilled to "live in people's hearts."

CHAPTER XIV

JOHN LOTHROP MOTLEY (1814–1877)

"LIFE is work or it is nothing," wrote Motley to Holmes from that busy workshop, his study, where he was toiling to recreate the dead and gone for living readers; and he certainly based his declaration on his own experience. Hard work, earnest purpose, and unflagging enthusiasm have rarely had a better incarnation than John Lothrop Motley, the leading historian of America.

Motley was born in Dorchester, Massachusetts, April 15, 1814, and died in Dorchester, England, the twenty-ninth of May, 1877. He was interred in Kensal Green Cemetery near his wife, whose death took place three years before his own.

John Motley, the great-grandfather of our historian, emigrated to this country from Belfast, Ireland; the ancestors of the Reverend John Lothrop, the historian's grandfather on the mother's side, were from England. The father and mother of the historian were reputed in their youth the handsomest pair in Boston, and were, besides, a vivacious, intellectual pair, — the father, a lover of books, having dabbled a little in literature himself. Thus the boy came honestly by his physical beauty and his passion for reading, being rarely seen in his early years without a book in his hand. Among his early schoolmasters was Bancroft the historian, then teaching at Round Hill, Northampton.

Motley was only thirteen when he entered Harvard. He was fond of languages, and learned them easily. He was a very ambitious boy, and had the reputation in his youth of being reserved, haughty, and cynical, after the fashion of what he had conceived of Byron. He spent his leisure writing poems and prose tales, and dreamed, as most imaginative youths do, of a fame in poetry and fiction that was never to be his. In 1832 he went to Germany, and continued his studies at the universities of Göttingen and Berlin. Bismarck was a student at Göttingen at the same time, and he and Motley soon became warm friends. The two students subsequently removed to Berlin, and lodged at the same house, living in the closest intimacy.

Returning to America in 1834, Motley took up the study of law, but he did not continue long in so uncongenial a pursuit; he was made for literature, and to literature he gave his attention. In 1837 he married Mary Benjamin, sister of Park Benjamin the poet and lecturer, and two years later published his first work, a novel in two volumes, entitled " Morton's Hope." The book was a failure. O. W. Holmes, in his biography of Motley, characterizes it as " a map of dissected incidents which has been flung out of its box, and has arranged itself without the least regard to chronology or geography." The young novelist did not take the failure of his book to heart, but continued to apply himself assiduously to his literary studies. He went to Russia in 1841 as secretary of legation, and took up his residence for a short time in St. Petersburg.   He found it an expensive place to live in, and went into society just enough, he says, to see its general structure, " which is very showy and gay, but entirely hollow and anything but intellectual."

He gave up his appointment, returned home, and began writing historical and critical essays for the " North American Review."   In 1849 he published a second novel, " Merry Mount, a Romance of the Massachusetts Colony," which had not much better favor with the public than its predecessor, and with the failure of which he was content to abandon fiction for the work in which he was destined to be successful.   " Did I not have two novels killed under me (as Balzac phrases it)," he writes to Holmes on the appearance of " Elsie Venner," " before I found that my place was among the sappers and miners, and not the lancers?   And was it not natural, having thus come to grief in the bygone ages, that I should feel solicitude when I saw you setting off on the same career ? "

" Among the sappers and miners," his work did really appear to be, from the laborious study and research it entailed.   He had planned a history to be called " The Eighty Years' War for Liberty," and it was designed to cover "a most remarkable epoch in human history, from the abdication of Charles V. to the Peace of Westphalia."   The history was to be divided into three epochs: I. " The Rise of the Dutch Republic; " II. " Independence achieved, from the Death of William the Silent till the Twelve Years' Truce (1584-1609) ; " III. " Independence recognized, from the Twelve Years' Truce to the Peace of Westphalia (1609-1648)."

Motley did not live to carry out fully this design. After completing the history of the first two epochs under the titles "The Rise of the Dutch Republic" and "The United Netherlands," he wrote "The Life and Death of John of Barneveld, Advocate of Holland," which was the last work he lived to publish.

In 1850 he had composed the first part of his history of the "Rise of the Dutch Republic;" but feeling the need of more material to work with, he went with his family to Europe the following year, settling successively at Berlin, Dresden, The Hague, and Brussels; working ten hours a day "as hard as a wood-sawyer," he says, "digging raw material out of the subterranean depths of black-letter folios, in half a dozen different languages." But a fine enthusiasm for his hero, William of Orange, sustained him in these tedious labors, and he writes to his father from Dresden: —

"I flatter myself I have found one great, virtuous, heroic character. This man, who did the work of a thousand men every year of his life, who was never inspired by any personal ambition, but who performed good and lofty actions because he was born to do them, just as other men are born to do nasty ones, deserves to be better understood than I believe him to have been by the world at large. He is one of the very few men who have a right to be mentioned in the same page with Washington."

He adds that he is working on his history not for money, but in the hope of making "some few people in the world wiser and better."

He anticipated having to publish the book at his own expense, and was not confident of success. He offered the manuscript first to Murray of London, who declined it, and then to Chapman, who published it in 1856 at the expense of the author. It appeared at the same time from Harper's publishing-house in America, and met with instant success. "The United Netherlands" followed in 1860, and the next year Motley received an appointment from Lincoln as minister to Austria. This appointment involved a residence in Vienna, where Motley had the pleasure of renewing his friendship with his old college friend Bismarck.

After the accession of President Johnson, Motley resigned the Austrian ministry, because he felt insulted by a letter of inquiry addressed to him by Secretary Seward, at the instigation of the President, concerning the truth of certain calumnious reports made against him by a venomous slanderer wholly unknown to Motley.

The proud-spirited author, every inch a gentleman and a patriot, was not more fortunate in his next appointment as minister to England, in 1869, under the Grant administration. He was recalled in 1871 because of an alleged failure to follow the instructions of his government in an interview with Lord Clarendon concerning the Alabama claims. According to Grant's alleged statement, Motley was explicitly charged to treat the subject in the gentlest possible manner, and, on the contrary, followed the lead of Sumner, who had offended the British government by a violent speech on the subject. But as Motley's alleged offence had not excited more than a gentle demur followed by a satisfactory adjustment of the difficulty at the time of its occurrence, and as a year had gone by before a renewal of the charge was made, Motley's biographer, Holmes, is inclined to think that the real cause of his dismissal was Grant's private animosity to Motley on account of the latter's friendship with Sumner, whose determined opposition to the annexation of San Domingo to the United States had antagonized Grant. However that may be, Motley keenly felt the injustice of the recall. He had served his country faithfully, and he had won the respect and admiration of the English nation, not only through his intellectual gifts, but through the courtesy and tact with which he had discharged his official duties. He now turned once more to his chosen work, and established himself at The Hague to collect material for the history of John of Barneveld, which was published in 1874, not quite three years before the author's death.

Speaking of Motley as he appeared in his college days, Holmes says : —

"In after years one who knew Lord Byron most nearly, noted his resemblance to that great poet, and spoke of it to one of my friends; but in our young days many pretty youths affected that resemblance and were laughed at for their pains, so that if Motley recalled Byron's portrait it was only because he could not help it. His finely shaped and expressive features; his large, luminous eyes; his dark, waving hair; the singularly spirited set of his head, which was most worthy of note for its shapely form and poise; his well-outlined figure, — all gave promise of his manly beauty, and commended him to those even who could not fully appreciate the richer endowments of which they were only the outward signature."

There was much of the poet in that fine organization of Motley's as well as in his appearance. He was excitable, impulsive, ardent in his loves and hates, subject to the depressions of the melancholy temperament; but he held these moods well in check. He had failed in his earliest efforts; he had been severely wounded by the lack of confidence his government had placed in him; he was diffident about the success of his later work in history. He was proudly reserved; his letters edited by George William Curtis fill two large octavo volumes, and not one letter reveals a familiar glimpse of the man. Descriptions of places and people make up the bulk of them, — rapidly sketched outlines of notabilities whom he has met, and he met many of them, but these sketches are limited to the external appearance. Whenever he feels obliged to speak of himself, he apologizes for his egotism, and gets rid of the necessity of such speaking in as few words as possible. But he has not so successfully kept himself out of his histories; he is not a cool, indifferent narrator of events. His pulse quickens, his color rises as he narrates the horrible atrocities of the Inquisition, and the cold, perfidious cruelty of Philip II. of Spain; and he loves his hero, William of Orange, grows tender over him, and spares no pains of research to pay a tribute to his greatness. Prescott wrote to him : —

" You have laid it on Philip rather hard. Indeed you have whittled him down to such an imperceptible point that there is hardly enough of him left to hang a newspaper paragraph on, much less five or six volumes of solid history, as I propose to do. But then you make it up with your hero, William of Orange, and I comfort myself with the reflection that you are looking through a pair of Dutch spectacles, after all."

But whether looking through Dutch spectacles or with his naked eyes, Motley never saw in tyranny anything but an outrage on humanity, and anything but a virtue in brave, resolute resistance to it. He thought Carlyle " a most immoral writer for his exaggerated reverence for brute force, which he was so apt to confound with wisdom and genius. A world governed *à la* Carlyle would be a pandemonium." Much of Motley's strength as a writer lies in this keen perception of moral distinctions. No mere worldly success or triumph can make wrong right to him. He had, too, the power of vivid description and lifelike portrayal of character. His style is by no means always above criticism, but it is always the dress of sinewy, fiery, living thought, and much may be pardoned the dress of a courier who brings us valuable information.

Of Motley's three histories, " The Rise of the Dutch Republic" is the most interesting, from the fact that its history is, as he himself says, at the same time the biography of William the Silent; and the reader follows the story of the hero with unabated interest from beginning to end. The history opens with a description of the territory and the early inhabitants of the Netherlands, followed by an account of the rise and expansion of municipal power. The history proper begins with the abdication of Charles V. and the accession of Philip II. to the throne of Spain. The subsequent struggle for religious and political freedom is narrated with spirit and fulness of detail, and the history concludes with

the assassination of the Prince of Orange, July 10,
1584.   The fine pen portrait of the Prince in the concluding chapter deserves to be transcribed entire, as
an example of Motley's sympathetic treatment of a
subject; but we can give but very little of it here: —

" His constancy in bearing the whole weight of struggle as
unequal as men have ever undertaken was the theme of admiration even to his enemies.   The rock in the ocean ' tran-
quil amid raging billows ' was the favorite emblem by which
his friends expressed their sense of his firmness.   From the
time when, a hostage in France, he first discovered the plan
of Philip to plant the Inquisition in the Netherlands, up to
the last moment of his life, he never faltered in his determination to resist that iniquitous scheme.   This resistance
was the labor of his life.   To exclude the Inquisition, to
maintain the ancient liberties of his country, was the task
which he appointed to himself when a youth of three-and-
twenty.   Never speaking a word concerning a heavenly
mission, never deluding himself or others with the usual
phraseology of enthusiasts, he accomplished the task through
danger, amid toils, and with sacrifices such as few men have
ever been able to make on their country's altar ; for the disinterested benevolence of the man was as prominent as his
fortitude.   A prince of high rank and with royal revenues,
he stripped himself of station, wealth, almost at times of the
common necessaries of life, and became in his country's
cause nearly a beggar as well as an outlaw.   Nor was he
forced into his career by an accidental impulse from which
there was no recovery.   Retreat was ever open to him.   Not
only pardon but advancement was urged upon him again and
again.   Officially and privately, directly and circuitously, his
confiscated estates, together with indefinite and boundless
favors in addition, were offered to him on every great occa-
sion. . . . He went through life bearing the load of a peo-

ple's sorrows upon his shoulders with a smiling face. Their name was the last word upon his lips, save the simple affirmative with which the soldier, who had been battling for the right all his lifetime, commended his soul, in dying, 'to his great Captain Christ.' The people were grateful and affectionate, for they trusted the character of their 'Father William,' and not all the clouds which calumny could collect ever dimmed to their eyes the radiance of that lofty mind to which they were accustomed to look for light. As long as he lived, he was the guiding star of a whole brave nation, and when he died the little children cried in the streets."

CHAPTER XV

HENRY DAVID THOREAU (1817–1862)

EVERY literature has a class of books whose merit is of a rarity so exquisite and delicate that they never become general favorites with the public. They require for their enjoyment a purity of taste that can detect beauty unadorned and a familiarity with the essential truths of human nature that underlie all the trappings of culture and civilization. These books have their warm admirers, who prefer for them, as Scherer says of a book he loved, just "that sort of half success, . . . that which a lover prefers for the woman he loves, dreading to see her the object of an admiration too noisy, too general, and therefore profane, but wounded in his feelings if he finds everybody indifferent to the charms that touch him to the bottom of his heart." Such admirers "rather congratulate themselves on the fact that the importunate noise of fame has not been heard around a delicate and discreet work. They would have been less sure of their impression had it been general. They have enjoyed more because they felt they were enjoying alone. The author appeared to belong more to them; the book remained for them more intimate and lovable."

No author of America has been so worthily the object of this tender, half-jealous regard in the warm appreciation of a select few as Henry D. Thoreau. The most original, the most purely spiritual, and most purely intellectual of all American authors; the freshest and in some essential respects the soundest and most tonic writer, — his very merits have contributed to retard the growth of a fame which slowly increases year by year. During his lifetime but two of his works were published, — "A Week on the Concord and Merrimac Rivers," in 1849, and "Walden," in 1854. So unsuccessful with the public was the first work, that four years after its appearance the author received from his publishers seven hundred and six unsold copies out of a first edition of one thousand copies.

"Walden" attracted more attention, but it contributed to a singular misapprehension of the author, whose two years' experiment came to be regarded as an epitome of his lifetime, and the author himself, as a hermit or recluse who passed his life in the depths of the forest far from the homes of men. Emerson's vigorous and characteristic sketch of him accentuated too strongly the stoical element of his nature, and further contributed to this misapprehension. But Thoreau left at his death forty volumes of manuscripts, from which successive publications have been made, until we have now in all eleven printed volumes, from whose tonic, wholesome pages there emerges the spirit of a man of such deep, underlying tenderness as puts to shame all surface emotionalism, and of so sweet and lofty a serenity, so exquisite a purity and so complete a truthfulness, that earth seems a fitter dwelling-place for all the virtues because he shared its life.

Henry David Thoreau was born in Concord, Massachusetts, July 12, 1817. Through his father, he was of French Huguenot descent, but the Celtic element in his nature is hardly apparent in anything except that happy unconcern for the morrow which makes the most of to-day; though in Thoreau's case there was no levity in this unconcern, and it seems rather the fine flowering of philosophy than the tendency of inherited temperament. The elder Thoreau was a pencil-maker, and the limited income from his trade sufficed for the needs of his family, but left nothing for luxuries. But the boy, Henry, had a healthy appetite for out-doors which made him independent of any artificial luxury for his enjoyment. He scoured field and wood and meadow; he collected specimens for the naturalist Agassiz. But the spirit of poetry even then, as always, was stronger in him than the spirit of science, and he was fond of going up the river to a cliff with his brother John to see the sun rise and gleam on the smooth, still waters, or of a Sabbath afternoon he liked to climb to the garret at home, in which he used to monopolize, he says, the little Gothic window that overlooked the kitchen-garden, in order to watch the clouds and the flight of birds. His seriousness in early boyhood earned for him among his schoolfellows the title of "Judge."

He entered Harvard University in 1833, taught school between college terms, and was graduated four years later. In 1834 he began keeping the diary from which selections were from time to time given to the public after his death. On his return home after his graduation, he taught for a short time in the Concord Academy, then mastered the secret of pencil-making. Having convinced himself that he could make the best lead-pencil in the market, he refused to make another, on the ground that he would not be continually doing what he had mastered, but must apply himself to learning what he did not know. He writes to a friend about this time : —

" I am as unfit for any practical purpose — I mean for the furtherance of the world's ends — as gossamer for ship-timber, and I, who am going to be a pencil-maker to-morrow, can sympathize with God Apollo who served King Admetus for a while on earth. But I believe he found it for his advantage at last, as I am sure I shall, though I shall hold the nobler part at least out of the service. Do not attach any undue seriousness to this threnody, for I love my fate to the very core and rind, and could swallow it without paring it, I think."

His keen, alert intellect, with its insatiable desire for knowledge, made such heavy demands upon his time that he early resolved that all his economies should be in the sphere of his material wants, and that he should reduce these wants to their lowest terms. He was poor, and dependent upon his own exertions for his livelihood. He coveted a broad margin to his life, an untrammelled leisure for mental growth. He was willing to give life only for life, and would engage permanently in no calling that could give him nothing but money in return for his time. Far beyond all the wealth of the world, he rated the wealth of intellect and character, and to acquire this imperishable wealth was his only aim. He bought strong, homely clothes, warranted to stand the wear and tear of hard service, and his trousers were made by the village sempstress in an old-fashioned style. He learned surveying, was an adept at gardening and fence-making, and varying these out-door employments with occasional teaching, he passed his early manhood in what his neighbors thought a manner wholly unworthy of his college training and his mental gifts. They looked askance, too, at his fondness for rambling in the woods on Sunday, and predicted no good of a youth who preferred the turf of the forest to the pews of a church.

In 1839 he and his brother John built a boat, and made a voyage on the Concord and Merrimac rivers. Thoreau afterward sold the boat in which the voyage was made to Hawthorne, who changed the name from " Musketaquid," the Indian name for the Concord River, to the " Pond Lily." In 1841 Emerson, always generously susceptible to intellectual qualities, invited Thoreau to make his home with him. Thoreau accepted the invitation, and was a member of Emerson's household for two years, rendering in his turn such services as required the aid of an ingenious head and skilful fingers. In January of the following year, Thoreau's brother John died from lockjaw, the result of tearing his hand on a rusty nail while leaping over a fence. What Thoreau seemed to feel in the death of this brother, which touched him deeply, was the exaltation rather than the despair of grief. It cleared away trivial events for him, set him face to face with a great reality, concentrated and purified his aim, and made him say what sounds at first hearing strange and heartless, but what is profoundly true: " Any pure grief is ample recompense for all."

In 1843 Thoreau left Concord for Staten Island, New York, to become for a time tutor in the family of William Emerson, a brother of Ralph Waldo Emerson. Hawthorne, who was living in Concord at this time, and had early learned to value Thoreau, makes note of his departure in his journal in the following manner: " I should like to have him remain here, he being one of the few persons with whom to hold intercourse is like hearing the boughs of a forest tree; and with all this wild freedom there is high and classic cultivation in him, too." But there was more than high and classic cultivation and wild freedom in him. The hunger and aspiration of the ideal haunted him. He sifted all that is coarse and trivial out of life, and would have but the finest flour of it. He asked from his friends no toleration of what was weak in him, but a constant challenge to keep his life in harmony with his highest aspirations. His letters to Mrs. Emerson breathe a lofty, ideal, chivalric spirit, very exquisite and very rare. He writes to her: —

" I thank you for your influence for two years. I was fortunate to be subjected to it, and am now to remember it. It is the noblest gift we can make : what signify all others that can be bestowed? You have helped to keep my life ' on loft,' as Chaucer says of Griselda, and in a better sense. You always seemed to look ·down at me as from some elevation — some of your high humilities — and I was the better for having to look up. I felt taxed not to disappoint your expectations, for could there be any accident so sad as to be respected for something better than we are ? . . . The thought of you will constantly elevate my life; it will be something always above the horizon to behold, as when I look at the evening star."

Thoreau returned to Concord in the following year. Besides a paper in the "Dial," a lecture, and two or three essays, he had as yet given nothing to the public, and in what he had written, no adequate expression of himself. Simple and unconventional as was his life, the problem of gaining a livelihood still absorbed much of his time, and he longed for seclusion and leisure to think and write. In 1841 he wrote to a friend: —

"I grow savager and savager every day, as if fed on raw meat, and my tameness is only the repose of untamableness. I dream of looking abroad summer and winter with free gaze from some mountain-side while my eyes revolve in an Egyptian shine of health; I to be nature, looking into nature with such easy sympathy as the blue-eyed grass in the meadow looks into the face of the sky. From some such recess I would put forth sublime thoughts daily, as the plant puts forth leaves. Now-a-nights I go on to the hill to see the sun set as one would go home at evening, — the bustle of the village has run on all day and left me quite in the rear; but I see the sun set and find that it can wait for my slow virtue.

But I forget that you think more of this human nature than of this nature I praise. Why won't you believe that mine is more human than any single man or woman can be? that in it, in the sunset there, are all the qualities that can adorn a household, — and that sometimes in a fluttering leaf one may hear all your Christianity preached."

This letter is the prelude to the Walden experiment, which was not, as some of his critics and biog-

raphers say, a deliberate attempt to prove that " man
could be as independent of his kind as a nest-building
bird; " but the act of a man with urgent business
on hand who knew how to shut himself away from
intruders. He says: —

" I used to see a large box by the railroad six feet long
by three feet wide in which the laborers locked up their
tools at night, and it suggested to me that every man who is
hard pushed might get such a one for a dollar, and having
bored a few auger-holes in it to admit the air, at least get
into it when it rained, and at night hook down the lid, and
so have freedom in his love, and in his soul be free."

Our Yankee Diogenes was not so hard pushed for
his tub. Emerson owned a few acres of woodland
on the shores of Lake Walden, about two miles from
Concord, and they were at Thoreau's service. In
March, 1845, Thoreau began building for himself a
small shanty on a beautiful knoll among the pines,
through which gleamed the sea-green waters of Lake
Walden. He dug a cellar seven feet deep in the side
of a sloping hill, cut white pines for foundation timber, bought an old shanty from an Irishman living
near the railroad, took it to pieces and transported
its boards, roof, and nails to his chosen site. His
shanty cost him $28.12½. It consisted of one room,
ten feet wide by fifteen feet long. It had a window
at each side, a door at one end, and a brick fireplace
opposite the door. His furniture, he tells us, consisted
of " a bed, a table, three chairs, a looking-glass three
inches in diameter, a kettle, a skillet, a frying-pan, a
dipper, a wash-bowl, two knives and forks, three
plates, one cup and spoon, a jug for oil, a jug for

molasses, and a japanned lamp." He thanked God that he could sit or stand without the aid of a furniture warehouse, and said that if he had to drag his trap he should take care that it was a light one and did not nip him in a vital part. A lady once offered him a mat, but considering that he had no room to spare in his house, and no time to spare within or without to shake it, he declined it, preferring to wipe his feet on the sod before his door.

He spaded up and planted about a third of an acre near the house, and moved into his new home on the Fourth of July, 1845. The pine wood in which he lived is intermixed with oak, hickory, hazel, and an undergrowth of low blueberry bushes and rambling blackberry vines. In summer the dark lustrous leaves of the wintergreen, and the graceful, trailing partridge-berry gleam among the brown pine needles on the ground. The golden-rod and aster brighten the steep wooded banks encircling the lake, and the air is fragrant with the balsamic odors of the pine. It is an idyllic spot to live in, and the visitor at first sight of it has a feeling of pleasant surprise and an impression that Thoreau's stay here was only a delightful and prolonged camping-out, the experience of which any one might envy him. The house is gone now, and only a trace of shallow excavation remains to show its site; but near it, in the direction of the lake, stands a cairn, piled up by visitors and yearly growing larger, so that there is no danger of its site being lost with time.

Thoreau's housekeeping cost him little effort. He scoured the knives by thrusting them into the earth;

he cleaned his floor by throwing water on it and scouring it with sand and a broom. He used neither tea, coffee, butter, milk, nor fresh meat, so that his food cost him in money but twenty-seven cents a week. He confesses to have made a satisfactory dinner off a dish of purslane, gathered in his corn-field and boiled and salted. For bread, he found a mixture of rye and Indian meal the most convenient and agreeable, and made it up without yeast on finding it palatable, after forgetting his rules and scalding his yeast one morning. But once, for more than a month he had no bread, owing he said to the emptiness of his purse, and got his satisfaction out of the experience by discovering that even the "staff of life" is not absolutely essential to life. Counting up his expenses and income at the close of a summer's gardening, he thinks he has been more successful than any other Concord farmer, because he has made $8.71½, and if his house had burned or his crops failed, he would have been nearly as well off as before. He was out of the reach of the power of fortune to make or mar him. By working six weeks in the year, he found he could meet all the expenses of living, and in the large leisure thus left him he himself could "grow like corn in the night" and "put forth sublime thoughts daily as the plant puts forth leaves."

He got ready for publication his "Week on the Concord and Merrimac Rivers." He made a trip to the Maine woods, recorded his daily observations of nature in his faithful diary; and never had nature a more loving, more patient, or more faithful observer than he. Says Lowell: —

" He had watched nature like a detective that is to go upon the stand. As we read him, it seems as if all out-of-doors had kept a diary and become its own Montaigne. We look at the landscape as in a Claude Lorraine glass; compared with his, all other books of similar aim, even White's Selborne, seem dry as a country clergyman's meteorological journal in an old almanac."

Concord was so accessible, and walking so agreeable, to Thoreau that hardly a day passed in which he did not go to town. On one of these visits to town in 1846, he was arrested and put into jail for refusing to pay his poll-tax. This refusal was Thoreau's emphatic way of protesting that he owed no allegiance to a government under which slavery existed, and when Emerson went to his cell and said, " Henry, why are you here? " he answered significantly, " Why are you *not* here? " His friends paid his tax, much to his disgust, and he was released. This obnoxious tax continued to be quietly paid by his friends, and he was never afterward imprisoned for withholding it.

Among the most welcome visitors at Walden of whom he makes mention are Alcott, "one of the last of the philosophers; " Ellery Channing the poet, with whom he made " a bran-new theory of life over a thin dish of gruel; " and Edmund Hosmer, the " long-headed farmer " of Concord.

As Thoreau's object in going to Walden was " to transact some private business with the fewest obstacles," there was no particular reason for prolonging his stay when the business was done: consequently, in September, 1847, Thoreau left Walden and went to live with Emerson's family again, while

Emerson was lecturing in England. There was between Thoreau and Emerson that genuine kinship of spirit whose depth and fulness makes mere kinship of blood seem shallow and impertinent. But this natural likeness has led to a mistaken and foolishly iterated charge that Thoreau either consciously or unconsciously imitated Emerson in the peculiar direction of his thought and in his manner of expression. Never was a charge more unwarrantable. Of the two men, Thoreau was the more essentially original, but he lacked Emerson's urbanity, that quality that soothes and conciliates and makes men popular. Emerson's love of nature was an acquired taste; with Thoreau it was born and bred in the bone: he came and went "with a strange liberty in nature, a part of herself." Both men saw through the surfaces and shows of things, and valued only the core of sincerity within; both would fain live " not for the times, but for the eternities: " but while Emerson saw the wisdom of compromise and tolerance, and gained in breadth thereby, Thoreau's life was one of complete and resolute renunciation of all that the world holds dearest. He did not play at philosophy and discourse the wisdom of the sages from a down cushion; he lived what he talked. To him a thing either was or was not, and he accepted or rejected it accordingly; he knew no half-way measures." He says : —

" As for conforming outwardly, and living your own life inwardly, I do not think much of that. . . . Just as successfully can you walk against a sharp steel edge which divides you cleanly right and left. Do you wish to try your ability to resist distention? It is a greater strain than any soul can long endure. When you get God to pulling one way and the devil the other, each having his feet well braced, to say nothing of the conscience sawing transversely, almost any timber will give way."

Neither Thoreau nor Emerson was social by nature; but while Emerson was eager to look at the world through as many eyes as he could in order to enlarge his own experiences with the experiences of others, Thoreau's own eyes served him to such good purpose that he coveted the use of nobody else's. He had absolutely no interest in man as a purely social creature, and would not have exchanged an hour's silent intercourse with an Indian for a day's converse with all the Benthams and Adam Smiths in the world. The events of the political world concerned him less than the flight of a hawk. It was only when he saw some principle of life, some hope of humanity in jeopardy, that he ceased to be indifferent, as when John Brown was hanged. Then he felt himself linked to our common humanity, and thrilled to the innermost core with the electric shock of sympathy. "Perhaps if I were to go to Rome," he says, "it would be some spring on the Capitoline Hill I should remember the longest." And yet there were springs of deep feeling in him, capable of overflowing into the purest tenderness for all who were worthy of sharing his solitude. "What if we feel a yearning to which no breast answers?" he writes in his journal. "I walk alone. My heart is full. Feelings impede the current of my thoughts. I knock on the earth for my friend, but no friend appears, and perhaps none is dreaming of me. I am tired of frivolous society in which silence is forever the most natural and the best manners. I would fain walk on the deep waters, but my companions will only walk in shallows and puddles; " and again he writes to a friend : —

" As for the dispute about solitude and society, any comparison is impertinent. It is an idling down on the plain at the base of the mountain instead of climbing steadily to its top. . . . Will you go to glory with me? is the burden of the song. . . . It is not that we love to be alone, but that we love to soar, and when we do soar, the company grows thinner and thinner till there is none at all. It is either the tribune on the plain, a sermon on the mount, or a very private ecstasy still higher up. We are not the less to aim at the summits, though the multitude does not ascend them. Use all the society that will abet you."

Society did not abet Thoreau; therefore he walked alone on the summits, and left it loitering on the plain.

Man and his relations to society as well as to nature are the themes of Emerson's pen. Nature and her relations to man are the subjects about which Thoreau writes. These men faced different ways: Thoreau looked toward the primeval forests; Emerson's eye was turned toward the populous cities; and the style in which each wrote is equally characteristic. Both well knew how to pack meaning into few words; but there the likeness ends. Emerson's sentences are like jewels that owe their brilliancy to the labor of the workshop. Thoreau's sentences are like the forest herbs, sometimes adorned with fragrant delicate and beautiful flowers, and sometimes owing their value to their bitterish tonic roots. Perhaps it is safe to say that if either of these men owed an inspiration to the other beyond that of a friendship based upon similar ideals, it was Emerson, not Thoreau, who was the debtor. Unconsciously Thoreau sat to Emerson for a model of the excellences so frequently lauded in his essays, — the beautiful indifference to material things; that self-centred, quiet strength that does not find recognition necessary to its preservation; that sincerity which belongs to simple and noble natures; the single-eyed devotion to the intellectual life, — and in our admiration of the artist it is an absurdity to accuse the model of a lack of originality, because he resembles the portrait.

In 1849 Thoreau published "A Week on the Concord and Merrimac Rivers," and made a trip to Cape Cod. The "Week" did not sell, and involved him in debt for its printing. Thoreau was neither disheartened nor disappointed by its failure to interest the public. The fact that the book existed, that it represented sincere life and earnest thinking, was success enough for him. But his genius was not entirely unrecognized. Horace Greeley discerned his uncommon wit and sense, and tried to bring him before the public, negotiating with publishers and magazine editors for him, but often with little success. "You may write with an angel's pen," wrote Greeley to him, "yet your writings have no mercantile money value till you are known and talked of as an author. Mr. Emerson would have been twice as much known and read if he had written for the magazines a little, just to let common people know of his existence." But Thoreau was in no haste to let common people

know of his existence. He would not write to order
simply to see his name in a magazine. He believed
that the writer who would permanently interest
readers must report so much of his own life. His
thoughts must be as much a spontaneous growth and
proper to him as the acorn is to the oak, and he would
give to the public no forced growths, no tumid hot-
house fruits, but only such as were hardy products of
the soil under the bare sun, the wind, and the rain.
"How much sincere life before we can even utter
one sincere word!" he exclaims.

In 1853 he took an active part in the antislavery
agitation, and from that time until his death he never
lost an opportunity, even if he did not deliberately seek
it, to denounce the evil he hated. His magnificent
plea for John Brown sets the ears tingling to this day,
with the fierce scorn of its passionate invective. Yet
this activity in public matters was wholly out of
harmony with his tastes. In 1861, when the rumble
of the war was heard, he said: " I do not so much
regret the present condition of things in this country
(provided I regret it at all) as I do that I ever heard
of it. . . . Blessed are they who never read a newspaper, for they shall see Nature and, through her,
God." A man of Thoreau's rectitude could shirk
no duty, no matter how sorely it burdened him: —

"The fact is, you have got to take the world on your
shoulders like Atlas, and put along with it. You will do this
for an idea's sake, and your success will be in proportion to
your devotion to ideas. It may make your back ache occasionally, but you will have the satisfaction of hanging it or
twirling it to suit yourself. Cowards suffer, heroes enjoy.
After a long day's walk with it, pitch it into a hollow place,

sit down and eat your luncheon. Unexpectedly, by some immortal thoughts you will be compensated. The bank whereon you sit will be a fragrant and flowery one, and your world in the hollow, a sleek and light gazelle."

Thoreau slipped his world into the hollow, and sat on the bank as often as he could honorably do it. In the summer of 1850 he made a second trip to Cape Cod, and in September of the same year he spent a week in Canada with his poet-friend, Ellery Channing. In 1853 he revisited the Maine woods, and four years later made his last journey there. He visited the White Mountains, and while at home haunted his own native woods and fields as if he were the incarnate spirit of nature. In November, 1860, he contracted a severe cold that developed later into consumption. He went to Minnesota for his health the following year, but with no avail. Returning to Concord, and conscious that the end was not far off, he set about the revision of his manuscripts with the aid of his sister Sophia. When at last he could no longer leave his bed, he continued to write while his trembling fingers could hold a pencil. He died on the sixth of May, 1862, and was buried in Sleepy Hollow Cemetery.

Thoreau's valuable collection of plants, Indian relics, and the like were left to the Boston Society of Natural History. At the death of his sister Sophia, in 1876, his journals and early essays were given to his friend and literary executor, Mr. Harrison Blake, of Worcester, Massachusetts. The published volumes prepared from these manuscripts are known as " Excursions in Field and Forest," "The Maine Woods," " Cape Cod," " A Yankee in Canada,"

"Early Spring in Massachusetts," "Summer," "Autumn," "Winter." Thoreau's familiar letters have also been published, and make an interesting and valuable volume.

In appearance Thoreau was short of stature, but long-limbed, with narrow sloping shoulders. His shrewd, homely face was ruddy from exposure to the wind and sun. He had a huge, aquiline nose, eyes that were blue in certain lights, gray in others, and his soft, abundant hair was dark brown in color. In later years he wore a beard, sometimes as a sort of fringe under his chin to protect his throat, and then as a covering to all the lower part of his face. " He believed and lived in his senses loftily," says Ellery Channing. Eye and ear were to him the avenues of perfect delight. The sight of budding woods, he tells us, intoxicated him. All the sounds of nature came to his ear as sweetest music. He loved the low hum of the telegraph wires, — or " telegraph harp," as he called them. His verses interspersed through his prose writings show that he had not an ear for metrical harmony, but he loved music and was a rather skilful performer on the flute.

Thoreau's love of nature was not the weak, sickly, clinging love of those sentimentalists who seek in her solitudes a salve for their wounded vanity; neither was it a mere sensuous delight in sweet odors, bright colors, and harmonious sounds. It was the healthy, virile, enduring love of one who discerns excellences and virtues which he would make his own. His love was one with his aspiration. Nature was as beautiful to him and he haunted her as ceaselessly in the bleak desolation of winter as in all the color, beauty, and manifold life of summer. He says: —

"I would be as clean as ye, O Woods. I shall not rest until I am as innocent as you. . . . There is nothing so sanative, so poetic as a walk in the woods and fields, even now when I meet none abroad for pleasure. Nothing so inspires me, and excites such serene and profitable thought. The objects are elevating. In the street and in society, I am almost invariably cheap and dissipated ; my life is unspeakably mean. No amount of gold or respectability could in the least redeem it, dining with the Governor or a Member of Congress. But alone in distant woods or fields, in unpretending sprout lands or pastures tracked by rabbits, even in a bleak and, to most, cheerless day like this, when a villager would be thinking of his inn, I come to myself. I once more feel myself grandly related. This cold and solitude are friends of mine. I suppose that this value in my case is equivalent to what others get by church-going and prayer. I come to my solitary woodland walks as the homesick go home. I thus dispose of the superfluous, and see things as they are, grand and beautiful. . . . I wish to get the Concord, the Massachusetts, out of my head, and be sane a part of every day. . . . I get away a mile or two from the town into the stillness and solitude of nature, with rocks, trees, weeds, snow about me. . . . This stillness, solitude, wildness of nature is a kind of thoroughwort or boneset to my intellect. It is as if I always met in those places some grand, serene, immortal, infinitely encouraging, though invisible companion, and walked with him."

This intense and peculiar love, this particular value of nature to himself, leads Thoreau into a minute record of the most trivial things that come under his observation. Finding men so engrossed with what was pitiful and mean to him, — mere money-getting, — he consoled himself "with the bravery of minks and muskrats." He would not "go round the corner to see the world blow up," but he would make a day's journey on foot to find what kind of a trail the muskrat leaves or to measure the length of a rabbit's tracks. But it is a fine moralist that is making these measurements and recording these observations, and if we often find them tiresome and sometimes even a little exasperating, we are rewarded with some fine, tonic thought, with the air of the hills or the breath of pine woods about it, and are refreshed for the day.

"Cape Cod" is the least interesting of Thoreau's works. It opens with an account of a shipwreck and the recovery of some of the drowned bodies, at which sight we feel that Thoreau is almost as indifferent a spectator as the old men who are carting away the sea-weed, concerned only in their harvest, which the waves wash ashore, and not in the useless dead bodies they cast up. The spiders, the shifting sand, the light-colored toads that have the hue of the sand they live in, the wreck, sketches of the fishermen on the Cape, — at intervals a dry, circumstantial description, a reflection on life, or a quotation from Greek, Latin, or some natural historian; — that is "Cape Cod." The "Week on the Concord and Merrimac" has much less description in it, but abounds with fine passages of reflection, notably those on Sunday, friendship, and reading. "Walden" is the most popular, and, as a whole, the best of Thoreau's works. He has given us in it what he himself required of every author, "a simple and sincere account of his own life." Perhaps there is not in all literature a manlier, more sagacious, and more truthful bit of writing on life in its noblest and most serious aspects than the conclusion of " Walden." To every man that frees us even for an hour from the slavery of material things and engrossing vulgar cares, we owe sincerest gratitude. No man ever freed himself more completely than Thoreau, and the inspiration of his life in the simple manly record of it left to us, is the noblest gift America has as yet received from her men of letters.

Not that Thoreau is not an extremist, and never falls into impracticable views. Men are more necessary to one another than Thoreau thought they were, and the progress of society is as much dependent on man's weakness as on his strength. In his disdain of inventions and increased facilities for intercourse, Thoreau forgets that we owe to them that breadth of mind and understanding of other nations and individuals, which come from a free exchange of thought and experience, and result in the decline of superstition and the growth of culture. It is the power of communication that has enriched and elevated the race. Each generation inherits the collective wisdom of its ancestors, and adding to the store, passes it on to posterity. If wisdom could not accumulate by such legacies, man's condition would be little better than that of wild beasts. But in his impatience at the restraints of social life, which would have trammelled his own intellectual development, Thoreau ignores his own immense debt to civilization. He himself was of the purely intellectual type of man. He lived in thoughts, not actions. He was perfectly true to his individuality, obedient ever to the inner voice, and not to that which came to him from the outer world. But he forgets that all men are not so richly endowed as he, that not one in a million can go to the woods as if he were going home, or ripen in solitude as he did. Yet he knew that a man must carry his own wealth within himself in order to be rich in poverty and isolation, for he once said to Ellery Channing concerning the Walden experiment:

"I have gained considerable time for study and writing, and proved to my satisfaction that life may be maintained at less cost and less labor than by the old social plan. Yet I would not insist upon any one's trying it who has not a pretty good supply of internal sunshine; otherwise he would have, I judge, to spend too much of his time fighting with his dark humors. To live alone comfortably we must have that self-comfort which rays out of nature, — a portion of it at least."

Thus, while we must admit the limitations and the extravagance of some of Thoreau's opinions, his life is none the less a fine example of the surpassing beauty and richness of the intellectual life, in comparison with the meanness and ugly vulgarity of those lives whose real poverty is in some measure concealed by the clutter of material luxury, and whose only aim is to conceal it still more effectually by further accumulations. The spread of modern luxury, and the discontent and feverish restlessness that follow it, the stifling of what is pure and disinterested, noble and beautiful in character in a greedy absorption in mere money-getting, are the dangers of this industrial age. These dangers, confined not alone to America, but spreading to every part of the civilized world, have been admirably pointed out to the French by one of their faithful critics, Émile Montégut.   In reading his arraignment of the evils attendant upon the love of show and the pursuit of gain among his contemporaries, we are in some degree warned to stop the spread of these same evils among ourselves.   He says : —

" The generations which preceded us still preserved some of those qualities which make us pardon many errors and vices; but the generations which are growing up every day, even those who have scarcely entered upon life, promise to atone amply for the softness and timidity of their fathers, who had not the courage to be boldly stripped of every vestige of moral sentiment, and every solicitude for interests that are not material.   These children make one shudder.   Look for nothing youthful in them, none of that charming thoughtlessness, none of those elevated illusions which characterize youth.   The age of chivalry long past was resuscitated each year, in some sort, with the birth of new generations.   But to-day prosaic realities have replaced for young men all the illusions with which they formerly nourished themselves. Ardent, rapacious, pitiless as usurers hardened by their trade, as devoid of tenderness as old soldiers who have seen too much pain, too many massacres to be easily stirred, they bring to their pursuit of wealth the same sharp eagerness that was formerly brought to the pursuit of pleasure.   They have no passions, no love ; their heart is empty, their very blood is cold. . . . It seems as if their fathers had bequeathed with their blood all the experiences, all the disillusionments, all the accumulated skepticisms of five or six generations. They have no other god but wealth, and recognize no other power.   Supple, adroit, cunning, they employ in making a fortune, in making their way, an activity, an energy, an assiduity, such as no monk ever practised in repelling the snares of the devil or in uprooting from their heart the instincts of the old man. Nothing troubles them, nothing distracts them from their aim, and what it does not include they abandon with indifference. . . . They know how to abstain, and they do not love abstinence. They are active, and they do not love work; dissolute, and they have no sense of pleasure."

From this sad and degraded picture it is invigorating and encouraging to turn to this brave, clean, noble, and beautiful life of Thoreau's. Not that he set himself up for an example, or belonged in any sense to the class of noisy reformers who have no conception that reform, like charity, begins at home. Of their reforms and all professional philanthropy, he had a healthy horror. To set about *doing* good without making it your chief business to *be* good and thus indirectly to illuminate the lives of others, while attending, like the sun, strictly to your own business, he thought a poor, cheap way of *seeming* to live and getting credit for *really* living. " What a foul subject is this of doing good, instead of minding one's life, which should be his business ! " he once wrote to Mr. Blake, " doing good as a carcass which is only fit for manure instead of as a living man; — instead of taking care to flourish, and smell and taste sweet, and refresh all mankind to the extent of your capacity and quality."

Thoreau did good to mankind in this way. His life tastes and smells sweet. It is the poem which he would have written, but could not " both live and utter it." And the melody of its unwritten verse, the purity and nobility of its unwritten lesson, will abide with the world a lasting possession.

CHAPTER XVI

JAMES RUSSELL LOWELL (1819–1891)

IT is not often that the critical faculty is associated with the gift of poetry. "Poets and men of strong feeling in general," says Ruskin, "are apt to be among the very worst judges of painting. The slightest hint is enough for them. Tell them that a white stroke means a ship, and a black stain a thunder-storm, and they will be perfectly satisfied with both, and immediately proceed to remember all that they ever felt about ships and thunder-storms, attributing the whole current and fulness of their own feelings to the painter's work."

Those who have seen Turner's "Slave Ship" wanting the Ruskin eyes, and recall the magnificent description of it in "Modern Painters," copies of which description in the Boston Art Museum, where the picture hangs, are put into the hands of the spectator to assist him to see, will have no difficulty in assenting to the above declaration. Ruskin is eminently a man of feeling, and he sees with his emotions as well as his eyes. What he says of judgments of painting by poets and men of feeling is equally true of all the imaginative arts. Byron thought Pope the prince of poets. Burns rated himself below Thomson and Shenstone. Scott's publishers declared that they liked well enough his own "bairns," but wished to be preserved from those of his adoption. Hawthorne wished for the talent of Anthony Trollope. Emerson shot wide of the mark in many of his critical estimates. Rossetti and a few other imaginative men in England and America call Whitman the greatest poet of the century. The list might be extended indefinitely, but it would carry us no farther than Ruskin's admirable explanation why poets and men of feeling are apt to be the very worst judges of art.

James Russell Lowell, poet and critic, is a notable exception to this fact. He had not only the quick responsiveness, the surcharge of feeling that go with the poetical temperament, but he had the self-poise and coolness along with the power of sympathetic self-surrender, the acuteness of observation, and the breadth of comprehension, the wide culture and the use of it, that make the strength of the critical faculty. "I am thankful," he once said, "for the immense ballast of common sense I carry. It sinks me too deep in the water sometimes for my keel to plough air as a poet's should, but it keeps my top-hamper steady when the wind blows as it has lately."

We should be equally thankful for that "immense ballast of common sense," for we owe to it some of the best criticism of the century, — fine, true, richly suggestive, and wholly delightful. And all this without surrendering the poet's higher privilege to give us winged thoughts that carry us into the bright heaven of invention. "The Biglow Papers," "The Vision of Sir Launfal," "The Harvard Commemoration Ode," contain some of the finest lines that our poets have written.

James Russell Lowell was the descendant of a family that came originally from Bristol, England. The city of Lowell, Massachusetts, was named after one of his ancestors, and another was the founder of the Lowell Institute, Boston. His father was an earnest clergyman of the Unitarian faith; his mother a sweet woman of Scotch descent, with a vein of poetry in her nature that showed itself in a love of old ballads and Scotch romances. James R. Lowell was born at Cambridge, Massachusetts, the twenty-second of February, 1819. He was graduated from Harvard in his twentieth year. An omnivorous reader, a hater of mathematics and regularly prescribed tasks, he did not acquit himself very creditably as a student, and was suspended for a few months in his Senior year, because he was wholly neglectful of such studies as did not interest him, and was sent for a short time to Concord to study under a clergyman. But the boy was not in reality idle; he was simply educating him-self after his own fashion, which happened not to be that of his college professors.

After graduating, Lowell studied law, but found it little to his taste. He was almost persuaded to try mercantile life, when, chancing to be in Boston to look for a situation, he stepped into the United States Court and heard Webster. The eloquent orator so charmed the youth that he returned to the study of law and took his degree in 1840. He opened an office, and while waiting for clients turned his attention to poetry. The clients never came; but a book of poems entitled " A Year's Life " found its way to the public in his twenty-second year, and the law was abandoned.

In 1843 he started the publication of a magazine

called "The Pioneer." Only three numbers of this magazine appeared, and it was discontinued on the failure of the publisher. Lowell's eyes troubled him about this time, and he spent the better part of the winter in New York for their treatment. A second volume of verse, under the title of "A Legend of Brittany," was published in 1844. This year was also made memorable by his marriage to Maria White, a beautiful, gifted young girl who also wrote verses. The happy young couple settled at Cambridge, in Elmwood, the house in which the poet was born; and from there, for a number of years, Lowell contributed regularly to antislavery journals.

The most celebrated of these contributions was the masterly satire in verse, "The Biglow Papers." The first series of these papers was written as a protest against the Mexican War, which Lowell, in common with the prevailing New England sentiment, regarded as a crime, inasmuch as it aimed at the unjust acquisition of territory for the sake of increasing the number of slave States. Lowell's patriotism was not of the vulgar sort that shouts, "Our country, right or wrong." Says his mouthpiece, Homer Wilbur, in the "Biglow Papers:" —

"Our country is bounded on the North and the South, on the East and the West, by justice, and when she oversteps that invisible boundary line by so much as a hair's breadth, she ceases to be our mother, and chooses rather to be looked upon *quasi noverca*. That is a hard choice when our earthly love of country calls upon us to tread one path and our duty points us to another. We must make as noble and becoming an election as did Penelope between Icarius and Ulysses. Veiling our faces, we must take silently the hand of Duty to follow her."

The first series of the " Biglow Papers " was published in book form in 1848, the year that also saw
the publication of " A Fable for Critics " and " The
Vision of Sir Launfal."

A volume of prose entitled " Conversations on the
Old Poets" had appeared three years before these
poetical publications, and though the book is weakened by a vast amount of padding and a superabun-
dance of imagery oftener far-fetched than true and
effective, it does reveal germs of the Lowell who was
to make his mark in criticism.   There is here, as in
all his prose, an ardent love of excellence as it shows
itself in strength, health, and beauty, a scorn of mere
sentimentality or surface feeling, a manly independence, a generous enthusiasm more willing to see
excellences than faults, and that dread of emasculated
speech that so often made him drop from the language of books into that of the streets.   " The muse,"
he says, " can breathe as august melodies through an
oaten straw as she can win from Apollo's lute."
True, but Lowell forgets that she cannot as successfully play a duet with them, which is what he often
attempts to do.

The following is a pretty and effective bit of writing
from this early book : —

" To open a volume of Burns after diluting the mind with
the stale insipidities of the mob of rhymers who preceded
him, reminds me of a rural adventure I had last summer.
Skirting in one of· my long walks a rocky upland which
hemmed in the low salt marsh I had been plashing over, I
came at a sudden turning upon a clump of red lilies that
burned fiercely in a kind of natural fireplace shaped out for
them in an inward bend of the rock.   How they seemed to

usurp to themselves all the blazing July sunshine to comfort their tropical hearts withal !   How cheap and colorless looked the little bunch of blossomed weeds I had been gathering with so much care !   How that one prodigal clump seemed to have drunk suddenly dry the whole over-running beakers of summer to keep their fiery madness at its height."

For the sake of Mrs. Lowell, whose health was failing, Lowell and his wife spent a year in Europe, passing most of that time in Italy, returning to America in 1852. In the autumn of the following year Mrs. Lowell died.

On the ninth of January, 1855, Lowell delivered the first lecture of a semi-weekly course of twelve lectures on the English Poets at the Lowell Institute, Boston. These lectures excited much favorable notice, in consequence of which Lowell was appointed to the chair of *belles lettres* and modern languages in Harvard made vacant by the resignation of Longfellow. He was granted two years' leave of absence, and went to Europe to prepare himself for his college duties. Of his difficulties with the grammatical intricacies of the German language, he writes humorously from Dresden to a friend : " If I die, I shall have carved on my tombstone that I died of *der die das*, — not because I caught 'em, but because I could n't." However, he caught them sufficiently well to enter upon his professorial duties in 1857. This same year he was married to his daughter's governess, Miss Frances Dunlap, a woman of rare spirituality. In addition to his college duties, he was editor-in-chief of the " Atlantic Monthly " from 1857 till 1862, and in conjunction with Charles Eliot Norton edited the " North American Review " from 1864 till 1873.

Lowell's college work was not congenial to him, and when he was released from it after twenty years of service, he wrote: —

"I never was good for much as a professor — once a week, perhaps, at the best, when I could manage to get into some conceit of myself and so could put a little of my *go* into the boys.   The rest of the time my desk was as good as I; and then, on the other hand, my being professor was not good for me — it damped my gunpowder, as it were, and my mind, when it took fire at all (which was n't often) drawled off in an unwilling fuse instead of leaping to meet the first spark.   Since I have discharged my soul of it and see the callus on my ankle where the ball and chain used to be, subsiding gradually to smooth skin, I feel like dancing round the table as I used when I was twenty to let off my animal spirits.   If I were a profane man, I should say, ' Darn the college ! ' "

But this must not be taken too literally in so far as Lowell's teaching goes. A man like Lowell, of exuberant spirits and tireless swift intellectual energy, is the best of all lessons and the finest of all inspirations in himself alone.   There was nothing of the conventional professor about him.   He was careless about the mechanical details of his work, the correction of examination papers, the making out of percents, the pedantic insistence upon the etymological and grammatical features of the text of a classic. For all that, he had no time and less inclination; but he knew how to get the heart and brain of a book and to hold them up quivering with life before his eager pupils.   He opened to them a vast new world of ideas and feelings, and left them richer than they knew, or he either.

We owe to these college years the best of his fine criticism in "Among my Books" (1870) and "My Study Windows" (1872). To a lady in London, in reference to the second volume of "Among my Books," he says: —

"I am never happy when I am writing about books that I like. I had much rather like them and say nothing about them, — for one should be secret about one's loves and not betray the confidence they have put in one. But I had to write because I had foolishly allowed myself to be made a professor, and you will understand better the defects of some of my essays when I tell you that they were patched together from my lectures, leaving out a great part of the illustrative matter, and compressing rather than dilating, as one should do for a miscellaneous audience."

But these volumes of criticism are not the only works which Lowell produced in his twenty years of college service. On the outbreak of the Civil War the "Biglow Papers" were renewed, and this second series was published in book form in 1867. "Fireside Travels," a delightful volume of prose, dedicated to his lifelong friend, the sculptor and poet, William Wetmore Story, appeared in 1864. Another volume of poems, "Under the Willows," was given to the public in 1869, the year that also saw the publication of his long, reflective poem, "The Cathedral." The best of the poems in the collection "Under the Willows" — "The Snow Fall," "Aladdin," "Pictures from Appledore," "The Dead House," "Auf Wiedersehen," "The Finding of the Lyre," "After the Burial," "In the Twilight" — are the expression of real feeling, and sing themselves without effort. The same may be said of the most popular of his earlier short poems, — "The Present Crisis," "Columbus," "To a Dandelion," "The Heritage," "My Love," "The Changeling," "An Indian Summer Reverie," and the fine sonnet containing the well-known lines,

> "BE NOBLE! and the nobleness that lies
> In other men, sleeping but never dead,
> Will rise in majesty to meet thine own."

The title "Under the Willows" was chosen in commemoration of a row of six large willows terminating what was called New Road, leading into Cambridge from the West. These fine old trees — "such trees Paul Potter never dreamed nor drew" — were the remains of a stockade erected in the early Colonial days as a defence of the settlement. "Three Memorial Poems" (1876) — the "Concord Ode," "Under the Old Elm," and "An Ode for the Fourth of July, 1876" — complete Lowell's literary work until his appointment as minister to Spain in 1877. After this event, which was a turning-point in his career, his published writings were chiefly of a political nature: "Democracy and Other Addresses" (1886), "Political Essays" (1888), a slender volume of verse, "Heartsease and Rue" (1888), and a volume of critical miscellany, "Latest Literary Essays" (1891).

Lowell's life in Madrid was by no means a life of social pleasures and official duties. He found time to read a great deal, and he took up a thorough study of the Spanish language. He writes from Madrid in the summer of 1878: —

"I have turned school-boy again, and have a master over me once more . . . who comes to me every morning at nine o'clock for an hour. We talk Spanish together (he does n't know a word of English), and I work hard at translation and the like. I am now translating a story of Octave Feuillet into choice Castilian, and mean to know Spanish as well as I do English before I have done with it. This morning I wrote a note to one of the papers here in which my teacher found only a single word to change. Was n't that pretty well for a boy of my standing?"

In 1880 Lowell was sent from Spain as minister to England, in which official capacity he served his country for another period of three years. He loved London. Many years before going there, he had written to a friend: "I fancy if I were suddenly snatched away to London, my brain would prickle all over as a foot that has been asleep when the blood starts in it again. Books are good dry forage; we can keep alive on them, but, after all, men are the only fresh pasture." Now, in the large free life of the world's metropolis, he enjoyed this fresh pasture to his heart's content. He was very popular in England. His social gifts, his happy facility in making public addresses, his fame as a writer, did honor to the country he represented, and delighted the nation to which he had gone. For nine years after his appointment to England, he regularly spent his summers in the romantic old town of Whitby, where the famous old abbey, the changing lights of the sea, and the moors purpled with heather were a source of endless delight to him. His wife died in 1885, and he rented the old homestead at Cambridge, feeling it too painful in the first sharp grief over his loss to go back to meet the ghosts of former happiness. But in the fall of 1889 he returned there to live with his daughter, Mrs. Burnett, and her family. He would

not have the leaves raked away from the lawn, " for
the rustle of them," he said, " stirs my earliest memories, and when the wind blows, they pirouette so
gayly as to give me cheerful thoughts of death. But,
oh, the changes ! "

He lived two years to enjoy this old home, from
which much of the joy to him had fled in those sad
changes over which he sighed, and after several
attacks of illness he died on the twelfth of August,
1891.   He was buried in Mt. Auburn Cemetery,
where the ashes of so many illustrious New England-
ers lie. His grave, on the lower slope of a grassy
ridge, is shaded by a large elm, and marked by a
simple, low slab of blue slate.

Of all American writers, Lowell had the largest,
warmest nature. A certain freshness, a buoyant and
youthful vigor, abound in him from his earliest to his
latest years.   In his beautiful poem commemorating
Agassiz, he says : —

> " He was so human! whether strong or weak,
> Far from his kind he neither sank nor soared."

One feels that the lines were made for Lowell,
too. He was so human ! Unconventional, full of
noble impulses that were translated into immediate action, generous, brave, loyal-hearted, cheery,
sparkling with wit, exuberant in spirits, full of affection and tenderness, and full of bright humor, too,
scornful only of what is base, unjust, and cruel,
— his is the most attractive personality in our
literature. His tenderness, his susceptibility, were
almost feminine. He once wrote in his earlier
years : —

"I pass through the world, and meet scarcely a response to the affectionateness of my nature. I believe Maria only knows how loving I am truly. Brought up in a very reserved and conventional family, I cannot in society appear what I really am. I go out sometimes with my heart so full of yearning towards my fellows that the indifferent look with which even entire strangers pass me by brings tears into my eyes."

And yet he had a virile contempt, mixed, he says, with pity for all the weaknesses of the poetical temperament, — the mawkish sentimentality that is so apt to sour into cynicism, the over-sensitiveness that responds so keenly to the merest trifles, and the solitariness and egotism that grow out of this morbid irritability. He might himself have been a victim of these weaknesses, had not the "immense ballast of common sense" with which he was endowed steadied him and helped to keep him rooted in the real. He says in one of his letters : —

"I find myself very curiously compounded of two distinct characters. One half of me is clear mystic and enthusiast, and the other humorist. If I had lived as solitary as a hermit of the Thebais, I doubt not that I should have had as authentic interviews with the evil one as they ; and, without any disrespect to the saint, it would have taken very little to have made a St. Francis of me. Indeed, during that part of my life in which I lived most alone, I was never a single night unvisited by visions, and once I thought I had a personal revelation from God himself. I can believe perfectly in the sincerity of those who are commonly called religious impostors, for at one time a meteor could not fall, nor lightning flash, that I did not in some way connect it with my own interior life and destiny. On the other hand, had I mixed more with the world than I have, I should probably have become a Pantagruelist."

An extraordinary youthfulness of feeling, the feeling that beyond all others belongs most peculiarly to genius, characterized Lowell all his life. Writing in his seventy-first year, he says: —

"Thank God, I am as young as ever. There is an exhaustless fund of inexperience somewhere about me, a Fortunatus purse that keeps me so. I have had my share of bitter experiences, but they have left no black drop behind them in my blood — *pour me faire envisager la vie en noir.*"

He loved the earth and the life on it, not with that melancholy need of seeking solace in nature which many modern poets feel, but with a love that was wholly sympathy with its joyous pulse-beats. Here is a characteristic outburst from one of his letters which will illustrate this feeling: —

"I wanted to tell you what glorious fall weather we are having, clear and champagny, the northwest wind crisping Fresh Pond to steel blue, and curling the wet lily-pads over till they bloom in a sudden flash of golden sunshine. How I do love the earth ! I feel it thrill under my feet. I feel somehow as if it were conscious of my love, as if something passed into my dancing blood from it, and I get rid of that dreadful duty-feeling, ' What right have I to be ? ' and not a golden-rod of them all soaks in the sunshine, or feels the blue currents of the air eddy about him more thoughtlessly than I."

Much of this fulness of life in him showed in his animated face and active figure. He was not above middle height, but was robust enough to carry the impression of health and endurance. His gray eyes brightened with his gayer moods and gave vivacity to a face framed by a full beard, lighter and redder in color than his dark auburn hair.

Lowell's letters edited by Charles Eliot Norton are the best record that we have of his personality in his social relations. Viewed in that light, they do not make too prominent the lighter, gayer side of his character. Glimpses we have, also, of that other, deeply serious side of him, but they are only glimpses. The revelation of that side is to be found in his works. "The Vision of Sir Launfal" is one of the finest expressions of it, as well as the most perfect of his poems. The subject is an original treatment of the old legend of the Holy Grail, the fabled cup out of which Christ drank at the Last Supper, and the quest of which was the favorite enterprise of the knights of the Round Table.

The prelude to the first part of the poem fairly brims over with spring juices and sunshine. In the universal well-being of this happy season,

> " 'T is as easy now for the heart to be true
> As for grass to be green and skies to be blue,
> 'T is the natural way of living ; "

and Sir Launfal remembers his vow to recover the Holy Grail. He commands his golden spurs and richest mail to be brought to him, and declares he shall not lie in a bed again until he has kept his vow; and sinking down on a bed of rushes, he hopes for a guiding vision, which comes to him in this wise:

From the frowning, gray old castle whose gates are shut to all but lord or lady of high degree, the young knight sets forth on his quest. A hideous leper at the castle gate begs an alms of him, and, in loathing of him as a blot on the summer morning, he disdainfully flings him a coin. The leper refuses to lift it from the dust, and reproaches him for giving worthless gold from a sense of duty, and withholding the richer alms of his heart's warm sympathy.

The prelude to part second begins with a description of winter in all its bleakness and bareness; and in part second, Sir Launfal, a worn old man, returns to his castle to find another heir in his earldom, and himself shut out from the Christmas cheer and ruddy blaze within the castle walls. He falls into a reverie, warming himself with the memory of desert heats in Oriental lands, when suddenly he is aroused by the voice of a beggar, and lifting his eyes, sees the leper before him again. Sir Launfal is touched with pity now: he has known sorrow himself, and heartache, discouragement, and despair; for he has come back from his weary search without the Holy Grail. He has no gold to give, but love and pity are in his heart; he shares his broken crust with the leper, and breaking the ice from the brink of a streamlet, he offers him drink from a wooden bowl, — when lo! the leper is suddenly transfigured into the image of Christ, the poor wooden bowl into the shining Holy Grail, and he hears a soft voice saying, —

> "Lo, it is I, be not afraid !
> In many climes without avail,
> Thou hast spent thy life for the Holy Grail;
> Behold, it is here, — this cup which thou
> Didst fill at the streamlet for Me but now ;
> This crust is My body broken for thee,
> This water His blood that died on the tree;
> The Holy Supper is kept, indeed,
> In whatso we share with another's need :
> Not what we give, but what we share, —
> For the gift without the giver is bare ;
> Who gives himself with his alms feeds three, —
> Himself, his hungering neighbor, and Me."

At this, Sir Launfal awakes, understands the beautiful significance of the vision, and orders his armor to be hung on the wall, saying that the Holy Grail is found here in his castle, and he throws its doors wide open to all, rich and poor alike, —

> "And there's no poor man in the North Countree,
> But is lord of the earldom as much as he."

The poetical part of the "Biglow Papers" is written in the Yankee dialect, a dialect which Lowell loved. "To me," he says, "the dialect was native, was spoken all about me when a boy at a time when an Irish day-laborer was as rare as an American one now. Since then I have made a study of it so far as opportunity allowed. But when I write in it, it is as in a mother-tongue, and I am carried back to long ago noonings in my father's hayfields, and to the talk of Sam and Job over their jug of *blackstrap* under the shade of the ash-tree which still dapples the grass whence they have been gone so long." That he used the dialect with the vigor and freedom of a mother-tongue, the witty, satirical, and sometimes pathetically beautiful lines in the "Biglow Papers" most unmistakably show.

The "Biglow Papers" is a political satire that has become a classic. What was local and temporary in its themes is so bound up in Lowell's treatment of them with what is universal and abiding in human nature, that it gives almost as lively a pleasure to-day as in the stirring times in which it was written. It is introduced by a ludicrous imitation of press-notices, among which is a capital parody of Carlyle's peculiar phraseology, entitled "From the World-Harmonic-

Æolian-Attachment." The chief characters in the satire are Homer Wilbur, pastor of the First Church in Jaalam, and his gifted parishioner, the young farmer poet, Hosea Biglow, of whom his pastor says that in mowing " he cuts a cleaner and wider swath than any man in town." And he can cut just as clean a swath with his pen through cant, injustice, and political quackery. Birdofredum Sawin, another character, represents the weak, easily influenced, time-serving politician who trims his sails to catch all the winds that blow, and has no other aim in life than his own immediate pleasure and profit. The public journalist who leads his sheep for the sake of the mutton; the poltroonery of the clergyman " who chooses to walk off to the extreme edge of the world and to sow such seed as he has clear over into that darkness which he calls the next life; " the presidential candidate's letter of acceptance that, like the ancient oracle, conveys no meaning at all or an accommodatingly equivocal one, being subject, like the beast in the Apocalypse, to as many several interpretations as there are minds brought to bear upon it,— all these are treated with admirable scorn, and help to keep the book alive. Then, too, it would be hard to match anywhere the pathos, the quick heart-throbs of agony and longing that tremble through the poem that Hosea Biglow addresses to the editor of the " Atlantic Monthly " in answer to the latter's request to be funny. Real tears watered the writing of that poem, and the glitter of them seems to rest on it still.

The deep feeling and high purpose that underlie the humor, the clever satire and the bursts of indignation in the " Biglow Papers," may be traced again in the Memorial Odes. The fine portraitures of Lincoln and Washington in the " Harvard Commemoration Ode" and in " Under the Old Elm," are quite un-equalled. They belong to a class of literary work in which Lowell excelled, and for which his critical faculty particularly fitted him. The " Fable for Critics," in spite of many lines that are hardly better than doggerel, contains, with the exception of the lines on Thoreau, wonderfully true and clever analyses of our principal writers.

To Thoreau, Lowell was always unjust. His own warm social nature and his indebtedness to his fellow-men for the broader development of his genius wholly unfitted him to understand or appreciate the colder temperament of Thoreau, whose peculiar gifts required an altogether different atmosphere for their development. He treats the Walden episode, not as such, but as the actual existence of the man, — as if he were a life-long hermit quarrelling with civilization. Yet, with singular inconsistency, he comments with charming indulgence upon the scholar's aloofness from the busy affairs of the world in his essay on Gray, where he notices Gilbert White's recording the awakening and coming forth from his dormitory of an old tortoise at Lewes, Sussex, when news of Bur-goyne's surrender must have reached England about that time. " It may argue pusillanimity," writes Lowell, " but I can hardly help envying the remorse-less indifference of such men to the burning questions of the' hour, at the first alarm of which we are all expected to run with buckets, or it may be with our can of kerosene, snatched by mistake in the hurry and confusion." He dwells lovingly on Izaak Walton's sequestered life during the tumult of civil and foreign war, saying : —

" So far as he himself could shape its course, it leads us under the shadow of honeysuckle hedges, or along the rushy banks of silence-loving streams, or through the claustral hush of Cathedral closes, or where the shadow of the village church-tower creeps round the dial of green grass below, or to the company of thoughtful and godly men. . . . Whether such fugitive and cloistered virtue as his comes within the sweep of Milton's gravely cadenced lash or not, — whether a man does not owe himself more to the distasteful publicity of active citizenship than to the petting of his own private tastes or talents as Walton thought it right and found it sweet to do, may be a question.   There can be none that the contemplation of such a life both soothes and charms, and we sigh to think that the like of it is possible no more.   Where, now, would the fugitive from the espials of our modern life find a sanctuary which telegraph or telephone had not deflowered?   I do not mean that Walton was an idle man, who, as time was given him for nothing, thought that he might part with it for nothing, too.   If he had been, I should not be writing this.   He left behind him two books, each a masterpiece in its own simple and sincere way ; and only the contemplative leisure of a life like his could have secreted the precious qualities that assure them against decay."

A little more indulgence in his criticism of Thoreau, who answers his question as to the possibility of finding a man, now, whom the world could not find, would have given us a truer portraiture of a rarely gifted spirit, whose contemplative life secréted the precious qualities, not of two only, but of many books that will live.   But with the exception of his judgment on Thoreau, and possibly his interpretation of Carlyle, there is very little to quarrel with in Lowell's criticism both in prose and verse. He had read widely and with keen appetite. He knew men, and had never shared the romantic dreams of the Transcendentalists. He tested what he read by his knowledge of life as he had seen and felt it. By that standard he detected instantly what was fine and true, and what was mean and false. It is the critic's only true standard, but it is safe only when the critic himself has a large nature and a clear eye. Lowell had both. How he rejoices in the hearty freshness, sincerity, and simplicity of Chaucer! He is always delightful when he speaks of him, yet not more so than when he writes of Dryden, who was almost Chaucer's antithesis, and of whom, when he reads him, he says that he "cannot help thinking of an ostrich to be classed among flying things and capable, what with leap and flap together, of leaving the earth for a longer or shorter space, but loving the open plain, where wing and foot help each other to something that is both flight and run at once."

Lowell has no sympathy with pessimism, cynicism, or sentimentality. His criticism stands for a wise optimism and a joyous sympathy with life. He calls the sentimentalist a —

"spiritual hypochondriac, with whom fancies become facts, while facts are a discomfort because they will not be evaporated into fancy. Theory is too fine a dame to confess even a country cousinship with coarse-handed Practice, whose homely ways would disconcert her artificial world. The very susceptibility which makes him quick to feel makes him also incapable of deep and durable feeling. He loves to think he suffers, and keeps a pet. sorrow, a blue devil familiar that goes with him everywhere, like Paracelsus' black dog. . . . We do not think the worse of Goethe for hypothetically desolating himself in the fashion aforesaid (Werther), for with many constitutions it is as purely natural a crisis as dentition, which the stronger worry through, and turn out very sensible, agreeable fellows. But whenever there is an arrest of development, and the heart-break of the patient is audibly prolonged through life, we have a spectacle which the toughest heart would wish to get as far away from as possible. We would not be supposed to overlook the distinction too often lost sight of, between sentimentalism and sentiment, the latter being a very excellent thing in its way, as genuine things are apt to be. Sentiment is intellectual emotion, — emotion precipitated, as it were, in pretty crystals by the fancy. . . . It puts into words for us that decorous average of feeling to the expression of which society can consent without danger of being indiscreetly moved. It is excellent for people who are willing to save their souls alive to any extent that shall not be discomposing. It is even satisfying until some deeper experience has given us a hunger for what we so glibly call ' the world ' cannot sate, just as water-ice is nourishment enough to a man who has just had his dinner. . . . True sentiment is emotion ripened by a slow ferment of the mind, and qualified to an agreeable temperance by that taste which is the conscience of polite society."

Elsewhere he says : —

" Poets have forgotten that the first lesson of literature, no less than of life, is the learning how to burn your own smoke ; that the way to be original is to be healthy ; that the fresh color, so delightful in all good writing, is won by escaping from the fixed air of self into the brisk atmosphere of universal sentiments, and that to make the common marvellous as if it were a revelation is the test of genius."

At its best, Lowell's prose shows unmistakable traces of the poet. He is never at a loss for an image or a picture. Writing of Chaucer, he says that —

"his best tales run on like one of our inland rivers, sometimes hastening a little and turning upon themselves in eddies that dimple while retarding the current; sometimes loitering smoothly, while here and there a quiet thought, a tender feeling, a pleasant image, a golden-hearted verse opens quietly as a water-lily to float on the surface without breaking it into ripple."

Speaking of that natural indifference to beauty in vulgar souls that cannot recognize it for themselves and feign an admiration for what is celebrated as admirable, he says: —

" I remember people who had to go over the Alps to learn what the divine silence of snow was, — who must run to Italy before they were conscious of the miracle wrought every day under their very noses by the sunset, — who must call upon the Berkshire Hills to teach them what a painter autumn was, while close at hand the Fresh Pond meadows made all orioles cheap with hues that showed as if a sunset cloud had been wrecked among their maples."

But his prose is not always so simple and fine as that. He dreaded above everything to talk like a book. "There is death in the dictionary," he says, " and where language is too strictly limited by convention, the ground for expression to grow is limited also; and we get a potted literature, — Chinese dwarfs instead of healthy trees." He is never tired of praising that simplicity of expression which "leaves criticism helpless by the mere light of nature alone." Yet he was himself by no means a simple writer. His vocabulary contains many unusual words as well as very many trite ones, and he is fond of piecing out his velvet with cotton, or of wearing the laborer's soiled blouse over the professor's gown. It is as if he were always fearful of playing the pedant, or carrying his learning as if it were an uncomfortable weight. This strain after ease that so plainly evinces uneasiness gives to his prose at times a disagreeable impression of incongruity, just as his humor is sometimes impertinently obtrusive and spoils a serious passage with its waggery. These faults are not to be found in his public addresses delivered in England, nor in his political essays, which should be read by every student of American history and every citizen of the United States. They are thickly sown with maxims of political wisdom, and are characterized throughout by uncompromising logic and common-sense, shrewd and biting sarcasm, and admit not a word for mere rhetoric's sake, not a playful relaxing by so much as a smile of tense feeling and earnest expression of it. They are as fine in their way as anything Lowell has written, and add lustre to those masterpieces of criticism and poetry that will keep his memory green.

CHAPTER XVII

FRANCIS PARKMAN (1823–1893)

FRANCIS PARKMAN, the son of a Unitarian clergyman, was born in Boston, Massachusetts, on the sixteenth of September, 1823. He was of a delicate constitution from his earliest childhood; but his intellect was so active and daring, and he threw himself with so much zest into whatever inquiry interested him, that his accomplishments even in his boyhood would have been remarkable in one of rugged health. Fond at all times of out-door life, his earliest interests were in the direction of natural history. He made extensive collections, and roamed the woods, learning to fish and hunt, and acquiring that acquaintance with nature which was to make him the most picturesque of historians. An eager interest in chemistry succeeded his passion for collecting, and for a time he devoted himself exclusively to chemical experiments.

In 1840 he entered Harvard College, and not long afterward formed the design of writing a history of the French in North America. In his preface to "Count Frontenac," he says of this design:—

"When, at the age of eighteen, I formed the purpose of writing a French-American history, I meant at first to limit myself to the great contest which brought the history to a close. It was by an afterthought that the plan was extended to cover the whole field, so that the part of the work, or series of works, first conceived would, following the sequence of events, be the last executed. As soon as the original scheme was formed, I began to prepare for executing it by examining localities, journeying in forests, visiting Indian tribes, and collecting materials."

During his college course Parkman's health gave way, and he went abroad; but, keeping in mind his purpose, he took lodgings for a time in a Roman monastery, that he might study the character of the religious recluse of whom the early French missionaries to the Indians were representatives. Parkman returned to Cambridge in time to be graduated with his class in 1844. After his graduation he made a feint at studying law for two years, then abandoned the subject to throw himself heart and soul into his chosen life-work.

He felt that a knowledge of Indian life and character at first hand was absolutely indispensable to his treatment of a subject in which the Indian plays so prominent a part; and to acquire this knowledge, he determined to spend some time among the wild tribes of the West. With this purpose in view, he set out from St. Louis on the twenty-eighth of April, 1846, for a tour to the Rocky Mountains. The site of the present Kansas City was then on the frontier, and the vast plains of the West were still a free playground for the buffalo and the Indian. Parkman was accompanied by a relative about his own age and, like himself, a college graduate, and by two guides of French descent.

The discomforts of primitive travel over the wild plains, drenchings from storms, frantic chases after galloping horses broken loose, anxious camp-fire vigils, rough and meagre fare, — all this told on the delicate constitution of Parkman, and before he had reached the village of the Dacotah Indians, he was so ill and exhausted that his life was in danger. But the dauntless spirit in him never faltered for a moment. He took up his abode with an Indian family, ate boiled puppy with them at their dog-feasts, watched their dusky figures flitting before the bright lodge-fires, listened to their weird cries, and gave no sign of his suffering. Of these discomforts and his illness, he says: —

"I was so reduced by illness that I could seldom walk without reeling like a drunken man, and when I rose from my seat upon the ground, the landscape suddenly grew dim before my eyes, the trees and lodges seemed to sway to and fro, and the prairie to rise and fall like the swells of the ocean. Such a state of things is not enviable anywhere. In a country where a man's life may at any moment depend on the strength of his arm, or it may be on the activity of his legs, it is more particularly inconvenient. Nor is sleeping on damp ground, with an occasional drenching from a shower, very beneficial in such cases. I sometimes suffered the extremity of exhaustion, and was in a fair way of atoning for my love of the prairie by resting there forever.

"I tried repose and a very sparing diet. For a long time, with exemplary patience, I lounged about the camp, or at the utmost staggered over to the Indian village, and walked faint and dizzy among the lodges. It would not do, and I bethought me of starvation. During five days I sustained life on one small biscuit a day. . . . I used to lie languid and dreamy before our tent, musing on the past and the future ; and when most overcome with lassitude, my eyes turned always toward the distant Black Hills."

Mark that, — these tired, sick eyes turning not toward rest and home, but toward the purpose yet unfinished. He wished to see an Indian fight, preparations for which were going on where he was; and when the camp broke up, although he was so weak and ill that he could only sit his horse by day "with the aid of a spoonful of whiskey swallowed at short intervals," he followed the Indian trail alone with one guide.

On his arrival at the Indian village he was attacked by all the curs in the settlement barking and yelling at his heels. One big white cur that he could not conciliate he bought of the squaw to whom it belonged for some beads, vermilion, and other trinkets, and had the dog served up at a feast to which the Indians were invited. He joined the Indians in a buffalo hunt to which his savage companions rode, each with a piece of buffalo robe for a saddle, and for a bridle a cord of twisted hair tied to the horse's lower jaw. He watched them surround the newly killed buffalo, cut it to pieces, crack the huge bones and devour the marrow, cut away collops of liver and eat them raw on the spot, their faces and hands smeared with blood. He watched the squaws rub the brains of the buffalo into its hide to render it soft, pliant, and fit for use as clothing or the covering of wigwams.

These Indians, the Western Dacotahs, with whom he lived were " thorough savages," he tells us, "living representatives of the stone age. . . . Hunting and fishing, they wander incessantly, through summer and winter. Some follow the herds of buffalo over the waste of prairie; others traverse the Black Hills, thronging, on horseback and on foot, through the dark gulfs and sombre gorges, and emerging at last upon the ' Parks,' those beautiful but most perilous hunting-grounds. The buffalo supplies them with the necessaries of life, — with habitations, food, clothing, beds, and fuel; strings for their bows, glue, thread, cordage, trail-ropes for their horses, coverings for their saddles, vessels to hold water, boats to cross streams, and the means of purchasing all that they want from the traders. When the buffalo are extinct they, too, must dwindle away."

The long painful summer with its rich but costly experiences wore away, and Parkman returned to civilization and the East to prepare an account of what he had seen for his first book, " The Oregon Trail, Sketches of Prairie and Rocky Mountain Life." He had paid dear for the material of this book, but he had paid it willingly. He had witnessed a form of life fast disappearing, and says of it : —

" The wild cavalcade that defiled with me down the gorges of the Black Hills, with its paint and war-plumes, fluttering trophies and savage embroidery, bows, arrows, lances, and shields, will never be seen again. Those who formed it have found bloody graves, or a ghastlier burial in the maws of wolves. The Indian of to-day, armed with a revolver and crowned with an old hat, is an Indian still, but an Indian shorn of the picturesqueness which was his most conspicuous merit. The mountain trapper is no more, and the grim romance of his wild, hard life is a memory of the past."

"The Oregon Trail" appeared in 1847 in a magazine, and two years later in book form. It is an ideal book for the young who love adventure; it is truthful, picturesque, full of the life of the prairie and the Indian lodge. It is intensely interesting, also, to the student of Parkman; being autobiographical in its nature, it introduces the author in such a way as to reveal his most prominent characteristics, — heroism, endurance, unwearied persistence, and conscientious fidelity to fact.

While his memory of Indian life was vivid, Parkman wrote the " History of the Conspiracy of Pontiac," and published it in 1851.   He said that he chose the subject because of the opportunities it afforded him for depicting forest life and the Indian character.   The book is intended as a sequel to "France and England in North America," which is the general title of Parkman's historical works, and it is one of the most interesting of the series.

Parkman was happily married in 1852; six years later his wife died, leaving him two daughters, and his sister took charge of his home in Boston.   He went abroad, spending his time collecting historical material in England, France, and Spain.   This research was carried on under very painful circumstances, and in the preface to his next work, " The Pioneers of France in the New World " (1865), he informs his readers that for eighteen years the state of his health has been such as to render close application to books suicidal; and that for two periods of several years his eyes had not permitted him to read continuously for more than five minutes, and often not at all.   Like Prescott, he was forced to employ a reader and to dictate what he had composed. His physician told him that he could not live and work as he did; but the threat did not make him idle, he simply worked on.

In addition to this labor of searching books and

manuscripts with borrowed eyes, he added that of
visiting all the chief localities mentioned in his
histories. He made in all five journeys to Europe
in the interests of his work. He travelled the ground
of the French explorers in Canada. He visited the
scenes of the great battles and sieges in the French
and Indian War. He journeyed over the country in
the line of march that the Spaniard, Menendez, took
on his way to butcher the French Huguenots at Fort
Caroline, Florida. He explored the scenes of La
Salle's discoveries. He chatted about Pontiac with
Pierre Chouteau, companion of La Clede, the founder
of St. Louis, at Chouteau's country-house near that
city. He visited Brittany that he might look at the
portrait of Jacques Cartier in the town hall of St.
Malo, and his rude stone mansion in the suburbs, and
see for himself if nothing more might be learned of
this intrepid explorer.

He desired to give life and form to his facts without abusing his fancy. "Faithfulness to the truth of
history," he says, " involves far more than research,
however patient and scrupulous, into special facts.
Such facts may be detailed with the most minute
exactness, and yet the narrative, taken as a whole,
may be unmeaning or untrue. The narrator must
seek to imbue himself with the life and spirit of the
time. He must study events in their bearings near
and remote; in the character, habits, and manners of
those who took part in them. He must himself be,
as it were, a spectator of the action he describes."

"The Pioneers of France in the New World" was
succeeded by "The Jesuits in North America" (1867);
"La Salle and the Discovery of the Great West"

(1869); " The Old Régime in Canada " (1874); " Count Frontenac and New France under the Reign of Louis XIV." (1877); " Montcalm and Wolfe " (1884); and " A Half Century of Conflict " (1892). The last-named volume is properly the sixth in the series concerning the struggle between France and England for possessions in the New World.

In the execution of this great work, Parkman turned once aside to write a novel; but the venture, like a similar one of Motley's, was without success, and he did not repeat the experiment.   As a relaxation from his studies, he cultivated roses so successfully that his gardens became famous.   He was chosen president of the Massachusetts Horticultural Society, and for two years was at the head of the agricultural depart- ment in Harvard College.   He was a man of simple, agreeable manners, fuller of deeds than words; tall and slender in figure, with a smooth face; pale, sharp, resolute features; gentle brown eyes, and thick hair. While he lived, his active spirit knew no rest, and his death on the eighth of November, 1893, followed close upon the conclusion of his work.

The recognition of the importance and significance of that work has been steadily growing since his death.   John Fiske declares that " it clearly belongs among the world's few masterpieces of highest rank, along with the works of Herodotus, Thucydides, and Gibbon."   Parkman himself indicates the importance of his theme when he says : —

" The most momentous and far-reaching question ever brought to issue on this continent was: Shall France re- main here, or shall she not? If by diplomacy or war she had preserved but the half or less than half of her American possessions, then a barrier would have been set to the spread of the English-speaking races : there would have been no Revolutionary War; and for a long time, at least, no independence. . . . A happier calamity never befell a people than the conquest of Canada by the British arms."

He dwells with a fulness of picturesque detail on all the conditions that preceded this momentous struggle and conquest; the daring explorations of the French, their efforts at colonization; the insufferable tyrannies of a paternal government that found the citizen a child and kept him so; the thankless labors of the Jesuit missionaries among the Indians, and the life and character of the Indians themselves. His theme necessarily involves much repetition of scenes of carnage and savage treachery; but he does not write history for the sake of relating bloody conflicts; it is man that interests him, — individual man, savage or civilized. Events are little to him unless they elucidate character; while the slightest personal detail that can give a more intimate glimpse of a man's nature, is of the first importance. His pages are alive; he tells us how his soldiers, missionaries, and explorers suffered; what they said, and how they felt and looked. For this reason his books abound in food for the psychologist. Here the great primitive passions of humanity have a fair field for their play. We seem to be spectators of a great moral drama, often a terrible drama. We see the influence of unrestrained license upon men, — the savage and brute reappearing as the superficial gloss of civilization wears away; we witness the strength of the hunger for life in mothers abandoning their children in moments of deadly peril, — Quakers abandoning their principles and taking up arms in self-defence. We note the vanity and selfishness that taint the ascetic as well as the man of the world; we see him preaching a gospel of love, and at the same time sowing the seeds of hatred and murder in the breasts of his converts. But we note, too, fine heroic qualities, for Parkman loves a hero. He watches with Wolfe racked with pain and disease, and listens with sympathetic attention while the hero says to the physician before the attack on Quebec: "I know perfectly well you can't cure me, but pray make me up so that I may be without pain for a few days and able to do my duty: that is all I want." In La Salle he finds another hero after his own heart, — a man whom no peril, treachery, or difficulty can daunt in the fulfilment of a resolve, — "an unconquerable mind" served by "a frame of iron."

La Salle had first undertaken his Western explorations in hope of reaching the Indies through a river communication with the ocean. Discovering that the Mississippi empties instead into the Gulf of Mexico, his next ambition was to explore and colonize the West for the French. The boundless, fertile prairies seemed to him the possible foundation of a great French empire. To realize this possibility, he underwent almost incredible labors, among others that of journeying on foot from his newly built fort, Crèvecœur, opposite the present site of Peoria, Illinois, to Montreal, Canada, — setting out on the first of March, wading through slush and snow, famishing at times and arriving at his destination sixty-five days later, on the sixth of May. Parkman follows this tedious and painful journey with minute description, unwilling that the slightest detail of so courageous an undertaking should miss its record.

Yet there is no undue heat in Parkman's enthusiasms, any more than in his disapprovals. He is always cool and unprejudiced. He espouses no cause but that of truth, and will tell it whether it be to glorification or to shame. He has a wise skepticism that will take no character for granted on the score of a reputation, but will sift all evidence *pro* and *con* to find out the real man clear of the false coloring lent him by gratitude or prejudice. He observes, in "The Old Régime in Canada": —

"Children are taught that the Puritans came to New England in search of religious liberty. The liberty they sought was for themselves alone. It was the liberty to prevent all others from doing the like. They imagined that they held a monopoly of religious truth, and were bound in conscience to defend it against all comers. Their mission was to build up a western Canaan, ruled by the law of God, to keep it pure from error, and, if need were, purge it of heresy by persecution ; to which ends they set up one of the most detestable theocracies on record. Church and State were joined in one. Church members alone had the right to vote. There was no choice but to remain politically a cipher, or embrace, or pretend to embrace, the extremest dogmas of Calvin. Never was such a premium offered to cant and hypocrisy ; yet in the early days hypocrisy was rare, so intense and pervading was the faith of the founders of New England."

Concerning the exile of the Acadians, he says: —

"New England humanitarianism melting into sentimentality at a tale of woe has been unjust to its own. Whatever judgment may be passed on the cruel measure of wholesale expatriation, it was not put in execution till every resource of patience and persuasion had been tried in vain. The agents of the French Court, civil and military and ecclesiastical, had made some act of force a necessity. We have seen by what vile practices they produced in Acadia a state of things intolerable and impossible of continuance. They conjured up the tempest, and when it burst on the heads of the unhappy people, they gave no help. The government of Louis XV. began with making the Acadians its tools, and ended with making them its victims."

As a people, he does not give an ideal picture of them, but truthfully represents them as "a simple and very ignorant peasantry, industrious and frugal till evil days came to disconcert them;" living in wretched huts, often crowded by more than one family and not over clean, gossiping and quarrelling among themselves, "sometimes by fits, though rarely long, contumacious even towards the curé, the guide, counsellor, and ruler of his flock. Enfeebled by hereditary mental subjection, and too long kept in leading-strings to walk alone, they needed him, not for the next world only, but for this; and their submission compounded of love and fear was commonly without bounds. He was their true government; to him they gave a frank and full allegiance, and dared not disobey him if they would. Of knowledge he gave them nothing; but he taught them to be true to their wives and constant at confession and mass, to stand fast for the church and King Louis, and to resist heresy and King George; for, in one degree or another, the Acadian priest was always the agent of a double-headed foreign power, — the Bishop of Quebec allied with the Governor of Canada."

While doing justice to the devotion, courage, and resolution of the Jesuits in their missionary labors in Canada, Parkman recognizes and declares that "the unchecked sway of priests has always been the most mischievous of tyrannies; and even were they all well-meaning and sincere, it would be so still." Commenting upon the failure of their missions among the Canadian Indians, with the fall of the Hurons, he says : —

" Liberty may thank the Iroquois that by their insensate fury the plans of her adversary were brought to naught, and a peril and woe averted from her future. They ruined the trade which was the life-blood of New France ; they stopped the current of her arteries, and made all her early years a misery and terror. Not that they changed her destinies. The contest on this continent between Liberty and Absolutism was never doubtful, but the triumph of the one would have been dearly bought, and the downfall of the other incomplete. Populations formed in the ideas and habits of a monarchy and controlled by a hierarchy profoundly hostile to freedom of thought would have remained a hindrance and a stumbling-block in the way of that majestic experiment of which America is the field.

" The Jesuits saw their hopes struck down, and their faith, though not shaken, was sorely tried. The providence of God seemed in their eyes dark and inexplicable ; but from the standpoint of liberty that providence is clear as the sun at noon. Meanwhile let those who have prevailed yield due honor to the defeated. Their virtues shine amidst the rubbish of error like diamonds and gold in the gravel of the torrent."

A passionate lover of liberty, Parkman can see that the full enjoyment of it does not belong to everybody : —

" There are no political panaceas except in the imagination of political quacks. To each degree and each variety of public development there are corresponding institutions, best answering the public needs ; and what is meat to one is poison to another. Freedom is for those who are fit for it. The rest will lose it or turn it to corruption. . . .

" The German race, and especially the Anglo-Saxon branch of it, is particularly masculine, and therefore particularly fitted for self-government. It submits its action habitually to the guidance of reason, and has the judicial faculty of seeing both sides of a question. The French Celt is cast in a different mould. He sees the end distinctly, and reasons about it with admirable clearness, but his own impulses and passions continually turn him away from it. Opposition excites him ; he is impatient of delay, is impelled always to extremes, and does not readily sacrifice a present inclination to an ultimate good. He delights in abstractions and generalizations, cuts loose from unpleasing facts, and runs through an ocean of desires and theories."

Parkman's work abounds in excellent characterizations like the above; but man does not play the only part in it: nature, too, has her place there, and he paints the setting to his great human drama with as much faithfulness and care as he places his figures in it. He loved October and its gorgeous coloring, calling autumn the most inspiring of American seasons. We find its colors in his books, but not more frequently than the more delicate beauties of spring, the snowy desolation of winter, and the fulness of summer in primeval forests. His books are as full of outdoors as Thoreau's. It is to the lakeside, the great prairies, or into the depths of tangled forests, that he leads us, and not into kings' cabinets and the boudoirs of intriguing women. The following ex-

ample of his descriptive power follows the account
of the peril and sufferings endured by Champlain
and his companions during the severities of a Canadian winter : —

" This wintry purgatory wore away ; the icy stalactites that
hung from the cliffs fell crashing to the earth ; the clamor of
the wild geese was heard ; the bluebird appeared in the
naked woods ; the water-willows were covered with their
soft caterpillar-like blossoms ; the twigs of the swamp maple
were flushed with ruddy bloom ; the ash hung out its black
tufts ; the shadbush seemed a wreath of snow ; the white
stars of the bloodroot gleamed among dank, fallen leaves,
and in the young grass of the wet meadows the marsh mari-
golds shone like spots of gold."

But better than anything else he has done is the
characterization of the Indian. The subject fascinated him, and whether he designed it or not, the
Indian is the central figure of all his work. He
paints him in every mood and form of his wild
life, — lounging on skins torpid after dog-feasts, in
the excitement of war and the chase, grave in the
council lodge, stoical in the endurance of torture,
fiendish in the application of it. He has no illusions
concerning him. " To make the Indian a hero of
romance is mere nonsense," he declares. He knows
him to be a grown-up child, lazy, improvident,
thoughtless, credulous, believing in charms, dreams,
and witchcraft, lying, thievish, living from hand to
mouth, cruel as death to his enemies. He does not
believe that he can be reclaimed from a savage state,
but is doomed to extinction under the efforts to
civilize him.

" Some races of men seem moulded in wax, soft and melting, at once plastic and feeble. Some races like some metals combine the greatest flexibility with the greatest strength. But the Indian is hewn out of a rock. You can rarely change the form without destruction of the substance. Races of inferior energy have possessed a power of expansion and assimilation to which he is a stranger ; and it is this fixed and rigid rule that has proved his ruin. He will not learn the arts of civilization, and he and his forest must perish together. The stern, unchanging features of his mind excite our admiration from their very immutability ; and we look with deep interest on the fate of this irreclaimable child of the wilderness who will not be weaned from the breast of his rugged mother."

Few histories leave upon the mind of an American reader so salutary an impression of progress as Parkman's. Dealing with a period comparatively recent, they depict a condition of things practically so remote that it is difficult to realize the imminence of the danger that threatened this country. Grateful to have escaped it, and conscious that other insidious dangers confront us, the reader echoes the fine passage with which Parkman closes his history of " Montcalm and Wolfe " : —

" Those who in the weakness of their dissensions needed help from England against the savage on their borders, have become a nation that may defy every foe but that most dangerous of all foes, herself: destined to a majestic future if she will shun the excess and perversion of the principles that made her great, prate less about the enemies of the present, resist the mob and the demagogue as she resisted Parliament and king, rally her powers from the race for gold and the delirium of prosperity to make firm the foundations on which that prosperity rests, and turn some fair proportion of her vast mental forces to other objects than material progress and the game of party politics.   She has tamed the savage continent, peopled the solitude, gathered wealth untold, waxed potent, imposing, redoubtable, and now it remains for her to prove, if she can, that the rule of the masses is consistent with the individual; that democracy can give the world a civilization as mature and pregnant, ideas as energetic and vitalizing, and types of manhood as lofty and strong, as any of the systems which it boasts to supplant."

CHAPTER XVIII

LATER WRITERS — WHITMAN, STODDARD, STEDMAN,
HOWELLS, JAMES

IN our survey of American Literature in the preceding chapters, we have chiefly confined our attention to the most eminent writers of our country, — to those whose work is done and upon whom time has passed a favorable judgment. But our literature is further enriched by other writers whose work eminently deserves recognition. Among these writers the most distinguished are the novelists Henry James and William Dean Howells; the poets and critics Edmund Clarence Stedman and Henry Stoddard; the sincere, manly essayist John Burroughs; the philosopher and historian John Fiske; and the popular humorist Mark Twain (Samuel Langhorne Clemens).

We have also in Walt Whitman another writer of peculiar interest, but one who holds an anomalous and equivocal position in American literature. Though unrecognized by the vast majority of thoughtful readers and conscientious critics, he is not lacking in a unique and interesting personality, and is not without a small band of enthusiastic admirers whose opinions deserve serious consideration and not the contemptuous silence with which they are usually received.

When Whitman's "Leaves of Grass" appeared in 1855, Emerson wrote the author a letter, breathing the very spirit of generous, enthusiastic approval and encouragement. Whitman's unconventionality, his immense egotism answering to that self-reliance and independence that Emerson himself inculcates, undoubtedly pleased him. Here seemed the man self-centred, erect, broad as the prairies of his country, of whom Emerson had written; and he hailed the new man as a prophet hails what answers to his word. His enthusiasm blinded his judgment; he wished so earnestly to see some living thing in the wilderness that he mistook a bush for a bear. But his enthusiasm cooled; he saw his mistake, and to the generous, unstinted praise of the letter to the author there succeeded a sober second judgment which made him regret sincerely Whitman's unauthorized publication of it.

Thoreau, too, records his admiration of Whitman's "Leaves of Grass," not so unreservedly as Emerson, but as heartily, saying: "I do not believe that all the sermons that have been preached in the land put together are equal to it, for preaching." This dictum is repeated in various forms by a few other distinguished Americans, notably, John Burroughs and Edmund Clarence Stedman, and finds an echo in England among a small number of liberal thinkers. Therefore no student of American letters can be excused from examining the claims of Walt Whitman as a poet and thinker.

WALT WHITMAN was born on the thirty-first of May, 1819, at West Hills, Long Island, about thirty miles from New York City. On the paternal side he was of Anglo-American descent, but his mother, Louisa Van Velsor, was of Dutch origin. "The Van Velsors," says Whitman, "were noted for fine horses, which the men bred and trained from blooded stock." Burroughs speaks of a paternal great-grandmother, "a large, swarthy woman who lived to a very old age. She smoked tobacco, rode on horseback like a man, managed the most vicious horse, and becoming a widow in later years, went forth every day over her farmlands frequently in the saddle, directing the labor of her slaves, with language in which, on exciting occasions, oaths were not spared."

Whitman inherited from this coarse and vigorous stock his healthy physique and love of the open air. He was thoroughly an out-door boy; clam-digging, eel-spearing, gathering sea-gulls' eggs, fishing excursions, chats with fishermen and sailors were the chief pleasures of his boyhood. Coney Island, then bare and unfrequented, was his favorite bathing-place, and when a lad in his teens, he loved to race naked up and down the hard sand, declaiming aloud Homer and Shakespeare. His father, a carpenter and builder, had a family of eight children, of whom Walt was the second son. The eldest son was mentally defective, and died insane a little past middle life; and the youngest, Eddy, was an imbecile. A third son was a poor weak creature who died in middle age, but Walt was a healthy, fast-growing lad, and at fifteen had almost the stature of a man. When his father removed with his family to Brooklyn, Walt became for a short time a lawyer's office-boy. A ticket to a circulating library was given him, and he devoured romances, novels, and poetry without discrimination.

He had no settled aim for the future beyond what is understood by the phrase " seeing life." He was a lover of crowds, had a particular fondness for ferries, and his favorite comrades were omnibus-drivers. He told Thoreau that he " loved to ride up and down Broadway all day on an omnibus, sitting beside the driver, gesticulating and declaiming at the top of his voice." He acknowledges his indebtedness to these Broadway jaunts as well as to the stage actors, singers, and public speakers of his time, for the inspiration of much of his " Leaves of Grass." The truth is, he had a prosaic and not a poetical order of mind. His imagination was too meagre to afford him pleasure or to lead him to knowledge, and he was wholly indebted to sensory impressions for his intellectual development. Hence the eagerness with which he sought such impressions, and the importance he ascribes to them.

On leaving the law office, Whitman learned printing, taught country schools and boarded round, resumed his trade, edited a paper in Brooklyn for a year, worked his way as a journeyman printer through many of the States, tried house-building for a time, and having reached middle·life without success in anything, resolved to become a great poet of a new order, a new time, and a new country.

He tells us that before writing he went thoroughly through the Old and New Testaments, Shakespeare, Ossian, the best translated versions of Dante, Homer, Æschylus, Sophocles, the Nibelungenlied, and one or two other masterpieces, and came to the conclusion that these giants had served their purpose with the past but were unfit to satisfy the demands of the future.   Democracy and America had come into existence since then, and must be sung in his own personality, — he, Walt Whitman, being their representative.   Then he looked over Poe's poems, which he did not admire, but in his prose works he found the theory that there can be no such thing as a long poem.   The idea made a strong impression upon him, and induced him to chop his "Leaves of Grass" into fragments; there is absolutely no other reason for such divisions as he makes, since theme and style are identical from beginning to end of his work, and he can give to his segments no other title than their first line.

"Leaves of Grass" appeared in 1855.   The publication of Emerson's private letter to Whitman attracted the first general attention to the book, but it met with almost universal condemnation.

The Civil War broke out; in 1862 news came to Whitman that his brother George had been wounded in the battle of Fredericksburg, and he went to the camp hospital at Falmouth, Virginia, to take care of him.   The sufferings that he witnessed among the wounded and dying soldiers touched his large warm heart, and he continued his ministrations among them at different camps until the close of the war.   Very beautiful, very manly, noble, and tender, was this camp duty; and the memory of it should not perish.   He wrote letters for the wounded; cheered them with hearty words of sympathy and hope; carried them gifts of books, magazines, newspapers, tobacco, fruits, or dainties, as he thought fitting, — often small sums of money which he received for that purpose from benevolent men and women.   On a hot, broiling July day he would give them an ice-cream treat.   He slighted none, Northern or Southern, white or black, and met, as he calculates, from eighty to one hundred thousand soldiers. He helped to dress their wounds, kissed them tenderly as a mother when the longing for home was strong in them. But the richest gift of all that he brought them was the gift of himself; the sunny wholesomeness and courage of his presence. Health, strength, and cleanness seemed to radiate from him; he had a magnificent physique,— tall, large-limbed, broad-shouldered, and his bright florid complexion was heightened in color by contrast with his hair and beard, which whitened early. His manner was calm and self-possessed; he was rarely or never excited; was not fluent in conversation, often hesitating for the right word and the idea, but he was a good listener.

After the war Whitman found employment in the Indian Bureau of the Interior Department at Washington. An ex-Methodist clergyman, then secretary of the Interior, turned him out for having written "Leaves of Grass." This unjust and pitifully childish behavior toward a man who had rendered valuable services to his country during the war, and who was still serving her as a faithful and competent official, secured for Whitman the stanch friendship and esteem of many worthy men and women. From Washington he went to his brother George's home at Camden, New Jersey. The terrible strain of three years' hospital service had sapped his splendid strength, and in February, 1873, he was stricken with paralysis. When he had sufficiently recovered to be about again, he spent his summers at a country farmhouse near Timber Creek.

There was a fine strain of heroism in the man, which showed itself in his hospital experiences, and now showed itself again in the resolute bravery with which he bore his sad affliction. He did not whimper, he did not dwell upon what he had been or might be, but made the most of the sources of happiness still accessible. "The trick is, I find," he says, "to tone your wants and tastes low down enough, and make much of negatives and of mere daylight and the skies." He lived as much as possible out of doors, making a gymnasium of the quiet woods, taking naked sun baths and brisk rubbings, exercising arms and chest by pulling on the tough flexible young boughs of beech, hickory, or holly, and swaying and yielding with them, exercising his lungs by shouting, singing, declaiming, as in the old Broadway days, living, in short, as he says, —

> " At vacancy with nature,
> Acceptive and at ease :
> Distilling the present hour,
> Whatever, wherever it is,
> And over the past, oblivion."

In these little excursions he carried a note-book, and found the woods in mid May and early June his best places of composition. He believed that, after all that is temporary in life, nature alone remains permanent to man, and that the ultimate serenity and happiness of mankind depends upon awakening " from their torpid recesses the affinities of a man or a woman with the open air, the trees, fields, changes of seasons, the sun by day and the stars of heaven by night."

The prose volume, " Specimen Days," resulting from the notes taken in these summer excursions, is filled with descriptions of brooks, clouds, trees, the flight of birds, the humming of insects, given in a succession of minute details, as is his method in what he calls his poetry, and like it wholly wanting in that picture-making power of selection that marks the true artist, and almost wholly wanting in that vivifying presence of the imagination which marks the true poet. Yet Whitman never makes nature an accomplice of human frailty, and the book is singularly free from any weak sentimentalizing.

Whitman never recovered his old vigor, and in 1888 he had so far declined in health as to require a wheeled chair and an attendant. He had been living for some time at his own plain little house on Mickle Street, Camden, New Jersey, where he received visits from many friends and admirers. All who met him found him the most cheerful of invalids, and testify to the singular charm of his personality. He was no student of books, but impatient of methods of learning that were not directly aimed at eye and ear. For that reason he liked best of all to associate with unlearned men and women of native vigor of mind. He had a strong, rugged, self-reliant, all-embracing nature, fearing nothing but " grace, elegance, civilization, the mellow-sweet, the sucking of honey-juice," and as a man he was altogether lovable, and in many respects admirable. But he was neither a profound and logical thinker, nor a poet, and he laid claim to these distinctions.

Whitman died on the twenty-sixth of March, 1892. His prose works are published under the titles of

"Specimen Days and Collect" and "November Boughs." What is called his poetry is published in a volume entitled "Leaves of Grass," to which many lines, some of them under the general title of "Drum Taps," have been added since the first edition.

In justice to those who cannot transform defects into charms, it is necessary to state that even Whitman's most ardent admirers have not arrived at a stage of uncritical enthusiasm without severe and continuous effort. One of them confesses that for eighteen years he has read Whitman, does not understand him yet, never expects to do so wholly, finds him "lighted with an almost unearthly splendor," and will continue to read him as long as he lives. Experience teaches us that there is no superstition so ugly, so foul, or so absurd, that it cannot find a following, if it be only asserted with sufficient gravity and vehemence for a certain length of time. There is no deformity of fashion, no native ugliness that having been looked at long enough will not eventually please the eye. In certain Alpine districts where goitre universally prevails, if a comely girl chances to escape this hideous affliction, it is said compassionately of her, "How pretty she would be, if she only had a goitre!" Fortunately for the reign of good taste in art and literature, the goitrous poet the "unearthly splendor" of whose affliction it requires eighteen years' steady reading to discover, will never be luminous to many readers.

Whitman's admirers are to be found, not among those for whom he professed to write and whose representative he called himself, but among those in whom an excess of culture has resulted in a revolt against good taste. Commenting upon this fact in his admirable lecture on " The English Novel," Sidney Lanier says of Whitman : —

" Professing to be a mudsill and glorying in it, chanting democracy and shirt-sleeves and equal rights, declaring he is nothing if not one of the people, nevertheless the people, the democracy, will have nothing to do with him, and it is safe to say that his sole audience has lain among such representatives of the highest culture as Emerson and the English *illuminated.*

" The truth is that, if closely examined, Whitman instead of being a true democrat is simply the most incorrigible of aristocrats masquing in a peasant's costume, and his poetry, instead of being the natural outcome of a fresh young democracy is a product which would be impossible except in a highly civilized society. . . . His democracy is really the worst kind of aristocracy, being an aristocracy of nature's favorites in the matter of muscle. . . .

" In speaking to those who may be poets in the future, I cannot close these hasty words upon the Whitman school without a fervent protest in the name of all art and artists against a poetry which has painted a great scrawling picture of the human body, and has written under it ' *This is the soul ;* ' which shouts a profession of religion in every line, but of a religion that when examined reveals no tenet, no rubric save that a man must be natural, must abandon himself to every passion ; and which constantly roars its belief in God, but with a camerado air, as if it were patting the Deity on the back and bidding Him *Cheer up* and hope for further encouragement."

Every honest, unprejudiced critic must echo Lanier's protest. Whitman himself declared to a group of friends that one main object he had from the first was to sing, and sing to the full, the ecstasy of simple physiological being. This putting of one's self on record, not by his best thoughts, his aim, his aspirations, but by his weight, the girth of his thigh or chest, and the state of his lungs and liver, is unique enough, and may be interesting from an anatomical point of view; but it is not with a man's liver and lungs that *literature* is concerned. Neither is it concerned with political and material success, nor have we Americans, by virtue of living in a large, fertile, and prosperous country under a democratic form of government, lost the instincts and desires common to humanity, lost all pleasure in noble, uplifting thoughts, all capacity for appreciating what is refined and beautiful in art and literature, and therefore must produce a new form of poetry to tell the world how well off we are in cattle and corn.

Whitman's method of writing " poetry " is very simple. His impatience of restraint, his incapacity for close attention, and his defective ear made rhyme utterly impossible to him, and he ignored it entirely, but substituted, instead, the mere form of it, — short lines and capital letters. Sometimes these lines have a certain rude vigor and rhythmic swing decidedly fresh and pleasing. " The Song of the Redwood Tree," for example, has melody, freshness, verve, and a wholesome sentiment. The last eight lines of " A Song for Occupations " are good and vigorous. The lines in " Drum Taps " entitled " Come up from the Fields, Father," contain a vivid and touching home scene when news of battle is brought to the old farmhouse ; and the poem on Lincoln's death, " Captain, O, my Captain," has been much and deservedly admired. But for the most part Whitman's lines are the veriest dry bones of prose, growing out of a note-book, a pencil, and a dictionary of technical terms.

No man ever pierced the surface of things so little as Whitman. He can do nothing but heap epithet upon epithet, call names and append an exclamation point to them or print them in italics; as if one were to call out stentoriously " rose, nightingale, forest," and believe that with this shouting of names he had caught color, perfume, melody, and majesty, and fixed them in immortal verse. Whitman's dreary cataloguing is as far from the method of the imagination as the rule of three from a Shakespearian sonnet. Amidst a confusing mass of details, the truly imaginative or artistic mind seizes upon the characteristic and suggestive features of a subject and reproduces them vividly. The true poet discriminates between what is essential to his theme and what is not. The world will not soon forget that storm in the Alps which Byron sung in a few short vigorous lines: —

<blockquote>
" Far along,
From peak to peak the rattling crags among,
Leaps the live thunder ! not from one lone cloud,
But every mountain now hath found a tongue,
And Jura answers through her misty shroud
Back to the joyous Alps, who call to her aloud."
</blockquote>

What movement, what crashing sound and exhilarating joy, are crowded into these few lines ! The telling points of the storm are seized, — the ragged lightning-flash, the startling peal, and its rolling echoes. The attention is concentrated on these, and is not weakened by crowding in details of which the spectator would be unconscious.

Whitman, on the contrary, in his " Proud Music of the Storm," drivels through six or seven pages about all the noises he ever heard, until the confused and wearied reader loses all grasp of his theme, and is reminded of the babbling old nurse in " Romeo and Juliet " who must recall the chief events of fourteen years to say that Juliet is near that age. No continuity, no clear settled purpose, distinguishes Whitman's dull, uncouth pages of words. He once told a friend that " Leaves of Grass " is " just four hundred pages of 'let fly,' " and so it is. Geographical catalogues make up a good part of it, and they continue for page after page in a dry enumeration unrelieved by a single reflection to show why they were copied from some school-boy's text-book.

When Whitman drops his inventory style, he frequently falls into the coarsest slang and most vulgar grammatical errors, or utters commonplaces in a strained, affected, uncouth garb singularly out of harmony with the democratic simplicity that he so constantly lauds. He plays all sorts of jugglery with language; throws words together in an incoherent jumble without subject or predicate; couples the most opposite terms and ideas in bold defiance of the laws of reason; and affects mutilated foreign words, trusting to the ignorance of his readers to give him credit for familiarity with various tongues. He has no definite expression for his thought, or rather no definite thought for expression; but ranges synonym after synonym in line, so that his ideas, instead of having a solid centre and firm outline, are enveloped in a nebulous cloud and fray out into the feeblest mist.

No man ever made so many promises and failed to keep them as Whitman. His " Leaves of Grass " is mainly made up of assertions that he is *going* to sing the song of this or that, that he is *going* to be the founder of a new religion, etc., but he never goes beyond the promise. He is the stentorian-voiced showman of a little side-show, where more is to be seen on the posters and heard in the braggadocio of the showman's tongue than inside the tent. He is like a little second-hand country shop that calls itself the " World's Bargain Store " and has the earth for its sign. Nothing is more absurd than the claim of some of his admirers that he " has dealt with the vast developments of the nineteenth century, all the teeming life and work of America," simply because he has crowded into his catalogues all the nouns and adjectives he ever heard of. Any un-abridged dictionary would be a more fitting subject of such eulogy than Whitman. As well might an artist lay claim to having painted a picture because he had said "trees, water, earth, sky, blue, green, red, brown ; " or a builder declare that he had put up a house be-cause he had collected the bricks for one. The truth is, Whitman has dealt with nothing, and our proud civilization would sink into a chaos of anarchy were his teachings to be universally followed. Noth-ing that stimulates his slow pulse is repugnant to him ; hence he falls into indecencies in which there is neither salt of wit, sarcastic lash, nor gleam of intellect to preserve them from putridity. He knows no distinction between good and evil, beauty and ugli-ness, or what is pleasant to the senses and what is disgusting. To what little purpose he studied nature not to learn that law, not license, governs all her works; that instead of the blind impartiality he attributes to her and would imitate, she is an inexorable discriminator! In her fierce struggle for the survival of the fittest, she takes by the hand the strongest; she pardons no lapse into weakness; she sends disease and death on the trail of broken law; she aims at growth and development, and in steady pursuit of that aim has ruthlessly blotted out type after type that has failed to meet the demands of environment.

In the presence of this solemn teaching, Whitman's "profound lesson of reception, nor preference, nor denial," that ranks the beetle and his dung-ball with Christ and Socrates, the murderer and the felon with saint and sage, but typifies the ignorant indiscrimination of the drivelling child that fills his mouth with dirt and buttons, candy or apples, as they happen to come within reach of his feeble, restless hands. An acceptation of Whitman's teaching is a denial of nature's lessons; it is a step backward: and as long as there is in human nature an instinct that impels it forward, a love of decency and order, a cheerful obedience to law in the knowledge that it is the foundation of all free, healthy life, a clear discrimination between what tends to human welfare and what tends to human destruction, a refined appreciation for the graces as well as the substance of art, — there will be no place for Walt Whitman among the great thinkers and poets of the world.

RICHARD HENRY STODDARD was born in the sea-coast town of Hingham, Massachusetts, July 2, 1825.

His father, a sea-captain, died in the poet's early boyhood. His mother married again, and removed with her family to New York, where the boy worked for a time in an iron foundry. We do not know the story of the struggle of this susceptible and poetical nature to grow to its full stature in the midst of circumstances so adverse, — the hard toil that exacts its full share of mental as well as physical strength, the uncongenial atmosphere of a crowded and noisy city, — but that it did grow we have abundant evidence in prose and verse.

"The Country Life," a beautiful little poem, gives us a glimpse of the poet's tastes and dearest recollections: —

> " Not what we would, but what we must,
>   Makes up the sum of living.
>   Heaven is both more and less than just
>   In taking and in giving.
>   Swords cleave to hands that sought the plough,
>   And laurels miss the soldier's brow.
>
> " Me whom the city holds, whose feet
>   Have worn its stony highways,
>   Familiar with its loneliest street,
>   Its ways were never my ways.
>   My cradle was beside the sea,
>   And there I hope my grave will be.
>
> " Old homestead !   In that gray old town
>   Thy vane is seaward blowing ;
>   The slip of garden stretches down
>   To where the tide is flowing.
>   Below they lie, their sails all furled,
>   The ships that go about the world.

“ Dearer that little country house
    Inland, with pines beside it,
Some peach-trees with unfruitful boughs,
    A well with weeds to hide it,
No flowers, or only such as rise
Self-sown, poor things, which all despise.

“ Dear country home, can I forget
    The least of thy sweet trifles, —
The window-vines that clamber yet,
    Whose bloom the bee still rifles !
The roadside blackberries growing ripe
And in the woods the Indian Pipe.”

.   .   .   .   .

The intoxicating and satisfying sense of beauty in the world is very prettily expressed in the poems “ Spring ” and “ Hymn to the Beautiful.” The opening stanza of the latter poem is particularly good : —

“ My heart is full of tenderness and tears,
    And tears are in my eyes, I know not why,
With all my grief content to live for years,
    Or even this hour to die.
My youth is gone, but that I heed not now,
My love is dead, or worse than dead can be,
My friends drop off like blossoms from a bough,
    But nothing troubles me, —
Only the golden flush of sunset lies
Within my heart like fire, like dew within my eyes.”

“ The Flight of Youth,” another happy rendering of a universal feeling, runs as follows : —

“ There are gains for all our losses,
    There are balms for all our pain,
But when youth the dream departs,
It takes something from our hearts,
    And it never comes again.

> " We are stronger, and are better
>   Under manhood's sterner reign,
>   Still we feel that something sweet
>   Followed youth with flying feet,
>   And will never come again.
>
> " Something beautiful is vanished,
>   And we sigh for it in vain;
>   We behold it everywhere
>   On the earth and in the air,
>   But it never comes again."

The poems we have noticed belong to Stoddard's less ambitious efforts; but they are the lines that have the staying quality, — the lines that touch some familiar and responsive chords in us, and are remembered longest. We find fewer of such lines in the poetry of Stedman, who in his early years was too powerfully influenced by Tennyson to do strong, original work. His satirical poem, " The Diamond Wedding," is very clever in its way; and his pretty little poem, " The Doorstep," has long been a favorite, and has its place in every representative collection of American verse. Stedman will probably be remembered as a poet by it alone, just as Bayard Taylor (1825–1878) will very likely live to the general reader chiefly as the author of the " Bedouin Love Song," with its passionate refrain, —

> " I love thee, I love but thee,
>   With a love that shall not die
>   *Till the sun grows cold,*
>   *And the stars are old,*
>   *And the leaves of the Judgment Book unfold !*"

EDMUND CLARENCE STEDMAN was born on the eighth of October, 1833, at Hartford, Connecticut.

He was educated in his native town, followed journalism in his youth, and later became a stockbroker in New York.   His first volume of poems was published in 1860.   But his reputation as a poet has been eclipsed in later years by his work as a critic.   His first volume of criticism, " Victorian Poets," appeared in 1875, and it was followed ten years later by a companion volume, " Poets of America."   As a critic, Stedman has done good work, but he lacks both sting and sweetness.   His criticism is almost uniformly laudatory, but it does not convey an impression of deep joy in what he praises.   The reader catches no warmth from him, feels no desire to read where he has been reading; yet he is himself eminently readable.   Where he cannot in conscience praise, as in his consideration of the extravagant affectations of the neo-romantic school, he deplores the lack of wholesome criticism, and is disposed to " cry out for an hour of Jeffrey or Gifford."   The reader, for his part, feels inclined to cry out to Stedman: " This is *your* hour; do not shirk its duty; do it, no matter how painful."   That he could do it, we feel sure.   Although his criticism deals more with technical execution than with subject matter, he has a right feeling for what is fine and strong in thought and emotion.   To be sure, he has pleasant words to say of what he so aptly calls the " stained-glass poetry " of the Rossetti school; but it is a kind of poetry which does not appeal to him strongly, and he overpraises Whitman in a natural reaction against extreme culture.   But he recognizes that this is the cause of his admiration, and confirms Lanier's statement quoted above, in an assertion that —

"Whitman's warmest admirers are of several classes : those who have carried the art of verse to super-refined limits, and seeing nothing farther in that direction, break up the mould for a change ; those radical enthusiasts who, like myself, are interested in whatever hopes to bring us more speedily to the golden years ; lastly, those who, radically inclined, do not think closely, and make no distinction between his strength and weakness. Thus he is, in a sense, the poet of the over-refined and the *doctrinaires*."

But Stedman is no lover of eccentricities for the sake of eccentricity ; and though he calls Browning "the most intellectual of poets, Tennyson not excepted," he does not feel that this excuses his offences against form, and says : —

"Eccentricity is not a proof of genius, and even an artist should remember that originality consists, not only in doing things differently, but also in 'doing things better.' The genius of Shakespeare and Molière enlarged and beautified their style ; it did not distort it. . . . A poet, however emotional or rich in thought, must not fail to express his conception and make his work attractive. . . . Ruskin has shown that in the course of years, though long at fault, the masses come to appreciate any admirable work. By inversion if, after a long time has passed, the world still is repelled by a singer, and finds neither rest nor music in him, the fault is not with the world ; there is something deficient in his genius — he is so much the less poet."

Stedman sees the immoral teaching of " Browning's emotional poetry," and significantly remarks : —

"That many complacent English and American readers do not recognize this, speaks volumes either for their stupidity or for their hypocrisy and inward sympathy for a creed which they profess to abhor. . . .

"The 'study' of Browning takes strong hold upon theorists, analysts, dialecticians, who care little for poetry in itself, and who, like Chinese artists, pay more respect to the facial dimensions of the muse than to her essential beauty and the divine light of her eyes."

Stedman does not believe that there is any necessary antagonism between poetry and science, declaring that "while all other arts must change and change, the pure office of poetry is ever to idealize and prophesy of the unknown," and that since "nature is limitless in her work and transitions, her book of secrecy infinite," poetry will always find a fair field for her idealizations and prophecies.

Stedman is thoroughly sound on the much disputed question of realism, which he thinks should be "just as true and faithful to the ideal and soul of things as to obvious and external matters of artistic treatment."   He believes in an "aristocracy of art which by instinct selects an elevated theme. It is better to beautify life by an illusive reflection in a Claude Lorraine mirror than to repeat its every wrinkle in a sixpenny glass."   And elsewhere he says : —

"The term realism constantly is used to cloak the mediocrity of artists whose designs are stiff, barren, and grotesque —the form without the soul. They deal with the minor facts of art, unable to compass the major ; their labor is scarcely useful as a stepping-stone to higher things; if it were not so unimaginative, it would have more value as a protest against conventionalism and a guide to something new."

Stedman rightly ranks the spirit of a work of art higher than its form, and declares himself in favor of "simplicity, impulse, sincerity as opposed to obscurity, didacticism and the affectation either of refinement or a ' saucy roughness,' — always in behalf of imagination and against the multiform devices proffered consciously or unconsciously in lieu of that supreme quality."

Such a feeling is the basis of sound criticism, and in so far as we have Stedman's faithful expression of it, he stands to-day among the foremost living critics of America and England.

WILLIAM DEAN HOWELLS and HENRY JAMES are the leaders of the realistic school of fiction in America. Howells is of Welsh descent on his father's side, and was born at Martin's Ferry, Ohio, on the first of March, 1837. His father was a printer and the editor of a country paper, a man of more than ordinary character, a lover of poetry, and a Swedenborgian in faith. Says Howells: —

"The printing-office was my school from a very early date. My father thoroughly believed in it, and he had his beliefs as to work, which he illustrated as soon as we were old enough to learn the trade he followed. We could go to school and study, or we could go into the printing-office and work, with an equal chance of learning, but we could not be idle; we must do something for our souls' sake, though he was willing enough we should play, and he liked himself to go into the woods with us and to enjoy the pleasures that manhood can share with childhood."

There was a small but choice collection of books in his home, and Howells read them with a delight that makes his recollections of his reading in " My Literary Passions" one of the most charming books he has written. Goldsmith, Cervantes, and Irving were the first authors of his heart, and when we listen to the fine tribute he pays to these old masters and feel how they enriched his boyhood " beyond the dreams of avarice," we are inclined to ask him what sort of influence the realistic books he now loves would have had upon him then, and whether youth can ever have better food than these old authors furnish. But he has answered the latter part of the question himself.

"Upon the whole, I am very well content with my first three loves in literature, and if I were to choose for any other boy, I do not see how I could choose better than Goldsmith, Cervantes, and Irving, kindred spirits and each not a master only, but a sweet and gentle friend whose kindness could not fail to profit him."

In his love for Cervantes, Howells taught himself Spanish when a boy, and at fifteen thought of writing a life of Cervantes. Pushing on with his studies alone, he taught himself Latin and enough Greek to enable him to read a chapter in the New Testament and an ode of Anacreon. He began to write verses in imitation, he tells us, of Moore, Goldsmith, or Pope, according as the fancy for each poet was uppermost. He took up German, plunged into Heine with the aid of a lexicon, and wrote poems and prose sketches in so clever an imitation of him that Lowell once wrote him : " You must sweat the Heine out of your bones as men do mercury."

In his twenty-fourth year, in connection with John James Piatt, he published a volume of verse entitled " Poems of Two Friends." The same year the publication of a campaign biography of Lincoln was followed by his appointment as consul to Venice. He took an Italian grammar on board with him when he crossed the Atlantic, and could soon read the language readily. "Venetian Life" and "Italian Journeys," the results of his experiences in Italy, were printed in a Boston newspaper after their rejection by the magazines.

On his return to America he wrote for the New York papers for a time, and then found employment on the "Atlantic Monthly" as assistant editor. His first novel, "Their Wedding Journey," was published in 1871. Since then, he has written many novels, the best of which are "The Rise of Silas Lapham," "A Modern Instance," "A Woman's Reason," and "April Hopes."

As a novelist, Howells is a faithful delineator of the ordinary phases of the social life he sees. His young women with their grace, prettiness, maidenly reserves and ideals, are natural creations, but we are a little impatient of the middle-aged and elderly society mammas, who all talk alike in a stream of broken, lively sentences, mingling sentiment, fashion, ailments, gossip, in an absurd confusion. Their talk, as one of them in "A Foregone Conclusion" says, "just seems to be going on of itself, — slipping out, — slipping out." We meet this woman again, young as well as old, and in an aggravated stage of slippiness, in Henry James, and note with a protest her appearance in the short stories of our minor authors. But even when this woman is on the scene, Howells is never dull. He has a good style; he manages his characters with a skill that comes from perfect understanding of them, and though an ultra-realist in theory, he is better than his theories.

As for these theories, we find them cleverly and lucidly set forth in a very readable little volume entitled "Criticism and Fiction." He tells us elsewhere that in his early days he had no "philosophized preference for reality in literature," and we are probably indebted to the influence of his former hearty enjoyment of the older giants in literature for what is bright and wholesome in his own work. In his "Criticism and Fiction" he says: —

"The young writer who attempts to report the phrase and carriage of every-day life, who tries to tell just how he has heard men talk and seen them look, is made to feel guilty of something low and unworthy by the stupid people who would like to have him show how Shakespeare's men talked and looked, or Thackeray's or Balzac's or Hawthorne's or Dickens's: he is instructed to idealize his personages, that is, to take the lifelikeness out of them and put the book-likeness into them. He is approached in the spirit of the wretched pedantry into which learning, much or little, always decays when it withdraws itself and stands apart from experience in an attitude of imagined superiority, and which would say with the same confidence to the scientist: 'I see that you are looking at a grasshopper there, which you have found in the grass, and I suppose you intend to describe it. Now don't waste your time, and sin against culture in that way. I 've got a grasshopper here which has been evolved at considerable pains and expense out of the grasshopper in general; in fact, it 's a type. It 's made up of wire and cardboard very prettily painted in a conventional tint, and it 's perfectly indestructible. It is n't very much like a real grasshopper, but it 's a great deal nicer, and it 's served to represent the notion of a grasshopper ever since man emerged from barbarism. You may say that it's artificial, but then it's ideal, too; and what you want to do is to cultivate the ideal. You'll find the books full of my kind of grasshopper, and scarcely a trace of yours in any of them. The thing that you are proposing to do is commonplace; but if you say that it isn't commonplace, for the very reason that it hasn't been done before, you'll have to admit that it's photographic.'

"As I said, I hope the time is coming when not only the artist, but the common average man who always 'has the standard of the arts in his power' will have also the courage to apply it, and will reject the ideal grasshopper wherever he finds it, in science, in literature, in art, because it is not 'simple, natural, and honest,' because it is not like a real grasshopper. But I will own that I think the time is yet far off, and that the people who have been brought up on the ideal grasshopper, the heroic grasshopper, the impassioned grasshopper, the self-devoted, adventure-full, good, old, romantic, cardboard grasshopper, must die out before the simple, honest, and natural grasshopper can have a fair field."

This is an amusing and fair protest of which every sensible man and woman will heartily approve, but it does not touch the real question at issue between idealism and the realism which we have from France, and in the latest fiction from the farming districts of the West, to which Howells gives his unqualified praise and encouragement. The question is not whether we shall have the real grasshopper or the mock one,—by all means let us have the real one,—but whether we shall have *nothing but grasshoppers* in our literature when we might have song-birds and butterflies as well. Are we to have snarling and cursing and the commonest vulgar slang in place of fair words and good English?　Are we to have the sentiment (if you choose to call the belief by that name) that a man may rise superior to his surroundings and be happy even if poor and in cheap clothes, supplanted by the sentiment that it takes broadcloth and money to make him a man?　Must we sentimentalize over a toad and blame nature for not giving him the feathers of a jay?　Even a photograph needs retouching to remove the accentuated lines and harshness of light and shade due to the absence of the softening play of life.　Must there be no retouching in realism?　Are we never to go deeper than surfaces?　Is the harsh crude realism, so hopelessly dull and vulgar and so drearily unreal that the soul sickens at it, truer than all that makes life worth living? truer than that which we feel in our own hearts when the blood in our veins is young and warm and pure?　If the question of imagination is to be left entirely out of art, then journalism which records the daily happenings of the streets and highways, and by preference the sins and crimes of humanity, will fulfil the office of the poets and novelists, and the sensational newspaper, the organ of realism, is destined to be the literature of the future.　Genius will not be required to write it; the only qualification will be a liking for bad odors and a prurient curiosity eager to sniff them out.

In that admirable series of essays entitled "The Relation of Literature to Life," written by Charles Dudley Warner, is to be found a timely and most sensible essay on Modern Fiction.　In the course of this essay Warner says: —

"In nature there is nothing vulgar to the poet, and in human life there is nothing uninteresting to the artist, but nature and human life for the purposes of fiction need a creative genius. The importation into the novel of the vulgar, sordid, and ignoble in life is always unbearable, unless genius first fuses the raw material in its alembic.

"When, therefore, we say that one of the worst characteristics of modern fiction is its so-called truth to nature, we mean that it disregards the higher laws of art, and attempts to give us unidealized pictures of life. The failure is not that vulgar themes are treated, but that the treatment is vulgar; not that common life is treated, but that the treatment is common; not that care is taken with details, but that no selection is made, and everything is photographed regardless of its artistic value. I am sure that no one ever felt any repugnance on being introduced by Cervantes to the muleteers, contrabandistas, servants and serving-maids, and idle vagabonds of Spain, any more than to an acquaintance with the beggar boys and street gamins on the canvases of Murillo. And I believe that the philosophic reason of the disgust of Heine and of every critic with the English *bourgeoisie* novels describing the petty humdrum life of the middle classes, was simply the want of art in the writers; the failure on their part to see that a literal transcript of nature is poor stuff in literature. . . .

"The characteristics which are prominent when we think of our recent fiction are a wholly unidealized view of human society, which has got the name of realism; a delight in representing the worst phases of social life; an extreme analysis of persons and motives; the sacrifice of action to psychological study; the substitution of studies of character for anything like a story; a notion that it is not artistic, and that it is untrue to nature to bring any novel to a definite consummation, and especially to end it happily; and a despondent tone about society, politics, and the whole drift of modern life. Judged by our fiction, we are in an irredeemably bad way. . . .

"The artist who so represents vulgar life that I am more in love with my kind, the satirist who so depicts vice and villany that I am strengthened in my moral fibre, has vindicated his choice of material."

The story of Howells's own life as he tells it in his various books of an autobiographical nature is the best bit of realism of the genuine, delightful sort, that we have had from his hands. Few narratives are prettier than his pleasant little reminiscence, " My Year in a Log Cabin." Howells's father had failed in a newspaper venture in Dayton, Ohio,, and after the failure removed with his family, in the fall of 1850, to a small log cabin on the Little Miami River. He had charge of a saw and grist mill there. The family lived in a very primitive way. The walls of the little log house were covered with newspapers; a rude ladder formed the stairway to the upper story, whose imperfect roof let the snow sift through in winter. But there was no consciousness of poverty in this richly gifted boy. The whole experience was a romantic episode to which he looks backward in manhood with fondness, and would not have missed it for much. It is this spirit of joy and triumph over material losses and wants that we miss in the literature of sordid realism, and which ought to be there because it is *true*, and the absence of which makes it the apotheosis of dulness. It is the same spirit that sings through Lowell's poem of " Aladdin,"

> " When I was a beggarly boy
> And lived in a cellar damp,
> I had not a friend nor a toy,
> But I had Aladdin's lamp.

When I could not sleep for the cold,
  I had fire enough in my brain,
And builded with roofs of gold
  My beautiful castles in Spain.

" Since then I have toiled day and night,
  I have money and power good store,
But I 'd give all my lamps of silver bright
  For the one that is mine no more.
Take, fortune, whatever you choose,
  You gave and may take again ;
I have nothing 't would pain me to lose,
  For I own no more castles in Spain."

It is that light and warmth from the fire in the brain that we ask for in literature; not sensationalism, nor vulgarity, nor silly romanticism, nor cold-blooded minute cataloguing of commonplaces. The great geniuses have always given us this warming light, and by that experience we are warranted in believing that they will continue to give it to us, and we have but to wait patiently for their coming again.

HENRY JAMES was born in New York City in 1843. His father was an author of distinction, and gave his son exceptional advantages in education. James has lived almost all his life abroad, and is probably more at home in Paris or London than in his native city. His writings are always the easy work of a man of culture, and would be always delightful if we were not sometimes irritated by a half-contemptuous, half-weary air and talk of "prigs" and "bores," as if from that superior height of worldly knowledge where one has sucked the marrow out of life and has nothing left but the dry bones. It is this unsympathetic, disillusioned attitude that makes Henry James at times the least satisfactory of novelists. His characters often catch his weariness and repeat it in wearisome dialogues, which with long pages of close analysis make up the bulk of his novels. His theory of fiction is that —

"character, in any sense we get at it, is action, and action is plot, and any plot which hangs together, if it pretends to interest us only in the fashion of a Chinese puzzle, plays upon our emotions, our suspense, by means of personal references. We care what happens to people only in proportion as we know what people are."

True; but to know what people are it is not necessary to pull them to pieces and put them together again, any more than it is necessary to understand the mechanism of a clock in order to tell what time it is by it. And a much higher degree of creative genius is implied in the delineation of a character which reveals itself in the conversation and action of a story, than in the analytic method, which is much like an artist's writing "This is a horse" underneath the picture of one. Then, too, the intelligent reader is deprived by over-analysis of making his own interpretation; he can have no curiosity about characters whose every emotion and thought is subjected to minute dissection, and is consequently satisfied with one reading of his story, and rarely takes it up again.

The best known of James's novels are "An International Episode," "Daisy Miller," "The Portrait of a Lady," "The American," "The Princess Casimassima," and "The Bostonians." The last-named book, though an extremely disagreeable novel, is a clever satire of woman's rights, mesmeric healers, and philanthropic humbugs in general; and it pleads, like its hero, against the " feminization of the age."   Says this intrepid and conservative hero to a pretty girl-lecturer on woman's rights and wrongs : —

" I am so far from thinking, as you set forth the other night, that there is not enough woman in our general life, that it has long been much pressed home to me that there is a great deal too much.   The whole generation is woman-ized ; the masculine tone is passing out of the world ; it 's a feminine, a nervous, hysterical, chattering, canting age, an age of hollow phrases and false delicacy and exaggerated solicitudes and coddled sensibilities, which if we don't look out will usher in the reign of mediocrity of the feeblest, the flattest, and the most pretentious that has ever been.   The masculine character, the ability to dare and endure, to know and yet not fear reality, to look the world in the face and take it for what it is — a very queer and partly very base mixture — that is what I want to preserve, or rather, I might say, to recover ; and I must tell you that I don't in the least care what becomes of you ladies while I make the attempt."

James has done exceptionally fine work as a critical essayist in his two charming volumes, "Partial Portraits " and "French Poets and Novelists." We find in these essays more intellectual shrewdness than in Stedman, and a more satisfactory interpretation of realism than in Howells, — a greater respect for truth without literalness, and a fuller appreciation of the personal element in literature.   On the question of morality in art, he has a word to say which it is good to hear and no less pleasant to remember as being in harmony with the spirit of the great bulk of American literature.

"To deny the relevancy of subject matter and the importance of the moral quality of a work of art strikes us as, in two words, ineffably puerile. . . . There is very little doubt what the great artists would say. These geniuses feel that the whole thinking man is one, and that to count out the moral element in one's appreciation of an artistic total is exactly as sane as it would be (if the total were a poem) to eliminate all the words in three syllables, or to consider only such portions of it as had been written by candlelight. The crudity of sentiment of the advocates of 'art for art' is often a striking example of the fact that a great deal of what is called culture may fail to dissipate a well-seated provincialism of spirit. They talk of morality as Miss Edgeworth's infantine heroes and heroines talk of 'physic,' — they allude to its being put into and kept out of a work of art, put into and kept out of one's appreciation of the same, as if it were a colored fluid kept in a big-labelled bottle in some mysterious intellectual closet. It is in reality simply a part of the essential richness of inspiration — it has nothing tt do with the artistic process, and it has everything to do with the artistic effect. The more a work of art feels it at its source, the richer it is ; the less it feels it, the poorer it is. People of a large taste prefer rich works to poor ones, and they are not inclined to assent to the assumption that the process is the whole work."

A GROUP OF FRENCH CRITICS

By MARY FISHER

12mo.   300 pages. $1.25

Those who are in the habit of associating modern French writing with the materialistic view of life and the realistic method, will find themselves refreshed and encouraged by the vigorous protest of men like Scherer and other French critics against the dominance of these elements in French literature in recent years. — *The Outlook*, New York.

The writer of this book deserves the sincerest admiration and praise for showing the healthy side of French talent; and those who have been asked to accept Zola and Verlaine as the last expression of French genius will be grateful to the author for leading them out of the dissecting-room into the pure open air. — *The Saturday Evening Gazette*, Boston.

An opportune and able book. — *The Chattanooga Times.*

" A Group of French Critics " deserves a friendly welcome from everybody who desires to know something of the best in contemporary French letters. — *The Philadelphia Press.*

Here is abundant evidence that the worst elements in French literature have not been without their censors close at hand, able to say " Thou ailest here and there " with as much precision as can be desired.   Once more we have brought home to us that folly upon which Burke animadverted, — the folly of bringing an indictment against a whole people. — *The Christian Register*, Boston.